I0822855

War of the Worlds

Battleground Australia

Conceived & Edited by

Steve Proposch, Christopher Sequeira & Bryce Stevens

First published by Clan Destine Press in 2019

PO Box 121, Bittern
Victoria 3918 Australia

National Library of Australia Cataloguing-In-Publication data:

Eds: Steve Proposch, Christopher Sequeira and Bryce Stevens

WAR OF THE WORLDS: BATTLEGROUND AUSTRALIA

ISBN: 978-0-6485236-3-5 (hardback)

978-0-6485236-2-8 (paperback)

978-0-6485236-8-0 (eBook)

Cover Design by Steve Proposch

Cover & Interior Art for Sections 1, 2 & 3 by J. Scherpenhuizen © 2019

Art for Before the Lights Go Down p7 Sholto Turner © 2019

Design & Typesetting: Clan Destine Press

www.clandestinepress.com.au

Dedication

This collection is dedicated to all those writers who have
shown us that social and humanitarian issues
can be the foundations of the most lasting
and significant of speculative fiction works,
a foremost example being H. G. Wells;
but on a roster which the editors of this volume
would also particularly include
Isaac Asimov, Kurt Vonnegut and Ray Bradbury.

Contents

Before the Lights Go Down

Written at about the same time as cinema was born, but before both world wars, the original story tapped into the primal fear of a ruthless invader. Between those conflicts, the residual horror of World War I and the dread of the crushing boot of fascism during Hitler's rise in Europe, was exploited by the other Welles. In 1938 Orson Welles used H.G.'s template to terrify America with a radio play, which caused a panic as many Americans believed there was a real invasion. Even now well, into the 21st century, *War of the Worlds* can still be read as a harbinger of contemporary fears of the invisible enemy and international terrorism.

Introduction

Alex Proyas

I DISCOVERED SCIENCE FICTION THROUGH THE MOVIES. *2001: A SPACE Odyssey* was the Holy Grail; at the ripe age of six, it made me decide I'd grow up to make movies. I went straight from wanting to be an astronaut to a film director. My parents became worried about their boy at that point.

I stumbled upon *The War of the Worlds* through the cheesy George Pal/Byron Haskin movie made in the 50's...the one for which they couldn't work out how to make walking tripod war machines, so they had them just float on 'electrified' air. Those visual effects have sadly not stood the test of time, though the film still scared the hell out of me as a kid.

About 10-years-old, I discovered books – science fiction books. Bradbury, Clarke, Dick, Asimov – and I realised it was more fun to read and make up movies in my head. Anything was possible; even lumbering Martian tripods. That's when I started writing too...though everything I wrote began with: FADE IN. It was too late for me; movies would be my fate.

H. G. Wells really started something with *The War of the Worlds*. There have been radio shows, movies, TV shows, even a rock musical (which I'm quite partial to, actually). Written at about the same time as cinema was born, but before both world wars, the original story tapped into the primal fear of the ruthless invader. Between those conflicts, the residual horror of World War I and the dread of the crushing boot of fascism during Hitler's rise in Europe, was exploited by the other Welles. In 1938 Orson Welles used H.G.'s template to terrify America with a radio play which caused widespread panic as many Americans believed there was a real invasion. Even now well, into the 21st century, *War of the Worlds* can still be read as a harbinger of contemporary fears of the invisible enemy and international terrorism.

What seemed most interesting in the novel, though, was how humanity would fight this unknowable, mysterious enemy, an enemy which seemed unbeatable, until of course (and famously) we were spared not by our own cunning and heroism but by the viruses we were immune to and which the enemy had not anticipated. That fate had befallen many ancient cultures when assaulted by the forces of colonialism. An idea which might seem like ancient history, but somehow it, too, has achieved different resonance now. Now we can see our own western culture more clearly as the face of the invader...The British Empire as the conqueror of native lands, and, more recently, America as the stomping 'Martian' invader laying waste to foreign territories with its 'heat-ray-shootin' drones. And the 'virus' spread as ideas on social media, often rallying entire nations to rise up against oppressors.

The tension between science/reason and religion as depicted by Wells, himself a man of reason (if not a sworn atheist), describes the religious as weak-willed; and in the novel religion crumbles when faced with calamity, unlike reason which fights and survives. Though it is interesting that humankind's salvation does not come through science, and both the villain and the saviour would become fashionable in 20th century science fiction, it is serendipity that is the saviour. Or could that be divine intervention? Perhaps the vestiges of Victorian thinking? Or a comment on humanity's ultimate weakness in the face of a superior species – a logical expression of Darwin's evolution, still fresh at the time Wells wrote the novel.

And now, 120 years later arrives this collection; and what a wonderful, lurid, wish-fulfilment it is! A collection of nail-biting suspense, social commentary, the dark and light, the erotic and perverse, and, of course, glorious bug-eyed aliens...stories set in some twisted alternative history (or multiple alternate time-lines – trying to make them all connect is probably impossible) all versions of *War of the World* starring Wells' war machines, supercharged for a new age.

The collection begins in 'The Past', events which occurred concurrently with the original time-line, but on the other side of the world, in the land down under:

In Re The Strange Fate of Samuel Langhorne Clemens by Jack Dann posits an unnamed reverend as the brunt of Samuel Clemens' jealous wit, but then the world is attacked by the Martians; perhaps as Wells' story assaulted literary status quo at the time? And even Wells himself plays a part in this fever dream, which illuminates the Martian's preferred 'fine-dining' and clarifies why they might catch an Earth-germ or two.

And with *The Saltwater Battle* by Lindy Cameron & Kerry Greenwood, war machines attack and it's 'Proto-Suffragettes versus the Martians!' in an amusing re-framing of Wells as a kind of girl's-own adventure; with some appropriately scandalous post-modern romance for good measure. Are the Martians ridding the Earth of 'toxic masculinity' or merely being pragmatic with future plans for sustainable industrial food production?

In Janeen Webb's *Apostles of Mercy* suspense is created by cross-cutting between deluded religious zealots and a group of arrogant colonialists, who both encounter an injured Martian and deal with it in their own foolish ways. Will the colonialists get a taste of their own medicine by this new superseding invading force? Or will the zealots be fooled by a new god to worship?

At the height of the invasion, cities lie in ruins in *Banjo's War* by Narrelle M. Harris. The bush is the only safe haven; the co-operation of black fella and white fella the last bastion of hope. This story captures the palpable desperation of the novel, depicting a near too fantastic wish-fulfillment, of an Australia and its many diverse peoples brought together to fight a common, non-human enemy. An alternate reality we'd all like to believe was somehow possible.

In *The Inconvenient Visitors; Or, An Unrestful Cure* by Lucy Sussex, residents of a hill-top guesthouse observe the first battle of the Martian invasion and the war machines, which easily dispatch the soldiers sent to battle them. But the tripods are unprepared for the dangers of the Australian bush.

Rick Kennett's *The Enemy of the Enemy* shows a proverbial Aussie larrikin's encounters with the unknown, and his primitive struggles to comprehend the superior Martian intellect.

Speed Bonnie Boat by Carmel Bird brings us fast-forward to "The Present" to describe the history of the failed alien invasion at the turn of last century, and juxtaposes it with the very real British invasion and genocide in Tasmania, narrated by a descendant of the original Palawa peoples. This is as much a commentary on Wells' work as seen through the political lens of 2019, as it is a story of the origins of a new threat to humanity.

In *Doctor Were's Son* by Dmetri Kakmi the aliens live amongst us. Or maybe the aliens are us? A disturbing tale of how a second invasion might manifest itself with a new breed of Martian. An enemy, defeated and demoralised, prepares to make a comeback in a most unexpected way.

Nothing Missed by Angela Meyer is a poignant story of loss and grief, and a yearning to not feel pain; where a dead Martian serves as the numbing stand-in for our 'connected' modern world. Or is the desire to join with the 'other' a metaphor for racial harmony? Either way this post-modern tale, though it has ephemeral ties with Wells, is thought-provoking and touching.

In *Even Less Than Zero* by Jenny Valentish the satirical integration of the Martian conquest it seems is complete as we meet a third generation Martian-Australian named Kali eking a living by starring in adult movies. Tentacle erotica is all the rage and Kali has embraced the hedonistic lifestyle of the LA porn industry because...well, that's what humans like watching Martians do.

Cat and Mouse by Bill Congreve is alien abduction with a twist. Inspired by Ivan Denisovich, a man stuck in his very own Martian gulag hatches a crazy escape plan. The tale comes complete with a visceral image of a hot-rod-driving, bad-furniture-building, 'Big

Daddy' Roth-like alien, last survivor of the original invasion, abducting folks in the Blue Mountains of New South Wales. Not just any garden-variety tree-change eccentric.

In *A Fair Go To Mars* by Jason Franks, a couple of unwitting EPA workers on a routine assignment in the middle of nowhere encounter the noxious Martian weed, a Martian war machine, and a country town politician who doesn't understand that 'alien invasion' is not part of an EPA officer's job description.

In the final part of this collection we are introduced to visions of the future. Incidentally the 'future' of Wells' novel was written once before in *The Tripod Trilogy* by John Christopher, with its wonderful plot device of teens being 'capped' when they come of age, ensuring the invaders control the population's thoughts, keeping them docile and submissive.

Back to our collection, *Riding the Snails* by Jason Fischer introduces us to a future where things get really weird. The invaders rule; displaced humans ride the backs of giant Martian snails, propaganda carved on their shells, feeding on lichen as they cross the desert. Yarni, a young human female, is tested as she rises in the hierarchy of the human servants, hoping to please her masters and avoid being demoted to the lowest fatal rank of cattle. But she ultimately plays a hand in preserving human culture. With a nod to John Christopher, even Burroughs' 'Barsoom' gets a reference in this engaging and imaginative story, which reminded me in a good way of so many great science fiction stories of the past.

The Sixth Falling Star by Kaaron Warren continues the themes of displaced people, with Jena who commands a barge for ferrying the dead along the canals; a grim journey towards some unknown sacrifice; a brokered peace with the invaders but at such great a cost. A new eco system functions so much better than the destructive, old human ways, but the purpose for it all is terrifying.

In *The Second Coming of the Martians* by Sean Williams a man tracks down the last surviving Martian in the wastes of Antarctica, hidden away since the original invasion, far from the bacteria which doomed its kind. The purpose of his quest is to understand the mystery – the 'why' of the Martian invasion – and to learn the identity of the true invaders. A satisfying conclusion to this collection, which builds upon and adds to Wells' great novel, as all good sequels should.

Great science fiction always speaks of the here and now, our contemporary fears and concerns. Wells' story did just that and continues to do so, as clearly expressed by this handful of talented authors, building on the past, and carrying forward and evolving ideas to resonate with a new audience and a new world. The notion of setting a series of stories of alien conquest and colonisation in a land troubled by the invader (in fact and fiction) in Wells' day, today, and conceivably for some time to come, is both rewarding and cautionary.

A most rewarding dramatic construct, both for the imagination of the storyteller and the enjoyment of the reader. I think H.G. Wells would have certainly approved.

Alex Proyas, Sydney, Australia, May 2019

Foreword: The Martians in Australia

Steve Proposch, Christopher Sequeira & Bryce Stevens

THE MARTIANS INVADED A HANDFUL OF YEARS BEFORE THE 20TH CENTURY was born. In H.G. Wells' *The War of the Worlds* they came from their red planet and crashed down to Earth, most famously in Great Britain.

In this book we propose the terrifying aliens with machines that stalked on three legs were also sent to Australia, the immense island continent in the southern hemisphere, still five years shy of Federation.

A huge brown land of climactic and geographical extremes, from desert to rainforest; home to a citizenry of both invaded indigenous natives and rudely-landed settlers – many of whom were convicts. For all these people blood, violence and hardship had been an integral part of Australian history.

Would invading Martians prove to be the greatest hardship of all?

The battle was fought and won. Martians were defeated in Australia, just as elsewhere on Earth, by pure biological chance;

bacterial misalignment. But there was not the extinction of Mars' children on the world's largest island continent. A small number survived, over years, decades, more than a century.

The Martians dwelt among us, in hiding at first, then gradually moving more into the open. They lived in shadows, watching us, studying us, becoming like us.

The destiny of Australia was changed forever, its potential altered by an intra-solar alien culture just as it had been by the human invaders who overran indigenous lands centuries earlier. The new, expanded culture develops. Life evolves.

Finally, we see what the horizon of time holds, as the impact of the Martians' existence in Australia plays out well past their secretive years into a time when they have shifted their influence out into the world and we know they are here. Naturally, they have no intention of departing, and the strangest riddles of co-existence face Earthling and Martian alike.

Section 1. The Past

In Re The Strange Fate of Samuel Langhorne Clemens

Jack Dann

Way! Way! The Martians are coming!

– H. G. Wells (*The War of the Worlds*)

I FIRST SAW THE REDOUBTABLE AUTHOR, SPEAKER, AND RACONTEUR SAMUEL Langhorne Clemens, otherwise known by his more recognisable *nom de plume* Mark Twain, when he spoke to a 'packed house', as they say, at the Melbourne Athenaeum Library Theatre on Collins Street in Melbourne City.

The invitation to hear and meet this man was proffered by his devoted wife (and my longtime catechumen and friend) Olivia Langdon, who had suffered from Pott's Disease as a child. I had been charged by my diocese and her influential parents to administer to her secular and religious educational needs when she could no longer attend classes at Thurston's Female Seminary in Elmira, New York; and we formed a lifelong bond, which we have maintained through a lively correspondence over the years.

As I was not able to comply with Olivia's request to perform her marriage to Mister Clemens – that back in 1870 – because I was administering to the aborigines of this great colony of Victoria, and as she had once again fallen ill and could not accompany him on this antipodean speaking tour to heal their finances, she was most insistent that her husband should finally make the acquaintance of 'the rector who had brought her ever closer to science and the Lord'.

I must confess to the reader that I have had but little to do with Olivia's literary, intellectual, and (it pains me to say) reformist accomplishments; and as I shall prove later in this recountal, I no longer even deserve to wear the clerical collar. Be that as it may, I fulfilled this particular obligation to Olivia by making the trip by rail from my parish in the gold mining town of Foster to Melbourne, where Mr Clemens had kindly reserved a suite for me at the Grand Hotel, which was but a short walk from the Athenaeum. And although I was greeted with the usual civilities by the hotel staff, I must admit I was surprised that Mr Clemens hadn't left me his card or a note to accompany the theatre ticket that the concierge handed me upon arrival.

'No, sir, I can assure you that the ticket was all we received,' and that was that.

Well, Mr Clemens must have had more on his mind than paying his respects to his wife's correspondent and former curate: I could not in good conscience have expected any more courtesy than the ticket and sumptuous hotel suite, the latter being certainly more expensive than anything I could afford on my own. As the lecture wasn't to begin until 9pm, I entertained the idea of exploring the Botanic Gardens, but thought better of it in case Mr Clemens might yet try to call upon me at the hotel. Olivia had told me that he was prone to 11th hour appearances. And as no such appearance eventuated, I dressed and enjoyed a stroll down Collins Street. I arrived at the theatre in plenty of time and, again, inquired as to the whereabouts of Mr Clemens, but was told that he never sees patrons before he performs. With that I gave my ticket to a uniformed porter who guided me upstairs to my seat in the exclusive section of the balcony dress circle.

The star performer was late, and only when every seat was filled and the audience began shifting in their seats and talking in louder and louder voices did Mr Mark Twain step out from behind a curtain decorated with the stars and stripes of the United States. The audience seemed to be struck dumb, for I could not hear a sound except for the breathing of the woman beside me and the general rustling of clothes as people shifted positions, suddenly coming to attention *en masse*.

Mr Clemens was dressed immaculately in evening clothes and his patent leather shoes flashed in the glare of the limelights, but his clothes belied his affect, which at first blush seemed unsure and seemingly provincial. His uncut gray hair looked like it was hastily combed, if it all, and he looked frail, far older than his years, and somehow unkempt. And yet...and yet, as I have just noted, he was perfectly dressed. Perhaps the combination of frizzy hair, thick moustaches, and bulbous nose gave me that impression...and the way he initially moved, as if he was surprised to have stepped onto a stage. He took a few awkward, tentative steps across the platform, blinked at the lights, and then suddenly pivoted toward the audience, as if he now recognised every soul seated before him and was absolutely sure of himself and his elevated place in the world. The audience roared in appreciation, and I found myself clapping along with everyone else.

'Now I know that all you good people are here to be entertained,' he said, walking purposely back and forth across the stage like a ship's captain pacing his quarterdeck. 'And I would guess that you're all probably waiting for me to tell a story or two, as it seems that I've been known to do that from time to time.' He waited for the laughter and shouting to subside, and then continued: 'Now I do not claim that I can *tell* a story as it ought to be told. I only claim to know *how* a story ought to be told. There are several kinds of stories, but there is only one difficult kind, and that's the humorous story, which is the one I'll talk to you about. And the humorous story is American...of course!'

After the applause died down, he called for a chair, which was brought out to him by a stage hand. Then he sat down, lit a cigar, and began talking to us as if we were at an intimate gathering. 'The art of telling a humorous story – understand, I mean by word of mouth, not print – was (as I said) created in America, and has remained at home. But I consider it my paramount moral duty to bring it here to you.'

Perhaps it was the temperament of the crowd, the anticipation of hearing the great man speak, the great man who had travelled so far to be here, but all those around me were ready to laugh at every intonation, at every calculated pause; and to my surprise, I found myself absorbed in the hilarity, if hilarity it was, for as I listened I could not help but understand that he was in actuality giving us an American version of an Aristotelian lecture on the nature of humour. I knew we were being mocked, but I could not ascertain exactly how he was doing it, nor could I prove what I've just alleged. I remember him saying, 'Let me set down an instance of the comic method, using an anecdote which has been popular all over the world for, oh, maybe 12 or 1500 years. The teller tells it in this way…'

And I was amazed, as transfixed as were my neighbours, as he took on the aspect and intonation of an elderly farmer from the Midwest of his country telling his story of a wounded soldier. I won't bore you with my fragmented recollection of the story: suffice it to say the tale received a standing ovation. What I wish to relate happened after the telling, after he explained (in what I considered a condescending manner) the art of stringing incongruities and absurdities together in a wandering and seemingly purposeless way.

As I mentioned earlier, I was comfortably seated in the exclusive dress circle: my seat was in the very centre of the centre section, first row. Mr Clemens crossed to a position directly before me and looking up at me – I'm certain he knew who I was as I was wearing my clerical collar – he said, 'When I was in Sydney I had a large dream, and in the course of talk I told it to a missionary from India who was on his way to visit some relatives in New Zealand.' He smiled, nodded (at me?), and continued: 'I dreamed that the visible universe is the physical person of God; that the vast worlds that we see twinkling millions of miles apart in the fields of space are the blood corpuscles in His veins; and that we and the other creatures are the microbes that charge with multitudinous life the corpuscles.'

I felt more than a little uncomfortable at this profane turn of his lecture, and I might add that his penetrating upward gaze actually felt hot on my face, as if he were directing poisonous igneous rays toward me from his squinted eyes. Did I detect the ghost of a smile? I could not be sure.

'Now this missionary, whom we'll call Mr X, considered the dream awhile, then said: "It is not surpassable for magnitude, since its metes and bounds are the metes and bounds of the universe itself; and it seems to me that it almost accounts for a thing which is otherwise nearly unaccountable – the origin of the sacred legends of the Hindus. Perhaps they dream them, and then honestly believe them to be divine revelations of fact. It looks like that, for the legends are built on so vast a scale that it does not seem reasonable that plodding priests such as myself could happen upon such colossal fancies when awake."

'And then,' continued Mr Clemens, 'when I asked my pious missionary about his personal belief, he told me that – and I quote – "There are many nations in the world, and each group of nations has its own gods, and will pay no worship to the gods of the others. Each group believes its own gods to be strongest, and it will not exchange them except for gods that shall be proven to be their superiors in power. Man is but a weak creature, and needs the help of gods: he cannot do without it. So, too, do we as Christians know when a man is working by God's power and not by his own. We know, for instance, that there was a supernatural property in the hair of Samson, for when it was shorn, he was as other men…"'

With that, the speaker shrugged and raised his hands in supplication, obviously enjoying the stunning effect upon his audience, which had suddenly become as silent as the proverbial mouse. However, I took his words and manner and intense, focused stare as a personal insult, as I'm sure it was meant to be. I know not why he had chosen to disparage me, although I must admit even now that he did it with such subtlety that no one else could have or would have guessed the insult or his motives. Nor could I understand his motives. Had I not been anything but friend and counsellor to his helpmate over the years? Surely it could not be jealousy on the husband's part. Surely not. I did find out the truth, but not on that particularly devastating night, for even as Mr Clemens looked up at me with such ferocious intensity, the world was about to come to an end, and resurrection would seem infinitely distant to those such as myself, who might be compared with the transient creatures that swarm in a drop of water.

For it was at that very moment that Melbourne exploded, or to be specific, I felt a change in temperature, as if I and the entire company around me had been transported into a boiling hell; and I heard a strange roaring, a machine-like stuttering such as I had never heard before. Then the theatre shook as if the hand of God had slapped it: surely, this must be an earthquake. But that would not explain the sudden, intense blast of heat.

A portion of the ceiling collapsed right before me, falling on the hapless assembly below, and I was literally thrown out of my seat as the balcony began shaking and cracking. Panicked neighbours to my left rushed toward the immediate safety of the exit door wing, while a heavyset woman seated to my right elbowed me back into my seat in her scramble to get to the doorway. As I struggled for breath, others pushed roughly past me and disappeared through the double-door exit. I got up to follow and felt a terrible stabbing pain in my foot, which had been stepped upon, and as I fell back onto the cushions of my chair, I experienced the prolongation of what could have only been seconds into a long moment: the stage and seats below were veiled in swirling plaster dust, and I looked for Mr Clemens – this occurring in an instant, mind you – but could not see him. Patrons behind me and below were shouting and clamouring to escape, and the heat...the heat was suffocating.

Someone shouted 'Fire!'

I heard crashing, saw the far wall to my right bulge, then crack open like an egg to reveal tongues of flame – this vision of the fires of Hell was my recurrent nightmare, and now it was fact! – and I pushed myself down into the aisle, foolishly and irrationally hoping for the protection of the seats, which were, of course, constructed of flammable fibre. I did indeed feel a fiery breath streaming above me. I closed my eyes tight and held my breath, as an overpoweringly acrid smell burned my nose and throat. But I certainly couldn't remain curled up in the aisle like a child; I had to face whatever the Lord had prepared for me.

Rising, I found myself staring right through a rupture in the ceiling and the wall behind the proscenium arch. I can only describe what I saw as some sort of enormous armoured spider, which must have been taller than a house. Although plaster dust impeded my view, I could see that the metal machine or creature had extended a long, flexible, glittering tentacle no thicker than a walking stick. It whipped across the stage and captured a pitiable figure trying to escape: I could only pray that it wasn't Mr Clemens.

But I had no time for further contemplation because I reflexively ducked as the shining silver spider directed a beam of intense heat and a contained stream of foul-smelling black smoke into the theatre. And then, wreathed in its *own* miasma of unearthly green smoke and still hoisting the poor soul caught in its grasp, it moved away into the distance, prancing on long, thin metallic legs as if it were wearing seven-league boots.

So the demonic phantasm had seemingly finished with us.

But, alas, it had left us a terrible offertory…

The stream of roiling black smoke the creature had ejaculated now covered the first floor. It was oily and shiny and heavier than the densest fog, and it poured smoothly over the floor, seats, stage, and what was left of the audience scrambling for the exits. What happened next is akin to a dream, a nightmare where cause might (or might not) follow effect, but perception is skewed in such a way that words might become objects and ears might see. It was in such a state that I watched the doomed people below me fall screaming into the poisonous black ocean of smoke, none to rise thereafter; but I couldn't *hear* their screams: I just *knew* the unfortunates were calling, pleading, shouting, for my psyche was so overwhelmed that my ears were stoppered and my eyes recorded their pleas for help as exudations of the poisonous sea that overwhelmed them. The black smoke moved like a living thing, or like carbolic gas pouring from a volcano until all the surfaces below me were covered; and even then it flowed rather than diffused as any earthly gas would be wont to do.

It pains me to relate that I could but gaze helplessly at the extinction below me. As I mumbled the first line of Psalm 46, I noticed that the gas was forming into layers: the bottommost streams were diminishing, turning a sickly ochre color, and settling. Perhaps the deadly stuff was dispersing! I experienced a small surge of hope and an obscenely selfish relief as I surveyed the dead and gauged my chances of getting out of this theatre alive. Then the balcony began to tremble as if it was a live thing; and I feared that in moments or perhaps seconds, it would indeed collapse…or the rest of the ceiling would collapse. I was, to coin a phrase, *incidit in scyllam cupiens vitare charybdim*: caught between Scylla and Charybdis. If I remained where I was, I would certainly fall to my death; and if I could manage my way downstairs, I would die of lung poisoning. But the gaseous, eddying lake *was* diminishing. I could see that where the gas had completely changed colour, it became transformed into floury dust.

Slowly, cautiously, I made for the exit. There was no one left at this level: those who had made their way downstairs were certainly already dead, although I comforted myself with the thought that they might have escaped the building before the metallic spider had released its heavy poison. I waited beside the exit, my back against the wall, as if a solid object could somehow protect me; and when I heard another portion of the ceiling collapse, I quickly made my way down the stairs. It was a miracle – if, indeed, such a word should even be spoken in such circumstances – that the stairway itself hadn't collapsed. Holding my soiled handkerchief over my nose and mouth, I then ran through swirling black dust, almost tripping over the corpse of the heavyset woman who had earlier elbowed me back into my seat, and escaped the theatre directly through its front door. Escaped into a blast furnace, for Melbourne was on fire. Buildings had exploded (and were exploding!). What had been Collins Street and Little Collins Street and Bourke Street were now rubble, and an unearthly green glow emanating from the heavens above illuminated this hellish transmogrified city.

People were running in every direction.

A patrol of soldiers shouting 'Out of our way, out of our way' pushed past me, and I barely escaped being run over by a hansom cab. I sought momentary shelter against a building wall so that I might get my bearings and found myself staring, transfixed, at the enormous armoured spiders, or tripods, if you will, that were moving steadily and purposely in the distance. I could but glimpse them through the smoke, fire, and glowing haze. I would learn soon enough that they were not automata, but buttressed war vehicles: the steely integuments that contained the octopoidal Martian invaders. Their movements gave the impression of synchronisation and choreography, but I admit to describing them in this manner because I have never served in the military. I'm sure a more astute observer would describe their movements more precisely in terms of manoeuvre and strategic advantage.

And as the tripods moved, they swept streets and lanes with their heat rays. Buildings exploded as if bombs had been placed inside them. Omnibus cable trams burned and melted, their tracks transformed into molten rivulets. Yet, perhaps, just perhaps, all was not lost, for I also heard the booming of artillery and saw one of the tripods come under fire. A projectile smashed into its silvery plating, and the tripod lost its footing whilst firing its heat ray from one of its metallic arms. As the monster toppled, the green-flashing heat ray voluted: not only did it set fire to the surrounding buildings, but it also struck one of its comrades. Both tripods collapsed to the jubilant shouts of everyone, including myself. This was a short-lived joy, however, for it was as if the creatures' minds were telepathically connected (which indeed they were) because other tripods immediately blasted our troops and converged upon their fallen comrades. Perhaps it was an afterthought, but then they turned their heat rays on everything around them. As children might whirl weighted skip ropes around their heads, so did the tripods deliberately and purposively begin to spray a large circumference with death. And I could see that the Martians' green-flashing heat-ray funnels were turning in my direction.

As did everyone else around me!

Chaos ensued. Horse guards appeared seemingly from out of nowhere and rode through the pedestrians as scythes through wheat. Motor cars and horse drawn vehicles rushed this way and that. Some were boarded, their drivers and passengers thrown into the street. Carriages were overturned. The screaming, frightened crowd had turned into a maddened mob. The hoi polloi as well as the more affluent pushed and punched each other in a mad rush to escape the oily flames; and I must admit that I was no different than any of the other panicked pedestrians. I ran, ran madly, pulling and pushing past others as the world turned red around me. I felt the searing heat, felt my face burn and itch, and the coins in my pocket became so burning hot that I screamed in pain. I tore the pockets open, all the while running with no sense of direction or purpose other than that given to all threatened, fleeing animals. But I was lucky: I had escaped the direct ray. I was only blistered: my frizzled beard came away like confetti when I touched my stinging cheek.

A cyclist careened past, knocking me down; and an instant later I found the cycle overturned. The rider's clothes were on fire, and the poor man stood up as if he could run away from the flames devouring him. Without considering right or wrong (although, may God forgive me, it was too late for him), I grabbed the bicycle, set it aright, and rode off as fast as my legs could push the pedals. And then I, too, was knocked off my perch, so to speak, by a drunkard, who swung an empty bottle at my head, then kicked at me. I got up as quickly as I could, lest I be trampled by those rushing past. The bicycle had, of course, disappeared.

I heard a woman's scream; and, finally, I regained not only my balance, but what I like to think of as my moral compass. I hurried around a corner and saw two men trying to drag two ladies out of their little pony-chaise while a third man dressed in what was no more than rags held the frightened pony's head. I could see that it was an older, stout woman who was screaming while her courageous, young companion was fighting a black-bearded tough off with her whip. A scruffy-looking red-haired man came around from the other side and tried to pull her out of the chaise.

I shouted 'Desist!' and ran toward them. Although I am now in my late middle years, I was an expert boxer in my youth; and when the wretch closest to me rushed toward me with brass knuckles, I gave him a roundhouse kick and a punch to the jaw. I then approached the one holding the pony. He let go of the chaise, and the young woman smacked the carriage horse with her whip.

As the carriage receded down the lane, I was struck from behind. I saw a brief yet brilliant flash of yellow light as I fell. Although I was dizzy and concussed, I remained conscious. And then I heard gunfire, or rather a shot being fired nearby. I looked up to glimpse my assailants running away helter-skelter.

'Well…?' asked a gentleman looking down at me as he leaned out of a charred, square phaeton buggy. He had been dressed in evening attire, which was now scorched and grey with ash; his black hair and moustaches were singed and frizzled, and his forehead and clean-shaven cheeks were burned and blistered. He was slender yet powerfully built and held a double-barrel howdah pistol, which was little more than a sawed-off rifle. 'The world is on fire, Vicar. Do you wish to burn or bolt? The choice is yours.'

As he spoke, he snapped his whip impatiently; and I gladly climbed into his carriage.

He told me his name: Herbert Wells.

'And what's yours, Vicar?'

'Langdon McDowell, at your service, sir.' I said, striking out at a thug wearing a torn Salvation Army jacket who appeared seemingly out of nowhere and tried to pull me out of the carriage: no doubt, intending to insert himself in my place. Every street, lane, and avenue was teeming with frightened, coughing people, many limping and bandaged, as most (including Mr Wells and myself) were burned and blistered by the Martians' fire. But I suspected that terror-stricken mass of humanity had its own intent and direction. Like iron filings attracted to a lodestone, pedestrians as well as the more fortunate in wagons, drays, cabs, carriages, and motor cars were heading south: away from the immediate conflagration and toward the monolithic Flinders Street Station: Melbourne's rail terminus.

We, however, moved east across the crowd. After seeing the destruction to the tram tracks, Mr Wells and I both agreed that our best prospect would be to find relatively near shelter and wait (and hope) for the Martians to move on...or for our armed forces to strengthen, regroup, and destroy them.

Thus did we travel through this unearthly cityscape as particles of dry red dust – the exudation of the Martians – roiled in the air, covering everything. We proceeded slowly and carefully, mindful of our stout-hearted horse, past Parliament House and into the Treasury Gardens. The red-hued atmosphere began to give way to true darkness, to the comforting susurration of insects and the leaf-crunching movements of ringtail possums. A cloud of flying foxes flew overhead.

Mr Wells and I did not utter a word in the woods; it was as if – for these few moments – we had escaped not only the Martians, but time itself. There were people running about (mostly soldiers), but their movements were hushed; and by the time we reached the broad avenue of Powlett Street in East Melbourne, the only indication that the Last Days were upon us was the boiling red sky behind us. The streets and laneways were empty; the terrace-style homes devoid of light. Had everyone left? Were the residents hiding? Could they be…asleep, unaware of the horror surrounding them?

We heard reassuring, rumbling noises and then artillery wagons materialised out of the dust. The wagons were flanked by Victorian Mounted Rifles, Rangers, artillerymen, and sappers in wide-brimmed slouch hats and small round caps. The soldiers' red, blue, or khaki jackets and dark trousers looked crisp and well-kept: they had not yet been stained with blood and the evil-hued dust produced by the alien invaders. Columns of fresh-faced volunteer and professional troops, all marching smartly toward us, marching down Victoria Street, Albert Street, Grey Street. A young fuzz-faced soldier shouted to us from a carriage truck hauling a huge Maxim gun, 'Halloo, we're the beast-tamers!'

And another: 'To the front…to smash the beasts!'

Laughter. 'Away with you, boyos' – this also directed to us – 'or you'll get eaten!'

Mr Wells waved back, then shook his head and said, 'They're green as twigs. They think they're going to a picnic. But there won't be enough ground to bury them all in.'

I nodded, admittedly feeling an appreciative security as I watched the troops massing and marching past, and listened to the ringing clop-clop of the cavalry horses: thickset stocky bays known as Walers, and the rumbling of numberless carriage trucks, wagons, and hospital carriages.

Mr Wells fell silent, for he suddenly had his hands full trying to quiet his carriage horse.

'Hey, you two,' shouted a sergeant in a practiced, stentorian voice, as he cut away from his men and rode over to us. His green and gray uniform was anything but well kept, and he looked grizzled, dirty, and exhausted; he wore a flapped ammunition bandolier and carried a lever-activated service rifle over his shoulder. 'Unless you've got state or military business here, off with you both! This area has been cordoned off, and you're not safe here.'

'We're safer than where we were,' Mr Wells said softly, glancing back at the western sky, which seemed to be on fire.

The sergeant stared fixedly at my companion, then nodded. 'I got caught up in Kew: we lost the 1st Militia Battalion there and most of the 4th in less than an hour. I just hope we can smash them's tripods before they can turn their heat rays at us again.' He shook his head, as if he had acquired an exaggerated facial tic; and although he continued talking to us, he seemed to be directing himself to some faraway presence. 'Yes, I know they's nothing but slimy octopus things once you get them out of their machines. They got no natural defenses. I killed one with my boot, yes I did: stepped right on its slimy head – they're mostly just big heads, anyway – and it squelched like a big huntsman spider.' He turned away and mumbled, 'Just like a big huntsman spider.' The sergeant had a welt that extended across his ruddy, sunburned face; and because his eyebrows had been singed away, he appeared goggle-eyed, as if he was in a state of constant surprise. He regained himself and told us that all the residents had been forced to lock up and leave their houses. 'Any that are still here…well, it's on them if they get burned out or eaten by them monsters.'

'Eaten?' I asked.

'That's what I said. Well, maybe get dranked rather than eaten. They're bloodsuckers. I seen it, I did.' Then his expression changed; he nodded blankly and mumbled, 'I seen them, I did. They burned out Kew, just like they're going to burn us down.' He now stood motionless as a store manikin.

Mr Wells thanked the sergeant and gently tapped the carriage horse on its rear with his whip and told it to 'Step'. Once we were away, he said, 'Seems the old soldier has a bit of war nerves, poor sod.'

I could but nod, and we rode: we rode past the troops moving west; and the forage capped artillerymen who were deploying medium field guns and old smooth bore brass howitzers were too preoccupied to notice us. Unlike the fresh-faced boys marching to the front, these men were as bedraggled and hollow-eyed as the sergeant who had stopped and cautioned us. Nevertheless they looked to be setting up their machines quickly and efficiently.

'How could we have been going about our business in Melbourne City when entire shires and townships were being destroyed by these...creatures?' I asked.

Although that was, of course, a rhetorical question, Mr Wells responded thoughtfully: 'If what we've experienced is anything to go on, I would suspect theirs is a strategy of containment.' He made a guttural, laughing noise. 'Destruction is certainly containment. And where ignorance is bliss, 'tis folly to be wise.' When I didn't react as he no doubt expected, he said, 'I should have thought you'd know Thomas Gray for his "Elegy Written in a Country Churchyard". He was quite a good poet.'

Under different circumstances I would have attempted some sort of persiflage; but as I was not in a proper state, I simply stared toward the ominously empty streets ahead. After we turned down Clarendon Street, I commented that the residents could not have all left the area. They must be ensconced in their homes, in their cellars perhaps. They must be too afraid to turn on a light or–

'Whoa,' Mr Wells said as we approached the imposing grand entry of a very dark, two story bluestone dwelling. 'Would you be so kind as to inspect this house, Vicar? If it is occupied, surely one of its neighbours will provide us safe haven.' Meantime, I will tend to the horse and hide the buggy from view.'

'Shouldn't we stay together?' I asked.

'I will find you.'

I knocked on the arched front door; and when no one answered, I found a rock with which to smash its stained-glass window and gained entry. Cognisant that my criminal activity would not pass unnoticed in Heaven, I guiltily felt my way through every floor, through every room of this sumptuous alcazar. I called out softly with each few steps I took, just in case the owners were hiding in one of the cavernous chambers, but I was certainly and surely alone...until Mr Wells found me when I returned to a drawing room that overlooked the north portico.

'I've investigated two of the other terrace houses on the street,' Mr Wells said. 'I sense something very wrong here, as if–'

'Yes...?'

'As if we're being watched. Can you feel it?'

'Do you mean here, in this particular room?' I asked. I could easily make out his features, red-tinged in the crepuscular light streaming through a high window.

'Yes,' he said impatiently. 'On this street, in this room, everywhere around us.' I looked around the shadowy salon with its velvet sofas and formally placed ottomans, its grand piano and pool table which awkwardly faced each other; but I could not sense anything other than a sudden pounding in my head.

'Well, except for a sudden mi–'

My suggestion that I might be experiencing the onset of a migraine headache was cut short by the muffled booming of artillery and the rattle of Maxims, and then the very floor heaved under us as the room seemed to explode into brilliant white light. And then deafening explosions as Martian heat-rays struck our artillery projectiles, melted our armaments, destroyed buildings nearby, and transformed cobblestones into the lethality of canister shot.

'Downstairs, quickly,' Mr Wells said, and we didn't stop until we reached the basement story. A small barred window near the ceiling allowed the sickly green light to suffuse the room, a portion of which was devoted to the storage of root vegetables, hanged meat, wine, and other foodstuffs.

'Well, at least we won't starve,' I whispered, as if the Martians were standing just outside the barred window.

'If we can survive long enough to experience satiation,' Mr Wells said, seating himself across two crates.

'Well–'

He told me to be quiet, and, of course, I acceded to his wish. We listened to the faint screams of men hurt or dying, to the occasional clatter of horse and wagon, to the distant roar of a fire: most likely the Treasury and Fitzroy Gardens we had passed through earlier. And the percussion of cannon, the dull distant noise of battle and death, and my own heart-stabbing fear and panic stretched all emotion into a sort of regularity, a metronomic steady beat of resignation.

It was in that state that I broke bread with Mr Wells, for we had found enough victuals in the larder cupboard to provide us with a rather sumptuous cold dinner of cured ham, smoked bacon, some limp lettuce, stilton, nesselrode pie, and a half-bottle of very good Madeira.

We ate sparingly, however, as we knew not how long we might have to take advantage of the bounty of our unknown hosts' home. And even though I was no better than a thief in another man's house, *Corinthians 9:27* flashed into my mind: "Discipline the body and keep it under control, lest after preaching to others I myself should be disqualified." Ah, the Lord is certainly capable of great irony…and that ironical thought was followed by a blinding glare of green light and then a punishing blast, a concussion that knocked me unconscious.

I woke up to see Mr Wells' green-shadowed face near my own.

'Well, after a cursory examination, I don't believe any of your bones are broken,' he whispered as he knelt over me. His breath smelled fetid 'Now, try to remain quiet, for there is smashed crockery everywhere. And if you move, you'll make a noise, and–'

I nodded, for I could see beyond the collapsed wall which had once supported the barred window, five or six crablike excavating machines with jointed legs, levers, and metallic arms that could reach, clutch, and dig were working in smooth coordination to turn the pit caused by the explosion into some sort of hippodrome or coliseum. Everything, including our prostrate selves, was bathed in the auroral greenish light of the open air, for the house had collapsed backward. The floor above was completely destroyed. All that remained was the scullery which we inhabited. We were in effect buried in the earth and ruins, buried on every side except that facing the excavation, of which we were now a part.

And we could clearly see, up close, as it were, the actual Martians denudated of their metallic integuments. The brain-addled sergeant who had stopped our carriage on Powlett Street was right when he said that the Martians were mostly just big heads. Their huge heads or bodies – it was difficult to discern one from another – were about four feet in diameter. Their faces had no nostrils, just great, owlish eyes above beaks that seemed to be composed of hardened flesh. And below their beaks were bunches of long reticulated tentacles arranged around small adipose lips the colour of raw liver. These sinewy appendages functioned as hands and feet do for us, but our greater gravity made it difficult for these creatures to use them propulsively. The Martians were gathered together in groups around open, makeshift pens, each containing equal numbers of inert and probably drugged human captives. Every once in a while one of the Martians would make a whistling noise, but for the most part they seemed to be communicating without words…communing telepathically, one head to another.

I thought at the time that perhaps my migraine symptoms and Mr Wells' earlier perception of "wrongness", of being watched, might be side-effects of the Martians' telepathic "noise". But such an errant thought – and, indeed, my need to describe it here – are symptomatic of my reaction to the horror I witnessed from the vantage of the basement larder. To this day I try to escape, to bury and suppress that terrible vision…that vision of Martians reaching into the pens with their proboscide tentacles and feeding on the human beings they had captured; and even as we watched this abomination in fascinated disgust, the Martians' crab-like automatons had begun to herd hundreds of men, women, and, God protect them, children into a newly finished and closed section of the pit. Presumably, the entire pit and many more like it would become holding stations for the cattle they had come to Earth to feed upon.

And Merciful Heavens feed they did.

They didn't need to chew flesh; there was no cracking of bones, no mastication; no, these foul, globular creatures simply inserted a dart-tipped proboscis into their living captives and imbibed their blood directly. They literally drank them dry! And their human fodder did not – or could not! – twist or shudder or utter a word.

Unlike we more composite humans, the Martians had no need for glands, digestive organs, and hormonal regulation: no need for what an astute author of my acquaintance had described as the organic fluctuations of mood and emotion. These creatures had left tooth and claw and emotion behind, along with their need for digestion. No ructions of love or fear or hatred for them. They were in simplicity and complexity giant brains, fleshy intelligences that could create ideas and machines to fulfil any and all of their ghoulish, dispassionate dreams…and they dreamed of us…as food.

Which they would cultivate and farm and slaughter.

I awakened to a wickedly roseate dawn tinged with the greenish aurora of the previous night. For a moment I could not determine where I was; and then memory overcame my mind's resistance. I felt ill as I gazed outward into the pit, which was now compartmentalised into holding pens, feeding and forcing yards, waiting bays, circulating catwalks, and gates. Beyond the processing facility a spherical unit arrayed with heat ray funnels burned blood-drained bodies into ash.

The smell of burning flesh was overwhelming.

Mr Wells was kneeling beside me; how long he had been there watching the machines, I could not tell.

'They've gone,' he whispered. 'They've all gone.'

True enough: there was not a Martian to be seen. Only their machines, which crab-walked around and through the facility as they executed their assigned tasks. We could no longer see any of the human captives, for the pens were empty and discarded, and the pit was now a completed walled facility.

'The Martians must only feed at night,' Mr Wells continued. 'That is only a guess, of course, as we have only been here for–'

'We must leave before they return,' I said, feeling a sudden, inexplicable surge of impatience. 'Right now.'

'No,' Mr Wells said, looking calm and focused, as if he were simply contemplating whether to move a bishop or a knight on a chessboard. 'I believe we should wait a bit longer. Get the lay of the land, so to speak. Watch and see if their machines are capable of surveillance, and if so, how we might best circumvent them.'

Then Mr Wells bent low so as not to expose himself to outside eyes – either machine or alien – and crawled away from me. I noticed that while I had slept, he had cleared a rough path free of any shards of glass, shattered crockery, plaster, and splintered wood: a path past where the larder cupboard had stood to the stairway which might give us entry to the uppermost tier of the excavation and possible escape.

But I did not have a chance to whisper, 'No, I don't think we should wait.' I didn't have a chance to tell him that I, too, had felt as if we were being watched...and that I felt the pitiless stare of something cold and calculating and very near right this very minute.

And thus we, or rather he, lost any chance of escape...

Unfortunately, Mr Wells was wrong: the Martians could and did feed day or night, for, as I was to learn later, they had no need for sleep as we know it; and as I watched Mr Wells carefully crawl past the area where the wan morning light streamed into what was left of the larder, I saw a grayish tentacle slithering silently down the stairs as fast as water sluicing into a well. Reflexively – and without even considering the possibility that I might endanger myself – I shouted to warn Mr Wells of his immediate danger.

No, that is a lie! Even now my mind still seeks to bury my misdeeds, even at the very moment my pen touches paper, even as I try to expiate myself by composing this true and scrupulous narrative. No, I did *not* warn Mr Wells of immediate danger!

I watched, transfixed and in abject terror, as the snaking tentacle paused in the stairwell for an instant before lashing itself around Mr Wells and evulsing him upward and out of my line of sight. And then my turn came, for two or three more tentacles slithered down the stairs, waving back and forth, searching, crawling, investigating, as if their extremities had eyes. I backed away, but there was nowhere to go except into the excavation itself. However, *anything* would be better than being seized by those grasping feelers.

It was then that I heard a strange, alien shrieking, a hellish sound that I can only describe as something like a combination of chittering cicadas and baying hounds. And at that instant the tentacles furiously began slapping against the ceiling, walls, and floor in what I could only imagine as some sort of convulsive death throe before being pulled – or so it seemed – back up the stairwell to where they had originated.

Then silence, except for my bellows-loud breathing. Silence and the greenish light of sunrise. But I could not hold back my guilt, disgust, and panic. I had to get away from this place, and as we had not seen anything but the Martians' automata in the pit, I thought to take my chances and find a gate or outlet through which I might escape. But as I stood up, a voice sounded in my head, as if I was hearing the internal vocalisations of my conscience.

Move away from the opening! Immediately!

Even as I did so, I thought I could recognise that voice and its particular accent. 'Who…or what are you?' I asked.

Come up the stairs where you will be safe, and I'll explain.

'Safe? My companion just–'

Mr Wells might well survive to tell the tale, even though I fear he will suffer a bit of amnesia for a time.

'How do you know who he is and what he is about? How–?'

Lower your voice. Just think what you wish to say, and I'll hear you. You might have already given your position away. You must choose: remain here and die, or trust what you are hearing and climb the goddamn stairs!

Then I heard the voice again and somehow I knew it was an afterthought: *What you believe to be machines working in the excavation are not automata at all. They are Martian slaves and can perceive any change in their surroundings as well as any armoured Martian. And I am not strong enough to protect you from the lot of them.*

I knew that voice! It was…Mr Clemens.

But how could *that* be possible?

Move!

After I heard the clank and creak of metal in the excavation beyond, I obeyed: I crawled to the stairway where Mr Wells had been seized and climbed the stairs.

Keep going.

'Can you see me?'

In more ways than you could ever imagine.

I climbed the stairs, then climbed over what seemed like a mountain of earth, bricks, plaster, and smashed and broken household objects. I tripped over the protruding leg of a buried settee and fell, sliding backwards down through the rubble. I might well have broken my back on the cement stairs below me, but my fall was arrested by tentacles that encircled me and drew me upwards to the relative safety of what was now high ground (and what had previously been street level). Shivering with fear and disgust, I nevertheless registered that the tentacles pressed and squeezed around me as if they were fingers kneading bread. And then, released by the tentacles that had saved me, I found myself as close as I ever want to be to a dead Martian: its two-story armour carapace was burn-blackened where it had been sheared almost in half, and its three metallic legs were bent, splayed, and broken. Although still partly connected to its lower carapace, gravity had brought down the torso; and the hood that had contained the Martian rested on the ground, which was saturated with a striated greenish-black ichor. The Martian – presumably the one that had attacked Mr Wells – stared upward with dulled owl eyes, as if staring at the kindred creature that had so recently felled it: the monster that kneeled before me on its tripod legs.

The monster that bowed until it was low enough to the ground to open its hood and reveal its dual nature, for the victorious Martian looked as pallid and dull-eyed as the creature it had destroyed; but tethered to this Martian was the limp, corpselike body of a man: Mr Samuel Langhorne Clemens.

'Mr Clemens,' I cried.

Direct yourself to me, parson…to the tentacled creature that has not yet breathed its last breath.

'But–'

Desist your verbalisation. For your safety and – I swear I could hear his sardonic laughter – *for mine.* Those thoughts hurt, as if every word, so to speak, compounded the migraine throbbing in my brain.

I nodded and said, or rather thought, *How have you become this…this thing?*

The 'I' which once inhabited the rusk of my body – my *body, which is barely alive and will not live for much longer – was poached, shall we say, by the Martian within whom I presently inhere. This Martian is, or rather was, special: a telepathist who could enter alien minds. Most Martians can only commune amongst themselves, but this one ranked high in their scientific estate. He and others like him would rule our minds and restrict our thoughts.'*

And yet…?

Ah, yes, said this composite Martian and Mr Clemens, *but these creatures have a tragic flaw: hubris. How could they even consider their cattle as their equals? But I am – or was – a very bullish sort of kine; and while the Martian drained my blood, drained just enough to pleasure himself and weaken me, while he probed and investigated my psyche, my thoughts and memories and knowledge, I insinuated myself into* his *psyche. I hid inside his great brain and twisted his thoughts into my own. Who is the slave and who is the master now? I ask myself. But such a question has no relevance, for both of us will soon cease to exist. My remains, which are strapped to this Martian body, are nothing more than a faded memory. And the Martian who talks to you now as myself is dying.*

(This sibylline conversation, which I have tried to render as just that: a conversation, was, in fact, more of an "immanence", an almost instantaneous sequence of revelations, which I don't believe lasted for more than an instant. I must beg the reader to forgive both this narrative intrusion and my inability to describe this singular experience.)

And we, continued Mr Clemens, *must ask you a favour in return for saving your life, Vicar.* I could sense a smile, which I visualised as a flower blooming and then dying, turning from resplendent red to black and rot. *And we, or rather I, have a confession to make.*

Yes...?

Do you remember when our eyes met during my talk at the Athenaeum Theatre? Of course you do!

Could you read my mind even then? I asked.

No, but I can now...and your memories: those I can read... Although Mr Clemens gazed at me, or perhaps through me, the Martian through which he communicated looked intently at me with its great owl eyes. *And I must acknowledge my jealousy of you, acknowledge that I have* always *been jealous of you. It was because of my misplaced jealousy and anger that I could not bear to rendezvous with you at your hotel, could not shake your hand nor welcome you to Melbourne. I can now but beg your forgiveness.*

But why on earth would you be jealous of...me? You who–

Because for all the years of our marriage, Olivia talked of you, talked incessantly about your faith and friendship and...

Yes?

Friendship and love.

Platonic love, I insisted. *Platonic love.*

The creature that had tethered Mr Clemens to itself did not have the facial musculature to express emotion, but those eyes drilled into my own; and I saw that he knew…he *knew* that I had been in love with Olivia, that every letter I wrote her was an expression of that extramundane love. And perhaps, just perhaps, she might have felt something more than a modicum of affection for me.

Again I insisted, *But it* was *Platonic!*

Yes, I can see that. The Martian's eyes seemed to change colour. *But as a last request, I must ask you to share your love with her.*

What?

Olivia is dying, Vicar.

Dying?

Her old enemy – Pott's Disease – has worsened considerably, Mr Clemens continued, *and she is now permanently bedridden. I will not be able to look after her. But you can…and must. Ironic, isn't it, that a Martian has given you your heart's desire?*

I won't burden the reader with the humiliating complexity of my emotions at that moment, if, indeed, this recountal – which tries to translate what occurred instantaneously into a sequential conversation – can even be considered accurate. I can say that before we – or I – returned to what we know as sequential time, I knew that I would do as he asked: I promised never to tell Olivia the truth of what had happened to her husband.

It was then that the Martian, that grotesque life form that now contained Mr Clemens' will and spirit, closed its metallic hood, rose to its full height, and released – or rather discarded – the now dead body of Samuel Langhorne Clemens. As he did so, armoured Martian slaves clambered over the lip of the pit compound, and Mr Clemens raised his metallic arms and melted the Martians with his heat rays as if they were glass. However, more slaves appeared, like insects swarming, as did their Martian masters: tripodal in their armoured integuments.

And the world seemed suddenly to be boiling and melting in the flames.

To this day I have no idea how I survived that doomed and abbreviated battle of the one against the many. All I remember is Mr Clemens, his incorporeal presence calm as a summer's day, whispering or perhaps shouting, I know not: *Run, Vicar…find my Olivia, comfort her, and tell her that I–*

Alas, I could not try to complete Mr Clemens' last sentence in Olivia's sweet presence, for she passed into the arms of the Lord while I was in transit to America; and after putting her affairs in order, I returned to Elmira, New York, where I once again became a tutor at Thurston's Female Seminary and preached on Sundays to a small congregation in one or another of the parishioner's homes.

And the Martians…?

Should they return, we who survived can envision their fate: by the blast of God shall they perish, and by the breath of his nostrils shall they be consumed.

Amen!

Postlude:
It was with great pleasure and trepidation that I read Mr Wells' excellent account of the Martian invasion of Australia, and I am most grateful that he referred to me as a physician named Doctor Moreau rather than Langdon McDowell the cowardly vicar. And although our paths have never crossed again, I can but wish him crowning success and long life.

Rev. Langdon McDowell
Woodlawn House
Elmira, New York
3 October 1901

The Saltwater Battle

Lindy Cameron & Kerry Greenwood

Tug Barker fumbled his grip on the barrel. It rolled from the cart, splashed through a puddle and slid slowly across the yard. Two women watched the big man as he stood still, head cocked, weighing up whether to chase it or wait to see where it stopped.

'Lazy sod is hoping it will make it all the way to the cellar drop.'

It didn't. The barrel of ale came to rest by the water pump.

'Come now, Mrs G, Tug's clumsy, not calculating. I swear he's got five thumbs; I've no idea how he dresses himself.'

'He doesn't, Miss Zoe. He sleeps in them clothes of his.'

'Tug!'

The carter looked around wildly – like he feared he was being spied on. It was Mrs Grainger's snorting laugh that revealed his spies, on the hotel's first floor balcony. His head swivelled from the women to the barrel and back, whereon he doffed his battered hat. 'Mrs G, Miss Vaughn. Dang thing just leapt out me 'ands, it did.'

'We saw that, Tug. I'll come down and give you a hand.'

'No need for that, Miss,' Tug said to Zoe Vaughn's already retreating figure.

'You take her help, Tug. We don't need that ale any more smacked-up than necessary.'

Zoe hauled herself into the beer cart, motioned for Tug to be the ground man, and rolled the remaining three barrels to the edge and onto the ramp that Tug had missed entirely with the first barrel. The many-thumbed-man still managed to dither the last barrel and didn't think to go after it until Mrs Grainger shouted, 'chase it, you lazy fool!'.

An hour later the barrels were safely in the cellar, and Tug and his Clydesdale, Edgar, were plodding away up Bunbury Street with a promise to return the next day with a replacement for the one that had split against the pump and leaked into the dirt.

An hour after that, Mrs Grainger was already serving guests and residents in the dining room of the Hotel Artemis when Zoe, after a quick change from her yard clothes, joined her three permanent residents, one weekender, and seven new guests.

The amiable Horatio Landers, who'd checked in two days previous, was regaling half the room with another tale of his recent trip to Ballarat where he'd been caught up in an unlikely escapade involving a travelling circus, a murder, and a spectacular meteor shower. The latter was no doubt an embellishment inspired by the strange local weather events and news from London, but the story was nonetheless entertaining, and its telling meant Zoe could sit quietly and observe her guests. Always one of her favourite pastimes, it had become more so since the intriguing Miss Harriet Brookes had decided to spend her weekends at the Artemis.

Zoe shifted her gaze from the voluminous and moustached Horatio L, on the far side of the room, to the slim and beautiful young Harriet – she of the fierce intelligence, quick wit and flashing green eyes – opposite her. This was the young woman's fourth stay at the riverside hotel since arriving from South Australia two months before. While it was simply a matter of convenience for Harriet, or 'Harry' as she preferred, it had profoundly changed the way Zoe regarded her days; her Fridays now rippled with a delicious sense of anticipation and Mondays were something of a disappoint.

Mrs Grainger handed a plate of corned beef, mashed potatoes and beans to Zoe, and gently placed another in front of their newest regular. 'And what did you learn at the University this week, Miss Brookes?'

Harriet raised an eyebrow. 'Possibly not a topic for dinner, this time, Mrs G.'

'There's naught that can turn my stomach, young lady. I'll just get my meal and you can divert us here on the sensible side of the room, with something that borders on the truth.'

Mrs Grainger collected her meal from the servery and joined Zoe, Harriet and an expectant circle of two hotel 'life guests', Oscar Jones and Ida McLeod, and Mrs Olive Dunkley who'd elected not to eat with her inebriated elderly brother tonight.

'Monday and Tuesday our classes were all about bones and muscles.' Harriet said. 'We got to work with an articulated skeleton for that–'

'A talking skeleton?' Oscar Jones gasped.

'Don't be silly, Oscar,' Ida McLeod said. 'Articulated in this context means artificial. You know, so the medical students can learn what's inside us.'

Harriet tried not to laugh. 'Actually Ida, it was a real human skeleton. Articulated means it all hangs together – like it should.'

'Well, I never,' Mrs Dunkley said. 'And they're letting an innocent girl like you close to something so, so–'

'Denuded?' Zoe said helpfully.

Harriet smiled. 'Oh, I'm not so innocent, Mrs Dunkley. I'm a farm girl, so I've seen birth and death and a variety of life in between; human and animal.'

Mrs Grainger tapped her plate. 'Yes, yes, but what about the gruesome things you learnt this week?'

'You are incorrigible, Mrs G,' Harriet said. 'Let's see – Professor Jacob's classes were all about poisons and their effects – deadly and otherwise – like spasms and vomiting and pus.'

Zoe snorted, Mrs Dunkley covered her mouth with her serviette, and Mrs Grainger asked, 'Deliberate or accidental poisons?'

Oscar Jones frowned. 'And why would you want to know that?'

'It would point to murder or misfortune,' Harriet said. 'The exciting rumour is that in a few weeks we will get to work on an actual' – she leant forward to whisper – 'dead body.'

'I can arrange one sooner if you'd like. You can have my husband.'

'Ida!' Zoe laughed. 'Your husband is missing not dead.'

'Ah, but when he's found he won't be long for this world.' Ida McLeod's eyes widened with…glee.

'Bertie's been missing for nigh on four years, Ida,' Oscar noted. 'I doubt he'll turn up in time for Miss Brookes' anatomy class.'

'And there'd be little doubt as to whether his demise was murder or–'

'Definitely murder; it is a little difficult to shoot oneself in the back.' Horatio Landers, standing by the servery to collect his bowl of apple pie and custard, naturally assumed his own tall tale of death was the only one taking place.

'We're plotting murder, Mr Landers, not investigating one,' Ida said.

'Pray tell,' Horatio said, 'so that I may get to solve two murders in a week. I'd give that Sherlock Holmes fellow a run for his money. You know he visited Ballarat a few years ago; stayed in the same hotel I did last week.'

Zoe smiled. 'You don't need great powers of deduction to solve a murder you witnessed, Mr Landers.'

'Nor one you hear being planned,' Ida added.

Horatio's moustache bristled, seemingly of its own accord, as he retreated with his dessert.

Harriet leant forward to draw in her conspiratorial audience. 'I met Sherlock Holmes when I was younger.'

Everyone sat back in astonishment and then forward again for the rest of the story.

'I'm surprised you didn't, too, Zoe,' she said. 'He was, after all, travelling with the man who was known to both our fathers; and who is the reason I am, in fact, studying medicine here in Melbourne.'

Zoe's puzzlement lasted a good four seconds before she leapt up from the table and left the room.

'Can anyone else hear that strange noise?' Mrs Dunkley asked.

'I can hear a whirring, but I thought your brother's wheeze had done a key change,' Ida said.

Zoe returned with a framed photograph. 'You mean this man?'

Harriet and Mrs Grainger peered at the group of eight men, all but one in British uniforms, posing with and without rifles, and somewhat informally, in a place that looked foreign to all but the one who wasn't British. There was desert beyond, camels lounging beneath a tree beside them, and a couple of canvas tents. Harriet grinned. 'Yes, that is Dr John Watson. Beside him is my father, Stephen Brookes, and–'

'Beside your father, is mine, Robert Vaughn.' Zoe said.

'What's going on in this photograph?' Oscar asked.

'These are members of the 66th Berkshire Regiment of Foot,' Zoe said. 'This was taken in July of 1880, about a week before the Battle of Maiwand. In Afghanistan.'

Harriet shook her head sadly. 'My father said that battle was a brutal and bloody disaster. The 66th lost half their men. Father and Dr Watson were both injured and sent home to England on the *HMS Orontes*.'

'And my Pa took a bullet to the leg in September that same year, at the Battle of Kandahar. He never returned to England, though,' Zoe said. 'He met my mother in her village on Mykonos and they sailed here instead.

'And that's really him? The Dr Watson who chronicles the adventures of Mr Holmes?' Mrs Grainger, who was seldom astonished, was clearly impressed.

'Yes. And I met them both,' Harriet's face lit up with the memory, 'when they visited our sheep station north of Adelaide six years ago.'

Zoe tugged on her earlobe to distract herself from the effect that Harriet's eyes – Harriet's everything – was having on her. The delicious shiver coursing around her body was surely visible to – ah, Mrs Grainger was trying her best not to laugh at her, as she posed another question to Harriet.

'And was the great Sherlock as moody and brilliant as the doctor portrays?'

Harriet turned her palms up as if weighing her answer. 'Yes. And also quite funny and endlessly curious. He even solved a crime that involve–'

Three simultaneous things drowned out whatever it was Harriet said.

Scooter Thomas, 13-year-old kitchen hand, burst into the dining room screaming, 'The sky's on fire. On fire, I tells ya. It's all bloody red out thar.'

Several deafening whiny-screams travelled from the front of the Hotel Artemis, but way overhead, towards the Maribyrnong River.

And – boom-be-de-crack-boom! boom-be-de-crack-boom! – a violent and repeating sensation like a thwacking of enormous drums shook the building as thunderbolts seemingly passed right through the walls.

All the guests, except Olive Dunkley's inebriated brother, instinctively leapt to their feet, although three were immediately knocked flat to the floor. Everyone else took hold in some way of the person nearest them, either in terror or the need for stability, as the very air around them, oddly thick and alive, shoved them this way and that.

'We need to see what that was,' Harriet said, her face close to Zoe's. She released her embrace of Zoe's waist and clasped her hand instead, leading the way from the dining room.

'The sitting room balcony,' Zoe suggested pulling Harriet towards the stairs.

Mrs Grainger, Oscar, Ida and Scooter followed close behind, and in a moment the six were staring aghast at a sight beyond belief.

The sky was indeed red, but it was reflected light from the three meteors streaking through the cloud cover from west to east over Port Phillip Bay, and from what was obviously fires to the north where the enormous space rocks had already struck ground.

'May the Good Lord save us,' Ida said.

Harriet, scientist and already-confessed non-believer, huffed. 'Mrs McLeod, your god is either responsible for this, in which case we're buggered; or nature itself has come to get us.'

'Language, dear girl!'

'Sorry, but…' Harriet waved her hands around at the burning night. 'Sometimes language is the best response.'

'I don't think it's nature,' Zoe said.

Harriet was unable to hide her surprise. 'You think they're heaven-sent?'

'In a way.' Zoe pointed with the hand that wasn't still holding Harriet's. 'Those meteors just changed direction.'

'That's impossible,' Oscar said. 'Isn't it?'

'And again,' Zoe pointed.

The second of three fiery balls hurtling together across the northern side of the city adjusted course enough so that when they all smashed to earth a moment later, they were seemingly an equal distance apart.

'Oh, My Lord, we're being invaded. Betty Naylor was right. She told me *The Argus* claimed London had been attacked and that's why we hadn't had news from there in three days.'

'Attacked?' Mrs Grainger said. 'England had a meteor shower too, Ida. That's all.'

'Attacked by who?' Oscar asked.

'Martians, of course.' It was Scooter, hanging on to Mrs Grainger's skirts but not taking his eyes off the destruction around them.

And destruction it was, for while it appeared many of the 'meteors' had landed in the countryside beyond the city, quite a few had clearly crashed into buildings in the inner suburbs. The distant shoreline near Sorento was also on fire; east around Hawthorn was a radiant red, and elsewhere the night was a sickly green.

Fire bells rang out across the night in every direction, as did the sound of people shouting. Amidst it all, those on the balcony heard Horatio Landers proclaiming, 'Oh, I'd say these are bigger than those that fell around Ballarat last week.'

Down on the riverside lawn of the Hotel Artemis, while Melbourne was assaulted by something terrible from the sky, Horatio was still regaling a captured audience of five with tales of his own adventures. 'The lads and I went out to investigate and found two blackened craters the size of two locomotives but empty of any burning rocks. We reckoned the meteors disintegrated on impact.'

'Martians,' Scooter said again. 'That's what Mugsy Bonner told Dave de Coite this arvo.'

Harriet raised an eyebrow. 'And who are these men that they would know such a thing?'

Scooter squinted, either to interpret the question or in wonder there was anyone in the world who didn't know 'these men'.

'They're captains, Miss – of the Tricolours and the Saltwater–'

'We're meant to be calling it the Maribyrnong River now, lad,' Oscar said.

'Oh, so these captains might have some knowledge of such things,' Harriet said.

Zoe snorted, and pointed to the river. 'Mugsy is skipper of the Saltwater punt, and De Coite captains our football team.'

'Dave knows aplenty,' Scooter said. 'He made Footscray the premier this year.'

'Sir George Turner is premier, lad,' Oscar corrected him; as usual. 'Our boys are the premiers. And Dave…'

Zoe sighed. Men and their football! For all the times she'd wished for anything at all to distract them from their incessant ball talk, she now knew even a fiery calamity from outer space would not stop them.

A far-off but approaching wheeze, that became a whine then a scream accompanied another set of three more-than-likely not meteors as they soared in from the east this time. They came low across the heart of Melbourne, over the water where the Yarra met the bay and slammed into–

'Good grief, that's Williamstown. They must have hit the docks.'

Everyone on the balcony stared in horror, hands to mouths or hearts, knowing – as fires broke out on the piers and buildings along the edge of Hobson's Bay – that Mrs Grainger was right.

'Oh my Dear Lord, those poor people,' Ida said. 'They couldn't survive that.'

'I cannot wait until morning as usual; I must go to Aunt Isobel's now.' Harriet tried to let go of her friend's hand, but Zoe held tight.

'The last train to Newport was at 5 o'clock, Harriet.'

'Then…then I will walk, Zoe. My aunt is all alone; she won't know what to do.'

'You can't do that, it's over four miles,' Zoe insisted. 'And it's dark.'

'But the sky is all lit up bright as day,' Scooter said. 'A spooky glowing-red sort of day, but–'

Oscar cuffed the back of the boy's head. 'That's not helpful, lad. And don't you talk such foolishness, Miss Brookes. You'll not be wandering the streets alone. It's not safe anywhere, with those Martian meteors flying around.'

'Thank you for pointing out I may be no safer here than on my way to Newport, Mr Jones.' Harriet wiggled her fingers, so Zoe finally let go. 'I will fetch a coat and change into my good walking boots. I will be perfectly fine. I've tramped much further than four miles before.'

As Harriet Brookes retreated inside, the four who remained on the balcony turned their gaze on Zoe, who raised her hands in surrender.

'What can I do? The woman is determined. And unstoppable.'

Mrs Grainger leant close. 'Of all her new friends here, I feel you would be most affected should something untoward happen to her.'

Zoe glowered at the woman she considered her second mother. 'And she's infuriating.'

'And adorable. And you cannot let her go alone.'

Zoe turned to the youngest amongst them. 'Samuel Thomas, are you big and bold enough to go with Miss Brookes?'

Scooter ran his hand through his mop of red hair and puffed up his chest. 'On my oath, Miss Zoe. I'll pertect her.'

'Excellent. Then go wake up old Billy and get him ready.'

Harriet had wasted no time. By the time Zoe passed though the first-floor sitting room and out into the hallway, Harriet was reshoed and half-way down the stairs.

'It really would be best if you at least waited until daylight.'

'I appreciate your concern, Zoe,' she said, as she pushed open the back door, 'but I am Isobel's only family here. I cannot leave her alone to…to whatever this may be.'

'Harriet.' Zoe caught up with her in the yard and gently clasped her elbow. 'Harry, please wait.'

Harriet Brookes turned into the restraining arm and fixed her beautiful gaze on Zoe's face. 'I am quite capable. I am much tougher than I appear. I am not afraid. I am–'

Zoe kissed her, quite passionately, on the mouth. And then, startled by her own boldness, stepped away.

'Oh my.' Harriet raised an eyebrow. 'Well, that's…'

'I'm sorry, that was quite–'

'Wonderful.' Harriet smiled a smile that lit up her eyes, and kissed Zoe back – with equal verve. 'I'm still going to check on Aunt Isobel,' she said, releasing her hold.

'Of course you are,' Zoe said, realising none of the cacophony caused by Martians, asteroids or exploding earthbound structures compared with the noisy carry-on of her own heart at that moment.

'I do like that you called me Harry.'

'Well, Harry, I will not let you go alone, only because you've only ever taken the train to Newport and you might get lost. I can't leave the Artemis, but they can.'

Scooter, grinning like a fool and leading the hotel's oldest horse, Black Billy, right up to them, announced. 'I will pro-teck you, Miss Brookes.'

Oscar, who was making his own way from the water pump, had clearly tried to correct the boy's English again.

'Oh, what an excellent idea,' Harriet said. 'But what if he gets startled by all those terrible noises.'

Zoe smiled. 'Billy is deaf as a post, so he's the best horse to carry you both.'

'Mr Jones there said I should look for a side saddle,' Scooter said, 'but as I can't magine what such a thing would be like, I'm afraid we probably don't have no such thing, Miss.'

Oscar groaned.

The sky to the east beyond the Melbourne flared red again as more things from the dark beyond crashed to earth, and the air reverberated from the impacts even from that distance.

'I promise to be careful, Zoe, especially now,' – Harriet kissed Zoe on the cheek, on the corner of her mouth, which implied so much more than farewell – 'now I have Scooter to protect.'

'That's my job, Miss.'

Harriet grinned at him. 'Me. To protect me. And, I will fetch my aunt back here, so we can all face this disaster together. With luck we'll be home for breakfast.'

'That's if home an'-all is still 'ere at breakfast,' Scooter noted, then rubbed the back of his head as he scored another whisterpoop from Oscar.

'Part of protecting Miss Brookes, young Samuel, is not scaring the beeswax out of her with notions like that.'

'He's quite right, though, Mr Jones,' Harriet noted. 'None of us know where the next of those whatever-they-may-be will strike.' With that she stepped easily into the stirrup, swung her right leg up and over and sat comfortably astride old Billy. 'Clearly I can't imagine a side saddle either.'

A bit of wriggling to resettle her skirts, then she reached down to haul Scooter up behind her.

Oscar handed up the small hessian water bag he'd filled for them.

'Scooter. Hyde Street to Somerville Road to Williamstown Road. It's the most direct way to Newport.'

'Yes, Miss Zoe.'

And then they were gone.

'If this is a Martian invasion, I reckon they better steer clear of that young woman,' Oscar noted.

Zoe laughed. 'Come, old friend. We'd better prepare ourselves too. Water, food and blankets down to the cellar.'

'And shovels and other tools to dig our way out again, should it come to that,' Oscar said.

OF THE 11 PEOPLE still occupying the Hotel Artemis, six worked a roster of two-hour vigils from the riverside gazebo, while the rest bunked together in the huge cellar, either sleeping or drinking tea. Oscar and Horatio announced the clackety-clack noises that began at around nine o'clock were more than likely guns and artillery, though what they were firing at and where was anyone's guess.

At 11 everyone recklessly rushed outside after something crashed on their side of the river, about half a mile north but close enough to the water that it sent waves downstream. Ida and Oscar reported that it most likely hit the tallow factory, or the rope works, beyond the jetty for the punt.

By seven o'clock in the morning, when Zoe and Mrs Grainger were on their second watch, it felt as if their whole world was in flames. Melbourne and its suburbs were no longer being assaulted, that had stopped around midnight, but the meteors – always in threes – continued to streak across the sky far to the north and east.

It was obvious the fire brigade was kept busy all night as the bell at the Eastern Hill Fire Station, on one of the highest points of the city, was clanging every 15 minutes until dawn.

'I swear I don't care what Dave said to Mugsy who told Scooter,' Mrs Grainger said. 'I'll not believe they're Martians until I see one myself.'

Zoe gathered her long hair into a coil and pinned it up out of the way. She had changed into her favourite working clothes – her father's old trousers, a woollen shirt and her sturdy boots – the ones she always wore to work with their two horses, one cow and several chickens. Granted, she'd more than likely wear them during the day even if she had no yard work to do.

'If this is an invasion of some kind, Mrs G, it's a strange one. These alleged Martians seem intent only on throwing large, hot rocks at us.'

Given the past hour had been relatively quiet, the odd noise that now hurried towards the hotel was disturbing. It was a rattle, a clack-clack, a peculiar and persistent scraping, and the strangled vocals of a desperate man who apparently couldn't decide whether to swear or sing. Then in through the gateway came Tug Barker, driving his horse which dragged what was left of his Carlton Brewery cart. It was a wonder the thing could travel at all, as the back end of the tray and its wheels were missing.

Following close behind, but driverless, was one of the Batties Concentrated Milk carts; its horse apparently having decided to tag along. Both horses sensibly pulled up without any help from Tug, who slid from the seat and into the dirt.

'Are you drunk, Thomas Barker?' Mrs Grainger asked. 'You know it's not even seven o'clock.'

'I was hiding but the drinking was accidental,' Tug said. 'I threw meself into your ale,' he pointed to the broken barrel tied to the back of his seat, 'and well, you know, one thing led to getting well and truly possum-faced.'

'What on earth were you hiding from?'

'Something that shouldn't be on this earth, Ivy Grainger. Them damn Martians are everywhere. I'm just glad you two are alive for me to tell you.'

Zoe helped Tug up off the ground and realised most of the beer smell that was emanating from him was from his sodden clothes.

'You mean you climbed into the barrel?'

'Yes, indeed, Miss Zoe. I know it was cowardly, but I figured if I was going to die I may as well be so drunk I wouldn't care if I was scorched to oblivion.'

'What are you talking about man? Surely it's easy to avoid a falling rock – if you can see it coming.'

'They're not rocks, Ivy Grainger. Them things have all been giant cylinders filled with Martian machines. Though John Fisher said the machines got built inside the craters, from what came out of the cylinders.'

'You've seen them?'

'I seen the machines, Miss Zoe. I seen what they did to…to John Fisher when he ran from his milk cart. It was all zap-zap with thin red lights and ploof he was ashes.'

Zoe and Mrs Grainger glanced at each other and back at Tug wondering if he was so inebriated he had no idea what he'd seen.

'Don't you go looking at me like that. I ain't that drunk; I just smell like it. Them three-legged metal monsters are stomping all over the place, blasting this and blowing up that. They got these whippy tentacles that grab people and yank them inside like they're eating them, except they're made of metal so that can't be so. I'm wondering if I could trouble you for a cup of tea?'

'Of course, we've a pot on the go in the cellar, where we all spent the night,' Zoe said. 'You take him over, Mrs G, and I'll unhitch Edgar from what's left of the cart. How long has the milk horse been with you, Tug?'

'Since Yarraville, about an hour ago. I spent the night there after collecting today's barrels from the Carlton Brewery warehouse. But them bastards, sorry, ladies, them Martians started wrecking all the factory buildings and half the houses there. And, oh my, I don't know how many they ate or collected or whatever they be doing with all them people they're just lifting off the streets; like they're picking apples or peaches or…' Tug plucked at the air. 'Me and Edgar parked ourselves under the rail bridge and waited until they'd moved on, before heading here this morning. We met poor John and his Nessie there just near where the Junction Hotel is, was. Maybe I need a rum. No tea.'

Zoe felt a coldness flush through her body. 'All this destruction was last night, not this morning?'

'Yes, Miss Zoe. Didn't you hear all the guns firing on them? The last of them monsters, that I saw, was heading westwards at maybe half-eleven.'

'Oh dear,' Zoe said.

Mrs Grainger gave her a motherly hug. 'Take the milk cart. Go find her.'

The destruction visited upon the streets and buildings of Footscray, five streets inland from the river, was almost impossible for Zoe to make sense of. Close to the waterway that separated 'the west' from the heart of Melbourne there was little evidence that anything untoward had taken place. But Zoe had been unable to turn down Whitehall, the street she told Scooter to take Harriet, because a smoking crater made it impassable. She urged Nessie on and then left into Hyde Street where she encountered a steady stream of people leaving town by the looks of it, headed she knew not where.

She spotted Reverend James Argyle and Father Bob Sweeney on the corner of Buckley Street working together – in itself a miracle – to stem the exodus. But folks were scared, and they'd packed what was precious to them in handcarts, and horse carts, on bicycles, and in suitcases and hessian bags and were aiming to get as far away from the city as they could.

Zoe wondered at the sense of that. Hadn't they seen that those things were falling everywhere about the countryside?

'Oh, not you too, Miss Vaughn,' Reverend Argyle said, as Zoe drew her small cart to a halt beside the two men.

'No, I'm not abandoning our town, gentlemen. I'm looking for–' Zoe realised only the residents of the Hotel Artemis would know Harriet Brookes. 'Have you seen our boy Scooter? You know, young Samuel Thomas.'

'You mean the red-headed orphan?' Father Sweeney said. 'Not since last week at the football.'

'I need to get to Newport. Any word on what danger or obstacles lie that way?'

'The mechanical beasts that attacked our neighbourhoods with their heat rays moved north-west after our soldiers and their artillery gave them a thrashing. Some say they're congregating around Braybrook Junction. Mayor Gallant said word came through the train station there was destroyed, and large sections of the track were ripped up and dragged off.'

'Dragged off by what?'

'The slug creatures inside the giant armoured heads I imagine,' Reverend Argyle said.

Zoe guessed the minister's imagination was being carried away, further than was healthy for a man of the cloth.

'What is that you're wearing, Miss Vaughn? Is it appropriate attire for a gentlewoman?'

'Now right there, Reverend Argyle, you have the reason why I don't attend church anymore. Here we all are going to hell in a wheelbarrow and you still worry about the things that don't matter.' She took her leave, with a sweet smile, and clicked at Nessie who was keen to escape the thronging crowd.

It took nearly an hour to reach the crossroads of Williamstown and Somerville, a distance of no more than two miles. Her progress was impeded by the rubble of buildings that had exploded across the cobbled roadway, mangled vehicles that blocked the smaller streets she tried to detour around, and the need to vomit, on three occasions, after coming upon the charred remains of people huddled in the ruins.

'What on earth are we doing out here?' she asked Nessie, knowing full well she would not turn back until she'd made it to Isobel Wright's home in Farm Street, Newport. She needed to know whether Harriet and Scooter had made it there. Or not. While she had no way of knowing which route they had actually taken, given the battles that had gone on overnight, she hoped they had made it through before the otherworldly danger had revealed its true self. Devastating meteor showers were one thing, but cylinders containing metal war machines – with heat rays no less – and which may or may not carry Martian slugs was something that had to be fought against, not endured.

She and Nessie continued along the pockmarked Williamstown Road, weaving around chunks of debris, deep holes, and odd stands of molten metal, which she eventually realised were canons. She began to wonder just how many soldiers had survived the thrashing they'd given the Martians. It also occurred to her that she'd not asked anyone how big the Martian machines were. Would she round a corner and come upon one lying in wait, big as a bear, and crouching ready to strike? With it's three legs. And its heat ray.

'Good grief, now whose imagination is being carried off.'

It took only 20 minutes to reach Spottiswoode, where the oddest sight in a day of peculiarities met her. There, gathered on one side of Hudson Street, a group of mostly women were heckling the crowd of men spilling out of the Grand Hotel; while on the corner diagonally opposite and, seemingly reluctant to step onto Williamstown Road – because any who did were pulled back – was another group of women, some carrying placards demanding 'the Vote'.

Suffragettes versus the Temperance League in a battle for what? Zoe wondered. The hearts and minds and of the local men who, understandably today, wanted a drink or ten? And again why, while the world faced an attack from somewhere beyond their comprehension, were they arguing about the small things?

With no interest at all in what the Temperance women had to say, she steered Nessie to the far side of the road. The suffragettes began shouting at her to stay back, to get away from them, until they saw that the driver of the milk cart was not a man.

'You may stay with us if you wish,' proclaimed a tall, buxom and imposing woman. 'I am Marjorie Blair, president of our group. And you are?'

'Zoe Vaughn, proprietor of the Hotel Artemis in Footscray, on a quest to find two friends.'

'Zoe Vaughn?' A woman pushed her way forward and peered into the cart. 'Are you looking for my niece, Harriet?'

'Mrs Wright?'

'Yes, dear. Harriet and the young boy left me here with my friends, knowing I'd be safe. She headed back to your hotel about an hour ago.'

Zoe shook her head. 'How does she know you'll be safe? Here on the street. In the open. With, with–'

'Unarmed women?' posed Marjorie Blair.

'Well, yes.'

'Because my brilliant niece worked out what those Martian things are after.'

'Conquest of the Earth?' While Zoe also thought Harriet Brookes was brilliant, it was doubtful she had worked out the motive of the invaders in the few hours since they had parted company.

'Quite possibly,' Marjorie agreed. 'But they also – oh, no. Nobody move,' she said as a hideous wailing filled the air. 'Do not panic. Do not run.' She took hold of Nessie by her bridle and gently threw her shawl to cover her eyes, whereon the horse settled happily.

The wail changed key to a low mechanical thrum as something began to emerge from the broken buildings beside the Grand Hotel. First there were a cluster of tentacles waving deliberately as if testing the air, then a great burnished hood crested what had been the roof of the single-story building.

It continued to rise.

The massive hood covered a lower metal section the size of steam engine.

So, a little bigger than a bear, Zoe noted. And then…

It stood.

Or rather it unfolded its three legs, pushing itself upwards until it towered over the three-story Grand Hotel.

While Zoe was unable to quell the rising panic, she could not have run anywhere even if it was the sensible thing to do. She was rigid with fear.

Some of the men outside the Grand were also rooted to the spot; some crossed the road to join the Temperance League, perhaps thinking they had drunk so much they were hallucinating; and others took off down Hudson Street.

The Martian got the runners first. The three thickest of its many tentacles lashed out and collected two men in each, passing them into a cavernous maw that opened beneath the hood. Other tentacles slapped men to the ground and even reached inside the hotel to drag patrons out.

'Do not move,' Marjorie whispered again.

And not one of the suffragettes ran away. They stood bravely immobile taking calming breaths and smiling encouragement at each other.

The women and few men of the Temperance League however shuffled this way and that, showing fear and indecision before making a collective choice to walk then run off down Williamstown Road back towards Yarraville.

The Martian whipped out a tentacle that snaked in the air above them, then retracted as if uninterested. A moment later the hood turned and revealed an aperture in its centre from which blasted a heat-ray, deadly in its accuracy. The Temperance League, in its entirety, was cut horizontally through the middle, stopping each dissected member for a brief moment before they burst into flames.

If she'd had anything left to bring up, Zoe would have vomited again.

The Martian, now with a strange green cloud billowing around its undercarriage, returned to its collecting, or feeding, of the Grand's patrons who could not escape its tentacles. When it was done it stepped into the street, set the hotel alight with its heat-ray and stomped right by the Suffragettes, its tentacles investigating its surroundings but apparently finding nothing of interest.

As soon as it was out of sight, the women relaxed into each other or collapsed to the ground, laughing with relief.

Zoe suspected they were all insane. 'Mrs Wright, which way did Harriet go?'

'Along Hall Street, so they could cross the fields to Yarraville.'

'She does know there's not much left of Yarraville?'

'Yes, dear.'

'Do they still have Billy?'

'No, they set him free in my farm paddock. It has a barn he can get into, and there's plenty of food and water for the old boy.'

Zoe smiled. 'Thank you. Are you certain you want to stay here?'

'As you witnessed, I am perfectly safe with my friends.'

The scorching heat from the incinerated hotel felt like bad sunburn on her face as Zoe urged Nessie along Hudson Street. She turned left down Hall at the still standing but deserted Spottiswoode Hotel and travelled as fast as possible in the hope of catching Harry and Scooter before they disappeared into one of the many damaged cross streets on the way home.

While this route contained the longest stretch of undamaged buildings she'd seen since crossing Whitehall two hours ago, for some reason she was troubled by the local penchant for planting the same ground covering plant in every garden. Until she realised it was a weed, red and strange, and it truly was everywhere. It grew up tree trunks, on fences, in crevices, on the road surface and encroaching into the otherwise empty land at the end of Hall Street.

She had two choices: cross the fields or backtrack. The latter would add another hour to her trek, and she did not want to waste any time in her search for Harry, especially now she'd seen first hand the damage the Martians could cause. The fact the fighting machines also lurked in strange places, waiting to attack, showed a cunning that was quite terrifying.

Nessie, untroubled by the red weed, plunged into the field of ankle-high red vegetation which seemed to spread ahead of them like a carpet being rolled out. By the time they reached Francis Street on the other side, the fields were completely besieged.

Zoe ventured down Ballarat Street but had not gone far when she realised she'd have to unhitch the milk cart or retrace her steps. The debris blocking her way could only be navigated on foot. She was soon threading her way around bluestone blocks, wooden doors, kitchen chairs, a Metters wood stove and scattered clothes. Nessie followed along, without being tethered.

'Where did it go?'

'Chase it the other way.'

'Bugger, Bugger.'

The owners of three different voices, two wonderfully familiar, were approaching along the ruins of Tarrengower Street. Before Zoe could make her presence known something else came rushing at her. It was man-sized, metal, three-legged and fast. It knocked her over and kept going, bumping into everything in its path until it disappeared into a house that had lost its roof and top floor.

A short human, dressed in a semi-tanned hide and reeking of

something vile, stood over her. 'What you doing down there, Miss Zoe?'

'Resting, Scooter. Why do you smell like a dead thing?'

'Cambaflarge.'

'Really? What are you camouflaged from?'

'The Martian battle-tripods and the scuttlers.'

'What on earth are the scuttlers?'

'Things like what just knocked you on your bum. They're the personal little tripods the Martians use for running around the ground.'

Zoe sat up. 'What are the big ones for?'

'Blowing everything up and shooting hot rays at people. They're bastards. And I ain't apologising for swearing.'

'Is that really you?' Harriet dropped to her knees beside Zoe and hugged her tightly. 'What are you doing out here in the streets?'

'Looking for you. Why aren't you covered in dung?'

'The Martians only seem interested in taking men. And boys. Male persons. They don't seem to be concerned with us – women, I mean – unless we're with men. Then they might collect us too; but mostly they incinerate any groups that contain men.'

'Or anyone who tries to run away,' Zoe said. 'You must have seen a lot of action last night to work that out.'

'You have no idea. It was truly awful, Zoe. Did you really come after me?'

"Yes. And I met your Aunt Isobel playing silly games with a battle tripod. I now assume she and the Suffragettes were testing your theory.'

'Oh no, is she alright?'

'Yes. I do believe your idea holds weight; it was almost as if the tripod couldn't see them.'

'I think it's smell. That's why I shoved Scooter and Petey – Petey, where are you? – into the stables at my aunt's place.'

'I'm here, Miss Harry.' Another boy dressed in horse manure loomed into view. 'Who's this then?'

'This is my very dear friend, Miss Zoe. Let's help her to her feet.'

Zoe wasn't quite sure where to wipe her hands once she was upright, but Harriet soon found her a shirt amongst the rubble to use as cloth. 'You get used to it,' she said. 'I can't smell them anymore.'

'And now we can sneak up on the scuttlers,' Petey said.

'And beat them senseless with our scuttler bangers,' Scooter said, raising a cricket bat.

"But aren't they metal, like the giant tripods?'

Scooter nodded. 'Yes, but not as metally.'

'The hood part is softer and easy to dent. And once we do that a few times, the squid bastards – again, not sorry – come out and we can hit them in the actual head.'

'Or stab them.' Petey waved a carving knife.

'I don't suppose you saw where the scuttler went?' Harriet asked.

'Into that blue house,' Zoe pointed. 'Why?'

'We damaged its…vessel, I suppose you'd call it. We have to finish it off.'

Zoe's eyes widened. 'Can't we just leave it?'

'It might be injured.'

Zoe raised her hands questioningly.

Harriet sighed. 'I've been questioning the general thinking that these Martians – if that is whatthey are – are here to conquer us.'

'Their intentions seem to be fairly obvious, Harry.'

'Yes, but we might be like mice or ants to them; quite inconsequential.'

'You may think it strange, my dear, but I don't find that notion at all comforting.'

Harriet laughed. 'I don't suppose it is. But I have seen the surface of the red planet through a large astronomical telescope and if there is a civilisation there it must be on the side that faces away from us. And what's more I imagine that the Martians are more likely escaping their desert planet for a better world, rather than invading ours for plunder to take home.'

This time Zoe laughed. 'You think they're migrants?'

Harriet shrugged.

'Who regard us as vermin? Or food?'

'Let's go get that thing,' Scooter said, and he and Petey set off for the blue house.

'Wait for us, boys.' Harriet clasped Zoe's hand.

'I must say, I prefer your other theory about how we survive this invasion simply by being women,' Zoe said, as the four of them entered the damaged residence.

'Or covered in manure,' Petey said.

'Shh.' Harriet put a finger to her lips then pointed to their right. There were few internal walls left and the scuttling noise was coming from the other side of one of them. Harriet indicated that she and Scooter would go one way; and Zoe and Petey the other.

The scuttler, crouched on its metal haunches, was leaning into the empty fireplace and rocking back and forth as if trying to remove its hood on the brickwork.

Zoe noticed tiny bits of debris – no, they were seeds – were being flung from the vessel every time it connected with the hearth.

And, disturbingly, the same red plant that had overtaken the fields was growing in the rivulets of water that snaked this way and that from a vase that had been smashed to the floor. As the water moved the weed grew. Or, the weed pushed the water so it could grow further.

Scooter wasted no time and was not in the least bit quiet about his attack, but the scuttler didn't stand a chance. He pushed it all the way into the fire place, then beat the legs off it with his bat. He and Petey dragged the incapacitated vessel back into the room and banged on the hood until the metal was dented so much it split open. Only then did they stand back and wait.

Moments later squid-like arms slid through the crack, forcing it further open, and then the Martian – a creature of mostly head, with oily-grey skin, two large eyes, and a tight and lipless V-shaped mouth – slid out onto the floor. It was badly injured and began a pitiful moan, which turned to a howl that travelled five notes up and down a scale, then shifted into a deafening ululation.

'It's bloody talking,' Scooter said.

Petey stuck his carving knife between the creature's bulbous eyes. 'Not no more.'

An hour later two women, two smelly boys, and a now-devoted horse walked through the gates of the Hotel Artemis. They were greeted by a relieved Mrs Ivy Grainger, full of hugs for everyone, even the smelly boys; Tug Barker, who appeared to be sober and no longer stank like a brewery; and Ida McLeod, who smiled broadly, kissed Zoe on the cheek, and went off to make more tea and inform the others of their return.

'Where's your aunty, Miss Harriet, did you not find her?'

'I did, Mrs G. I left her with her dear friend, Marjorie Blair, president of the western branch of the Victorian Women's Suffrage Society.'

'A stalwart woman is Marjorie Blair,' Mrs Grainger said. 'A friend of mine, and a great support to Henrietta Dugdale, co-founder of our suffrage movement.'

Zoe smiled. 'When I last saw your friend, Mrs G, she was striding along Williamstown Road with 12 other suffragettes, including Harry's Aunt Isobel. They had just survived a Martian encounter – as had I – and were off to rescue as many women as possible.'

'Oh, do tell,' Mrs Grainger said, 'but over a cup of tea. We're all still in the cellar.'

'WE NEED TO TELL the government and the military and police your theories,' Ida said, after the day's adventures had been recounted.

'I don't believe it's safe for any of us to leave here again, until the Martians have been dealt with,' Olive Dunkley said.

'But we're quite likely the only people who know how to survive those very Martians,' Harriet said, 'while the government and their troopers work out how defeat them.'

'If you're a woman,' said Horatio Landers, as if it was the most preposterous thing he'd ever heard.

'And how splendid is that,' – Mrs Grainger snapped her fingers – 'for once. And you can venture anywhere you like, Mr Landers, if you're prepared to roll in our dung heap first.'

'Or soak yourself in perfume,' Harriet suggested. 'I think that would achieve the same result in masking the way you smell.'

'Is that why Tug wasn't attacked by the Martian who killed John Fisher?' Zoe asked. 'Because he'd sat himself in a barrel of ale.'

"More than likely.'

'Then I have a plan how we can get to the Premier–'

'Sir George Turner!'

'Good memory, Scooter,' Mrs Grainger smiled.

'And anyone else who needs to know, as quickly as possible,' Zoe continued, 'and without anyone – man, woman, or boy child – who wants to come with me getting hurt.'

'I'm not leaving here, but I'll help get you ready,' said Mrs Grainger. 'What do you need?'

'Is the Saltwater Punt still operational?'

'I believe so,' Oscar said. 'And I will join your expedition, Miss Zoe.'

'Then we need the punt, and Mugsy Bonner, too, if you don't know how to operate it, Oscar. A variety of weapons would be good. Cricket bats and large knives have proven quite useful, but a gun, if anyone has such a thing might come in handy.

'We need food and water, Mrs G, because we don't know what's been happening on the big city side of the river. And finally, Oscar and our two young Martian hunters can choose how they'd like to smell.'

Harriet leant in close and whispered against Zoe's ear. 'I plan to go wherever you go, Miss Zoe.'

Zoe inhaled deeply and glanced at her future. 'I was hoping you would say that, Miss Harry; my love.'

Apostles of Mercy

Janeen Webb

> The Tasmanians...were entirely swept out of existence in a war of extermination waged by European immigrants...Are we such apostles of mercy as to complain if the Martians warred in the same spirit?
>
> – H.G. Wells, *The War of the Worlds*, 1898

IT WAS THE DARK OF THE MOON WHEN THE MYSTERIOUS CYLINDERS FELL TO earth: a blazing cascade that burned through the clear, black, star-spangled velvet of the Australian night sky.

High up in the Blue Mountains, at the summit of the resort town of Katoomba – staging post for visitors to the famous Jenolan Caves – the fashionably attired clientele of the luxurious Carrington Hotel took their after-dinner port out onto the balcony to enjoy the spectacle, but they were caught unawares when a red-hot fireball flamed across the peak. The heat was intense. Paint blistered on nearby weatherboards and singed gumnuts rained down upon the hotel's corrugated iron roof like hot hailstones, bringing with them the sharp smell of scorched eucalyptus.

And then the ground shook.

There was a distant *crack*: a huge eucalypt had exploded somewhere in the deep valley below. Gouts of fire erupted into the darkness. The astonished onlookers soon heard the hiss and crackle of flames as the fire took hold, racing through the dry bushland scrub. The Scenic Lookout was backlit by the fire's lurid glow, and throat-stinging smoke began to fill the air.

The hotel guests scurried back indoors to the comfort of closed shutters and restorative brandies.

In the little township below the hotel, the watchman was ringing the fire bell. There was a surge of activity: horses were harnessed; water wagons were filled; people began to assemble with ropes and shovels, ready to form bucket brigades. For the working folk of Katoomba, it would be a long night.

Pastor Jedediah Carpenter was the first person to locate the crash site. A stocky, raw-boned Irishman, he'd harnessed up his horse and dray at dawn and set out from his small holding outside Oberon, a mere 15 miles from the Jenolan Caves. He was a dirt-poor farmer, a religious zealot, and mad as a cut snake. He followed the smoke, searching for salvage.

The bush was strangely silent. The birds and animals had fled the firestorm that raged through the valley. The only sound that reached Jedediah's ears above the slow clop of his horse's hooves and the creaking of his old wagon was the soft *ping* of cooling metal. He pushed back his battered hat from his unruly mop of brown curls and wiped the sweat from his bloodshot blue eyes as he surveyed the smoking ruin of the landscape.

He tethered his horse and trudged up slippery scree to the lip of the new crater. And then he just stood there, stock still, staring into the pit, peering at the wrecked lumps of melted, twisted metal now embedded in the wounded earth. One of the strangely mottled missiles had split open on impact, and something had crawled out, only to die in the conflagration that had engulfed it.

Jedediah could hardly comprehend the horror of what lay before him: the charred remains of a bulky creature at least the size of a bull, a creature with what must surely have been a massive head with huge apertures for eyes and mouth, a creature with multiple, bunched tentacles that had twisted and shrivelled in the intense heat of the flames.

Jedediah almost gagged on the overpowering stench of burned blubber that emanated from the corpse, mixing with the acrid smell of smouldering vegetation. He fell to his knees, pulled his dog-eared bible from his coat pocket, and held it up in front of him with both hands, keeping the cross on the cover facing outwards towards the body – perhaps in defence against evil, perhaps in supplication.

'Here I am, Lord,' he cried. 'I see before me the body of the Beast of the Apocalypse, the harbinger of doom! Armageddon is upon us! The end is nigh!' He drew a shuddering, stinking, smoke-filled breath. 'Last night I witnessed the fall of Your fiery angels, Lord! Today You have led me here to the burning wilderness. Command me, Lord. I am Your servant. I will do Your bidding.'

His mouth fell open, forming a perfect 'O' of surprise, when a voice answered: *Help me.*

The words reverberated inside his head, a resonance that set his teeth on edge and amplified the buzzing of his perplexed, scattered thoughts.

At the Carrington Hotel, the guests were enjoying a leisurely start to the day. The warm smells of bacon and coffee and toast wafted through the comfortably appointed dining room. The talk around the breakfast table was all of last night's excitement.

Annie Fraser was cheerfully buttering her second slice of hot toast when her aunt arrived.

'I see your appetite has recovered, dear,' Lady Fraser said.

'Quite recovered, thank you Aunt,' Annie agreed, tucking into her heaped plate of scrambled eggs and crispy bacon. 'I had a bad headache, nothing more. All I needed was an early night. I'm perfectly well this morning.'

'Glad to hear it,' said Lady Fraser.

Charles Jackson, a visiting American geologist, looked up from his devilled kidneys. 'You missed the most spectacular meteor shower, Miss Fraser,' he said solemnly.

'Not at all, Mr Jackson.' She dimpled a smile at him. 'I watched from my bedroom window. But I couldn't come down to join you all – I was hardly dressed for company.'

'Quite right, dear,' said Lady Fraser. She nodded her thanks as she accepted a cup of tea from her daughter, Elizabeth.

'There will certainly be a large crater somewhere down in the valley,' Jackson went on. 'I'll look forward to investigating that. I should be able find it by triangulating the trajectory of the meteors.'

'You won't need much triangulation to find *that* crash site, Mr Jackson,' Elizabeth remarked. 'The fire will leave a big enough mark for anyone to see.'

'It will indeed, Miss Fraser,' said the Honourable Frederick Urquhart, cheerfully helping himself to more bacon and another grilled tomato. 'I've never seen the like,' he added, his soft Scottish accent contrasting sharply with Jackson's nasal whine. 'And you must admit we've witnessed the most spectacular astronomical events these past few nights.'

Elizabeth laughed. 'Nobody can deny that, Mr Urquhart,' she said. 'I must say I quite liked those green flares we saw the night before the meteor shower. They were definitely coming from the vicinity of Mars. I checked my almanac.' She paused for a moment, concentrating on stirring her coffee. 'I thought meteors were supposed to be always red and orange,' she said. 'Something about them burning up as they enter the Earth's atmosphere.'

'Quite right, Miss Fraser,' the geologist replied. 'You are a most remarkably well informed young lady.'

Elizabeth bridled. 'I assure you that ladies read the scientific journals quite as much as gentlemen, Mr Jackson. I have a selection sent directly from *Cole's Book Emporium*, in Melbourne: Mr Cole imports a most comprehensive range. There really is no need to assume ignorance on my part.'

'Elizabeth…' Lady Fraser shot her daughter a warning glance.

'It's quite all right, Lady Fraser.' Charles Jackson was powerless to control the red blush that now spread past his starched white collar and up to the roots of his carefully barbered blond hair. 'My apologies, Miss Fraser. The science involved is relatively recent. I meant only to indicate that I enjoy such up-to-date conversation.'

'Of course you did,' said Elizabeth.

'Anyway,' Jackson rushed on, 'there must be some contributing atmospheric conditions to make those gas explosions appear green to us. There may be high level atmospheric winds, or dust clouds, or even some chemical element in the gases themselves to create that strange effect.'

'Or,' said Freddy Urquhart, 'those fiery things falling from the sky aren't meteors at all. They could be something else altogether.'

'Such as?'

'Don't get all irritated, Charles,' said Freddy. 'You know the London papers have been reporting green flares emanating from Mars for days now. I've been following the story in *The Katoomba Times*. I must say the telegraphic system here is very efficient: news from overseas reaches Sydney within a day or so.' He tapped his newspaper for effect. 'There's a lot of speculation that your meteors are actually some kind of space missiles launched from Mars.'

Jackson shook his head impatiently. 'The chances of anything coming from Mars are a million to one,' he said. 'I'm a man of science, and I wonder that a respectable paper like *The Times* should bother to print such fanciful nonsense.'

Freddy was unrepentant. 'Unless it isn't quite so fanciful,' he replied. 'It says here that *The Washington Post* is reporting it too. Perhaps you'd find that more convincing?'

Jedediah Carpenter shook his head as if to dislodge the reverberating words, but he could not. He heard them again: *Help me.*

He realised that the cry must be coming from the one undamaged cylindrical shape he could see at the far edge of the crater. 'There's something trapped in there,' he muttered under his breath. He crept closer to the edge of the pit. 'Hello?' he called. 'Who are you?'

There was a slight pause while the Martian processed the thought patterns of this strange example of Earth's semi-sentient wildlife.

It drew deep upon its telepathic powers, working to decipher the muddle of Jedediah's mind, searching for the words that would trigger the desired response.

Help me, it sent at last. *You have been Chosen.*

That was enough for Jedediah. If the Lord had spoken to Moses from a burning bush, why wouldn't He speak to His humble servant Jedediah from a smoking crater?

'Hold on,' he called. 'I'm coming.'

Charles Jackson tried, unsuccessfully, to hide his annoyance. 'Well, Freddy,' he said, 'I'll soon find out if there's any truth in your rumours. I was preparing to ride down to the Jenolan Caves in any case: the underground limestone formations are said to be superb. I've brought my plans forward.'

'So have we,' Elizabeth said. 'Annie and I were intending to ride down the bridle track to see the famous caves next week. The hotel manager has already arranged for us to stay at the new Caves House guest lodge near the main entrance – everyone says the accommodation there is most comfortable.'

Lady Fraser frowned. 'And what are your plans now, may I ask?'

'I had a word with Mr Evans before I went to bed last night,' Elizabeth said. 'He assured me there will be no difficulty about bringing our excursion forward, and he offered to secure the best available horses for us first thing this morning.'

'And so he has,' said Jackson. 'I had the same thought last night, and I gave the same instructions. The mounts are ready – though I'm told that a couple of them are quite lively.'

'Annie and I will ride those, then,' Elizabeth said promptly. 'We like a bit of spirit.'

'Fine by me,' said Freddy. 'I ride well enough, but I must say I prefer my horses quiet.'

'Then we shall all get along famously, Mr Urquhart,' said Annie. She smiled brightly at him over the rim of her rose-patterned porcelain teacup. 'Does that mean you will be joining us?'

Freddy smiled back. 'It would hardly do to allow two such charming young ladies to ride unescorted,' he said gallantly. 'And besides,' he added, 'I'll confess I'm intrigued as to what we might find.'

'Good,' said Elizabeth. 'We can all go.'

'I haven't given my permission yet,' Lady Fraser said. 'I need to know exactly what's involved here.'

Freddy was suddenly serious. 'I'm told it can take up to three days to get to the caves,' he said. 'The trip is 46 miles by road. The bridle path down the cliffs – the one you mentioned, Miss Fraser – is undoubtedly faster, but I wonder about its serviceability: it looks straightforward enough on the map, but Mr Evans assures me it is steep, rugged and treacherous. I gather that it follows paths made by the wild horses, the brumbies that roam these mountains.'

'Just the thing for a brisk ride, then,' said Elizabeth.

'But if it's a treacherous track…' Charles Jackson began.

'Don't worry, Mr Jackson,' Elizabeth said sweetly. 'Annie and I will help you with the more difficult bits.'

Lady Fraser laughed. 'I'd recommend you *don't* suggest the ride might be too much for my daughter and my niece, Mr Jackson,' she said. 'They are both superb horsewomen.'

'We grew up riding,' Annie added. 'Elizabeth and I can outride most of the stockmen on our property.'

'And is it a large ranch?' Jackson asked.

'My husband and his brother, Annie's father, have adjoining holdings. We measure them in square miles,' said Lady Fraser.

Jackson mentally admitted defeat. 'Splendid!' he said, a little too heartily. 'It seems the issue is settled. We'll be able to get underway much sooner than I had anticipated. It turns out that Evans has already arranged our supplies, as well as bedrolls and blankets, and he's sent a groom ahead to apprise the Caves House manager of our impending arrival.'

'Excellent,' said Annie.

Elizabeth turned to Lady Fraser. 'Mother? Do we have your consent?'

'I suppose so,' said Lady Fraser.

Jedediah heard a low-pitched humming sound. He pulled his scarf up over his nose and mouth against the stench emanating from the pit and crept closer, his old hobnailed boots slipping and sliding on the loose rubble. He edged around until he could see more clearly. The end of the cylinder was slowly rotating – it was being unscrewed from inside. He almost jumped out of his skin when a hollow *clang* resounded in the still morning air: a hatch fell off and rolled down the furrowed slope to lie amidst the reeking remains of the incinerated Beast.

The Martian inched a questing, snaky grey tentacle over the rim of the cylinder. And then it began to heave itself up, its huge, monstrous form glistening like wet leather in the early morning light.

Jedediah recoiled in horror. He brandished his bible once more. 'Protect me, Lord,' he cried. 'I call upon Thy mercy.'

The Martian instantly withdrew. It ransacked Jedediah's memory until it came up with a suitable image, rapidly transforming its outward appearance to suit its needs.

When Jedediah dared to look again, an impossibly tall angel was emerging from the cylinder – complete with golden curls, flowing white robes and a shining halo. It was a perfect, living replica of the stained-glass angels he remembered from the old family church back home. He fell to his knees again.

'Command me, Lord,' he said.

I am Gabriel, Archangel of the Lord, Angel of Mercy, the Martian said. *You have been chosen to lead your people out of the darkness of their sin and into the light of salvation.*

Jedediah was overwhelmed, but he was not surprised. His heart was beating fast. He bowed his head. He'd always known he was born for nothing less than this.

You will do my bidding, said the Martian. *Your reward will be a land overflowing with milk and honey.*

'Just tell me what you need, Lord,' said Jedediah. 'I hear and obey.'

I need a place of healing, the Martian said.

Jedediah thought for a moment. 'I'll take you to the Caves,' he said at last.

'Caves?'

'Jenolan Caves. They're not far from here. The old tribal people use them as a healing place,' Jedediah said. 'They have a story about it. They say the water there is the purest you'll find anywhere on Earth.'

That is acceptable, said the Martian.

'As you will, Lord,' said Jedediah.

You must also keep secret the news of my arrival, until the way is prepared, the Martian added. *You must not betray my presence.*

Jedediah's brow creased in consternation. 'Surely, Lord, I may tell my flock?'

Your animals?

'My congregation, Lord.'

The Martian was starting to get the hang of this strange, elliptical discourse, beginning to understand that this particular sub-species of wildlife relied upon a set of shared stories for guidance – stories about a completely different tribe. This was useful information.

That is acceptable, it said, still sifting Jedediah's tangled thoughts. *Your flock will understand that you have been Chosen. Your flock will become my Apostles.*

'In the Mercy of the Lord,' Jedediah responded.

Apostles of Mercy, yes, the Martian said.

Jedediah positively beamed. 'Your Apostles of Mercy will live only to serve you.'

Then know that my safety is paramount, the Martian said. *The future of this world depends upon it.*

'I hear and obey, Lord.' Jedediah bowed again, uncertain of what exactly was expected of him. Sunday preaching was one thing – actually conversing with Angels was something trickier altogether. He glanced back at the charred remains of the monstrously tentacled *thing* in the pit.

'But the beast that fell from the sky…' he began.

A devil, yes, said the Martian. *Be not afraid: the Lord has sent his Angels to defend his people from…*it hesitated, momentarily puzzled as it scanned through Jedediah's memory for an appropriately biblical phrase…*from the servants of the Prince of Lies*, it finished. *I am come to protect you.*

That did the trick.

'I understand, Lord,' said Jedediah. 'Two different kinds of beings fell last night from the heavens: Satan's attackers, and the Lord's defending Angels.'

Yes, said the Martian. *The battle for Earth has begun.*

'I knew it,' said Jedediah. 'The end of days is coming.' It seemed perfectly right to him that the two opposing sides should arrive together. He counted himself blessed that he had found an injured archangel, and not the living spawn of Satan.

'I know a back way into the healing caves, Lord,' he offered. 'It's likely there'll be busybody sightseers around that Guest House they've built at the main gate. We can avoid meeting the likes of them until you are ready to lead the faithful to victory over the powers of darkness.'

That is acceptable, said the Martian. *Bring this.* It pointed to the cylinder. *Its contents are beyond price.*

'As you will, Lord,' Jedediah said again. His shoulders sagged. Getting the cylinder out of the pit wouldn't be easy.

Fear not, said the Martian. *Your strength will be sufficient unto the day.*

'Right,' said Jedediah. He squared his shoulders. He reckoned it'd be no worse than hauling logs, and he was well used to that.

Freddy glanced sideways at his folded newspaper, but held his peace, concentrating deliberately on the upcoming travel arrangements. He toyed with his orange marmalade – his toast was getting cold. 'I do hope everything will be alright,' he said.

'Of course it will,' said Jackson. 'We're in luck today. It transpires that Peter Cameron, the chief mining engineer, has decided to inspect last night's fire damage. He is travelling with one of his colleagues, a chap by the name of Robert Hatfield, and they have kindly invited us to join them. I understand that Cameron's miners maintain a hut for shelter about halfway down the bridle path.'

'That's right,' said Annie. She fished a crumpled piece of paper out of her pocket and smoothed it out beside her breakfast plate. 'The hut is marked quite clearly on our sketch map.'

Jackson was not to be interrupted. 'We shall easily reach the campsite before sunset if we leave with Cameron later this morning,' he said. 'My scientific gear is all packed. Do you think you ladies could be ready by late morning?'

'Of course we can be ready,' said Annie. 'We are probably more used to horseback expeditions than you are.'

'I didn't mean–' Jackson began.

'Of course you didn't,' Elizabeth said. 'But truly, we have only to change into our riding clothes, and we'll be ready to go.'

'And don't forget to load your pistols,' Lady Fraser said firmly.

'Of course not, Aunt,' Annie said.

Jackson and Urquhart exchanged glances.

Lady Fraser noticed. 'Before you ask, Mr Jackson,' she said, 'my daughter and my niece are both crack shots.'

Freddy smiled. 'All part of growing up on a large country estate,' he said. 'I was taught young, too.'

Annie rewarded him with another warm smile.

Lady Fraser was suddenly interested. 'A country estate, Mr Urquhart?'

'In the Scottish Highlands, yes,' Freddy said. 'My father is Lord Urquhart.'

Lady Fraser nodded. 'And shall you inherit the title, may I ask?'

'Not unless my brother dies without an heir,' he replied. 'I'll probably always be just an Honourable.'

'Ah,' said Lady Fraser. 'So you are the younger son seeking solace in the Colonies.'

'Something like that,' Freddy agreed.

'Mother!' said Elizabeth.

'It's quite alright, Miss Fraser,' Freddy said ruefully. 'I'm used to being the spare. And besides, I *am* very much enjoying my sojourn in your delightful colony.'

'There you are then,' said Lady Fraser. 'One must always be clear about these things – I find it saves potentially embarrassing misunderstandings.'

Annie shifted uncomfortably in her seat: her aunt's matchmaking interest in Urquhart was all too transparent.

Elizabeth, too, felt uneasy. She changed the subject, anxious to avoid the awkward topic of potential husbands. 'If there *are* Martians about,' she said lightly, 'I certainly want to meet one.'

'Me too,' said Annie. 'Will they be green, do you think?'

'Don't laugh too soon, Miss Fraser,' said Freddy. 'I've merely glanced at the morning edition of *The Katoomba Times*, but I can tell you that the telegraphed reports from England are still talking about Martians. It says here that observers on Horsell Common saw huge creatures emerge from metal cylinders that landed there.' He shuddered. 'And artillery men on the ground recorded reliable accounts of military-style weaponry – it seems the Martians are armed with a terrible *heat ray* – a device that can kill at a great distance. It says here that a whole platoon of soldiers was wiped out – incinerated.'

'I say, that's dramatic,' said Elizabeth.

'And *I* still say it's all nonsense,' Jackson retorted. 'It simply can't be true!' Jackson's countenance reddened again. 'The scientific advancement required to facilitate travel through space would be vastly superior to anything we have ever done.'

'And why is that so unthinkable, Mr Jackson?' Elizabeth asked. 'We're happy enough to assume that other human races are inferior to ourselves – why shouldn't the creatures of Mars have evolved beyond us?'

Jackson shook his head.

Elizabeth pressed her point. 'Mars is further from the sun,' she said. 'It would have cooled before the earth, so life might have begun there first. In which case, the Martians would have a huge head start on us.'

'Now you really are abandoning any semblance of scientific theory,' said Jackson. 'It's perfectly clear that the lesser gravity of Mars…'

Lady Fraser interrupted before he could warm to his theory. 'If there really is the slightest danger of Martians down at the caves,' she said coolly, 'I shall change my mind and forbid the girls to go.'

'In that case, Mother,' said Elizabeth, 'I'll admit that we were just teasing Mr Jackson.'

'Then I suggest you stop it at once,' said Lady Fraser. 'The very idea is too alarming – especially so soon after breakfast. You'll ruin your digestion.'

'Yes, Mother,' said Elizabeth. She took a last sip of her rapidly cooling coffee. 'I'll just go and get my things.'

The Martian watched, as fascinated as any anthropologist by the display of primitive technology it was witnessing. Its pre-launch briefing had indicated that certain species of Earth were capable of using tools, but this went beyond expectations.

Jedediah released his horse from the shafts of the dray and then clambered down into the pit to loop a set of long chains around the cooling cylinder. He reconnected the rig, ploughing style, and the patient horse took the strain: it began plodding forwards, slowly hauling the Angel's precious luggage up the steep slope. The Chosen One was sweating profusely by the time he finally set to work with his hand winch, utilising the dray's wooden shafts as a ramp to roll the cylinder up onto the wagon bed.

The Martian, unused to the smell of unwashed human pheromones, moved back a pace. It decided to risk a touch of levitation to speed things up.

In the end, the whole operation was accomplished in a couple of hours.

'That wasn't so bad,' Jedediah said. He watched closely as the Angel inspected the cylinder, satisfying itself that the precious contents were unharmed. 'That metal thing was much lighter than it looked.' He smiled. 'Or maybe the Lord has given me extra strength after all.'

But he was given no time to bask in his achievement. The Martian needed to get out of the rising heat of this shadeless Australian morning: it was feeling the sharp pinprick of sunburn on its glistening octopus-skin hide, and its tender tentacles were already drying out. The Angel illusion was no defence against the reality of the elements. A nice damp cave would be an ideal location for the task it had been sent to perform.

You have done well, Apostle, it said briskly. *And now we must leave this place. Take me to the caves.*

'As you wish, Lord,' said Jedediah. He set to work again, re-harnessing his horse. 'Not long now, Bill,' he whispered into the horse's ear. 'I'll get you a drink at the stream near the caves.'

The horse tossed its head.

'Good boy, Bill,' Jedediah said.

When he turned again, the ungainly Angel was already sitting on the driver's bench, waiting.

Let us go, Apostle, it said.

There was no mistaking the impatient tone. Jedediah flicked the reins and Bill set off at his usual slow walk, straining to pull the weight of the heavily loaded dray.

Can't he move faster? the Martian asked.

'I'm afraid not, Lord,' Jedediah replied.

This wasn't how he'd imagined the Chosen of the Lord would be treated: it didn't feel quite right somehow. He'd never heard of Archangels travelling with tin trunks. And the Bible stories hadn't said anything about Moses sweating to death hauling heavy baggage under a baking hot sun. This Angel was beginning to look suspiciously like hard work – the very thing he'd spent a lifetime avoiding. But Jedediah still trusted in the Lord: he twitched the reins and Bill moved a fraction faster. It was all the long-suffering animal could manage.

The sun was high in a cloudless blue sky by the time the Katoomba riding party finally mounted up, ready to head out. Cameron's workmen had set out earlier in drays loaded with engineering equipment and explosives for the mines, taking the safer, longer road down the mountain to Caves House.

Peter Cameron eased his horse alongside Charles' black gelding. 'I understand you are a geologist, Mr Jackson,' he said.

'Indeed I am, sir,' Jackson replied. 'I'm looking forward to seeing the caves.'

'They certainly won't disappoint,' Cameron replied. 'The limestone formations are truly astonishing. And our mining operations may be of interest to you as well. I'll be pleased to escort you to visit our workings.'

'Thank you,' said Jackson. 'I'd welcome the opportunity to see how you have managed the terrain. I must say your Scenic Railway is quite a feat of engineering. Some of those gradients are incredibly steep.'

Cameron smiled. 'It was a challenge to build it,' he said. 'The tram lines started as a convenient way to transport coal and shale kerosene, but now the network itself has become quite fashionable for the views it affords the traveller. We keep a sharp eye on its operation.'

'Is that why you are riding down today?'

'Partly,' said Cameron. 'This is a precautionary expedition to check on the extent of last night's fire, and to make sure the meteor strike did not impact any of our workings. I'm not anticipating any serious problems.'

'Mr Urquhart is worried that the meteors may prove to be missiles from Mars,' Jackson said.

Cameron snorted. 'I read the papers,' he replied, 'but I'll believe in Martians when I see one.'

'My thoughts exactly,' said Jackson.

Freddy interrupted them. 'I say,' he said, 'would you mind if I record the occasion?' He held aloft a folding pocket Kodak camera, the very latest thing in photographic technology.

Jackson grinned. 'Always ready to oblige,' he said.

The group duly posed for the photograph, and Freddy could not help but notice that the two young Fraser women made a very pretty picture on their high stepping mounts. Elizabeth wore a split-skirted dark red riding outfit, and had tied her dark curls back with a red ribbon under her felted hat; beside her, Annie was equally fetching in a deep-blue outfit that set off her trim figure and her shining blonde hair. And if Freddy was surprised that they were not riding side-saddle, he was far too gallant to mention it – these were modern women, after all.

Freddy put his hand to his heart. 'Exquisite,' he breathed. 'Simply exquisite. I am completely smitten.'

Annie favoured him with a warm smile as the four of them set out, pacing easily through the township, a little way ahead of

Cameron, who was already deep in a technical discussion with Hatfield.

The initial descent on the bridle path was easy going, and Jackson soon rode up beside Elizabeth. He cleared his throat, obviously getting ready to lecture. 'Jenolan is known as an *impounded karst,*' he said. 'Which means…'

'Which means,' Elizabeth said promptly, 'that the limestone receives most of its water from the surrounding insoluble rocks.'

'Indeed. And I assume you know the properties of limestone itself?'

'It's a biologically-based sedimentary rock,' Elizabeth said. 'The caves are formed…'

'Stop it, you two,' said Freddy. 'You're giving me a headache. It will be a very long ride indeed if the pair of you are going to bicker over scientific theories all the way down the mountain!'

'Sorry, Mr Urquhart,' Elizabeth said.

'Sorry, Freddy,' said Charles.

'Mr Urquhart is right,' said Annie. 'This is simply too boring. It's a beautiful day. I'll race you all down to Nellie's Glen. It's the first stop marked on the map.'

She didn't wait for an answer. She dug her heels into the flanks of her bay mare and set off down the hill at a cracking pace, her golden curls shining in the sunshine.

Elizabeth gave a most unladylike whoop and followed suit, urging her dappled-grey mount to jump a fallen log that lay in her path as she raced after her cousin.

Freddy stared after them. 'Magnificent,' he said. 'I wouldn't care to try that myself on such a steep slope.'

'No,' said Jackson. 'Those girls will cause trouble if we're not careful.'

'Nonsense,' said Freddy. 'Don't be such a stick-in-the-mud, Charles. I like a woman with spirit – and these two are superb.'

'If you say so,' said Jackson. 'I just don't want to find myself rescuing them from whatever ravine they happen to fall into.'

Freddy grinned. 'They're more likely to rescue us, I think.'

Jackson sighed heavily. 'I hope not,' he said. 'But I suppose we'd better get after them.' He patted his holstered hunting rifle. 'Best to be prepared,' he added.

'Are you expecting trouble?'

'Not really,' said Jackson. 'But we're heading out into the bush: who knows what we might find?'

'Oh,' said Freddy. 'I've only brought my Colt revolver.'

Jackson pulled back his jacket to reveal his shoulder holster. 'I have mine as well,' he said.

Freddy laughed. 'We're well defended, then. That gives us 12 quick shots between us. The Martians won't be expecting that.'

'And *I'm* not expecting Martians,' Jackson replied. 'But if you're right, Freddy – and I'm not saying you are – I want to be the first to bag a specimen. That'd be quite a coup in scientific circles.'

Freddy's face fell. 'Wouldn't it be better to capture a live specimen?'

Jackson shook his head. 'Better safe than sorry,' he said. 'Let's go. The trail seems well-enough blazed, but it won't do to let the Miss Frasers get too far ahead.' He didn't wait for an answer: he urged his horse forward and set off at an energetic trot.

Freddy settled his wide-brimmed hat more firmly. Fair-skinned and red-haired, he'd already learned to be wary of sunstroke in this part of the world. He sighed deeply, shook his reins, and started off at a more sedate pace.

Jedediah's journey to the caves was hot, slow, and uncomfortable. The old wooden dray sagged under the weight of the Martian. The creature could manipulate its outward manifestation easily enough, but beneath its ethereal angelic appearance it still weighed a ton, and it was suffering in Earth's greater gravity.

More speed, Apostle, it said.

Jedediah didn't want to contradict an Angel, but Bill the horse was already panting from exertion. This was another puzzling thing: Angels were creatures of air, they weren't supposed to be heavy. He wondered if the cylinder was a lot weightier than it had seemed when he loaded it onto the dray.

'Forgive me, Lord,' he replied. 'I'm doing the best I can.'

The Martian sifted the man's thoughts, but found only simple truth. *Very well*, it said.

They travelled in stony silence until Jedediah reined in the horse beside a small pool where a stream tumbled through a jagged fissure in the rock face. A few straggly gum trees arched above, offering a patch of welcome shade.

Bill immediately bent his head to drink, blowing through his nostrils in relief.

'Here we are, Lord,' Jedediah said. 'We have to leave the horse. The rock paths are too steep for animals. I have a lantern. I'll take you to the special cave, and I'll come back for your things.'

That is acceptable, said the Martian.

As they entered the passageway to the caves, the temperature dropped sharply, much to the relief of the suffering Martian. It smelled a welcome dankness in the moisture-heavy air. But the narrow rock paths were slippery, and it had to levitate to manoeuvre its unwieldy bulk down the rough-hewn rock stairs.

Jedediah didn't notice. He was so focussed on finding the right tunnel that if he glanced at his Angel at all he saw only trailing white robes. At last he found the cave he was seeking. 'I always knew an Angel would come here,' he said. 'Behold! The earth has prepared this temple for you, Lord.'

He raised his safety lantern, revealing one of the hidden wonders of the world. The roof of the cavern was at least 130 feet high, and dripping with spectacular crystalline white and brown stalactites that sparkled wetly in the flickering light.

'See,' said Jedediah. He pointed to a massive shawl-style formation with folds and points that hung a good 30 feet down from the ceiling. 'It looks just like an Angel's wing.' He swung the lantern to reveal the crystal-clear lake that filled the bottom of the cavern, surrounded by rising stalagmites and rocks crusted with glittering crystal helictites. 'And here are the waters of healing, Lord,' he said, his voice trembling with emotion. 'Your sacred temple will protect and restore you, Lord.' His words echoed strangely in the vast dampness of the cave.

The Martian scanned the vast underground complex, but found

nothing untoward. It realised they were now very deep underground, and calculated that the water here must have dripped through several tons of limestone that filtered out impurities.

The old people, whoever they were, were right: this water was perfectly safe to drink. It was a good start. The semi-sentient indigenous creature had chosen well: the Martian would be safe down here, safe to recover from its injuries, safe to fulfil its mission. But soon it would have to feed. It didn't like the tainted, adult-male smell of Jedediah.

Are there young in your congregation, Chosen One? it asked.

'Children? Yes, Lord,' said Jedediah.

Bring them to me, said the Angel. *To be…blessed.*

Jedediah beamed. 'Yes, Lord,' he said. 'Thank you, Lord.'

That is acceptable, said the Martian. *But first you must fetch my belongings. You have left my goods undefended. That is not acceptable.*

Jedediah scratched his head. 'Nobody much comes out here, Lord,' he answered. 'Your luggage is safe enough.' He held up his hand. The Angel was radiating displeasure. 'But I'll go and get it, Lord.'

At once, the Angel said, adopting a tone that sounded remarkably like Jedediah's mother in one of her less tractable moods.

Jedediah jumped to obey. As he toiled back up the slope, he consoled himself by rehearsing his triumphant return to Oberon. He was tired, but exultant. He could hardly wait to tell Jethro, his cranky father-in-law, that he'd have to show a bit more respect to the Chosen One. And he decided that his patient wife and the other women of his tiny congregation would become Sisters of Mercy. His children would be blessed. His following would grow. The Apostles of Mercy would save the world. He was looking forward to that. But first, he'd have to manhandle the Angel's metal cylinder down to the temple cave.

Bill was cropping the spindly, dry grass when Jedediah emerged, blinking, into the harsh sunlight. Without the Angel's intervention, the cylinder was much heavier. The Chosen One needed all his strength just to push it off the back of the dray, and it made a deep dent in the earth before it rolled to a stop. He thought about using chains to drag it, but finally he decided he'd just roll it down the slope, and turn it end over end where the path was steep and narrow inside the caves. The strange metal seemed pretty strong. He reckoned if it had survived a fall to earth, a few more knocks and scrapes wouldn't hurt it.

When Freddy finally caught up with the waiting Jackson girls, he immediately reached for his camera: Nellie's Glen turned out to be a fern gully to rival any on earth – a misty, romantic beauty spot set within a mountain vale filled with a myriad of cascading fern species in every imaginable shade of green. Tiny, honey-scented flowers perfumed the air, birdsong was all around them, and dappled sunlight fell gently on fallen tree trunks and rocks padded thickly with moss the colour of emeralds.

'Simply spectacular,' Freddy said, carefully choosing the best angle for his photograph. 'The ride will have been worth it if only to see this place.'

Annie smiled at him. 'I gather we are also in for a treat when we climb the next mountain,' she said. 'We will be able to see for miles.'

'I'd settle for this,' Freddy said dreamily. 'It reminds me of a line from Marvell: *...a green thought in a green shade.*' He turned to Cameron and Hatfield, who had just reached the glen. 'I don't suppose we could stop here for a while?' he asked.

Cameron shook his head. 'I'm afraid not, Mr Urquhart,' he said. 'I'll grant you this is a pretty place, but we must press on if we are to reach the hut at Little River before nightfall. I promise there are many more beauty spots along our route.'

Freddy sighed. 'As you will,' he said. 'I'll just have to return another day. Perhaps I'll arrange a picnic.' He looked straight at Annie. 'Would you like that, Miss Fraser?' he asked.

Annie blushed. 'That would be lovely,' she said. 'Perhaps I could bring my watercolours.'

Jackson spoiled the moment. 'Come along, everyone,' he said. 'We don't have time to admire the scenery. We really must get on.'

Cameron laughed. 'Indeed we must,' he said. 'But easy does it on these mountain paths. There's no reason we can't enjoy the view along the way.' He shook his reins and began to move out.

The noise was almost deafening as the Martian cylinder bumped and crashed and rolled its way to the bottom of the stone stairs, the racket of its passage echoing loudly along the narrow passageways.

Jedediah had to dive for cover as a huge flock of bats came wheeling through the steep cutting, disturbed by the noise, adding their high-pitched squeals to the cacophony. He was struggling for breath by the time he got to the Angel-wing cave. He pushed the Martian cylinder – now heavily scratched and dented – down the last steps until it rolled to a stop at the feet of the waiting Angel.

The Martian exuded irritation. The cylinder's descent into the underworld had been brutal. Now its tender cargo must again be inspected for damage.

Leave now, Apostle, it said. It added a touch of compulsion. *Go.*

Jedediah found that he had no choice but to turn around and begin the long, hard ascent all over again. He needed a drink, but he figured he'd stop by one of the trickling streamlets for that. Right now he just wanted to go home.

Alone in the vast, dripping labyrinth of Jenolan Caves, the Martian exulted. It had survived landfall, and now it had an underground place of safety and a clean water supply. The wildlife specimen had proved surprisingly easy to dominate, and soon it would bring fresh food. All was well. It sent its first telepathic message to its fellow colonists: *Arrived Southern Continent. Co-ordinates follow. Wildlife docile. Escort team perished on entry. Nursery pod intact, secure in underground location. Await instructions.*

It settled back to tend its burns and wait for a response. The precious Martian embryos were still safe and sound inside the shielded cylinder. Earth could be seeded after all.

The track from the foot of Nellie's Glen wound its way around the mountainside, and as the riders picked their way over fallen rocks and tangled grasses they could hear the gentle murmur of the Cox River running hundreds of feet below them. The twisty trail finally meandered down to a shallow ford where clear mountain water eddied and flowed, running swiftly over flat stones.

The riders crossed easily, and Cameron led the way back to the bridle path. 'The terrain changes now,' he said. 'You'll see wilder bushland.'

As if to mark his words, at the next bend a mob of wallabies hopped away in fright as the riders approached, startling a flock of kookaburras which flew off, calling raucously.

'I always think they are laughing at me,' Freddy said.

'Don't worry – they're laughing at all of us,' Cameron replied. 'It's part of their charm.'

The bridle path led to another steep climb, and, after a long and tiring ride, to an equally steep descent to Little River.

Jackson took out his spyglass. 'I can see the hut,' he said.

'Not before time,' Robert Hatfield muttered, flexing his tired shoulders.

'Cheer up, Bob,' Cameron said. 'It's not far now.'

THE FIRST RESPONSE THE Martian received from its fellow colonists was alarming: *Arrived Northern Islands. Co-ordinates follow. High losses sustained on entry. Local wildlife is sentient, armed and aggressive – a competing indigenous species to be eliminated. Report your supply status.*

The Martian thought for a while, then sent: *Current cave location has extensive supply clean filtered water, good air. Sheltered damp conditions ideal for embryos. Indigenous semi-sentient species is co-operative. Nutrition value of local food supply is still unknown.*

WHEN JEDEDIAH RETURNED TO the caves later that afternoon, bringing with him his wife and son, all was not well. The return trip had not been easy. He was bone-tired from his morning's exertions, and his wife had responded to his story of the Archangel with unexpected scepticism. The Chosen One was struggling to maintain his vocation.

'If I hadn't seen the fireballs fall from the sky with my own eyes,' Molly said, 'I wouldn't waste my time coming out here at all. We have a farm to run, in case you'd forgotten.'

'I haven't forgotten, dear,' he said. 'But the end of the world is nigh. What does it matter if I don't fix the fence?'

'We'll just have to see about that, won't we?'

They were still arguing half-heartedly when Jedediah lit his safety lantern and led the way down into the depths of the underworld, where sounds of hammering were coming from the back of the Angel-wing cavern.

'It is I, Lord,' he called. 'I have brought my firstborn child, Adam, to be blessed, as you desired.'

The hammering ceased, and the Angel appeared, holding what appeared to be a thin metal wand. It hovered greedily above the glistening cave floor, sniffing the clean food-scent of the untainted boy.

You have done well, Apostle, it said.

'This is my wife, Molly,' said Jedediah.

Molly bobbed a curtsey. She stared at the Angel with unabashed curiosity.

The Martian ignored her, completely focussed on the boy. *Welcome, child*, it said.

Jedediah gave Adam a push. 'Bow to the Lord,' he whispered.

The child bowed dutifully, his sun-bleached brown curls falling around his face, his blue eyes wide with wonder.

Come with me, child, the Angel said. *You will receive such blessings as only I can bestow.*

Adam shook his head and backed up towards his mother.

She put a protective arm around his skinny shoulders. 'Can't you bless him here, with his parents, Lord?' she asked. 'My son is afraid.'

Be not afraid, child, the Martian replied firmly, ramping up the compulsion. *The firstborn of the Chosen One has nothing to fear.*

The parents were powerless to resist. They could only stand and watch as their son was led away into a small side tunnel at the back of the Angel-wing cave.

'This can't be right,' Molly whispered.

'Just wait,' said Jedediah. 'We must put our trust in the Lord and His Angel.'

It was not long before Adam came staggering back from the

depths of the cave. He clung to his mother, shaking. He was very pale.

'He looks ill, Jedediah,' she muttered.

'He looks more angelic,' Jedediah responded. 'A full blessing is bound to be overwhelming for a child.'

'But what about the blood spot on his neck?'

Jedediah shrugged. 'The Lord moves in mysterious ways, my dear, His wonders to perform,' he said.

'That's as may be, but I'm taking Adam home,' Mrs Carpenter said firmly.

'I saw little teddies back there,' Adam whispered into his mother's skirts. 'Rows and rows of teddies with tentacles.'

'He's delirious!' She put her hand on his clammy forehead. 'And he's cold as ice.' She looked up at her husband. 'I don't know what's going on here, but whatever it is I don't like it. It's getting late: we'll lose the daylight soon. If you don't want to come home, Jedediah, that's fine by me. I'll take the dray – and you can stay here for the night with your precious Angel.'

The Martian reappeared.

Jedediah looked to it for support. 'May I depart, Lord?' he asked.

The Martian had just fed. It wanted to rest, and rest in its own form. It waved a barely-disguised tentacle. *That is acceptable, Apostle*, it replied. *You may go*. It hesitated. *Return tomorrow*, it added, *and bring more of your kind for… blessing.*

'I hear and obey, Lord,' said Jedediah.

The camping spot was picture perfect. The timber slab hut was situated beside a clear, swift-flowing stream in a little gully surrounded on every side by high mountains. The air was still, and graced by the liquid song of a native thrush.

Freddy was enchanted once more. 'I never imagined such glorious scenery,' he said. 'Why on earth didn't anyone tell me there are such lovely trails here – in all my time in this country, I've never seen such a variety of plants and birds and animals.'

'I don't think many people know about it,' Cameron replied. 'And, to tell you the truth, we engineers tend to see the landscape in much more practical terms.'

'That's a shame,' said Freddy.

'Not altogether,' Jackson said. 'See – there's a fire pit and stack of cut firewood over there by the hut, all ready for use.'

'We keep everything in good order and prepared for the next traveller,' Cameron said. 'The weather up here is extreme in winter. It wouldn't do to have any of my men stranded without shelter. If you'll excuse me, I'll go and help Bob with our arrangements.'

Freddy glanced around, realising, belatedly, that the other members of the party were busily making camp. Hatfield was all efficiency. He already had a fire going, and had set up a tripod over the flames to hold the billy can he had filled with water from the stream – an arrangement that promised a welcome cup of tea. Jackson was unsaddling his horse. Elizabeth and Annie had taken possession of the hut, and were moving their bedrolls and blankets inside.

Elizabeth suddenly began stamping her feet. 'Out you go!' she said. 'Shoo!'

A six-foot long red-bellied black snake slithered guiltily across the doorstep and disappeared into the lush undergrowth.

Freddy shuddered. 'That's a nasty surprise,' he said.

'It's always a good idea to check the corners,' Elizabeth replied.

At that moment, the lovely campsite seemed a lot less romantic to Freddy Urquhart. He looked around warily, re-thinking his initial choice of sleeping spot near a clump of long grass. 'I suppose every Eden has its serpent,' he said at last.

'Don't worry,' Annie said, laughing. 'We'll defend you from the wildlife.'

By the time Freddy had composed himself to spend a night under the stars, the two engineers were baking whole potatoes and fresh damper in the ashes of the fire, and Elizabeth and Annie were happily unpacking the useful assortment of tin plates, mugs and utensils that came with the hired camping gear. When they turned to the hamper that the packhorse had carried, they found that the cook of the Carrington Hotel had filled the basket with cold sliced meats, a wheel of cheese, a raised veal pie, little covered dishes of plum preserves and her special rhubarb chutney, fresh-baked shortbread biscuits, and the makings for tea and coffee. She had also provided a drawstring calico bag containing carefully wrapped fresh peaches for dessert.

Elizabeth undid the string and inhaled the ripe peach scent. 'Heavenly,' she said. 'This won't be bad for a camp meal.'

'Indeed it will not, Miss Fraser,' said Jackson. 'We are very well provided for. I've taken the liberty of bringing along a couple of bottles of decent claret.'

'And I've brought an extra flask of a most respectable brandy for after dinner,' Freddy added. 'It will be a small but useful contribution to our comfort.' He dug into the depths of his coat and came up with a heavily engraved silver hip flask.

'That's beautiful silverwork,' Elizabeth said admiringly.

Freddy grinned. 'One should always camp out in style, don't you think?'

'Indeed I do,' said Annie. Her expression was suddenly thoughtful as she watched Freddy unpack his expensive travelling kit.

Sunset came quickly in the mountain glen, and the riding party was soon gathered around the fire, cheerfully eating and drinking.

'I really must thank you for joining us,' said Cameron, sipping the last of Freddy's brandy from a battered tin mug. 'We rarely have such luxuries on working trips.'

'Hear, hear,' said Hatfield. 'Much appreciated.'

'Our pleasure,' said Jackson.

'Indeed,' Elizabeth added. 'Since you are kind enough to be our guides, the least we can do is offer you a decent meal.'

'And we shall dine together again tomorrow evening at Caves House,' said Freddy. 'It's good that we are all staying there.'

Cameron laughed. 'We can hardly avoid it,' he said. 'It's the only decent accommodation for miles around.'

Freddy reclined, looking up at the constellations blazing brightly above them. 'The night sky is so much prettier here,' he said. 'Look, there's Orion – upside down, of course. And I can see the Milky Way quite clearly. I never see this many stars at home.'

'That's because the southern hemisphere looks into the heart of the galaxy,' Jackson said. 'The northern hemisphere faces outwards.'

'Are you always so unromantic, Charles?' Freddy asked.

Jackson had the grace to smile. 'I guess so,' he said.

'Then let's look at Mars,' said Elizabeth. 'It's very red tonight.'

'No more green flares?' Annie asked.

'Not that I can see,' Jackson replied.

'So no more Martians coming our way this evening, then,' said Elizabeth.

Jackson was so easy to tease. 'I don't think…' he began.

Freddy intervened. 'And there's Venus, named for the Goddess of Love,' he said. 'Venusians must be a happy race.'

'If you follow that logic, Martians must be a very aggressive one,' said Elizabeth. 'Mars is the God of War, after all.'

'Let's hope *that* doesn't hold true,' said Cameron. 'I'm sceptical about a lot of recent newspaper reports, but I have to say I found today's accounts of Martian weaponry most unsettling. It's pure speculation, of course, but if Martians do exist, and if they do have science advanced enough to permit them to travel to Earth, it stands to reason that their weapons must be far superior to ours. One can only pray that their intentions are benign.'

'How could they be benign?' Freddy asked. 'Think about our own reasons for colonisation. Our early settlers did not behave well towards the indigenous peoples here, by all accounts.' He shrugged. 'British colonists arrived with superior technology. They used shot and muskets against spears and clubs, which could hardly be considered a fair fight.'

'That's a sobering thought,' said Elizabeth. 'There have been rumours of massacres, but…'

'Let's talk about something else,' Annie said firmly. 'This has been such a pleasant evening. I don't want it to end in nightmares about people being murdered by monsters from Mars.'

Freddy grinned. 'Your wish is my command, my lady,' he said. 'Let me divert you with amusing tales of the foibles of my family back in Scotland.'

Annie returned his smile. 'That will be most agreeable, Mr Urquhart,' she said.

Directly beneath their mountain camp, deep down in the dark of Jenolan Caves, the Martian was assembling its exoskeleton, patiently building the metal carapace it would need to withstand the extreme gravity and harsh sunlight of this too-bright world. The discordant pounding of metal on metal reverberated through the stillness of the permanent night of this limestone underworld, penetrating even the depths where strange, eyeless creatures lived their secret lives. The resident bats were restless, wheeling through the absolute darkness of their domain, screeching their blind alarms, shrieking their warnings.

The Martian was unperturbed. It scanned the fecund caves, wondering which of the inhabitants would prove edible. Tomorrow, it would experiment.

The riding party broke camp early next morning, sharing a frugal breakfast of hot, sweet tea and cold damper with the last of the Carrington cook's plum preserves.

'We need to stick together for this next part of the track,' Peter Cameron said. 'It's narrow, so we ride single file. The Black Range is a steep ascent.'

'How steep?' Jackson asked.

'About a 1500 foot rise in the next mile or so,' Cameron replied.

Jackson drew a sharp breath. 'Point taken,' he said.

Despite the difficult terrain, the group reached the summit without mishap, relieved to find that the bridle path now led them into the welcome shade of a thick forest of tall trees, where the ground was carpeted with fallen leaves.

Elizabeth breathed in the strong scent of eucalyptus that arose as the horses walked the track. 'Wonderful,' she said. 'There's nothing like this smell anywhere else on earth.'

'I'll grant you that,' said Jackson. 'I feel much the same about riding over pine needles back home.'

Before long, the riders emerged from the dim forest and into the blazing sunshine of the roof of the world. The path led for several astonishing miles across the top of the mountain before it plunged once more towards the valley floor.

'We're making good time,' Cameron said cheerfully. 'We'll get our first glimpse of the caves at Carlotta Arch.'

'And we should be able to find the meteor's crash site,' said Jackson. He raised his spyglass once more. 'The burning seems most intense over that way,' he added, pointing.

Elizabeth pulled a face. 'We only need to follow our noses,' she said. 'The smell of smoke and char is still very strong.'

'Indeed,' said Cameron.

'But what if there really *are* Martians in the vicinity?' Freddy said nervously. 'Do we really want to ride right up to them?'

Jackson snorted. 'You know *my* opinion on this subject,' he said. 'Let's at least find the crash site.'

'I second that,' said Cameron. 'We'll soon see what's what. We can always err on the side of caution if anything looks untoward.'

'I suppose that will be alright,' said Freddy.

They rode in silence for a while, concentrating on picking a safe way down the precipitous track. The horses were skittish, and the riders were anxious.

Jackson was scanning the terrain, his expression intense as they finally reached level ground.

'There!' he said at last. 'I think that must be the crater. The surrounding ground has certainly been disturbed.'

'And all the trees are broken,' Elizabeth said. 'I can see one that's split clean through and burned out. There's our fire site.'

'And it's still smouldering,' Hatfield said, noticing that intermittent blue-grey wisps of smoke were rising from the pit and drifting away.

'Then I suggest we tether the horses here and take a closer look on foot,' said Cameron.

'After you,' said Freddy.

Unstable rubble made the sides of the newly formed crater treacherous, but after half an hour's careful walking all six riders peered over the edge.

Freddy gasped. 'Good Lord,' he said, pointing to a patch of melted metal that had run down the steep slope before congealing into a twisted lump. 'That doesn't look like a meteor to me,' he said. 'That's more like an iron ingot.'

Jackson scratched his head. 'Some meteors may contain a high percentage of ore,' he muttered.

'But not usually in manufactured shapes,' said Cameron. 'See over there? That one hasn't completely melted. It looks like some sort of cylinder, though I couldn't tell you what the metal is.'

Hatfield whistled. 'And will you look at that?' he said, pointing at the charred remains of the Martian. 'Whatever was in there, it died trying to get out.'

After two days lying in a smoking pit under the hot Australian sun, the corpse was in a bad way, bloated and split. To make matters worse, the crows had been at the carcass. Shreds of pulled meat dangled from what was left of the open cylinder.

Elizabeth held her handkerchief over her nose and mouth. 'How horrible,' she said. 'It smells disgusting.'

'Revolting!' said Annie. 'What do you think it was?'

'Beats me,' said Hatfield. 'Whatever it was, it wasn't human.'

'Well,' Cameron said at last, 'whatever it was, it's well and truly dead.'

'For which we can be grateful,' said Freddy. 'Nothing could have survived that fire.'

'I wouldn't be so sure about that,' Elizabeth said. 'I can see tracks over there. It looks to me as if something heavy has been dragged out of the pit.'

'You're right,' said Cameron. 'There are deep wheel tracks leading away from the crater.'

'And those hoof prints aren't from our horses,' Elizabeth added.

'So,' said Hatfield, 'it looks safe to say that somebody dragged something out of the pit and carted it away. But who, or what, or why, it's impossible to tell.'

'That about sums it up,' said Cameron. 'You've gone very quiet, Mr Jackson,' he added. 'Is there something more you wish to see? I, for one, am anxious to escort these ladies out of this dreadful stench.'

'I find this all very puzzling,' Jackson replied.

'Are you ready to concede this could be the wreckage of a Martian cylinder?' Freddy asked.

It was Cameron who answered. 'Let's not leap to conclusions, Mr Urquhart,' he said. 'It could have been anything at all.' He turned to Elizabeth and Annie. 'Are you ladies ready to make your way to Caves House?'

'Absolutely!' said Annie.

'Please,' said Elizabeth. 'We've seen what there is to see here.'

'You go on ahead,' said Jackson. 'I'll just gather some soil samples, and I'll catch up with you. I assume I just follow the main track.'

'That's right,' said Hatfield. He glanced around. 'But I'll wait for you, all the same. Whatever has been happening here, I don't like the feel of it.'

'Much obliged,' said Jackson, his relief showing clearly on his perspiring face. For all his scientific bravado, he had no wish to meet whoever – or whatever – might still be in the vicinity.

When the group finally made it to Caves House, they found that Mr Evans had been as good as his word: he had sent a groom ahead, and they were expected.

The housekeeper showed Elizabeth and Annie to their comfortably appointed room on the top floor. 'You'll be wanting a bath,' she said, indicating the tin tub standing before the fireplace. 'I've sent a maid to heat water.'

'Thank you,' Elizabeth said. 'Much appreciated.'

'Very thoughtful,' Annie added.

The housekeeper smiled. 'All the ladies ask for a bath when they arrive from Katoomba,' she said. 'It's such a long ride.'

'It is indeed,' said Annie.

When the door had closed behind the housekeeper, Elizabeth bent to unlace her boots. 'I'd never admit it to the men,' she said, 'but that last descent was a bit of a stretch. My horse wasn't happy about it at all.'

'Neither was mine.' Annie rubbed her aching back. 'I know the smoke from a bushfire is always unsettling, but something else out there was spooking them.'

'I know.' Elizabeth grinned. 'Martians, do you think?'

'Don't even joke about it,' said Annie.

'Sorry,' said Elizabeth, 'but there's something very strange going on around here. I can feel it.'

'So can I,' said Annie.

A little later, washed and brushed, they re-joined the gentlemen when the riding party assembled in the candlelit dining room for the evening meal. Tonight, Caves House offered a simple baked dinner: roast lamb with mint sauce, boiled potatoes and peas, with apple pie to follow.

'I don't think I can eat a roast,' Annie said. 'Not after the smell of that burned thing we saw in the pit.'

'I know what you mean,' said Freddy. 'It's put us all off our food. But at least allow me to offer you a restorative glass of claret.'

'Thank you, yes.'

'Excellent idea,' said Cameron.

The claret proved to be rather thin, but it had the desired effect. The riders relaxed, and soon discovered that they really were quite hungry at the end of such a long day. They made short work of the meal, and retired to the sitting room for a nightcap.

Freddy offered the port decanter to Jackson. 'Did you learn anything more from testing the soil in the pit, Charles?' he asked.

'I'm afraid not,' Jackson replied. 'The impact crater is consistent with a meteor strike, but the ground is full of splinters of a metal that my field kit cannot identify. I've packed up more samples to take back to Sydney for better analysis.'

'So you're keeping an open mind,' said Elizabeth.

Jackson's reply was solemn. 'I really see no other option, Miss Fraser,' he said. 'The whole thing is quite baffling.'

'Well,' said Freddy, 'at least we'll finally get to see the famous caves tomorrow. I'll take my camera, of course, though photographing anything rather depends on how much light is available.'

'Not much, I'm afraid,' said Cameron. 'You'll only have lantern light.'

Freddy shrugged. 'I'll set the aperture as wide as possible. You'd be surprised what this little camera can capture.'

'In that case,' said Elizabeth, 'I'm sure we'll all be extremely interested to see the results.'

'And I'm afraid we'll have to leave you to it,' said Cameron. 'My workmen will be here in the morning with our wagons. Bob and I plan to ride out to the mine at first light. We shouldn't be away for long.'

'Then we shall hope to dine with you tomorrow evening,' said Jackson.

Next morning Jedediah was up early, urging his tiny congregation to come with him to worship at the caves.

His father-in-law was unconvinced. 'I know you have a vocation, son,' he said, 'but this is a big ask.'

'I truly am the Chosen of the Lord,' said Jedediah. 'I'm offering to prove it to you. Come and see the Angel for yourself.'

'There really is an Angel, Dad,' said Molly. 'He blessed Adam yesterday.'

'And now the child is talking nonsense,' Jethro replied. 'I think he's ill.'

'Please, Dad,' said Molly. 'If only to keep the peace. The others will come if you do.'

Jethro gave in. 'Alright,' he said. 'I suppose we need to seek out the truth of this, for all our sakes.'

'You won't regret it,' said Jedediah.

The Guest House provided a walking map of Jenolan Caves for sightseers, and Jackson spread it out on the breakfast table while the others were finishing their toast and tea.

'The cave I think we should visit first is said to contain spectacular stalactites, especially a formation called Gabriel's Wing,' he said. 'The route is one of the most accessible, through a passageway called the Dragon's Throat.'

'Steep, then,' said Elizabeth.

'I'd say so. The cavern itself is known locally as The Temple of Baal.'

'Ah,' said Freddy. 'Elijah's temple of false gods. Shall we find Jezebel, do you think?'

'I doubt it,' said Jackson. 'But I see from the map that Michael's Sword is down there.'

'Then I think we should all go and see it,' said Annie. 'A walk through the caves will make a pleasant change from yesterday's discomforts.'

The Dragon's Throat turned out to be a spectacular, rough-hewn staircase that twisted and turned as it wound down to the depths of the Angel-wing cave.

'This isn't too bad,' said Freddy, 'but I must say I'm not looking forward to the walk back up.'

'We'll do it in easy stages,' said Jackson. 'I want to collect mineral samples in any case. And I'll take some of that red weed for analysis – the stuff that's spreading everywhere the limestone is wet – I've never seen anything like it before.'

'Me neither,' said Freddy. 'It's very odd.'

'Why not collect your samples now?' Annie asked.

'I'd only be carrying them downhill in order to carry them back up. I see no need to make extra work for myself.'

'Sensible,' said Elizabeth. 'Though that rifle must be heavy. Why did you bring it?'

Jackson shrugged. 'After yesterday, I just don't feel safe without it,' he said.

'Quite right,' said Freddy. 'I brought my pistol too.'

Annie laughed. 'So did we,' she said. 'I guess we're all a bit nervous.'

They were still laughing as they rounded the last corner to the Angel-wing cavern: and all smiles suddenly stopped.

'What the devil?…' Jackson began.

'Quiet,' said Freddy. 'We don't want to spook them.'

They stared in disbelief. Below them, on a natural raised dais surrounded by the flickering light of safety lanterns, a monstrously glistening creature holding a silver sceptre loomed over a row of kneeling supplicants.

The Martian was instantly aware of the intruders. It probed their minds, recognising a different order of scientific understanding. It was caught. It needed to keep up the Angel appearance for Jedediah and his congregation, but it realised that such a primitive image would not convince these newcomers, who must surely be members of the rival species it had been warned about. At first, it did not react. It hoped the interlopers would leave.

Annie put her hands to her face. 'It's like I have double vision,' she said under her breath.

'I know,' said Elizabeth. 'I can see a strange creature, with a church angel superimposed on top of it.'

'Protective camouflage,' said Jackson. 'How fascinating.'

'I'd be willing to bet the worshippers see only the angel,' Freddy said. 'I'll try for a photograph.'

The Martian sent a warning to the intruders. *Leave*, it said. *Leave now. Leave before you are hurt.*

They all looked at each other, the Martian's message echoing inside their heads.

'Intriguing,' said Freddy. 'It's using telepathy. It must be highly intelligent.'

'It's highly alarming,' Jackson replied. 'This creature, whatever it is, is threatening to harm us.'

'All animals show their teeth,' Freddy said mildly. 'We've disturbed it. Let's give it a chance to settle down.'

'I don't trust it,' said Jackson. He unslung his rifle from his shoulder.

The Martian targeted him, increasing its coercive mind-pressure. *Go!*

The pain in Jackson's temples was excruciating.

Freddy could never remember exactly what happened next. It was all so fast, and he was fiddling with his Kodak, taking photos by lantern light. But Elizabeth and Annie saw the whole thing.

Jackson raised his hunting rifle, sighting along the barrel.

'Don't!' Elizabeth hissed.

Jackson ignored her.

Jedediah glanced up, and saw.

'No!' he shouted, hurling himself forward to protect his Angel. 'No!'

It was too late. Jackson fired. The sharp crack of the rifle shot ricocheted in the confinement of the cave.

Jedediah fell to the ground, stone dead.

Jackson re-loaded, ready to fire again.

The Apostles saw the Angel raise his fiery sword.

Annie and Elizabeth saw the Martian aim a thin, silver tube in their direction.

The heat ray arced across the cave. Cold crystalline stalactites fell to the floor, sizzling hot, sliced neatly where the searing beam had touched them.

Jackson was incinerated where he stood, the heat so intense that his bones simply vaporised.

Annie grabbed Freddy by the hand, and fled.

Elizabeth was right behind them.

They did not look back to see the Martian extending a grey, snaky tentacle to probe Jedediah's body: the Chosen One was about to be recycled as sustenance for the growing Martian embryos.

One of the women put her arm around Molly Carpenter's shoulders. 'You'd better sit down, love,' she said. 'You've had a terrible shock. I'll get you a drink of water.'

'I'm alright,' Molly said. She stroked her son's shaking curls as he huddled close to her, sobbing. 'But I must get Adam out of this place. He's just seen his father killed.'

'I'll help you,' the woman said. She turned to Molly's father. 'Can you deal with the body, Jethro?' she whispered.

'No need,' Jethro whispered back. 'The Angel is taking the Chosen One unto himself.' He pointed to where the Martian was, indeed, in the process of dragging Jedediah down towards the lakeside for re-processing. 'See?'

The rest of the apostles remained kneeling, praying for their departed pastor.

The Martian accessed Jethro's mind for acceptable phrases: *Be not alarmed*, it said. *I have destroyed one of Satan's minions – one who would hamper your good works.* It paused. *The Chosen One will be raised up on high to take his rightful place in Heaven,* it added.

The worshippers didn't look up. They didn't dare.

You may go, the Martian said, exuding equal measures of comfort and compulsion. *I shall see to the elevation of my faithful Apostle.*

'Your will be done,' Jethro intoned. He stood, gesturing to the others to do the same. 'Your apostles will return tomorrow to see to your needs.'

That is acceptable, said the Martian.

Freddy and the Fraser girls laboured up the shadowy, steep passageway of the Dragon's Throat, desperate to reach the faint glimmer of daylight that marked the exit from the caves. They did not stop when they made it to level ground. They dashed through the gate and sprinted toward the safety of Caves House, running as though the very hounds of hell were at their heels.

'Whoa!' Cameron almost collided with them as they neared the dray loaded with engineering equipment that he and Hatfield were now checking in the yard. 'What the devil is going on?'

'You look as if you've seen a ghost,' said Hatfield.

'We have,' Elizabeth gasped. 'Mr Jackson is dead. We saw him die.'

'And we are running for our very lives,' Freddy wheezed, struggling for breath.

'It's true,' said Annie. She leaned heavily on Freddy's arm, panting from exertion.

'You'd better tell me exactly what happened,' Cameron said. 'We'll need to send someone for a constable to see to the body.'

Freddy shook his head. 'There is no body,' he said.

'How can there be no body?' Hatfield asked. 'You said you saw Jackson die.'

'We did,' said Annie. 'He was killed by a beam of heat. He simply burst into flames – flames so hot he turned to ash and steam. There's nothing left of him at all.'

Cameron's expression was pure incredulity. 'Heat ray?' he said. 'You're saying you saw a *heat ray*? Like the thing the London papers reported?'

'Yes,' said Elizabeth.

'You're telling me there really *is* a Martian down there?'

'Yes.' Freddy's voice was barely a whisper. 'It has to be. We didn't believe it either, until we saw it. We all saw it. It was hideous.'

Elizabeth and Annie nodded their confirmation.

'You don't have to take my word for it. I'm pretty sure I got a picture,' Freddy said.

'But we can't develop a photograph out here, can we?' said Hatfield.

'Then go down and see for yourself if you don't believe us,' Elizabeth said sharply. Her voice was harsh with unshed tears.

'I'll go,' said Cameron. 'You must admit your story is pretty far-fetched.' He squared his shoulders. 'If Jackson is dead, the authorities will need evidence. I'm a practical man. I'll go and assess the situation. If what you say is true, we must decide what's to be done, and quickly.'

'Then for heaven's sake don't upset the monster,' Freddy said. 'It's a repulsive-looking beast, but it didn't strike until Jackson took a pot shot at it.'

'And there are other people down there too, worshipping it,' Annie added. 'Mr Jackson accidentally shot one of them, but the Martian hadn't harmed them.'

'Worshipping it?' Hatfield said.

'That's what it looked like to us,' said Elizabeth. 'The Angel-wing cavern is vast. They really are using it as a temple, kneeling before the creature with their heads bowed in prayer. It's very strange.'

'If you say so, Miss Fraser,' said Cameron. He turned to Freddy. 'Mr Urquhart, if you will escort the ladies back to the guest house, I'll make it my business to investigate the cave.'

'I'll come with you,' said Hatfield. 'Best you don't go alone.'

'Thanks,' said Cameron. 'In that case, we'll be on our way.'

The Apostles of Mercy had left the Temple of Baal through the back tunnels by the time Cameron and Hatfield made their way down the Dragon's Throat. The engineers were used to the darkness of the mines: they kept their safety lanterns turned low, and they moved stealthily.

'There!' Hatfield whispered. He pointed to a huge shape that bulked large beside the cavern's crystal lake, outlined against the dim light of a glowing lantern.

'I see it,' Cameron replied. 'Though just *what* it is I have no idea.'

Now that its apostles were gone, the Martian had dispensed with its protective disguise. It registered the shadowy presence of the mining engineers, but dismissed them as non-threatening. It had crucial work to do while the Chosen One's corpse was still fresh.

Cameron and Hatfield stared in horror as the octopoid creature set about reducing the body of Jedediah Carpenter to its component proteins. It used its long, strong tentacles to strip the flesh from the bones. The soft organs – heart, liver, lungs, kidneys – were tossed into an oozing red heap – and then the Martian began using a thin metal tube to siphon the blood and bodily fluids into a clear container.

Cameron felt his gorge rise. 'Enough?' he whispered.

Hatfield spat. 'More than enough,' he answered.

The deeply shocked engineers did not speak as they crept away into the cold darkness of the tunnels under the mountain. But by the time they re-emerged into the safety of daylight, both had come to the same conclusion.

'I'll get the dynamite from the dray,' Cameron said grimly.

'Right,' said Hatfield. 'I'll help you lay the charges – it's a two man job.'

'We'll have to seal the cave completely,' said Cameron.

'I know,' Hatfield replied. 'But we've probably got enough time. The monster seems preoccupied at the moment. I don't think it's planning to leave soon.'

'I dread to think what it's planning,' Cameron said. 'Let's just get this done.'

They worked methodically, moving as quickly as they dared, until Cameron finally straightened up, holding the T-bar plunger of a black ignition box.

'Well, Bob,' he said, 'we've used everything we have. If it isn't enough – if the creature escapes – it's been good working with you.' He held out his hand to shake.

Hatfield did likewise, clasping vigorously. 'And you too, Pete,' he said. 'Ready?'

'Ready as I'll ever be.'

Peter Cameron took a deep breath and pushed the plunger home. Seconds later, a huge explosion rocked Jenolan Caves. The sound was strangely muffled in the damp caverns, but the pressure wave was deafening. Suddenly, it was raining stalactites, the slow work of millennia eclipsed in a few violent seconds. And then everything was shockingly silent. When the glittering dust finally cleared, the access tunnels had completely collapsed, filled by tons and tons of rubble. The entrance to the Angel-wing cavern was sealed under a mountain of beautiful, fractured limestone.

Trapped in the ruins of the cave, the Martian had air and water, but little food. It sent a last, urgent telepathic message to its fellow colonists: *Warning. This operative is no longer viable. Current location – co-ordinates below – buried under rock fall – escape equipment inadequate. Embryos remain secure. Hibernation option is now activated. Re-activation setting: opening of caves. Future seeding of Earth remains possible. Message ends.*

Banjo's War

Narrelle M. Harris

We have buried the dead where the ghost gums stand
At the foot of the Eaglehawk
A grave for the many in stony land
Where few other men did walk.
I carved their names on a broken board
To honour those here deceased
Underneath, 'At peace in the arms of the Lord'
Instead of 'Slaughtered like sheep by a beast'.

– Andrew Barton 'Banjo' Paterson,
'The Defender's Rest', 1896.

Published in *The War Against the Martians*, 1897

Andrew wondered that any birds could still sing, in this devastated landscape. Yet there was a currawong's burbling, ringing call somewhere beyond the tangle of the choking red weed and angular legs of the fallen Martian tripod.

Men had sung too, for a short while after that singular victory: about the brave ones who had broken cover to lure the monster into the muddy, tunnel-riddled hillocks of the old goldfields; about the ones who dared death as they set off the explosives.

The Martian fighting-machine had stumbled into the tunnels thus exposed, those long, spindly legs staggering off balance, falling through the wet crust of the earth again as they tried to right themselves.

Then its legs bent and spasmed, trying to find purchase, while the men took to it with ropes and nets to entangle the tentacles that whipped out from its metal head. Others fell on the machine with pickaxes, spears, rifles and fire: any weapon they could find. Some threw muck over the hood of the machine, blinding it, and cracked the hard egg of the tripod's engine. Its heat ray, bursting out at desperate random, killed many. A puff of poisonous black smoke saw to many more before the machine fell into the mud, which neutralised the gas.

Two score men – whitefella, blackfella, Chinaman; miners and police; clerks and farmers and one formerly gentle vicar – came to fight it. The handful still alive after the melee hauled the Martian from the engine out onto the churned soil. They took their revenge on its soft body, flaying it to pieces.

One brief celebration of victory they'd had. Revelry and beer and the feeling that, despite the cost in lives, their combined might and intelligence and ferocity would preserve their world.

The dead Martian's comrades had come, then. A second tripod fell, but not fatally. Two others set upon the men who had fought so valiantly. Few of them escaped.

Andrew had only survived the encounter thanks to the courage of Jackie, the tracker who had pulled him into a tunnel exposed by the skirmish. They'd huddled there in terror until the screams of their fellow warriors had ceased, and the sound of the tripods striding the landscape had vanished.

Jackie, weeping, had sung a native song. Andrew crouched beside him in the tunnel, shaking. In Sudan in the 1880s he thought he'd filled up to the brim on horrors, only to discover the world could deliver worse nightmares. He longed to pour those horrors out in words, to fill his journal and empty his head, but somewhere in the fight, he'd lost his satchel and the journals he'd already filled with observations since the Martians had come.

In the weeks since the first pods had landed, Andrew's spirit had gorged on such terrors, from Eaglehawk to Ballarat. His body was gaunt and numb with what he'd witnessed: the brutal mastery of the Martians, to whom humanity was no more than livestock.

Andrew picked through the battlefield of that bittersweet and short-lived victory. Barely 10 days old, it was, and the red weed was already softening the landscape. The bodies of his friends were underneath it somewhere. The bent legs of the Martian's broken machine rose above it, twisted scaffolding for the alien plant growing all around.

A faint but rank smell rose from the weed. Where it brushed against his canvas trousers, it left smears of grey.

So, it had begun to rot where it grew here too, like it had wherever he'd been these last few days – where it grew at all. The ugly plant normally clustered around rivers and waterholes, but long stretches of New South Wales and Victoria were dry, and there the strange, cactus-like creeper failed to thrive.

A faint sound to his right snatched Andrew's attention back to the here and now. The currawong sang on, but the sounds of movement had been unmistakable. A snake, perhaps? A wallaby lost among the dying weeds? All the same, Andrew clutched his replacement satchel with his left hand, and reached for his pistol with his right.

A man stepped suddenly from a knot of red weed and tea tree. 'Mister Andrew.'

'Jackie! My god, I nearly shot you!' Andrew cried.

Jackie, wearing only battered trousers, held a spear with easy confidence. A rifle was slung across his back. The length of cloth that acted as a belt for those grimy breeches supported a hunting knife.

Jackie grinned, teeth white in his dark face, and let the spear tilt upright again. 'No you didn't, Mister Andrew.'

Andrew found Jackie's confidence in the quickness – or perhaps the slowness – of his reflexes both amusing and comforting.

'Quite right, Jackie,' he agreed. He holstered the gun and met his old comrade in a spontaneous, robust hug. 'You're alive, by God.'

'Not by God, Mister Andrew,' replied Jackie sombrely.

Andrew nodded soberly. 'No. Quite right again. And enough of *Mister* Andrew. We're brothers in arms, aren't we? Andrew is enough.'

'Andrew.' Jackie nodded. 'And you call me Moorabool now, eh? Come with me.'

'Is that your tribe name?' Andrew asked as he followed his friend.

'New name,' said Moorabool. He carried his spear lightly, as though he might need it.

Andrew found he was still smiling, despite everything. He'd never thought to see this man again. 'It's good to see you,' he said, buoyed by their encounter. 'I thought you must be long gone.'

'I been looking for my mob,' said Moorabool.

'Any luck?'

'The aunties took the bubbas inland, to Djab Wurrung country.'

'And the rest?'

'I don't know. Fighting. Dead. Still looking.'

'I'm sorry.'

He and Jackie – no, he must start thinking of him as Moorabool – fetched up at an old miner's hut. The A-frame roof was rusted, and no door hung on the opening, but the windowless stone walls seemed sturdy enough. A mound of earth at the rear gave some protection too. It was rude and filthy, but it at least offered shelter from the weather.

It would hardly offer shelter from the invaders, but Andrew knew no Martians had been in these fields for days. They'd come to Ballarat from the cities to extrude gold into coils of wire, the use for which nobody could fathom, except that it must have some use in their infernal machines. They'd done with that work for now, it seemed, and they had departed again, leaving Ballarat in ruins.

Andrew had seen the Martian fighting-machines striding on their three spider-legs, morning and night, back towards Melbourne. He dare not even think what that city now resembled.

Moorabool offered Andrew a water skin and Andrew drank gratefully. He passed the skin back and contemplated his companion's troubled expression.

'Jac- Moorabool?'

Moorabool dug at the ground with the blunt end of his spear. 'You whitefellas came and took our land.'

Andrew stared at his hands. 'Yes. We did that.'

'My mob thought we were done with losing it. Dying for it.'

Andrew could only think to apologise again, but shame and sorrow held his tongue.

Moorabool jabbed the spear down again, then seized Andrew's hand. Tugged on it. Andrew looked at dark fingers entwined with pale in the fading light.

'We all one mob now, fighting for our land.'

Any reply clogged in his throat with the sudden surge of feeling. Grief and humility, determination, thankfulness, fear. He nodded.

'You remember Mister O'Keefe?' asked Moorabool suddenly, dropping Andrew's hand.

'I remember he was a cruel bastard,' said Andrew.

'That cruel bastard man gave blankets to my cousin's mob. My cuz and all his family, they all got sick and died.'

Once more Andrew was reduced to only, 'I'm sorry.' It was too big a crime with no words big enough to encompass its horror.

'It's a sorry thing, but I'm not saying it for sorry,' said Moorabool, a light in his eyes. 'All us mobs around here, we think about what kind of blanket can we give the Martians.'

'They don't want anything of us but our planet.'

'They feed on us.'

Andrew blinked at him.

'I met a mob three days ago. Their old woman, sick as dogs, you whitefellas say. The typhoid. She stood and shouted at a Mars-fella to come get 'er, while her mob ran. The Martian ate 'er up, like a honey ant, sucked 'er dry. And then that Martian, he howled.'

Moorabool tipped his head back and mimicked an uncanny sound: '*Ulla ulla ulla ulla.* Then he fall down dead.'

'My god.'

'That auntie, she was a brave warrior.'

Andrew couldn't imagine the courage such a thing might take, even for one so sick: to stand and shout for death to take you.

'What happened next?'

Moorabool dug his spear into the dirt again. 'The Martians learned. They always learn. We kill this one here, but not another. That auntie use herself to poison one, but they stop eating blackfellas.'

'That's…something, at least.'

Moorabool grinned again, but this time it was a sharp and angry expression.

'I'm here looking for my mob. Why you here, Andrew?'

Andrew opened his satchel. He drew out his journal. 'I used to be a journalist,' he said. 'I wrote about the war in Sudan. I thought…if humankind survives this, it might help if there was a record.'

He wasn't sure he could articulate the deeper reason. His heart, his soul, were in the words of those journals. Parts of him all through those pages. He needed them back, if he was ever to make sense of this new world they all lived in. The need to retrieve those journals had burned in him all the way here from Eaglehawk. Even if he died in the attempt, he had to have his words back.

Moorabool peered at the journal and traced his finger over the cover, mostly clean and still very new. 'You had old books like this when we bring that Mars-fella down.'

'I lost them during the battle.' So much chaos in those hours. The strap of his satchel had broken. He, striking at the fallen machine with an axe, hadn't noticed until he and Moorabool were hiding in the darkness of the mining tunnel.

'Months of work are in them. The start of the invasion and the weeks that followed. All buried in the goldfields. I've seen the Martians leaving for the coast. I thought I might be able to find my books again.'

Moorabool rested his palm on the new notebook, then patted it. 'It's late now. We look tomorrow.'

They shared a meagre meal of stale damper, which Andrew fetched from his satchel, wrapped in cloth, supplemented with a few strips of smoked meat that Moorabool carried in a dilly bag. They sipped from the water skin again, and settled in for the night.

Andrew woke suddenly with his hairs prickling stiffly upright all over his head, his arms. He would have cried out only Moorabool pressed a hand over his mouth. The tracker's eyes gleamed in the darkness and he pointed through the doorless gap.

A spindly shape with a globular head lurched, silhouetted against the horizon of eucalypts and the wash of bright stars. The ground shook with the vibration of the fighting-machine as it stamped over this old battlefield.

The tripod stamped again, and swayed. Its tentacles unfurled from beneath the head and waved before it in a peculiar, slow fashion, almost delicately exploring the air.

The Martian was on its way to the coast, no doubt; or returning for some unknown reason. Surely, Andrew thought, he and Moorabool were not so important that the Martians came especially to hunt them.

The machine stamped a third time, its hood jerked up and its deadly heat-ray was suddenly burning a vicious sweep across the landscape, reducing red weed, plants, creatures to ash as it passed. The devastation halted and suddenly resumed in another direction. Rocks cracked and shattered into blackened fragments under the ray.

The third slashing arc of fire swept directly towards their little shelter. No choice remained but to break cover and flee.

Moorabool hefted his spear, crouched low and darted out of the hut. Andrew's hair crawled with the horror of it, but he took up his pistol and followed his friend into the night. If death was coming, neither of them would die like rats in a burrow.

The ray cut through the hut, reducing it to cinders and shards of stone. It continued its momentum, ignoring them, then abruptly ceased. The Martian did not fire its weapon again. Its metallic tentacles waved frantically for several minutes, then they too ceased to move.

Andrew and Moorabool were too exposed where they crouched in the moonlight. To move could attract the Martian's brutal attention again, but to remain cowering in the dirt was unthinkable.

Moorabool flicked the tip of his spear towards a furrow in the ground that offered slightly more protection. Andrew's boots made only slightly more sound on the earth than Moorabool's bare feet as they inched towards safety. They crept between the mounds of earth and the slowly rotting red weed, weapons ready, watching the progress of the Martian.

The fighting-machine resumed its passage, and its metallic tentacles began to wave again, with more agitation than before.

The spark of Andrew's hopes that they would escape the Martian's attention a second time guttered, however, as the thing's hood swivelled slowly in their direction. The machine began to walk inexorably towards them, spindly legs uncertain but unceasing on the treacherous ground.

The hood tilted up and light flickered about it. The Martian strode closer, tentacles still waving, until it loomed over them. It was almost as if the Martian couldn't see them. But then the hood tilted down again, as though at last it had pinpointed where they crouched. The light gathering in the hood intensified.

Andrew waited for the heat-ray to burn them both to ashes.

Moorabool rose up with a wild battle cry in his own tongue, and threw his spear. Before it had even struck the underside of Martian's hood, the rifle was in his hands and Moorabool fired at the tentacles which reached for him. Andrew leapt to his feet and waved his arms. 'Hey! Hi! Here, you brute, over here!'

As Moorabool's last bullet was spent, Andrew fired his pistol at the hood of the Martian. 'This way, blast you!'

The hood tilted in his direction. The glittering tentacles waved in the air, then reached for him.

Andrew darted to one side. He stumbled over a hollow but righted himself before crashing to his knees. He glanced back to see the Martian staggering on its legs as it twisted towards Moorabool.

Andrew fired at the beast's carapace again. 'Come along, you foul thing. Here! This way!'

Another shot and the Martian lurched towards him.

'Andrew! Come away!' cried Moorabool.

'Run! Hide!' Andrew called back, running through the weeds. 'Find your family!'

Moorabool wouldn't run. Instead, he took his hunting knife in hand and darted beneath the fighting-machine.

Andrew waved at the Martian again, distracting it from Moorabool's futile attack. He zig-zagged, and the Martian lurched after him. Once, it fired, spending the heat-ray uselessly on the ground. The stink of cindered weed and soil spurred Andrew on, but when he heard Moorabool cry out he turned.

Moorabool had plunged his knife into the lowest joint of the machine's spidery legs, then flung himself wide as the Martian stumbled.

The knife snapped and the machine righted itself. Its tentacles sought Moorabool, weaving above him but not seizing him.

Andrew took up a stone and flung it at the Martian. 'Over here, you devil!'

Once more the invader diverted its attention to the noisier target. It raised a leg and stomped it down, yards from where Andrew shouted his defiance.

'This way!' Moorabool beckoned Andrew to join him.

Andrew, heart thundering in his throat, trusted wholly to his friend's intent, and ran beneath the Martian machine, between its legs, to Moorabool's side. Moorabool caught at Andrew's reaching arms, and with his wiry strength dragged them both behind a great hillock of dirt.

'Wh-?'

Moorabool pressed his fingers to Andrew's lips for silence, then bobbed slowly up to spy on the Martian. Andrew rose with him and they peered through the tangled weeds.

The tripod stomped one leg, then another. One leg sank suddenly, well below the level of its fellows, as it stepped into one of the old mine tunnels. The tentacles flailed then went still.

'That fella sick,' whispered Moorabool with confidence.

One moment the machine stood tall against the sky; in the next it fell, toppling like a blue gum. The crash and clang as it collided with the rocks and soil rang through the air like a clarion cry.

Andrew and Moorabool watched – curious, silent, daring to hope.

The alien machine had cracked on impact with the ground. From within, a soft thing with a round body dragged itself out of the breach. Its tentacles twitched and writhed. From its fleshy beak rose a chilling cry.

Ulla ulla ulla ulla.

Anxiously, Andrew searched the horizon for any sign of the Martian's fellows, and found none.

'Mars-fella dying,' pronounced Moorabool.

They kept silent vigil over the thing that filled them with so much terror and revulsion until long after the Martian's death cries had faded.

They continued the vigil until the sun rose, and with it the morning songs of the currawong and a chattering flock of budgerigars that surged and swirled like a cloud.

The flock eddied and parted as one black shape angled in from the pale blue sky, and then another, and a third. The glossy black birds alighted on the corpse of the Martian and pecked at it.

'Crows,' said Moorabool, with a respectful nod towards the birds. 'And eagle.' He looked pleased, like it was a favourable sign. He rose and turned his back on the Martian, now dotted with carrion birds.

Andrew rose too, and turned away from the scavenger feast. He thought he saw a dog, perhaps a dingo, stalking closer. He shuddered, as though the Martian might suddenly move and cry out its *ulla ulla ulla ulla* yet again, but the only sound was the call of the Australian bush. A kookaburra's peculiar cackle fell from the trees, and it sounded to Andrew like a victory call. It sounded like home.

Moorabool grinned at him. 'You run fast, like a goanna!' He swooped his hands, zig-zag. 'Goanna-man!'

Andrew stared as Moorabool began to giggle, then suddenly they were both giggling, guffawing, gulping for air, tears running down their faces.

'Goanna-man!' shouted Moorabool when they found their breath, and they fell about laughing again. Moorabool mimicked a goanna's hind-legged sprint – legs and arms akimbo, stepping comically wide on each side and waving his hands as he referenced Andrew's courageous zig-zag dash – until Andrew was on his back, clutching his belly, hooting with laughter.

His friend fell on the ground beside him, and the two of them grinned up into the blue, blue, blue sky.

Finally, Moorabool rose up again, and Andrew too.

'Come,' said Moorabool, and Andrew followed.

They picked among the mounds until the tracker clambered into a hollow in the earth.

'I see this fella yesterday,' said Moorabool, nodding at the gaping mouth of a tunnel fringed with the root of fallen trees, a chunk of pale, veined quartz lodged at its mouth. 'You remember, eh?'

Andrew remembered. Moorabool had found the tunnel where they had sheltered 10 days ago. Moorabool stooped inside the opening. He scraped at the dirt with his spear, revealing a battered, soiled fold of leather.

With a heartened cry, Andrew got to his hands and knees and dug his old satchel out of the mud. Within, there were his journals, dirty but unharmed.

'Thank you,' he said, over and over, clutching the books to his chest and rocking them like a child. 'Thank you, oh thank you. Thank you. Thank you!'

Later, they filled up on fresh water and tubers roasted over a fire. On the horizon they saw another Martian stumble, its outline dark against the sky, and fall. Its distant cry – *ulla ulla ulla ulla* – reached them, then faded to brief silence, before the birds descended.

'Are they all dying, do you think?' asked Andrew, cautious with his optimism.

'I think the typhoid make 'em sick and die,' said Moorabool. 'The pox too. All kind of blood poison.'

Andrew nodded. 'I think you may be right.'

Moorabool glanced up to the eagle still wheeling across the sky, and to the cloud of budgerigars. The shape of the flock swelled and shrank, swelled and shrank, as they followed the river eastward. Andrew realised today was the first time in weeks that he'd seen and heard such flocks in all his travels.

'Where will you go now?' he asked his friend.

'My father is dead, but I'll look for my uncles and aunties, the rest of my mob,' said Moorabool. 'But first I'll go to the Djab Wurrung and my family there. Bring them home. You?'

'Sydney,' said Andrew. 'I want to be certain all the Martians are falling. I want to report on everything I've seen. I want to make sense of it all. Humans aren't alone in the universe. It changes everything.'

Moorabool nodded, as though he understood more than Andrew's words.

They shook hands and parted, Andrew east, Moorabool west, each to reclaim their country.

From city block to cattle run
From Broome to Hobson's Bay
Each native and adopted son
Stands straighter up today

The Koori spear, the Chinese sword
The European guns
All stood against the Martian horde
Earth's good, courageous sons

We of many nations fought
With courage, side by side
With our chances seeming nought
And side by side, we died

No more we judge by coloured skin
No more by hatred led
By battle forged, we all are kin
And all our blood is red.

Our flag, the symbol of our bond,
A spray of wattle-bough
Our discords we have stepped beyond –
We're all Australians now.

– Andrew Barton 'Banjo' Paterson,
'We're All Australians Now, 1896.

Read at the opening of the first Australian Parliament in Melbourne, 1899, by Wadawurrung elder, Moorabool, inaugural Parliamentary Representative of the Kulin Nations, under the terms of the Treaty of Birrarung, 1898.

Author's notes: The indigenous characters in 'Banjo's War' are not based on any real person, living or dead.

'The Defender's Rest' is adapted from 'The Swagmen's Rest', published 1895. 'We're All Australians Now' is adapted from the original 'We're All Australians Now', published 1915.

The Inconvenient Visitors; Or, An Un-Restful Cure

Lucy Sussex

All sorts come to Hazelmere, we've seen them all. That's what happens when a man of business like me, with an eye for the comforts of life, sees potential in a property. The advertisement in the *Argus* caught my eye first: Guesthouse for sale, Easter Hills. I took the train to Yarraman, hired a horse and rode up through farmland then bush, the trees to either side bowing in the wind. Between the wrought iron gates I went, up the drive to the house on the hillcrest, seeing stables, croquet pitch, kitchen gardens. It had potential, for what, I did not know, until I was sitting on the shady verandah, with a bottle from a local vineyard uncorked, and a rich fruitcake cut into wedges with my penknife. I gazed over the valley, the river below like a lady's silver belt, the little bush-birds hopping after my crumbs, and I felt something unusual: completely at peace.

What a place for a rest cure! I thought, and that was how I advertised it. A bit of refurbishing, a first-rate cook and soon the customers came flocking for luxurious respite. Look at the visitors' book and see: French Counts to opera singers and even a Princess from Samoa.

We just weren't expecting something so foreign, nor so much

trouble. I can't say that I had much inkling. Among the visitors, we had one solitary astronomer. He was a convivial chap, and I took up his suggestion to install a telescope. Never used it, since I keep my eye on business, not the skies.

Some of the guests did, but it meant nothing much, even when the weekly papers in the breakfast room were left open at the astronomy section. Mars to me was only a book donated to our small library by a grateful customer, Mr Fraser the phrenologist: *Melbourne and Mars: My Mysterious Life on Two Planets*. A bit of a rum title, I thought. He'd actually written it, too.

Our inconvenient visitors made their arrival after a long and hot period. The dam by the gates was lower than usual, and so was our custom. With the extended days of heat, people tended to linger at the beach, enjoying the bathing huts and donkey rides. I had been hoping for a cool and rainy time, the sort that would draw the trampers and the mushroom fanciers, but holidays neared, and still I mopped my brow with my handkerchief.

What we had at Hazelmere then were an odd company, of whom the following figured: old Colonel Schmidt and his wife; Mr Mowbray, a journalist, who mostly sat in his room working on a novel of Australian Life; Curate Pentland, afflicted with the nerves; Miss Royce, a lady not in her first youth, whom rumour said had been sent to recover from an unsuitable attachment. Then there were the staff: besides the three maids, myself and my dear wife, who was housekeeper; Job, the ostler, an Australian of the original type; Ah Kee the Gardener, who was Chinese and nicknamed Archy; and Monsieur Didier the chef, as nervy as any of our customers.

I was, I admit, not enjoying the best of days. Breakfast came with yet more relentless sun, followed by a row in the library. I subscribe to the best periodicals and Robertson the bookseller regularly sends a parcel of fashionable novels. Now Colonel Schmidt had mislaid *The Yellow Wave: A Romance of the Asiatic Invasion of Australia*, and intemperately accused Miss Royce of stealing it.

'As if I would read such rubbish!' the lady retorted loudly.

'Rubbish?' shouted the Colonel. Outside the window Archy was watering the geraniums, pretending at being oblivious.

'Yes, rubbish that is all jingo and UnChristianity!' she continued.

I frantically scanned the library shelves, for something, anything of the futuristic ilk, even if it was *Melbourne and Mars*. Then I literally put my hand on the solution.

'Perhaps you might like *The Battle of Dorking*, Colonel Schmidt?' I proffered, and next moment regretted it deeply.

Miss Royce laughed out loud. 'Colonel *Schmidt*, you would prefer a German invasion of England to an Asian invasion of Australia?'

Mrs Colonel, an anxious little dove, promptly had hysterics. When all the shouting was over, the Schmidts decamped down to the station, driven by Job in the trap. Archy, now weeding near the gate, raised his conical hat to them. I was having deep suspicions about the fate of *The Yellow Wave*.

The only person unaffected by the row was the journalist Mowbray, who witnessed the disturbance without pausing in his breakfast.

'Might have been worse,' he said. 'You could have offered him *The Coming Terror*, that's written by a genuine anarchist. I've interviewed Mr Rosa.'

'Something or someone I would never have in the house!' I replied stiffly.

Miss Royce laughed again, from the verandah hammock in which she had ensconced herself, with a plate of Monsieur Didier's madeleines and, I noticed, *Melbourne and Mars*. I wished her joy of it – I had work to do. The day went on, baking heat, the milk going sour, and Job returning and giving notice.

'Is this one of your Australian walking-abouts?' I asked. I had heard of such things during my two years in the colony but was new chum enough never to have encountered it before.

His face assumed an expression I had seen before. It usually meant trouble coming, in the ostler line of things: a horse was in a kicking mood, or a wheel was about to come off the trap.

'It's these hills,' he finally said. 'What they're called.'

'They're called Easter,' I said. A sere little breeze had arisen, sending a scatter of dried gum leaves dancing on the gravel path.

'You call 'em that,' he said, drawing a line in the gravel with one bare black toe. I saw his determination and let him go down the drive. At the gate he turned and called:

'I'll be back, if there's a job for me.'

Two steps on, he turned again, with a parting shot.

''Nother thing. Somebody's coming.'

'What does he mean?' said the wife, appearing with a basket to cut what flowers were in the garden, though they were fast tending to dry arrangements.

'Customers, I hope.'

Miss Royce, from her hammock, raised one eyebrow. 'He sounded ominous.'

'Don't care, so long as they pay,' I muttered.

Thankfully she did not laugh, but merely returned to *Melbourne and Mars*.

Night came, with a cold collation, since Didier had a headache. The guests scattered to their rooms, fanning themselves, with moths forming a pattern of silhouettes against the muslin curtaining. I stayed on the verandah in a deck chair, smoking my cigar and listening to the soft, busy noises of a warm bush night. The bird they called the Tawny Frogmouth, like a sawn-off owl, sat on a tree branch and watched me.

Then all of a sudden it happened, a whoosh, a trail of fire across the sky, passing over Hazelmere and down into the valley. The frogs stopped pobble-bonking in the dam and the frogmouth flapped away. The wife came to our bedroom window, voluminous as the curtains in her nightgown.

'That's not Archy setting off fireworks for his Chinese feasts again?'

'No,' came a voice from the darkness beyond the verandah. 'Something much bigger.'

I turned my head, towards the plinth where the telescope stood. My eyes taking their time adjusting, I did not immediately see Miss Royce in her dinner-dress sitting on the ground beneath the telescope.

'My legs gave way from the astonishment,' she said coolly.

I went over and helped her to her feet, just as Mowbray made an entrance, in dressing gown and tasselled nightcap.

'What in heaven was that? Falling star?'

'Stars do not fall, in astronomy,' Miss Royce said.

'A meteorite?'

She said something that sounded remarkably like: 'If we're lucky.' Then louder: 'It landed in the valley. Near the pine plantation, from the trajectory.'

'There's a story in that,' Mowbray said, ducking back into his room. 'For the *Argus*, or whoever pays the most.'

Miss Royce's hand was on mine, and it trembled slightly. Whither your arch looks and laughter now? I thought, but led her to the verandah. Mowbray reappeared, dressed in haste and stuffing a notebook into his coat pocket.

'Where's that Jonah?'

'Job's given notice. I suppose you want *me* to drive down to the valley in the middle of the night.'

'Not middle anymore,' said Miss Royce. She released my hand. 'I can pay extra for your time and trouble, but I must accompany you.'

'What the mischief does a petticoat want with a meteorite?' Mowbray said.

'Woman though I am, I have made a particular study of them,' she said simply. 'Nobody for miles can inform your journalism so well.'

'Then you will need a chaperone, young lady,' said my wife from her window.

What with the womenfolk needing to get suitably dressed, and me buckling a sleepy and reluctant horse into his harness, it was the grey of pre-dawn by the time we got down the hill to the valley. Between the trunks of the pine plantation we could see a great hole in the ground beside the racetrack, with mist or smoke arising from it. Everyone in Yarraman was awake, it seemed, and we followed a procession – children in goat-carts, maids pushing perambulators, young lovers arm in arm – towards what Miss Royce proclaimed the impact crater.

A meteorite it most certainly was not.

Until the cablegrams arrived from the Old Country, none of us who witnessed the events at Yarraman had any idea our experience was shared half a world away. We had to come to our own conclusions. Mowbray started making shorthand notes immediately, pen sketches of the crash site. They made his name, eventually, and my wife pasted them into an album. In them Miss Royce appeared as an anonymous authority, supplying the necessary astronomy. Until then I had no idea of the mysterious lights and gases that had been seen on Mars, at the opposition when our two planets are closest. I thought Opposition was loyal, and in Parliament…

We four crowded into Yarraman's little telegraph office, securing our primacy with pound notes from Miss Royce and Didier's best madeira cake, which my wife had thoughtfully packed. 'Move on, nothing to see,' the local mounted constables had declared to the crowd, a complete lie. They were chiefly concerned with securing the site, and as we left the telegraph office, the train drew in, packed with more police.

Mowbray elected to stay in Yarraman, tired but keen to report any further developments. I had my doubts about that. Even if some canal-building Martian were inside the big tin can at the centre of the crater, he surely must have been smashed or cooked by the fall to earth. My wife yawned repeatedly, and Miss Royce looked pale as her blouse, with dark shadows under her eyes. I saw it was my duty to get the womenfolk back to Hazelmere, and to their beds. Miss Royce shook her head slightly but let me help her back into the trap.

'Cheer up,' I said. 'We have the best view thanks to our elevation, and the telescope, which we can turn from the heavens to earth.'

The night might have been warm, but the day proved clear and hot from the moment the sun rose. There was a stillness in the air, as if a breath waited to be exhaled. The trap crackled over dead gum leaves on the dirt track, the only sound, for the birds seemed struck silent, not even a dawn serenade of squawks. Then, in the distance I heard a slow and steady thump-thump, receding away from the valley.

Miss Royce roused a little. 'Wallaby. Out late.' She glanced around. 'I know you are a new chum, but have you ever noticed how all the animals on these hills are much the same colour as the old trees?'

Now I too glanced at the trees and stumps as they passed. Ash-grey the trunks were, nearly black. I did not pay the comment much attention, more fool me. The events of the last few hours had taken an invisible toll, manifesting now in sore joints, and an increasing weariness. So it was that when we drove through the guesthouse gates the women shucked off their tiredness like pea-shells, and it was I who collapsed into my bed and a deep sleep.

I woke, hours later, in a tangle of sweaty sheets, with strange dreams in my head: a can opening, to reveal something worse than sardines, but I knew not what, for I ran away before I could see it. The awning had been pulled down on the verandah, but the sun shone bright as diamonds through its interstices. Outside I heard soft voices, my wife and Miss Royce:

'If you believe Mr Fraser – and there is no other book about Mars here – the Martians are human as us, but better. I fear his phantasy may be optimistic.'

My wife sighed. 'The poor man was both nervous and dreamy.'

'But progressive! He imagined a Mars both Socialist and with equality of the sexes.'

'No unsuitable attachments there?' enquired my wife.

A distinct pause, then Miss Royce said: 'My unsuitable attachment was to university education, above all astronomy.'

'Ah. Never was one for book-learning myself,' said my wife. 'Still, I read in bed, if I have time at the end of the day.'

'An excellent habit,' said Miss Royce.

'And I signed the monster petition for women's suffrage, not that my husband knows. Oh, to move to New Zealand and vote!'

I thought, from my darkness: I would never hinder you, not even from the ballot-box.

When I came out dressed, I found them on the verandah, now joined by Archy. The flooring was piled with old sacks from the stable.

'Where are the maids?' I said. Tilly, Mary-Anne and Daisy were sturdy local farm-girls, reliable until now.

'Gone home,' said my wife. 'Said they were needed, just in case.'

'To gawk at Martian-men, you mean.'

'Oh no,' said Miss Royce. 'Tilly saw a native bear climb down from a tree, to drink from the watering-can. So dry were the leaves, his usual fare! Tilly said it was a sign.'

'Of what, for heaven's sake?'

'Do you not hear the wind?' and as she spoke a gust from Hades rattled the awnings. I understood, then. Down at the Art Gallery in Melbourne, I had seen the great painting of Black Saturday, people, animals and birds, scared and dying, trampled underfoot while fleeing conflagration. Surely a day from Hell, and a day like this.

'You can flee the fire, or fight it,' she said.

I took a breath. 'An Englishman's home is his castle.'

'Then I will show you how to defend it,' she replied.

'What a day!' I said, exasperated. 'As if tin cans from Mars were not enough…'

'You should ask the men about that,' she said, with a sideways flick of her head. I squeezed between the awnings, to find Curate Pentland, clerical collar donned despite the heat, at the telescope. By his elbow was Didier.

'The redcoats have arrived,' he greeted me. I could see with my own naked eye the scarlet of the uniforms, the colony's finest regiment, gathering around the hole in the ground.

'Martial meets Martians,' he added. 'The God of War.'

'Ready for a scrap,' said Didier, forgetting his French accent. He rubbed his hands.

'I was an army Chaplain,' said Pentland. 'My duty is down there, to minister to the wounded.'

'Including any men from Mars?' said Miss Royce, all ironical again.

'They too are God's creatures, for He has made everything in the universe.'

'Including the Tasmanian indigenes, Job's kin? Who met a superior force, though arriving in boats, not shot across the ether between the planets?'

'That is irrelevant.' He swallowed, glancing at me. 'We must make haste.'

'No, you can't take the horse and trap!'

'It's not a hard walk down through the bush,' said Didier. 'Done it often enough, shooting ze possums for pie.'

They left not long after, two unlikely comrades suddenly finding their nerve at the whiff of warfare. I gave them a flask of water, and Miss Royce saw them on the way with her ironic laugh.

'I would not walk in the bush today. It is too like what my father recalls of Black Saturday.'

'May God preserve them,' said the wife, who can be pious on occasions.

In fact we forgot them quickly, as Miss Royce turned pedagogue, on how colonists prepare for wildfires. She and my wife donned their stoutest skirts and the maids' boots. We collected buckets, rakes, brooms and mops, and together carried the piles of sacking down to the dam, to dampen them. Archy got the ladders out, and we two cleaned the gutters of leaves. The women swept from the paths what I was now seeing as inflammables everywhere; and Archy climbed the trees, hacksaw in mouth like a pirate, to cut off any overhanging branches. We were soon all soaked to the skin with sweat, but that moisture would not be enough to save us.

Busy as we were, we managed the occasional glance valleyward, or a peep through the telescope. I could see the regiment drawn up, in a formation, and were those gun carriages being unloaded from the train? How unlike, though we did not know it yet, the response of our Northern hemisphere compatriots to the Mars-men, the doomed Deputation with their white flag. The Australian colonists did things differently, perhaps remembering the Tasmanians, as Miss Royce had. Or, what I had heard a Queensland squatter talk of one night when drunk after dinner: the dispersals, a bloody business.

We had done what we could against conflagration; I had even given the horse water and strapped on his double saddle, so the womenfolk could flee if necessary. Now Miss Royce marshalled us in front of the verandah, a troop armed only with water in buckets and mops.

'The spot fires come first, on burning leaves carried by the wind. You must dowse them as soon as they touch ground, or the house.'

While she demonstrated with the mop, I glanced down at the dam, hoping it would hold all of us, including the horse. Miss Royce had said we could expect the local bush creatures, from wombats to snakes, to join us in the watery mud if the fire rolled over the hill to engulf Hazelmere. That was our last resort, and our last chance to live.

Down in the valley, if you read Mowbray's reports, they had other concerns: the increasingly restive soldiers, the can itself restive, showing signs of life, what sort of life nobody knew. He describes the fear, the oohs and ahs as the can slowly opened, then the shock as the Martians emerged.

'I had thought that these Mars-men might be red, like their planet, and had even sketched in my mind some futuristic Red Indian. Tentacles I could never have imagined in my wildest dreamings, nor those hideous faces, the slimy brown skin. White man will always trump a brown, was the mutter of an old Colonist within earshot of me, but I had my doubts: these brown-skinned creatures had travelled between the planets, something beyond any white man.

'I cannot say for certain who started firing, some nervous foot-soldier, or a hasty young officer. All I can say is that the shot rang out, and pandemonium ensued, more shots, and then the Martians responded.'

Up at Hazelmere we heard that first shot, and the following. We crowded around the telescope, forgetting the mops and buckets, and so it was we saw clearly the flash of light.

'Lightning,' cried Miss Royce. 'A sure sparker of bushfire.'

'Too low,' I said. 'And also, too green!' for such was my impression, which as I blinked lingered lurid still against the red of my eyelids. As we gazed down – Archy had the telescope and would not let go – we saw the redcoats rally, shooting a volley. Next the green ray struck at them again, and they fell writhing to the ground, like bull-ants burnt out of their lair. Those men at the regimental rear turned prudent and retreated, becoming a rabble as the Martian ray struck again and again at them. Their fire reached beyond the crater, to the town and beyond, taking the roof off the Yarraman Arms in an incandescent burst, sparking a grass fire in the graveyard, and even striking at the base of the Easter Hills, the steep wooded slopes below us, which immediately went up like a bonfire.

Archy let go of the telescope, cursing in Chinese; my wife for the first time in our married life crossed herself; Miss Royce actually shed a tear. Me, I felt nothing but the certainty that that small dam would soon hold us all, to drown or boil, whichever came first. I reached out for my wife's hand and held it fast, feeling the warm metal of our wedding rings.

Miss Royce, in one of her scientific papers, has since theorised there are no trees on Mars. Which means no eucalypts, that tree which is a good servant when you need to boil a billy, but a bad master with a fiery, murderous temper. Yet the Australian bushfire is capricious and can be merciful.

The Martians, on their dry, cold planet, did not know that. They were intelligent, far more than us, when they took to the skies to invade us, using machines far beyond the current capacity of humankind. Certainly they had the wit to use their fire in a high wind blowing away from them. They did not know, nor I either, that a southerly change had been blustering up from the coast, and would suddenly change the course of the conflagration – towards the Martians in their hollow, with their tin can voyager.

We four, up at Hazelmere, had the best view of what happened: how the fire, the flames already high and speeding up the slope towards us, changed direction, striking through the bush at the northern end of Yarraman, escalating through the pine plantation, the trees exploding like Archy's rockets, and across the crater. We saw a Martian try to run, ungainly because of our heavier gravity on earth, said Miss Royce. The fire set him alight like a Roman candle, tentacles and all, and he fell in a blackened, twitching heap. Then came the explosion as the Martian's green fire machine met a greater enemy, sounding loud as a thunderclap.

When the town's photographers got their courage up to record events, no doubt at the insistence of Mowbray, they discovered at the centre of the crater a blackened, burnt-out can, which had survived the space journey from Mars to Earth, but not an Australian bushfire. We saw Mowbray later, when he came up to collect his bags: a conquering journalistic hero, with singed hair, and a broken arm, not his writing arm, for he got his reports in.

Miss Royce's parents came the next morning to collect her, in a fine carriage, so glad that she had survived that an unsuitable attachment to science could be tolerated. The curate and Didier we never saw again, no doubt among the heap of corpses from the Martian flame, burnt beyond recognition.

I threw the guesthouse open to visiting journalists and sightseers, playing ostler myself. Archy took over the cooking and proved a dab hand at it. We had a full house, a healthy balance sheet, and even the maids returned.

Last but not least, Job came strolling up the drive, swag on back. The horse had just bitten me, so I was more than glad to see him.

'You were right,' I said. 'Somebody did come.'

It was only at the end of that long week that I finally had the time and peace for my late night cigar on the verandah. When Job and Archy came looming out of the darkness, I passed them the cigar box. We sat there and smoked, united in what I could not put words to, but which might be called brotherhood. Invading Martians and bushfires can do that to you.

'Lucky escape, Boss,' Job finally said.

'Don't I know it!' Then something struck me. 'You said it was what these hills are called. What are they called, apart from Easter?'

'In language it means Fiery Hills. See them trees, the bark still black from the last fire? Hot day, big wind, lightning – the hills burn!'

Archy stubbed out his cigar.

Job spread out his hands. 'Long as my people 'member.'

'Longer than my people,' said Archy.

I thought: Job, why did you not tell me? Then I remembered the Tasmanians, with no bushfires to protect them from an invading force.

I got up. 'Excuse me a moment.' I went to our bedroom, where my wife was tucked up with her bedtime reading. 'Like to vote, dear heart?' I said.

And that is why the wife and I sold Hazelmere, to invest in a sanatarium in Te Aroha, New Zealand, a green, wet land, without bushfires.

And without Martians, I hope.

The Enemy of the Enemy

Rick Kennett

FROM HIS SOLITARY CAMPFIRE JIM HOPKINS WATCHED THE GREEN LIGHT sparkle across the starry outback sky of western Queensland and plunge below the horizon with a flash of emerald sheet lightning, all in ghostly silence.

And that was that. He should've forgotten it; he'd seen many shooting stars while working as a boundary rider for the Danley Downs cattle station. But this one was green, and he was sure it'd come down – actually landed – some distance to the north. A day's ride, he guessed, but still within the boundaries of Danley Downs. That, he told himself with his bush-bred curiosity making excuses, made it part of his job: mending broken fences, rounding up stray cattle, shooting predatory dingoes and chasing down green shooting stars. A detour like that wouldn't be noticed by the station manager, a blow-hard stand-over man by the name of Mitchell, a hero to himself and nobody else. At any rate Mitchell had no authority over the independence of a boundary rider, no matter how much he swaggered about the station itself.

Jim had heard stories of stones falling from the sky, heard they sometimes held star-smelted gold and were clotted with jewels of incalculable value. He rubbed his bristled chin, wondering.

Just before he'd left the homestead some days ago he'd read a newspaper story about something big falling out of the sky and burying itself into a great pit at some place in England called Horsell Common. As far as he knew that was the beginning and end of it. News from the outside world took time to reach remote places like Danley Downs, a long journey by cart or bullock dray from the nearest railhead and telegraph wire. The newspaper had already been several days old when he'd seen it. Anything could've happened since then, anything could've been discovered about it by now. Not that he really believed a hoard of gold and jewels had just fallen from the sky a day's ride away. But he knew he'd curse himself as a galah forever after if he didn't at least go take a squint. And Mitchell could go to the devil.

After a breakfast of johnnycakes next morning he saddled his horse and rode north. He smoked a couple of Woodbines, and in-between drags whistled a tune he'd heard once in a Brisbane music hall he'd attended with a girl named Molly. He'd walked out with her twice and had utterly failed to impress both times.

'What does "gauche" mean anyway?' he asked the memory of her parting words to him.

The west was ablaze with sunset and the stars to the east were already coming out by the time he arrived within a mile or two of a large stand of gum trees. Either within it or just beyond, he estimated, was where the green star had fallen. He stopped and made camp as there was no point searching in the dark.

Jim was jolted awake by a loud *crack* shattering the immense silence of the night.

He flung off his blanket and sat up, listening. His campfire had long since died and the dark all around was quiet once more, save for the uneasy stirring of his horse. Then, just as he was beginning to think it was a dream noise the *crack* came again – the unmistakable sound of splitting timber. He stared toward the trees, silhouetted against a glory of stars, and saw three or four of those stars blink in momentary eclipse. In the same instant a prolonged tumult erupted, as if a herd of bullocks were bashing about the trees and trampling down the undergrowth. Jim jumped to his feet, watching the dark, seeing the stars blink. Something was moving out there, something big and tall and stumbling.

A dark mass outlined itself for a second against the stars, there and gone. Then a succession of stars blinking off and winking on showed him it was turning around and coming his way.

Standing there in the night, faced with the approaching unknown, Jim suddenly felt more alone that he had ever done on any of his long, lonesome rides. His first impulse was to swing up onto his horse and gallop away. But this was blind, unreasoning panic, a sure recipe for death in a dark landscape of wombat holes and rocks. He fought down this urge and held onto his nerves, watching, listening.

Once more the stars blinked, to left, to right, as something out there – something huge – swerved and swung. Bush and scrub crackled and smashed as if trampled by a lurching giant. The horse whinnied and stamped. Jim patted the animal's neck, whispering calming words into its twitching ear, though calm was not at all what he felt right now. The thing in the dark was nearing, its thudding approach louder and now louder, accompanied by a metallic clangour and intermittent hisses as of jetting steam. The ground trembled as overhead he glimpsed an ill-defined swaying shape. The horse whinnied again, reared and bolted, knocking him down.

Far above something he took to be a water tower swung out of the dark, loomed a leaning moment over him. Dirt flew up in clods as the monster thudded by, clanking and hissing. A beam of light struck down, strong and wide like a warship's searchlight, dazzling Jim in sight and mind before snapping out again, leaving lines of colour running amok across his eyes. The night roared and crashed and thudded as the madly dancing titan wheeled around him in a staggering circle. Instinctively, uselessly, Jim wrapped his arms over his head, sure he was about to be stomped flat.

Something pounded like a pile-driver into the dirt close by, lifting, passing, receding in an uneven rhythm of gigantic footfalls, *thudthud-thud*.

Jim jumped up, uttering an inarticulate cry of relief, followed by a surge of consuming white-hot anger. He spun and reached down in the dark for where his saddle should be, for where his rifle should be. His fingers found its trigger. He fired into the dark, once, twice, three times, feeling great satisfaction at each recoil.

The whining *ping* of a bullet ricocheting off something solid answered the third shot. He smiled like an idiot, laughed like a madman. He fired three more shots, and when his ears finished ringing he could hear the irregular *thudthud-thud* of the thing stomping into the night.

Taking deep breaths he shouldered his rifle and dusted himself down. He whistled for his horse but it didn't come. He guessed it was now far off and still galloping. He didn't blame it in the least.

Feeling about on the ground he found his hat and for some time stood, listening to the returned silence, his mind in a whirl.

Striking a match he checked his pocket watch. It was exactly three o'clock. He sat down against his saddle, rifle across his knees, smoking three Woodbines in quick succession with twitching fingers and deep drags. Eventually he slipped into a troubled sleep haunted by dancing water towers with fiery, grinning faces.

First light showed the countryside as it should be: yellow grass, huddle of gum trees a mile or so away. Even his horse was not far off, quietly grazing. But here and there the grass had been flattened in circular patches about a yard across, and in places the scrub had been stamped down and crushed. There was no getting round it by calling it a nightmare or a bout of the DTs; he hadn't had a pull of grog for days. He fetched his horse and rode bareback over to the trees, watchful lest they suddenly explode with more reeling giants.

Tethering the horse to a branch and slinging his rifle over his shoulder, he followed a path of broken boughs, leaning trunks and the smell of fresh sap. He'd gone only a short distance in when it struck him how quiet it was. No laugh of a kookaburra, no lazy aark-aark of a crow. His noisy tramping as he waded through the smashed undergrowth startled nothing that flew, hopped or ran. But then something monstrous had burst out of here only a few hours before, so it wasn't that surprising.

What was surprising was that apart from the smashed undergrowth there was a strange red weed underfoot, like creepers or vines with little scarlet leaves. He'd never seen the like. And though he was no botanist, he was sure this red weed was foreign to outback Queensland.

Towards the centre of the trees the ground rose in ravaged heaps.

Branches and roots and whole trunks were sticking out of the upheaved earth like bones from out of burial mounds. Topping one of these he found himself on the lip of what at first glance he took to be a large mineshaft.

Then he saw it for what it was – a deep and elongated pit, maybe 30 yards across and at least 200 long, littered either side with the splintered and pulped remains of trees. The further end was a steep slope while the closer end was piled up almost to the size of a hill. And at the bottom of this hill, in the pit itself, was what looked like the end of a boiler or cylinder 30 or 40 yards across.

'I've heard the cry of the Benajilla banshee,' Jim said aloud to himself, tilting back his hat. 'And I've seen the Mulla-Mulla lights dancing in the night. But this beats them all by five country miles.'

He clambered down the slope where the red weed grew thickest, his mind a battlefield of wariness and wonder, curiosity and avarice. Those not-quite-believed yarns of gold and gems were becoming more believable by the minute.

Walking down one side of this massive cylinder he found an opening that reminded him of the mouth of a railway tunnel, though taller than it was wide. Its edges were angular as if hexagonal plates had been removed. The morning light, filtering through the riven trees, lit the interior dimly, grey grading to absolute black. He walked back to his horse – was it imagination or had the red weed grown thicker in the past 10 minutes – and returned with the bullseye lantern he used to hunt dingoes in the night. With its limited light he could not see the far walls of this cylinder's interior, though he could feel its vastness. Jim was so reminded of a cathedral in its stillness and size that he took off his hat. Then, feeling foolish, he put it back on.

He cupped his hands to his mouth.

'Cooo-*eee*!'

His bushman's call echoed with a metallic ring and sung away into the dark.

The place felt dead, like the ghost towns he'd ridden through while droving cattle in younger days. Sad and lonely ruins, they'd been, and perhaps haunted; as this place was perhaps haunted. He couldn't shake the growing feeling that a sinister purpose underlay all this silence and mystery.

He was about to cooee again, then thought better of it. No one had answered his call. Perhaps there was no one to answer. At any rate he didn't think he'd like to meet those who would dwell in such a place, who could crash down from the sky in green lightning, who were in any way associated with dancing water towers.

That last idea needed some thought, so he lit another Woodbine. As the match flared he glimpsed a big black box only a step or two away. In the light of his lantern it showed itself to be made of metal, maybe a foot by a foot-and-a-half long. There was a glass eye set flush into the end facing up, with grips or projections, curved and thin, on the sides. It was heavy and cumbersome, and with some difficulty Jim turned it over, then tipped it back so that the eye once more stared upward. He peered into it.

'Must be a camera,' he said, and laughed at recognising such an ordinary object in such an extraordinary place. Then he frowned, confused. Was it a camera? Most cameras, he recalled, had their lenses at the end of concertina-like affairs. And didn't they have slots at the back for photographic plates? This camera had no slots, was solid all the way around, except for the lens in the front. Weren't they supposed to have a little window at the back for the photographer to look into under his black cloth? And a squeeze bulb for the "Watch the Birdie"?

'It's a caution,' said Jim. 'So...perhaps it's a *moving* pictures camera.'

Not that he had any idea what a moving pictures camera looked like, but it was as good a guess as any. He'd only been to a picture palace once, and that'd been the second time he'd walked out with Molly, the Brisbane girl he had failed to impress. They'd gone to see *Train Pulling into a Station.* He remembered the title because he'd fled from the theatre, terrified that the oncoming steam engine was about to rush out of the screen and into the audience.

'Maybe *that's* what "gauche" means,' he said, and chuckled at himself.

He peered closer into the lens. Still thinking on girls and the big city, he wondered if this might be one of those shadow-play machines with such tantalising titles as *What the Butler Saw.* He grinned at the idea and felt his pulse race at the thought that here might be glimpses of feminine ankle...or more. But didn't those machines have a handle to crank? Didn't they have a penny slot? Not that he had a penny or carried any money at all out here in the back of beyond.

Something shifted under his fingers. Something clicked inside the box. He pushed and pulled at the curved projections, thinking they might slide. Already his mind's eye was flickering with images of a young lady rising from her bath.

The box clicked again and began to hum. He saw the lens blink a rapid red, saw the red grow bright, felt the metal grow warm against his hands.

He looked closer into the lens but saw only this red glow. So he tilted the box, shaking it. His hand slipped and the box fell heavily onto the floor. The humming stopped. The bright lens went dark.

'Bloody hell I've buggered it!'

He stood and glanced about, feeling in equal parts guilt and shame. Nothing came out of the dark to admonish his clumsiness.

'If ya ain't a camera and if ya ain't a damned peeping-show, what the devil are ya?'

A few steps further into the dark he found what he at first took to be a bullock's head, a great bulbous shape with large staring eyes, the brown flesh glistening like wet leather in the lamplight. Then he saw it had an upside down V-shaped mouth, and out of this mouth snakes were crawling.

He un-shouldered his rifle and brought it to bear on the snakes, squinting down the barrel. His finger tensed on the trigger…then relaxed. He lowered the gun.

'Ya actin' like a skittish kid, Hopkins!' he grunted to himself.

It was nothing but a head. A very big head, but without horns or a bullock's snout – more like a great leathery bag. No need to get scared. He'd seen worse than this: dead cattle disembowelled by dingoes, dead 'roos fly-blown and stinking with entrails dangling from them, which was probably what these unmoving snakes were. By the light of his lantern it was clear they were thin tentacles like those of an octopus, only smooth and without suckers. Some were splayed out before the head, some were bent behind it into shadow, eight each side of the mouth, each ending in a pointed tooth or claw.

For a long moment he watched the large unblinking eyes, the limp tentacles, and the grotesque mouth which he was sure was about to speak and say hideous things.

He stepped to the side to nudge the head with the barrel of his rifle and saw the figure sprawled behind it, which up until then had been hidden by the leathery bulk and its shadow. Only in comparison to the head did Jim think of it as human at all. It was prone, about seven feet long. Its skin was like grey tissue paper crinkled over bones like spun glass, the strings of sinews showing through. The skull was almost perfectly round with a lump of a nose, thin lipless mouth and dead eyes in flinty sockets. Its neck was stick-like and its papery skin had been ripped by the claw ends of the octopus's backward-reaching tentacles. It in turn had killed the octopus with something like a scythe, whose long handle its claw-like fingers clutched and whose blade was buried deep in the leathery brown flesh.

Jim swung the lantern about, certain he was about to be likewise attacked. Nothing came at him from the darkness behind. He looked again at the two corpses.

'Octopus...skelinton bloke...What yer killed each other for?' he asked in a tone of irritation used, he well knew, to cover his fright. It was plain the octopus had been chased, overtaken and killed by the skeletal figure even as it had reached back and clawed its attacker to death. Jim looked at them in turns, trying to find a reason why. He saw only that the skeleton was smiling.

Jim had a think, then cast his light back on the black box. Had they been racing for that?

Once again he felt a twinge of guilt at having dropped it and possibly broken something these creatures had killed each other to possess.

The mere size of the cylinder bespoke great value. Big as a battleship it was; and battleships, he knew, cost tens of thousands of pounds. Someone had gone to a lot of trouble and expense to build this and at least one other, if the newspaper yarn about the thing falling onto Horsell Common in England was true.

'I mean,' Jim said to the dark, to the dead, to himself, 'it has to contain *something* of value.' Recalling the green lightning of its descent and the dancing water tower, he added in quiet awe, 'Maybe magic.'

He'd seen magic – real magic – performed by a koradji man at a blackfella corroboree, and he'd witnessed the Mulla-Mulla lights dancing on the horizon and heard the cry of the Benajilla banshee sounding across an empty plain, so he was willing to believe there might be actual sorcery here.

'But still,' he reflected, 'we've got electricity and gramophones now and moving pictures and horseless carriages. Once upon a day *they* would've looked like sorcery. The world turns so fast now that science and sorcery gets mixed.' He waved an arm around. 'What if all this is just more of the same, only more mixed? What if it comes from a place where science moves faster than it does here?'

The thought was wondrous and terrifying, perhaps even blasphemous, that this cylinder and all it contained was beyond the mind of Man, perhaps beyond the *spirit* of Man. But how did the smiling skeleton and the thing that was all head and cuttlefish limbs fit into it? He instinctively disliked the octopus but felt only sympathy for the skeleton. It looked more human, and – if it'd killed that monster for ownership of the camera – it'd done something recognisably human too.

He moved off a few steps, then abruptly swung the light back behind him. The octopus had not moved, the skeleton had not stirred. Nothing was following.

He turned and found himself brought up against a rack of great orbs, like giant tear drops, gleaming in the lantern light. They were about a yard in diameter at their bulbous end, tapered to a tail at the other, translucent like murky water. Jim rapped his knuckles on one, expecting it to be wet and soft like jelly. Instead it was as though he'd knocked on polished glass, hard but warm as though filled with fire.

Another glance back at the bodies caused him to rethink the situation. Rather than the camera, had they been racing for these orbs, the octopus *with* the camera, the skeleton with murderous intent?

'It's a caution,' he murmured, and moved on.

At intervals his light showed shapes fastened to the wall: cubes and oblongs and canisters. There was something like a metallic spider or crab, big as a traction engine, that gave him a start as it loomed out of the dark. But close up he saw it was a mechanism, its claws glittering in the lantern light but silent and dead as everything else.

Presently he came upon four oval recesses in the curving wall, and beyond them a circular, hushed glow. Lifting his lantern, Jim saw the ovals as something like shallow cupboards. The first two were empty. Lengths of cable ending in open or broken loops depended from their back walls. But as he moved his light to the next two their inner shadows slid away revealing a sagging skeletal figure in each, manacled at wrists and neck. Their lipless mouths were open as if howling in soundless, endless pain. They were pale and the skin was tight against the bones giving these corpses a collapsed look, as if drained of blood. Lengths of thin tubes were inserted in their necks.

Jim backed away, shocked, disgusted. He'd seen enough. There was no treasure here, only death of a particularly ugly kind. And if there were treasure...well, he'd seen enough all the same.

But there was that circle of light just beyond the cupboards, obviously a portal of some kind. He didn't want to look, but with his rifle at the ready he stepped through into a room lit by softly glowing walls.

Three octopuses were piled in a wet heap like discarded baggage at one end, splashed in blood from gaping wounds inflicted with obvious violence and passion. Blood in great gouts stained the walls and smeared the floor in three wide lines leading to the dead things. They'd been mutilated, tentacles chopped, large eyes gouged, leathery hides torn open, massive brains exposed, cleaved and oozing grey-red.

And the smell...there was no smell. Jim knew well what a slaughterhouse smelled like, and here there was not the slightest whiff of corruption or putrefaction or even the peculiar odour of blood despite the wash of it all around. The air was fresh and clean and utterly unnatural.

Standing there staring, Jim was reminded of rumours he'd heard in the long ago of Jack the Ripper's last victim, Mary Kelly, surgically sliced to pieces on her gore-soaked bed, and of photographs that would not be released for 99 years. If they were anything like the scene before him now he knew why the Ripper photographs had been locked away. Though slaughtered cattle and dead and rotting animals in the bush were a commonplace to him, what he looked at now made him almost sick.

For a moment he couldn't understand his squeamishness. Then he realised. Animals reacted to the moment and nothing more; but what he'd seen in this cylinder showed that the octopuses were beyond animals, as were the skeletal men in the cupboards who'd been drained of their blood...some of whose number, so it seemed, had escaped and killed their tormentors. This deliberate cruelty and murderous revenge appalled him because they were all too human traits in this all too *unhuman* place.

The significance of the three smears ending at the heap came to him then as he imagined the massacre. They'd all been killed before the cylinder had landed and their bodies had slid forward, still bleeding, when the cylinder hit the ground.

'So that means…' Jim muttered and stopped, amazed at how his thoughts were arranging themselves. 'So that means the octopus and the skelinton bloke killed each other *after* the crash or they would've fetched up against the wall too.'

It occurred to him then that he'd made deductions like that detective in the English story magazines, working out conclusions with observation and reasoning. He felt a moment of justifiable pride at his own cleverness, though his pride was quickly dampened by the fact he had no idea what his conclusions amounted to. Three octopuses had been slaughtered before the crash, while a fourth had been killed and had killed its attacker after the crash and in a desperate chase for the camera or those teardrop orbs.

While pondering this he noticed a number of fist-like shapes in silver brackets on the wall opposite. Jim stepped across, ignoring what crackled under his boots. The objects were smooth and opaque but sparkled with inner light. They looked for all the world like emu eggs made of worked crystal.

He picked up one of these crystal eggs and then another, felt them heavy in his hands. But unlike the large teardrop-shaped orbs these were cold against his callused palms. He stared into them, and their opaqueness rippled and formed pictures.

The crystal in his right hand showed the land outside with its stand of smashed gum trees and his horse standing to one side, morning shadows lying long across the yellow grass. Both the trees and the horse were foreshortened as if viewed from a height of perhaps 20 or 30 feet. The crystal in his left hand also showed a view from a height, but here moving in a steady, fluid roll – a night time view of a city lit by fires with something indistinct and tall walking in the middle distance. Sometimes these walking things shone a moment with a red metallic lustre in the firelight and sometimes they were glimpsed as stalking stick insect silhouettes. A stately building with square towers at each corner moved past in the foreground, and Jim realised he was looking at the Houses of Parliament in far away London. Though he'd never been there, he was familiar with the great building with its square towers from the labels on bottles of Parliament rum.

Suddenly one of the sullen fires in the image erupted into a huge fireball, as if with the detonation of an armoury or gasworks, and reflected a lurid red on a stretch of water below.

'The Thames?' said Jim, trying to remember his schooling from long years ago. As if in a dream he didn't question how he was seeing what he was seeing. It just *was*. Sheer wonder had overcome all, and even as he looked the fire grew brighter and still brighter until it lit all too well a tall tripod structure. A cluster of arms or tentacles waved from just below a hood of shining metal surmounting the three legs, and the whole contrivance was wading down the centre of the river.

Two of these tentacle arms were wrapped around a bulky object, black and squarish. Behind the hood was a conical basket holding things that writhed and struggled. For an instant another tentacle swung close by Jim's field of view, only a few feet from his eyes it seemed, and it too was holding something that wriggled.

Now the tripod ahead raised the arms holding the black, squarish thing. The Houses of Parliament roared into flames and the crystal in his hand vibrated with an exultant cry of '*Aloo! Aloo!*'

Watching in horrid fascination the destruction envisioned in the left hand crystal, Jim did not immediately see what was occurring in the right hand crystal.

And then he did.

He saw the waving bone-thin arm, the long-fingered hands. He saw the spectral skull face, the eyes in their flinty sockets looking straight at him.

He never heard the crystals hit the floor.

His dash from the room, his headlong rush through the darkness of the cylinder, were dim blurs in his panicked flight – past the oval cupboards, the rack of teardrop orbs, the black box, the dead octopus, skeleton man, spurred by an animal need to reach the distant daylight of the opening, to run and run and run from all this madness.

So intent on escape was he that he didn't see the mechanism emerge from the dark to his left, straight lines of glittering metal rising and swinging, something big as a traction engine advancing on six legs in a crab-like scuttle, a crab-like claw reaching out, clutching.

Instinctively Jim dropped and rolled, his rifle clattering across the floor and into the dark. He didn't care. He was up and running again for the light in an instant, hearing behind him metal grating on metal in a tight scuttling turn.

He leapt from the hexagonal hole, fearing a giant's grasp on his back. He almost flew up the dirt walls of the pit while heavy noises clanged close behind. Grabbing and grabbing at red weed and raw earth he climbed, unheeding of broken nails and his own desperate animal sounds.

Into the trees, running, red weed squelching, slippery, crashing through the undergrowth, running, colliding with branches like arms outstretched to catch him.

He heard his horse before he saw it, whinnying in terror, pulling at its tether because it could see what Jim Hopkins dare not look round to see.

He wrenched the reins from the branch, swinging onto the horse as something heavy and large trampled the trees at his back. Then he was galloping for his life, out of the trees and across the plain in headlong flight.

For a full mile he let the horse have its head, and only then did he dare look back. He glimpsed something among the trees flash silvery in the morning light. Then nothing. No claws, no crab big as a traction engine.

By now his horse was tiring and he had little trouble easing it to a trot, reining it to a stop. His heart thumped and adrenalin raced in his blood. But he was sure now he was safe. At no point did he consider returning for his saddle, for his food and water, for his rifle.

He took a another, longer look behind. Nothing pursued. The sun shone strong and bright and a breeze sprung up, rustling through the grass. Crows flapped squawking from a nearby stand of trees. Everything seemed so normal again, almost as if nothing extraordinary had happened.

And so it was as he sat upon his horse, trying to remember where a billabong or other water source might be, that he didn't see what stepped quietly from the trees behind him until it wrapped a tentacle around his waist and hefted him neatly off his horse and into the air.

With a thump Jim found himself sitting in an oversized seat. Beside him sat a skelinton bloke, regarding him with its inscrutable skull face. Jim, who had experienced far too much that morning, could only stare at it, numb of all emotion.

The skeleton pointed ahead, then placed two fingers above its head like horns and chirped in a thin voice, 'Moo…moo' in distinct imitation of a cow. It pointed at Jim, then once more it pointed ahead.

Vaguely, Jim grasped the idea that it was indicating Danley Downs cattle station, about two days horse ride straight ahead. Without further comment the creature reached bony arms down to levers grouped like those in a railway signal box, pulling some with surprising agility, pushing others forward.

At this Jim grew conscious of a gentle rocking motion as if he were in a boat in a swell. In front of him was a wide window or port giving a view of the countryside moving by as if seen from a cantering horse, but here from a higher elevation. Below this window were several crystal eggs, all but one showing swaying scenes of tripods marching along what were clearly English city streets. Black smoke poured from canisters and heat rays blazed from boxes raised in steel tentacles. England, he saw, was being invaded by these fire-wielding tripods, destroying and trampling. For a moment he thought the skeleton men were doing this, but memory of what he'd found in the cylinder, not to mention the size of the seat he occupied, made him realise those tripods were being driven by the octopus things, those great loathsome leather bags. This skeleton and its dead mate had risen up against the cruelty of their masters and...

'You plucky little devil!' Jim exclaimed, and shook the skeleton vigorously by its clawed hand.

The creature looked startled by this sudden display of comradeship. Then, recovering, it pointed at the images of fire and destruction in the crystal eggs, then to Jim and then at itself.

'Us? But what are we to do?' said Jim. 'We're only one and a long way away.'

The pointing finger moved to the window and traced out the shape of a teardrop on the glass, reminding Jim of the larger crystals, those orbs heated with inner warmth. To his astonishment the skeleton spread its arms wide and roared explosively.

Manipulating the crystals shelved below the window, the skeleton showed Jim images flowing within them like picture palace cinematography.

He saw a world of red sand plains, saw distant cliff faces and terraced architecture, buildings that were door-less but studded with circular windows. He watched wide canals of shining water flowing by while great butterfly birds winged in crimson skies, and insect-like vehicles scuttled along paved roads. Octopus beings in tripod machines strode across red lands to conquer the skeleton men, enslaving them, preying on them in vampiric ways. Cylinders were fired from a massive cannon towards a distant blue-green star; and these cylinders, he saw, were filled with glittering machineries and occupied by octopus beings provisioned with skeleton men, some already with tubes inserted in their necks.

Jim glanced at his companion. Yes, it had a wound on the side of its stick-like neck.

As their machine strode along they conversed: Jim in his country vocabulary of horses and Molly and life in the bush; the skeleton in its bird-like twittering of things unknown and unknowable, neither understanding the other.

The crystal eggs showed only one cylinder loading with the tear shaped orbs. Jim reasoned they were likely the only ones brought to Earth, a special cargo; and remembering the extraordinary explosive gesture the skeleton had made in connection with them he concluded that they were bombs. Hard upon this came an understanding of why the skeletons had brought their cylinder here instead of to England – there had to be no chance of the octopus monsters recapturing these bombs. Along with the tripod they now rode, these were the weapons with which to defeat the invaders. But how powerful were these bombs? Like the blasting cartridges used to clear tree stumps? No, surely something bigger like artillery shells. Or something almost unimaginable? Like the eruption of Krakatoa a few years ago that ripped a hole in the ocean and took more than 30,000 souls?

His mind shied away from that possibility. What perturbed him more was the thought he was the go-between for the skeleton to deliver these weapons to mankind.

'Strewth,' Jim muttered, rubbing his bristled chin. 'If Molly could see me now.'

The tripod marched through the night, green vapour jetting from leg joints. Jim dozed fitfully, and just after sunrise he awoke from uneasy dreams, feeling wrung out, thirsty and hungry – he'd not drank nor eaten since breakfast the day before. His companion had had nothing to share as it apparently neither ate nor drank…unless it also drank blood.

At this thought Jim cast a wary glance sideways, but the skeleton was staring steadily forward as he guessed it had been doing for hours. If he could read any expression at all on that skull face it would have to be grim determination; and remembering what he'd seen in the crystals Jim knew why. It was the enemy of the enemy, and any who battled those octopus monsters was a good mate of his – and mates don't drink mates' blood. For all he knew it existed on sunlight like a plant.

Jim, not existing on sunlight, searched in his coat for any forgotten bits of food, finding none. Among the things he did find, however, were a scrap of paper and a stub of pencil. With these he made a crude map showing the location of the cylinder. Now he had something to show Mitchell before that blow hard station manager could start throwing his weight around.

The scenes glowing from most of the crystals now showed the tripods in England either slowing down or stopped, their tentacle arms limp at their sides. This to Jim was a bad sign as it could only mean the war there was ending with the octopus monsters victorious.

In their own tripod Jim and the skeleton man marched over a hill and into the home paddocks of Danley Downs cattle station. It was precisely nine o'clock on a cool Queensland morning. The sky was cloudless and the air keenly warm. Ahead were fences and hay sheds and grazing cattle. But where were the stockmen who should've been busy among them? There was no one to be seen, either on horseback or on foot. Had they seen the tripod coming and run? In truth Jim half expected to be shot at, especially if Mitchell were about.

'Not that it'll mean anything to this tin bucket,' he told his uncomprehending skeletal friend. 'Gawd oh mighty! We'll be like Ned Kelly in his suit of armour! Bang! Clang! Bang! Clang!'

Then to his great joy he *did* see Mitchell...at least he hoped it was Mitchell because he dearly wanted to show up that great self-important swaggering galoot. There was a horseman maybe a couple of hundred yards ahead. Yes, it had to be Mitchell because only Mitchell would be galah enough to stand in front of an advancing tripod. Yet even as Jim recognised him Mitchell turned his horse about and galloped away.

Jim yelled a dry-mouthed ragged yell. He pointed. The skeleton understood. It pulled and pushed levers. The tripod gathered pace, its legs flexing, green steam jetting, round feet pounding though the grass, steely tentacles rising, reaching out.

But Mitchell had had a good head start. Already several seconds ahead of the charging tripod he raced past a hay shed one side, a stand of trees on the other.

Within the madly rocking hood Jim ripped off his coat and attempted to wave it out the bottom opening with one hand while hanging on to the seat with the other. *'Mitchell! You wombat-headed galah!'*

Startled cattle stampeded to left and right. The distance between pursuer and pursued lessened as the tripod charged between hay shed and trees.

There was a sound like the twang of a mighty bowstring as a line of heavy fencing wires sprung up out of the grass. The legs of the tripod hit the wires and tangled, the machine itself hanging a moment suspended at an angle. A human cry and a bird-like shrill. The great glittering machine fell, smashing to the earth, sliding a dozen yards to a stop. It lay there, misted for a moment in green steam and a cloud of dust.

In ones and twos figures emerged from their hiding places among the trees and behind the shed where a jury-rigged lever system had raised the wires. They were drovers and station hands, a mixture of whites, native blacks and one or two Chinese. Some had rifles.

By now Mitchell had returned. He dismounted, pushed through the milling men and, brandishing a revolver, approached the hood of the prone machine. Through an opening in its underneath a man's arm protruded holding a riding coat. Mitchell looked closer, then flinched back with surprise. 'Jesus bloody Christ!' he muttered.

'What is it?' asked one of the drovers, pressing closer.

Mitchell waved them back with his free hand while keeping the revolver pointing into the hood's interior with the other. 'Look for the heat ray projector, like a big black box, like a camera. It's bound to be among the tentacles. The papers said those in England each carried one!'

'But what's in there, Mr Mitchell?' another drover asked. 'Is it a leather octopus big as a bear?'

'It's Hopkins with his neck broke. And something not human like a dried up mummy escaped from a pyramid. Hopkins must've been closer to the green shooting star than I was the other night. Gawd knows what he thought he was at, siding with these bloody things. Should've come back to the station, help set defences like I did. The man was a fool – or worse, a traitor!'

'He left before the papers from Brisbane got here,' said the drover. 'He couldn't have known-'

'He *should've* known to come back straight away regardless.'

'Maybe he was bringing this machine to us.'

'Eh? So how did he know to build it up? How did he know to make it work without those monsters to help? And what's that skeleton thing doing with him?' Mitchell shook his head. 'No, t'ain't natural. Now go find the heat ray.'

Later, while the bodies were being removed from the hood, several crystal eggs were found. They showed nothing but a milky cloudiness that seemed to shift within its depths. Mitchell ordered them destroyed in case they really were eggs.

'No bloody Martian's hatching on *my* station!' he said.

In Jim Hopkins' coat pocket they found a crudely pencilled map. Mitchell immediately took charge of it and retired to a chair on the verandah while the crash of hammers pounding crystal miracles to dust resounded from the smithy.

Hopkins had not been much of a map maker. His scrawls and lines were hard to decrypt, which didn't help with Mitchell's already cross-grained mood over his men's failure to find a heat ray projector in the tripod's wreck.

At intervals he snapped to one of the hands to 'get ya damned finger out' and get along the track to look for the weekly supply cart which was expected about now from the railhead.

'When you see it grab the papers and ride like hell back here! What…yes, gallop all the way…I don't care about the bloody horse! Gallop, ya lazy son of a gin!'

The last newspapers from Brisbane, arriving a week before and then already three days old, had told of the advance of the tripods across the south of England. Infrequent telegrams from Brisbane were quicker but added little more.

Three men had been sent off in succession but by early afternoon only one had returned, with no news of the cart or even the train.

Mitchell jumped up and called some of the drovers to get their horses ready and draw rations for a three day ride.

Daring greatly, one asked, 'To where, Mr Mitchell?'

'Where ya think! Out where I saw that green star fall.'

Before leaving, Mitchell gave orders for Hopkins' to be "planted" in the station's graveyard and "the unchristian thing" found with him to be burnt.

'Likely crawling with germs,' he said.

His party of seven whites and two blacks had only ridden a mile when the second man who'd been sent galloping to the railhead caught up with them. He handed Mitchell a copy of *The Brisbane Echo*, only two days old. The headlines screamed:

HOME COUNTIES UNDER THE HEEL OF THE INVADERS! HEAT RAY THREATENS LONDON!

Full Particulars from Our Special Correspondent.

Mitchell read aloud:

'A Martian fighting machine has wantonly obliterated Leatherhead and all its inhabitants–'

'I got family in Leatherhead!' said one of the drovers.

'– on Wednesday night. Further fighting machines with their Heat Ray and Black Smoke are advancing through Ealing, Richmond and Wimbledon, sweeping the populace before them. The streets are littered with the dead and rivers are clogged with floating rafts of Red Weed. It is truly the beginning of the route of civilisation, of the massacre of Mankind.'

An uneasy silence fell over the group of horsemen. Then one of the native drovers said quietly, 'Now you mob know what it's like.'

They rode off, following the pencilled map, following the distinctive yard-wide footprints the tripod had trod into the ground.

At sundown they camped, and those who could read passed the copy of *The Brisbane Echo* among them, and read it aloud to those who could not read.

They learned that many English towns and villages had been burned by the heat ray, poisoned by the black gas and trampled under, if not by the tripods then by the thronging hordes fleeing for the coast. Hundreds of men, women and children were being snatched up by the Martians and carried off in baskets for purposes that did not bear speculation.

Around midnight Mitchell and his men saw the Mulla-Mulla lights leaping and swooping in the distance, floating and shining for an hour before suddenly disappearing. They'd all seen those lights before, mysterious, inexplicable, silent. And it always drew a cold finger of fear down every spine, though none would ever admit it.

THE NEXT DAY THEY lost the track of the tripod in rocky ground, and Mitchell got confounded by the map. So they were still short of their goal when night fell.

An hour after they made camp a low keening like the mournful singing of a woman lifted out of darkness to the south, growing to a gentle sobbing on the night air. It strengthened, gaining music in its lilting lamentation rippled through with a hint of quiet, malicious glee, rising and falling, rising and falling.

'Ya know what that is, don't ya,' whispered a drover who called himself Smith. 'It's a banshee.'

'Ain't nothing but the wind,' said Mitchell, watching with the rest.

'No, I swear, it's the truth. I've heard it before. So had Hopkins, he told me.'

'Banshees is Irish,' said someone.

'Banshees be the soul of the country,' said Smith. 'Any country that has a need to cry out – be it Ireland or Australia or Timbuk-bloody-tu.' He stared into the dark, his face red lit by the campfire as the soft song continued to croon in the night, rising and falling.

'Ain't nothing but the wind,' said Mitchell.

'God save us from such wind,' said Smith.

'Amen,' said one of the native drovers.

The cry twisted into a soft laugh and stopped abruptly.

Before sunrise five of their number, the two blacks and three of the whites, including the man who called himself Smith, had slipped away.

'The devil and the desert take them for all I care!' was Mitchell's only comment, and after breakfast the rest continued on.

A few hours later they found the gum trees. It stood out like a wipe of pink on the horizon. This strange colouring presented a puzzle until closer they saw it was due to vivid red vines and wide scarlet fronds engulfing the trees, softened to pink by distance and by the fact some of the vines and fronds were turning white as if succumbing to a spreading disease.

Within the trees they found the pit and in the pit the half-buried cylinder. They entered with their rifles and lanterns. Presently they came upon the corpse of the octopus which Mitchell shot three times before realising it was already locked in mutual destruction with the skeletal figure. They didn't stop to ponder its implications because here Mitchell discovered his sought-after black box.

As if in prayer he knelt down and ran his hands over its metal casing and queerly shaped projections. He smiled into its single lens, too absorbed with his new acquisition to notice that the days-dead bodies beside him lacked any smell of decay or putrefaction.

'See what else is here,' he snapped at the others. 'Shoot any octopuses you find.' They hesitated, still staring at the dead things before them. 'Go on! Stop gawking!'

They moved off, rifles ready, slow footsteps echoing, their lantern beams swinging.

'First thing,' murmurred Mitchell to himself, 'is put that tripod back on its feet and learn how to work it. Then take it to England. Take the fight to the Martians. Use it to kill their tripods and maybe capture some too. Tripods striding right and left, but not a Martian in them. Not a Martian but me and other men! Sweeping the heat ray high and wide, smashing *them* to smithereens, making *them* run!' Yes, he liked that idea, liked these images of revenge. In a spasm of passion he hefted the box by a handle, feeling it grow hot in his hands, seeing the single lens eye glow red. 'Slither and scuttle ye monsters from Mars! Man on top again! Bang! Rattle! Smash!'

And the black box clicked.

And the black box hummed.

The air burned *crackle swish*. Sunshine streamed through a sudden hole in the cylinder's side and molten metal splashed to the floor. Mitchell was astonished…and then delighted.

'My god! My god!' he laughed, feeling the backwash of heat on his face.

Footsteps came running. He barely heard, drunk on pure power.

Crackle swish!

Another hole, more hot splashing metal, more sunlight illuming the dark.

Someone was speaking in a high frightened voice, telling of a room of dead monsters and crystal eggs showing immobile tripods with hanging limp arms.

The word 'eggs' caught at Mitchell's attention at the same instant the new fan of light showed up the rack of giant teardrops, smoky white and glistening.

'Eggs!' He swivelled the camera about. 'By god! No bloody Martian's making a hatchery of *my* world!'

He manipulated the handles. The heat beam hit the crystalline orbs and detonated them all simultaneously.

From its sun-like centre the blast expanded with the energy of an impacting asteroid, obliterating the cylinder, the trees and a vast swathe of the Queensland outback. It gouged out 100 mile wide crater in a single second. A titanic mushroom cloud towered into the sky. Far away Brisbane saw the explosion as a false dawn in the west. Minutes later the hell-wind struck the city. Buildings imploded and disintegrated. Rivers boiled. Shock waves rippled around the world thrice and thrice again.

Mars, watching, bided its time.

Section 2: The Present

A Fair Go To Mars

Jason Franks

THEY'D BEEN IN THE TRUCK FOR THREE HOURS BEFORE TAVISH ASKED her about the hat.

'No, it's a Stetson,' said Horrocks, keeping her Aviators fixed on the road ahead. The country on both sides was wide and flat; all scrub and saline yellow dirt and sparse groves of pale native trees. The late morning sun was high overhead, bright through the dusty glass of the windshield.

'I heard the Akubras are, you know, better,' said Tavish, peering at her hat through his stupid little rectangular sunglasses. Is this what he thought country folk talked about? Horrocks had done her engineering degree at Melbourne University; she knew that tone well. Next thing, he'd be asking if she had a horse.

'I like how the Stetson looks.' Mostly, she liked that it didn't look like the hat she'd worn in the Army.

Tavish looked at his phone, tapped the screen. 'Where are we again?'

She'd warned him there was no signal out there, but either he thought she was a liar, or he just couldn't accept that he'd have to be without the internet for a few hours. Horrocks glanced at him, sidelong. Was she being unfair? Being on the internet was the better part of his actual job. Tavish couldn't have been with the Environment Protection Agency for long; no way anyone with even the tiniest bit of seniority would have made this arduous journey, just to generate some content for the website.

No, fuck it. Horrocks decided she was in fact being perfectly fair.

'Same highway we were on last time you asked.' She pushed the map at him. Tavish floundered around trying to unfold it for a good 40 seconds before he gave up and set it helplessly on his lap.

'Look,' said Horrocks. 'We've got at least another hour of driving before we get to the site – assuming it's where Johnny Redneck says it is.' She was half convinced this was a prank by one of her ex's mates; part of an ongoing campaign to make her look bad in the custody battle over Marty. But HQ had insisted, and they'd even sent along this dipshit to see if they could get some good PR out of it. 'I'll get some samples for the eggheads, you can take some pictures, and then we have to drive all the way back. It's gonna be a long day, so you'd best get used to sitting there.'

Tavish thought about that for a minute. 'You think the Turnip will show up?'

'No way he's driving all the way out there to have a look at a bunch of weeds,' said Horrocks. 'Some babies will need emergency kissing, or something, and he'll have to stay in town. But you can bet he'll be waiting for his photo op at the pub when we get back.'

'Oh.' Tavish sounded disappointed.

'Not to worry,' said Horrocks. 'When you meet him, I'm sure Abernathy James will be happy to talk to you about his Akubra.'

Tavish sighed with audible relief when Horrocks pulled the truck over. 'Is this it?'

'Roughly, yeah.'

'How do you even know where we are? I haven't seen a sign for, like, an hour.'

It had been 10 minutes since they'd passed the last sign. Horrocks tapped the dashboard. 'Odometer says how far we've gone.'

She was out of the car and was halfway down the embankment to the creek before he even popped his door. Tying his shoes, looking for his hat, applying new sunscreen…whatever it was he was doing. Horrocks didn't care. She had her job to do and he had his.

The creek was only a couple of metres wide there. Clumps of

strange brown scum swirled slowly across its surface, just like in the report. Horrocks squatted down and captured some in a specimen jar.

'What is it?' said Tavish, still a couple of metres behind her and panting for breath already. He had his phone out and was taking pictures, or maybe shooting video. Horrocks wanted to tell him not to, but instead she just turned her face away.

'Don't know.' She lowered her sunglasses and squinted into the jar. 'I thought it might be some kind of algae, but it looks like it has a vascular system.'

Tavish leaned in and she handed him the jar. 'It looks like it *is* a vascular system,' he said into the phone, juggling it and the jar awkwardly between his hands.

'Whatever,' said Horrocks. 'I'm not a botanist.'

Tavish handed the jar back and she looked at the specimen one more time. Held up to the sun, the fronds looked more red than brown. She tucked the jar into a case and turned back to the truck. 'Let's head upstream a bit.'

'You think there's more up there?'

'I think there's something,' said Horrocks. 'See that mud?'

'Oh yeah. I see it,' said Tavish, looking down ruefully at his fancy hiking shoes. There was mud on the cuffs of his pants, which were cut high enough to show off his fashionable socks.

'That was the creek bed until…not very long ago.'

'Isn't there a drought on?'

'There is,' said Horrocks, 'But this looks too…sudden, for that. I bet whatever's choking the creek has something to do with this bloom.'

Tavish touched the brim of his cap in mock salute. 'Lead on.' He started to follow her up the slippery embankment.

'Try to keep up,' said Horrocks.

HORROCKS DROVE A FEW more kilometres up the highway and then turned off the road. The suspension squawked as the truck jounced over the uneven ground. Tavish gripped the Jesus handle nervously until she stopped near a stand of trees.

'Here we are.'

He had no idea why or how she knew this was a place worth

stopping, but, he supposed, that was why she was an Authorised Environment Protection Officer and he was a writer for the comms department. He knew he was better paid than she was, but Horrocks exuded a competence that nobody in his entire building could match.

Down past the trees the creek forked off the river that was thick with the red bloom they'd seen further up. Horrocks followed it up around a bend and suddenly drew to a stop. Tavish rushed to see what was there.

The river bed was full to overflowing here, but not with water. The growth was at a different scale here: thick crimson blades growing in snaggled clumps; bristling with hooks on the top edge. Tavish pulled out his phone and panned across it, capturing video. Horrocks was crouching down at a nearby outcropping.

'What are those?' said Tavish. 'They look like…weird…cactuses?'

'No,' said Horrocks. She actually addressed the phone-camera this time and didn't look like she wanted to take it out of his hands and smash it. 'See these dark veins? They're not any kind of succulent.'

Tavish scratched his head. 'Are those flowers, or leaves?'

'I don't know,' said Horrocks. 'But I can tell for damn sure it's a weed, and it's not native to this part of the world.'

Tavish brightened at that. 'Great!' he said. He hadn't hoped for anything nearly as exciting as a biosecurity breach on this little jaunt. 'So what happens now?'

'Now,' said Horrocks, 'we're going to see if we can find where it comes from.'

Horrocks climbed up into the bed of the truck and put one foot up on the tailgate. She tucked her sunnies into a breast pocket and raised the binoculars to inspect the terrain upstream.

Almost immediately Tavish started up. 'What do you see? Anything good?'

He was like her five year old, in a designer shirt. Horrocks panned the binoculars over the terrain for another half a minute. Then she lowered them deliberately and put her sunnies back on. Tavish was hopping from foot to foot.

She pointed a few metres away. 'See that?'

'What?'

'In the scrub.'

'It's just scrub…'

She sighed. 'You see anything unusual?'

'Yes?' No he didn't.

Horrocks swung down from the truck bed. 'You see those runners?'

He went blundering in the direction she had pointed, eyes down, and suddenly stopped. 'Holy shit,' he said. 'They're red.'

'Looks like they're coming from up yonder.' Horrocks pointed to the northwest with the blade of her hand.

'Cool,' said Tavish.

Horrocks cut a piece of it, stashed it in a ziplock bag and put it in the specimen case along with the samples from the cactus-algae-weed, or whatever the fuck it was, that she'd taken from the river.

Tavish stood looking at her expectantly.

'Get in the truck.'

He did as she said.

THEY HEADED SLOWLY AND deliberately to the northwest, moving away from the river. At first, Tavish was annoyed. He felt like his teeth were going to come loose from the vehicle's rattling, and he couldn't see anything special where they were headed. Mainly, though, it was because Horrocks had no interest in holding a conversation. It was a long boring ride and she'd laughed at his idea of streaming some tunes on the car radio, which, it turned, out didn't even have Bluetooth.

Tavish was half-convinced that Horrocks was just tearing around off road to make him feel uncomfortable, but the red crap in the river had been real. Then, out the window, he noticed more and more of the runners. After a few klicks there was more red grass than yellow, and soon it was like they were driving through a pool of clotted blood.

'Holy shit,' he said. 'How come nobody has noticed this before?'

'I think it's only been like this a few days,' said Horrocks. 'This stuff grows fast.'

They came to a chainlink fence, topped with rolls of barbed wire and threaded with more creeping red vines. Horrocks followed it around until they came to a gate, which was covered with signs saying:

> PRIVATE PROPERTY, NO TRESPASSING and DANGER – LIVE MUNITIONS.

Horrocks stopped the truck.

'I guess we should call it in,' said Tavish.

'Call it in?' said Horrocks. 'How? There's no signal, remember.'

'Don't we have a radio?'

'Even if we did, we're a thousand klicks from anyone who remotely gives a shit about what we're doing.'

'We should have a radio.'

Horrocks just shook her head. She opened the door and jumped down out of the truck. Tavish climbed out and followed her around to the back, where he found her fishing a pair of bolt cutters out of an old toolbox.

'You're not,' he said.

Horrocks set the blades of the bolt cutters on the padlock on the gates. 'We damn sure are.'

She hunched over the bolt cutters and strained at the handles.

'But the sign says…'

The lock snapped and fell in the dirt with a muted thud and a puff of dust. 'I'm an Authorised Environment Protection Officer,' said Horrocks. 'I can go anywhere it's my business to go. You want to wait for me out here that's your call.'

By the time Horrocks had put the bolt cutters away, Tavish was back in the truck.

The gravel road that led through the gate wasn't as bumpy as the bare earth they'd followed, but it was noisier under the tread of the tyres. It was better than trying to make conversation.

After about 20 minutes they could see some buildings in the distance. Tavish fiddled with the map, but Horrocks just shook her head. 'Whatever this place is, it's not on there.'

'Ummm…' said Tavish, as they came closer to the buildings.

This wasn't some old abandoned town. It was like the CBD of a prosperous regional town, but without any outlying suburbs or farmsteads. Office buildings, some of them 12 storeys high. Four-lane streets with traffic lights. Just a few urban blocks, dropped here in the middle of nowhere. A mock city, festooned with creeping red vines.

Horrocks had slowed the truck and turned the wheel, and Tavish assumed this was in order to survey the perimeter before they went to see what was inside. He pulled out his phone and filmed through the dirty windshield. He was so fixated on keeping the phone steady that he was completely off guard when Horrocks slammed on the brakes.

The truck lurched to a stop and Tavish frowned at her. 'Hey, I'm trying to–'

'Put the phone down.' Horrocks was staring past him, through the windshield on his side.

Tavish lowered the phone and followed her gaze.

First he saw the shadow; cast huge upon the upper storeys of one of the taller buildings. Then, a glimpse of something dull but metallic moving between tower blocks. A scalloped, hooded machine rose above the skyline. It moved gracefully, like some kind of sea jelly, with tendrils from its underside hanging loose but not limp. It had three longer, thicker limbs, which it used to brace itself against the sides of the buildings or the ground as it navigated the mock city. Even when the limbs were quiescent it was able to move through the air, like a helicopter or a drone, but with no evidence of rotors. Its engines were utterly silent and the only sounds it made were when its limbs struck off against a hard surface. Tavish wondered how fast it could go.

'Holy shit,' said Horrocks.

Seeing the shock on her face drove the wonder from Tavish and replaced it with fear.

'Do you know what that is?'

Tavish shook his head slowly.

'It's a Martian fighting machine.'

'Bullshit.' He knew she was right even as the words escaped his lips. He'd seen the old sepia-tinted photos – they all had – but the short-lived invasion had taken place almost 120 years ago. Once it was over, governments globally had immediately whisked away all remnants of Martian technology. The machines had survived longer than their pilots, but there was more organic matter in them than anyone had expected and they had rotted away in fairly short order. It was rumoured that MI7 kept some pieces in a secret bunker somewhere, preserved in formaldehyde, but nobody knew for sure. The Martian secrets had never been declassified and, with humankind's complete lack of success in finding signs of life on the invaders' purported home-world, most discussion about the events that had almost destroyed a hundred major cities around the world had devolved into superstitions and conspiracy theories.

Were they really Martians, or just some sophisticated aggression from rival political powers? Were they terrorists? Anarchists? The only people who seemed certain about what had transpired were the hordes of socially maladjusted men who professed allegiance to the Intellectual Dark Web.

Horrocks put the truck in gear and resumed her slow circumnavigation of the model city.

'What…what's it doing out here?' asked Tavish.

'You ask me, it looks like manoeuvres,' said Horrocks. 'Getting used to operating in a proper city.'

'So you think it's, what? The army? The defence force has recreated one of these old machines?'

Horrocks blinked slowly. 'They'd probably outsource this kind of technical work.'

'So, like, civilian contractors?'

'Either that, or actual Martians.'

He couldn't tell if she was joking or not.

On the far side of the model city and separated by a wide flat yard there was a group of flat, domed buildings made of some smooth, dull material. They looked like soup-dishes turned upside down.

'Ceramic,' said Horrocks. 'Smart in these conditions. Durable, low heat profile. Hard to spot.'

Fifteen more of the tripods stood in the yard, motionless amid the thick coils of red vegetation, formed up in two ranks. Smaller machines scrambled over them like spiders with too many legs, performing maintenance on the fighting units.

'This…is definitely military,' said Tavish.

'It sure as shit isn't a hippy commune,' replied Horrocks. 'Come on, let's see if we can find out who's in charge here.'

Tavish hesitated. This looked like a secret facility and he didn't have the clearance of a dog fart in a vegan pub. 'But…are we…allowed–'

'I was in the army for eight years,' said Horrocks, 'and I don't care what toys they have. These pricks have caused a biohazard. That means we're allowed.'

The EPA was a poorly funded and put-upon organisation barely tolerated by the conservative coalition government. Tavish was quite certain that the bureaucrats in head office would not be willing to butt heads with the defence sector…but Horrocks seemed to have some kind of an authority complex and her confidence was infectious. He sat back in his seat and continued to film through the windshield as she drove the truck brazenly up to the closest of the soup dishes.

'Let's see who's home,' said Horrocks, popping open her door and climbing down out of the truck.

A sector of the dome began to open and an armoured figure emerged. Luminous green mist swam around the ankles of its three triple-joined metal legs. It was probably eight feet tall, with a fringe of mechanical tendrils hanging from its attenuated torso. The head was the only fleshy part protruding from the armour: grey and soft-looking, as though its skull was made of cartilage. Two large black eyes gleamed wetly above a breathing apparatus that covered the lower part of its face. Metal structures that crawled up the head out of the collar were either some kind of instrumentation, or reinforcement for the skull. Possibly both.

Horrocks just stood there, transfixed, as the figure turned its head towards her. Behind it, the dome kept on opening.

Tavish waved his phone at the apparition, terrified and unsure what to do. 'It's a fucking Martian!'

Horrocks shook her head and scrambled back into the vehicle. The hat came off her head and she slammed the door on it. She opened the door again and let it fall out, yanked it shut, and turned the key in the ignition.

The Martian continued to regard them but made no move towards them. As light fell upon the exposed insides of the dome, Tavish could see that it was filled with dully gleaming machinery. Somehow it was less pants-shittingly awful if he looked at it through his phone camera, so he kept on filming. He was no expert but it looked like some of the machines in there might be artillery pieces. Others looked like throwing stars grown to the size of fighter jets.

Horrocks mashed the accelerator and spun the steering wheel. The motion threw Tavish against his seat and his hand whipped back into his face hard enough to smack his phone against his glasses. The lenses didn't crack, and neither did the phone, but it left him dazed. A few moments later he had recovered from the shock and they were barrelling down the gravel road. Tavish found his mind wandering. The pain, the bumpy drive, the flashing scenery. Had he just seen something important? Martians and guns? What the fuck was even happening? Horrocks was craned over the wheel, but kept glancing back in the rear view mirror.

Tavish put his phone in his lap and gazed out of the windshield, not really seeing the landscape in front of him. 'Is there someone following us?' he asked.

'Not yet,' said Horrocks.

There was still no sign of pursuit by the time they got back onto the highway, but that didn't make Horrocks feel any better. She didn't know how fast the tripods could move, but if they could mobilise one of the fighter jets she'd seen inside the hangar, they were toast.

Tavish gave a huge sigh and shook his head. 'Those…those were fucking Martians.'

'You already mentioned that.'

'But how did they get here? How did they survive?'

'Maybe they were here all along,' replied Horrocks.

'And they never bothered to invade?'

'My guess? The ones that landed in England were marines – this is an engineering battalion.'

'Well, fuck.'

'It makes sense,' said Horrocks. 'Lots of natural resources out here. Uranium. Iron ore. Even coal, if you're that way inclined. And it's a million miles from anywhere. You could spend decades out here doing whatever you like and nobody would notice, if you were careful.'

'I bet they'd show up on satellite photos,' said Tavish.

'I bet they wouldn't.'

Tavish fell silent while he chewed that over.

'Here's what doesn't make sense,' said Horrocks. 'I thought they couldn't survive on our filthy ball of mud, but here they are with an airfield and a munitions factory, walking around like they own the place.'

Tavish shrugged. 'I guess these ones lived long enough to figure out vaccines. Those red weeds seem to be surviving pretty well.'

Horrocks squinted through the dashboard. 'Well, now.'

'What?' said Tavish.

'I smell bacon.'

A pair of blue and white highway patrol cruisers appeared in the distance.

'Is that good or bad?' said Tavish.

'Bad, I'm guessing,' replied Horrocks.

It was another minute before they were close enough to hear the sirens.

Even behind his wraparound Raybans, the patrolman looked surprised to see Horrocks behind the wheel and Tavish in the seat next to her. He put one hand on the open driver's window and leaned in, so the bill of his cap was inside the vehicle and his face was close.

'Was I going too fast, constable?' She knew she had been right on the speed limit, because she'd set cruise control once she was sure there weren't any giant alien Parkour war machines following her.

The patrolman could see on her face that she wasn't taking bullshit, and his cap retreated a couple of inches. 'No, mate,' he said. 'There's a traffic hazard up that-a-ways,' he gestured back the way they'd come, 'and we just want to make sure you get to safety.'

'Well, I don't know if you are confused or something, constable, but right now we happen to be heading this-a-ways.'

'Which is, you know, the opposite direction to that-a-ways,' piped up Tavish.

Horrocks shot him a look and he shut his mouth.

The patrolman set his jaw. 'Mate, we just want to make sure you get where you're going safely.'

'And where is that?'

'Just come with us. We'll let you know when you're clear.'

The patrolman unhitched himself from the window and stood by expectantly. Horrocks rolled up the window.

'So what now?' said Tavish.

'I guess we're about to find out,' she replied.

The highway patrol escorted them all the way back into town; one car following and the other preceding them. They rolled to a stop at the Royal Victoria Hotel, a country pub that had been renovated to attract the road-tripping hipster crowd: old-timey bric-a-brac on the walls, a shiny new Marzocco coffee machine behind the bar, and a menu full of kale, wagyu beef, and heirloom fruits. A chalkboard on the bar boasted that they had half a dozen craft brews on tap.

Still no internet, though. The wifi didn't work, and Tavish supposed the local cell tower must be down. But then he didn't think the owners of the pub were too concerned about lost Trip Advisor ratings today.

Seated by the picture window, under looming aluminium signs advertising ironing starch and canned vegetables, Senator Abernathy James was tucking in to an early dinner. He had a pint glass of beer in front of him, a napkin tucked into the collar of his shirt, and a half-eaten hamburger on his plate, which he was working on with a knife and a fork. A pair of uniformed police bracketed him: one male, one female. James was wearing his trademark Akubra hat, indoors.

The senator smiled at them and gestured for them to come and join him. 'Beer? Something to eat? You two look like you've had a long, hot drive.' Although he was sitting there in air-conditioned comfort, his complexion still had the famous purple hue that had let to him being nicknamed the Turnip.

'I'll have what you're having,' said Tavish, seating himself opposite James.

Horrocks took a moment to glare at him before she sat down. 'Not for me.'

James spread his arms, still holding a utensil in each hand, and said, 'I'm so pleased to see two fine officers of the Environment Protection Authority out here, looking after our precious natural resources.'

'That's why they pay us the big dollars,' said Horrocks.

A young man materialised from nowhere with a pint glass for Tavish, although Horrocks hadn't seen the Turnip issuing any orders. Tavish ceased his fidgeting under the table and gratefully took up the glass.

'I'm glad you're pleased with your compensation package,' said James, smiling to show that he was in on the joke. He had the private school elocution overlaid on a broad country accent that you only heard coming out of cattle barons and politicians. 'See anything worth reporting out there? Putting our tax dollars to good use?' He cut another wedge of hamburger and forked it into his mouth.

Tavish sipped his beer and looked grateful for something to do.

'Bunch of strange red weeds choking up the creek,' said Horrocks. 'Some unusual runner grass.'

The Turnip finished chewing and swallowing his mouthful, and then his smile returned. 'I suppose you're going to tell me that's...what do you call it...*anthropocentric climate change*.' He chuckled to himself, like he was humouring a child who believed in Santa Claus.

Horrocks wasn't much younger than the patronising fuckwit and she was having none of that. 'No, actually,' she said. 'I'm pretty sure this is anything but.'

James raised an eyebrow. 'I thought basically anything that went wrong in our environment was the fault of, you know, Western Civilisation. At least that's what your liberal media tells me.'

'Well, in this particular case it was your Martians that caused it.'

Tavish spluttered but the Turnip did not even blink. It was impossible to tell if he was ever blushing through that purple complexion.

'If this is one of those...what you call 'em? *Internet memes*? Then I'm sorry, but it went right over my head.' James skewered a pair of potato chips on his fork, cut them down to bite size, and put them in his mouth.

'I mean literal Martians. A secret base, three-legged war machines, the works. Don't bullshit with me, Senator. I know you know they're out there.'

James made a show of chewing his mouthful while considering Horrocks' accusation. His smile spread slowly across his lips even as he swallowed them down. 'Let's say it's true,' he said. 'Let's say there are Martians out there, building war machines–'

'And polluting the environment,' interjected Tavish.

Horrocks shot him a look, but James only shrugged and nodded.

'Sure,' he said. 'Building their war machines and polluting the environment – let's say it's true.'

'It is true,' said Horrocks. 'Otherwise, why'd you have the fucking Highway Patrol drag us in here?'

'Even if it's true,' said James. 'Is it really a problem?'

'Well, yeah,' said Tavish. 'The environment–'

'Can be managed,' said James. 'These things happen. The EPA has procedures for dealing with exactly this kind of thing, right? Or else what do we need you for?'

'We deal with environmental damage,' said Horrocks. 'Not extra-terrestrial invaders.'

James shook his head, disappointed. 'Come on,' he said. 'What a terribly bigoted thing to say about our hypothetical guests.'

'They ran rampant all over the world, burning people alive, letting off chemical weapons, and drinking human blood,' said Horrocks.

James shrugged. 'Even if those old slanders are true,' he said, 'that was more than 100 years ago. The Germans and the Japanese killed a whole lot more Australians, in living memory, and we've long since forgiven *them*.'

Tavish stared at him. 'We have this humanitarian crisis brewing over the government's refusal to let asylum seekers enter the country,' he said. 'And you're allowing Martians to set up a military base here?'

The Turnip shook his head. 'We let in refugees in every day,' he said. 'We only turn away those who arrive by boat, from the north.'

'Well, that makes perfect sense,' said Tavish.

'It's not perfect,' admitted James. 'And if you were paying attention you'd know that I've often spoken up in defence of refugees, when…other people…say they're all terrorists. If there were Martians, I'd say the same for them. Everyone deserves a fair go in this country.'

Tavish couldn't believe what he was hearing. 'They're building war machines. Running military manoeuvres. They're not terrorists; they're an invading army.'

James cut the remaining portion of his burger in half and picked up one of them between his thumb and forefinger. 'You really don't understand anything, do you?' he said. He popped the piece of burger in his mouth, chewed a couple of times, and then continued with his mouth full. 'These Martians pay their way. They buy mineral resources from us. They're good for industry and the economy.'

'They make political donations, huh?'

'Of course,' said James. He swallowed, pursed his lips to suck a stray morsel out of his teeth, swallowed again. 'And not just to my party. They're smart operators, these…these supposed Martians.'

'So you're *letting* them build a…an army…here,' said Tavish, rising a few inches out of his chair. This appeared to startle him and he sat down again.

The Turnip picked up the last piece of hamburger off his plate. 'Don't be naïve,' he said. 'This is a huge country. The Martians aren't the only foreign military presence here.' He flicked the piece of burger into his mouth off the back of his thumb.

'So there's a – treaty?' said Tavish.

James took a swig from his beer glass; swished the fluid around his half chewed mouthful.

'More of a commercial arrangement.'

'Contractors,' said Horrocks sourly. 'They're defence contractors.'

James patted his mouth with a heavy linen napkin. 'They're here to keep our borders safe,' he said. He belched softly behind closed lips.

'Mercenaries,' said Tavish, wide-eyed. 'You have Martian mercenaries on your payroll.'

'Why not?' said James.

'How do you know they're loyal?' said Horrocks. 'They're not here to setup a new invasion?'

'Because,' said James, 'there's only five of them.' He threw the napkin on the table and stood up. 'Now, please. Take a moment to relax. Finish your beer. Enjoy the AC.'

'And then what?' said Horrocks. 'You'll take us out the back and have us shot?'

'Rubbish,' said the Turnip. 'We have some nice accommodation waiting while the PM and I work out what to do with you.'

'With a lovely view of the bushland through a razor wire fence,' said Horrocks.

Abernathy James shrugged. 'It's not luxury, but I'd say it's a solid three stars.' He stepped back and the police that flanked him moved in. 'Now Tavish, mate, please be good enough to hand that phone you've been fiddling with to Constable Wilkins over here.'

Tavish looked at his beer, drank it nervously, put it down on the table. 'Umm–'

'I made sure the cell towers are off,' said James. 'So there's no way you can send off that recording of our conversation.'

Constable Wilkins put her hand on the pouch containing her extendable baton.

'Don't be stupid, Tavish,' said Horrocks. 'You can hand it over peacefully or she'll break your jaw. And then take it.'

Tavish miserably took the phone out from under the table and handed it to the policewoman.

'Good lad,' said Wilkins. She put it in a pocket and lowered her other hand from the baton.

'Yours too.'

Horrocks fished the ancient clamshell phone out a thigh pocket. 'Mine doesn't do internet,' she said. She had a call she needed to make. Wilkins made a 'hand it over' gesture and Horrocks dropped into the constable's palm with a sigh.

The Turnip had gone over to the bar. He was standing there with one boot on the foot rail, his hat pushed back high on his head. 'Would you like another beer? For the road?'

Tavish looked like he was about to say yes, but he shut his mouth when Horrocks shot him a glare.

The Turnip shrugged. 'Right, well, I'm having one, so I guess I'll stay here a bit longer. Enjoy the ride, will you?'

Wilkins and her partner led them out to the cop car. It was still hot outside, but the temperature had dropped a good five degrees since they'd gone into the pub. Once they were seated in the back, Tavish started giggling.

Horrocks felt the urge to join him and clamped down on it hard. 'What's so funny?' she said.

'I forgot to ask him about his Akubra.'

THEY'D BEEN RIDING IN the back of the cop car for about 15 minutes when Tavish's phone started to bleep. They were back in a serviced area and all of his missed calls and texts were coming through. Wilkins, in the front passenger seat, took the phone out of her pocket, frowned at it, then set it on the dashboard.

Horrocks grunted and looked out the window again. It was getting dark out and she was worried about her boy. She wanted her phone back so she could call the childcare centre, but she knew it was already too late. By now they would have called her ex to come and collect Marty. She knew this would hurt next time they had a custody hearing. What was she going to say? 'I ran into some Martians at work, and the Turnip had me arrested?'

Tavish nudged her excitedly.

'What?'

'Internet's back,' he whispered. 'And they didn't turn off my phone.'

'So what?'

'So, now everything that's on there is backing up to the cloud.'

'So what?'

'So, my partner will see it all when she gets home and syncs up the iPad.'

Horrocks didn't give a shit about Tavish's domestic arrangements and it took her a moment to realise what he as saying.

'Shh!' she hissed.

Wilkins glanced back over her shoulder at them, narrowed her eyes…and then nodded slowly. A local copper who wasn't a complete bastard. That was refreshing.

Tavish and Horrocks settled back.

'What a day,' said Horrocks.

'Well, it wasn't as boring as I thought it would be,' said Tavish.

'I'm glad you were entertained.'

'Holy shit,' said Wilkins from the front. 'What's that?'

Horrocks looked out of her window to see a streak of green fire slicing through the wide night sky. Moments later there was a concussion strong enough to bounce the car on the blacktop.

Wilkins' partner steered the vehicle into the skid. They slid off the side of the road and came to a jarring stop. Horrocks couldn't hear the squeal of the tyres, but she could smell the burnt rubber.

Wilkins looked over her shoulder. 'You two alright?'

'Yeah,' said Horrocks.

'Think so,' said Tavish.

Horrocks turned her head to orient herself. Through the windscreen she could see a luminous green mist rising from what was the probably the site of impact.

'Oh shit,' said Tavish. 'Is that what I think it is?'

'Some more of the Turnip's friends coming to help shore up the economy,' said Horrocks.

Another streak of green slashed down from the darkness, and another.

'Looks like it's gonna be a long night,' said Tavish.

Horrocks could only agree.

Speed Bonnie Boat

From *The Chronicles of Carillo Mean*

Carmel Bird

I AM WRITING THIS STORY FROM A YACHT OFF THE COAST OF WESTERN Australia, on my way to the island of Mauritius where I have been invited to undertake some historical research in the Sir Seewoosagur Ramgoolam Gardens. You may wonder why I would choose to go by water instead of air. Well, these days, water is safer than air. Hear me out.

I remember with a vivid pleasure the long hours I spent in childhood devouring the books in my grandfather's library, which contained what seemed to me to be an infinity of volumes. My grandfather was aptly named 'Philosopher Mean', and he was a prominent local character in the small Tasmanian mining town of Woodpecker Point, near Smithton. I like to think I have in some ways taken up the mantle of Philosopher Mean, who died in 1960 at the great age of 99. His library, named the Charles Dickens Library in honour of my grandfather's favourite writer, was home to a broad collection of unpublished memoirs by people known and unknown to history. It was one of these, the short journal of a British-Australian soldier who was killed in the second battle of Ypres on 25 April 1915, that recently caught my attention. The soldier's name was Wilfred James Bryant.

The journal begins when Wilfred, at the age of 24, took a ship from Southampton to travel to Tasmania in 1901, and ends when he was about to set off for the war in Europe. His original journey was undertaken in order to escape from the ravaged landscape of much of England following the failed invasion of creatures from the planet Mars late in the 19th century. Wilfred's family had died in the invasion, and he, a budding mining engineer, had decided to put the tragic and sorrowful past behind him and to begin a new life in Woodpecker Point.

The poignant fact that his life was spared during the Martian invasion, only for him to die in battle in Flanders, struck me as starkly ironic. (His case is not as ironic as that of the deaths of boys called Victory who were born on November 11th 1918, and who died in the war that began in 1939.) Between the two terrible events – the Martian invasion and the First World War – Wilfred had become a respected and successful contributor to the Tasmanian mining industry. I searched for his details in *A Comprehensive History of Mining in Tasmania 1847-1910,* where I discovered the following entry:

> *Mr W.J. Bryant was born in Esher, Surrey, in 1880, and he studied metallurgy at the Mason Science College in Birmingham. He arrived in Hobart in 1901, transferred to the gold mine at Beaconsfield from where he later moved to take up a position at the mine in Woodpecker Point. Since that time he has resided with the manager of the Golden Goose mine, Mr G. E. Bannister, and has worked as an assayer at the mine.*

The words were accompanied by a small, formal, oval black and white photograph of a handsome Wilfred, his eyes large and clear, his beard short and carefully trimmed, a slight upward curl at the ends of the dark moustache, the ghost of a smile on his lips. There is no explanation of what might have caused Wilfred to emigrate, the little paragraph leaving such matters to the imaginations of readers who might well have conjectured that he was lured to the faraway island by the promise of riches. Or perhaps he was adventuring in the wake of a heart broken by the refusal of his suit. Was there a shy or haughty young lady who had toyed with his affections?

Personally, I imagine his life was so blighted by the tragedy of the loss of his parents and sisters in Esher, while he was safe in Birmingham, that he decided to proceed in the hope, or expectation, of a happier life, a better fate in the distant colony.

Wilfred's own journal does not refer in any way at all to the horrors of the Martian invasion that passed through Esher. It is as if he is a single organism sprung from the classrooms of the Mason Science College, ready to find his way, make his fortune, on the goldfields of Tasmania.

I consequently searched the shelves of the library for a copy of *The War of the Worlds* by H.G. Wells, which I re-read for perhaps the fourth or fifth time, on this occasion in search of scenes that Wilfred might have experienced. At the very least they must surely have been experienced by members of his extinct little family in Esher. Perhaps he was not in Birmingham but in Esher when it all happened; perhaps he undertook a journey not unlike that taken by Wells' narrator. This book is one of the fullest accounts of that curious, historic, unexpected and devastating series of events of 1896. So far as I know, the first Martian invasion is the only earthly invasion undertaken by beings who were not of the planet Earth, and I commend *The War of the Worlds* to anyone who is interested in the phenomenon of invasion *per se*, something that is common enough to be 'natural' among the peoples of Earth.

In prehistoric times the Celts invaded the islands of Britain. Romans, Vikings, Goths and so forth all left deep and indelible marks on the British Isles. Looking mainly at British history, you can trace the beginnings of the invasion of other countries by Great Britain back to the 17th century and the founding of the British East India Company under Queen Elizabeth I. In fact the name 'Great Britain' was first used by King James I in 1603. But this is not the place for a full history of Britain's invasion and colonisation of other parts of the world; I will skip to the time of Queen Victoria, when the sun never set on the British Empire.

The British established a military outpost at their New South Wales colony on the Derwent River in Tasmania (then known as Van Diemen's Land) in 1803. The plan was to establish a British camp run by soldiers and manned by convict-slaves in order to dissuade others such as the French and the Dutch from developing a base in the area. In 1644 the Dutch had already claimed the island when Abel Tasman's ship's carpenter swam ashore and planted the Dutch flag at Frederick Henry Bay, named for Prince Frederik Hendrik of Orange.

Because I am Tasmanian, when I hear the word 'invasion', I think, more often than not, of this invasion of the island by the British in 1803. To the indigenous peoples of the island, this operation was less abrupt than the Martian invasion of England, but it was considerably more deadly, and was, of course, successful in that it gave the British dominion over a decimated indigenous population. Whereas the Martians quite quickly succumbed to bacterial infections, the British brought their bacteria with them to Tasmania, as well as their gunpowder and their poisons and their cracked and convenient belief that the inhabitants of the island were dispensable because they were not really human. There developed a myth that the indigenous people had been completely killed off, removed from existence by the genocidal operation of British imperialism. However, I myself am living proof of the blind inaccuracy of this legend, for my great-great-great grandmother was a member of the Palawa peoples, and her blood is in my veins. So what occurred here in Tasmania was *unsuccessful* genocide.

There is a short section early in *The War of the Worlds* concerning the invasion of Tasmania by the British. I think it is best if I quote it here in full, since it is an example of the determined perpetration of the myth. Reflecting on the destructive onslaught of the Martians, the narrator of the story says:

> *And before we judge of them [the Martian invaders] too harshly we must remember what ruthless and utter destruction our own species has wrought, not only upon animals, such as the vanished bison and dodo, but upon its own inferior races. The Tasmanians, in spite of their human likeness, were entirely swept out of existence in a war of extermination waged by European immigrants, in the space of 50 years. Are we such apostles of mercy as to complain if the Martians warred in the same spirit?*

Note the blind and chilling phrase 'in spite of their human likeness', and the use of the term 'inferior races'. I might remind my reader that in the official government writings of Australia, and in the minds of non-indigenous Australians generally, the ancient indigenous peoples were, until recently, described and classified as being part of the flora and fauna, not part of the human population.

But I must return now to the journal of Wilfred the young assayer, for it is in this record that I discovered, woven into the account of life at sea, one of the most disturbing and alarming pieces of information you will ever hear.

On board the steam ship *Outhwaite* he befriended the ship's doctor, Henry Swift, who was travelling to Hobart with his 10 year-old daughter, Mercy, and her governess, Adelaide Jones, his wife and two sons having been killed in Barnes during the Martian invasion. It is Mercy Swift who is in fact the real focus of my interest here.

According to Wilfred, Mercy was a dreamy, intelligent, engaging child who loved to play quoits, sew, read and tease Adela Jones who was sweet, charming, long-suffering, with a cloud of soft brown curls, pink cheeks, and deep brown rather mournful eyes. Wilfred was clearly fascinated by Adela, while Adela was clearly in love with Henry Swift. I can add a footnote to all this, for I know that Henry and Adela married in Hobart and raised a large family in a house that I have in fact visited in Davey Street. If Wilfred knew of the marriage, he forbore to mention it in his journal.

So Mercy and Adela shared a cabin on board the *Outhwaite*. And it was in this cabin that Mercy housed her pet white rat, a secret to be kept from the ship's authorities, although the Captain, it seems, had his suspicions. There was also a precious box of dead insects from which Mercy could not be parted. She would take them out of their box and set them out on a table in the saloon and invent little stories about them. She was a prodigious storyteller, and in later life she wrote several books for children and illustrated them herself. The rat was known, somewhat unimaginatively, as Rattie.

But it was another of Mercy's treasures altogether that captured Wilfred's attention, and, I have to say, mine. This was the dormant creature known as Buddie who lived, snuggled in a grey silk shawl, inside a battered leather satchel which Mercy kept with her little collection of books. Adela was unaware of the existence of Buddie, believing the satchel to be for the purpose of carrying some of the books and Mercy's embroidery cloths and threads. Indeed it did also serve this purpose.

However, folded carefully into the depths of the satchel was a sleeping, breathing creature which can only be described, in a language possibly unfamiliar to Wilfred, as a deadly time bomb. Buddie was an immature Martian on his way to the New World.

As the narrator of *The War of the Worlds* explains, the Martians are highly adaptable, being principally made up of one huge, round brain. They are able to alter their bodies as the situation demands, and they communicate telepathically with each other. Their young are produced by budding off from the adult body, 'just as young lily bulbs bud off'. In moments of danger these buds drop into a dormant state, waiting for the telepathic message from Mars for their instructions to wake up and take on adult characteristics and duties.

I will quote a section from Wilfred's journal. At the time of writing he was recovering from a fever for which Henry Swift had treated him, and he was partly of the opinion that he was suffering from an hallucination.

> The child Mercy entered the cabin, carrying her leather satchel. She was humming the *Skye Boatsong*. 'Speed bonnie boat, like a bird on the wing'. She has a very pretty voice.
>
> 'Are you awake, Willow?' she said softly. I opened my eyes and murmured, unable to articulate any sensible words.
>
> She sat down on the floor beside my cot and proceeded to fish out her sewing. I perceived she was embroidering on calico an elaborate design of bees and pansies, and I recognised this as a pattern one of my sisters used to make. I uttered an involuntary sob as the thought of Agnes sitting by the fire with her needle flashing in and out, back and forth, purple and green, gold and black, roused in me a great sorrow at my present lonely state in this world. I closed my eyes as a few tears trickled across my cheek. Mercy continued her humming, and soon enough I recovered myself and lay there gazing at her. As I did so, she took Rattie from the satchel and placed him on her shoulder, where he

perched quite peacefully. Then, putting aside her sewing, Mercy drew from the leather mouth of the satchel a bundle of grey silk, which she proceeded to unfold with great care and precision. Finally, lying on her lap was a sleeping creature, brown and slightly wrinkled, a great round head with two enormous hands, and no body to speak of. Its huge bulbous eyes were closed; it had no nose; a sharp beak-like feature served it for a mouth.

'Good morning, Buddie,' Mercy whispered. As she did so she sprinkled the creature with little handfuls of red seeds which pattered onto its skin and settled in the folds of the silk. I almost sat up, and but for my fevered weakness, I would have done so. For I have seen those seeds before; they are the seeds of the red weed that proliferated across the south of England during the invasion. How can it be that this child is carrying around with her the very objects, animal and vegetable, that can destroy the world? Then she began to sing to Buddie. She sang the French lullaby, *Fais Dodo*, and I gulped and uttered another great sob and a kind of croak, for the song was one my mother used to sing to me when I was a child.

Mercy quickly flung the grey silk cloth across the creature in alarm.

'Oh Willow, are you ill again. Shall I call Papa?'

But I was speechless, and weak from the fever, and dazed by what I had seen, or what I had imagined seeing.

With the practised skill of a stage magician, Mercy methodically parcelled up her sleeping pet, her seeds, and her sewing, cupped her hand around Rattie, and slipped everything into the satchel.

'I think perhaps I should read to you, Willow. We were just beginning Chapter Three.' And she took from the pocket of her pinafore a soft paper copy of *Alice's Adventures in Wonderland*, and began:

'They were indeed a queer looking-party that assembled on the bank.'

I listened as if in a dream. What had I seen? What had I heard? I recalled the story of the young Martian that was born on Earth during the war. It had been still attached to its parent, having not quite budded off. And I heard that the scientists Charles Foster and Sir Percival Swope, in their exhaustive studies of the Martians, decided, or at least seriously speculated, that the young are able to exist in a dormant state outside the parent's body for considerable lengths of

> time, waiting until they are needed, fully instructed from and in communication with the authorities on Mars, for any contingency. Sir Percival wrote a paper, which was more or less dismissed as far-fetched and possibly deluded, on the possibility that the sleeping young could remain in a suspended state for, as he said, a hundred years. And he likened this notion to the story of the Sleeping Beauty. His reference to a fairy tale was mocked in the press and also in scientific circles.
>
> Is it possible that I actually observed Mercy Swift remove from her satchel a sleeping baby Martian? The seeds of the red weed? Surely it is not possible. If I report this to her father, I will surely only prove to him that the fever has entered my brain and destroyed my reason.
>
> I have decided to dismiss this whole episode from my mind. I believe it must have been a vision born of the fever, and referring to the horrors and tragedies I suffered as a result of the Martian invasion. I will never confess any of this to a living soul.

Ah, is it wisdom or folly that compels human beings to confide in their journals?

I am now certain that what Wilfred dismissed as a fevered vision was something that truly occurred in that cabin on board the *Outhwaite* as it made its way to Hobart.

In December 2019, Tasmania was experiencing catastrophic floods and bushfires, in temperatures of 40 degrees Celsius. My grandfather's library was the coolest, most comfortable place in Woodpecker Point, and so I spent many hours quite happily reading whatever took my fancy. For some reason I kept coming back in fascination to Wilfred's journal, to the page about the Martian bud in Mercy's satchel, to the part about the red seeds. And then…

My TV reception and internet connection here are not great, but on Christmas Eve I began to see intermittent disaster news items reporting the strange happenings in Davey Street, Hobart. A peculiar red weed had apparently grown up overnight in the garden of the house where the celebrated children's author and illustrator Mercy Swift had lived as a child.

This house is now a kind of museum where they display Mercy's books, her toys, her sewing, and so forth. I have myself been there on one occasion, and it is a popular place with tourists and groups of schoolchildren. I think I might have observed the leather satchel on a shelf in a glass display case. Did it at the time still contain the sleeping Buddie in his silk parcel?

The red weed was unstoppable by any method, chemical or physical. It had exited the garden and overtaken the road, blocking the traffic as people were attempting to drive to the cathedral at the bottom of Davey Street. The doors of the cathedral were open, and the red weed went marching boldly in where it completely filled the building, broke the windows, and continued on its rampage.

At first people thought the news items were some kind of bad taste hoax. People these days are quite accustomed to 'fake news'. I suppose *The War of the Worlds* radio broadcast Orson Welles made on Halloween in 1938 was one of the first, big, fake news stories of recent history.

But I realised that the red weed story had to be real, and I feared that there was worse to come. The direct slaughter of the people by the Martians, people killed in falling buildings, people succumbing to the poison of the black smoke.

Wilfred's account of Mercy's visit, his view of Buddie and the red seeds, it was all true and hideously ominous.

What to do?

I needed a friendly and seriously receptive ear. I phoned Gustav Fortescue, who is an old friend and who works in the Geology department at the University of Tasmania in Hobart. He was at the airport waiting for a plane to Canberra. I explained what I knew, and what I thought I knew. I imagined the scenario for him: it's time for the Martian invasion of Earth to begin in Tasmania. On Mars they have perfected a telepathic immunity which is sent to Buddie so that earthly diseases are of no consequence. The instructions go out to Buddie who has been sleeping, yes, just like Sleeping Beauty, for over a hundred years. They activate the red seeds. Buddie gets going, poisonous black smoke billowing around him. He produces hundreds of buds which leap into deadly life. Should Gustav call the police? The army? What would he say?

Gustav heard me out with a kind of unearthly patience. And

then he said quietly, 'It's already happened. They have taken over. I am hoping to get to the mainland, although God knows, they are probably heading there. Get out while you can.'

I was fortunate enough to be able to charter an aircraft from Smithton to Perth from where I set off for Mauritius in the yacht. Of course, it is possible that nowhere on Earth is safe. Time will tell. Human life is perhaps about to go the way of the dodo that was hunted to extinction on Mauritius by the Dutch in 1681.

You will have realised by now that the invaders have disabled the air routes. So, as Mercy sang to the dreaded Buddie all those years ago, I say: 'Speed bonnie boat, like a bird on the wing'.

Carrillo Mean
January 2020

Doctor Were's Son

Dmetri Kakmi

CONSTABLE ANN ROBINSON LED DANDO TO THE POLICE CAR IN FRONT of the cottage. Dando was naked, spattered with blood and wrapped in a brown blanket. It was night. A half-moon sailed in a clear sky and the ocean churned below the lighthouse.

Constable Robinson opened the car door and stood aside. 'Watch your head.' She put a hand atop Dando's crown and helped him in.

When the boy was seated, she slid in beside him, buckled him up and saw to her own seat belt. The white stone cottage was visible through the windscreen, the porch light spilling yellow down the wall. All else was dark.

Constable Phillip Badcock emerged from the house, locked the front door and made his way across the circular gravel drive to the waiting vehicle.

'You right?' he said to his partner through the open window.

She nodded and they both cast wary looks at the boy beside her. Dando shivered, despite the warm night.

Constable Badcock got in the car, started the engine, flicked on the headlights and manoeuvred an expert u-turn.

As the car drove away Dando turned in his seat and looked at the building with the lighthouse behind it.

How quickly things change, he thought. This morning life had been as he had always known it. Now everything was turned on its head, casting him alone in the world. As the house disappeared from view around a bend in the road, he sat forward in his seat and thought back to the beginning of the end. Was it only this afternoon?

'Hold still, Dando.'

'Am.'

'You're fidgeting.'

'Hurts.'

'Because you're fidgeting. It will be easier if you look away. Just a small jab.'

Dando clenched his teeth, but he didn't turn his head. He wanted to see what happened.

The hypodermic punctured the tender skin inside his right elbow and he watched with fascination as the clear plastic barrel filled with dark-red. Quarter full. Half full. Full. He sighed with relief when it was over, the sharp needle withdrawing from his arm, removing the dull stinging pain and the heaviness in his quivering limb.

Doctor John Were disinfected the puncture site with a cotton ball and held it in place with gauze. Dando rolled down his long T-shirt sleeve in a businesslike manner. He was 12, thin and small-boned, with straight black hair cut in a bowl shape. His compelling dark-green eyes seemed too big in the oval face that came to a pointed chin with a dimple.

'Drink your chocolate milk,' Doctor Were said. 'It'll do you good.'

The doctor sat on a stool beside the fold-out bed they had brought up to the lighthouse earlier. Turning his back on the boy, he rolled up his own shirt sleeve and applied a tourniquet to his lower right bicep. With trembling fingers, he picked up the hypodermic to pump all of Dando's blood into his own body.

He stared at himself in the mirror on the wall opposite. The effect was instant. His rapid heartbeat slowed and the three large polyps on the right side of his neck retreated. The skin on his face went from pale and gelatinous to firm and pink, the wide staring eyes and the ugly triangular mouth with the pointed upper lip took on its former human aspect; and, finally, the four tentacles atop his head retracted into the skull, leaving behind the bald pate that Port

Fairy's human denizens associated with their much loved and trusted general practitioner.

Dando observed this with satisfaction. Then he picked up the tall glass and downed the sweet milk in one long gulp, a liquid moustache remaining on his upper lip. He stretched out on the bed to alleviate a sudden dizzy spell.

'What happened?' Hands folded over his stomach, Dando stared at the ceiling, waiting for his father to speak.

Doctor Were faced the boy. It took a while to gather his thoughts. Fear and puzzlement warred. Finally, he said, 'I don't know. For some reason the carapace collapsed – only briefly – revealing my true shape.'

Doctor Were still found it hard to believe. He had lived within the shell for almost a decade and it hadn't failed him once. And then, without warning, it happened twice that afternoon.

'Why?' Dando asked, still examining the mould-spotted ceiling.

The doctor shook his head. He was a scientist; he ought to know. He had pioneered the technology, after all, had introduced it to a select few brethren, the most prized Martians strewn across the globe. It meant they could continue to live in secret. To survive. He ought to know what was going on. But he didn't.

A troubling thought: had it happened to anyone else?

'The carapace is linked to my DNA,' he said. 'If it is indeed failing, it must be on a cellular level.'

'Don't forget willpower,' Dando put in. 'Your will holds it in place and creates the illusion of a human body where none exists.'

'There is that.' The doctor rose. 'I have to contact the others.'

Dando sat up tentatively and placed his bare feet on the floorboards. 'What happened at the supermarket?'

The doctor resumed his seat and, taking a deep breath, told Dando what had occurred.

In the supermarket carpark that afternoon, as he prepared to leave the car, his face had turned pale and viscid, and just as quickly reverted to normal human skin as befitted a man of 45 years. He saw it happen in the rearview mirror. Doctor Were knew he should have buckled up and driven home, but he had arrogantly, stupidly, proceeded to the supermarket where the transformation occurred again in front of Helene Loos, the checkout woman. He felt it as a quivering vibration beneath his right eye, the shifting, the slipping. It was momentary. Even so the woman's surprised expression spoke volumes. Was his cover blown? It was impossible to say.

He raced to the car with the groceries and by the time he arrived home at the lighthouse, 11 kilometres from town, the tentacles writhed on his distended cranium. Thankfully, there had been no one on the isolated road to see.

Given what he had observed in Dando of late – the lengthy and often painful experiments on skin and blood cells – his first thought was that the boy's blood might provide a solution. It had proven to be the case. At least for the time being.

'Kill her,' Dando said in a calm voice.

It was Doctor Were's day for shaking his head. He did so wearily and said, 'If she's going to talk, she's probably done it already.'

A year ago, Dando knew, his father would not have hesitated to end the human's life in the fastest, most efficient manner. Now there was hesitation, lenience. What did it mean?

Picking up Dando's empty glass, the doctor walked to the stairs. 'I'll bring your dinner shortly,' he said.

'How long do I have to stay here?'

Dando took in the circular upper floor of the abandoned lighthouse. Above was the room with the disused lens and the spectacular 360 degree views of the Pacific Ocean. Although the prospect from up there was impressive and Dando found it endlessly diverting, he would rather be downstairs where he had greater freedom. But he didn't dare openly defy his father. Yet.

The doctor sighed. 'You know why. It's important no one knows you exist. If they come for me, you'll be safe. Even if they do come up here, you can easily escape.'

Dando nodded and picked at the blanket.

Doctor Were hesitated. Then he re-crossed the floor, set the empty glass on the chair and sat on the bed beside Dando. He put his hand tenderly on the back of the boy's neck and looked directly in his eyes.

'Don't be afraid,' he said. 'I swore to your mother I would protect you. I won't go back on my word.'

He held the boy in his arms for a moment and added: 'You're more precious than you know.'

Dando pulled away. 'You say that every time you want me to obey, but you never tell me why.'

'I believe you are the answer to Martian survival on Earth. That's why not even other Martians can know about you.'

'Is that all?'

There was a moment's hesitation before the doctor nodded. 'Yes.'

Dando counted each footfall as his father left. Quietly, the boy crossed the room and stood at the railing. He watched the top of his father's bald head as Doctor Were descended the three levels to the ground floor. The effect of the circular iron staircase was to make it appear as if he was being sucked into a swirling vortex. After the door between the lighthouse and the keeper's cottage closed, there was the sound of the door being locked. Then silence, apart from the moaning of the wind and crash of waves on the rocks.

Satisfied that his father would not return for the next little while, Dando turned his concentration inwards.

'Are you there?' he said. 'I need to talk.'

Well over a century after the Invaders arrived from the Red Planet – so seemingly invincible for so short a time – there were only 1400 left on Earth. The 300 who hid in plain sight thanks to Doctor Were's carapace technology were 'the Skins', the finest Martian minds left on this watery planet. The survival of these doctors and scientists, strategists, and thinkers, had been deemed of prime importance. The rest, those that remained visibly Martian, were mainly menials and low value pawns. It hardly mattered that they were rounded up by humans, to be killed or placed in concentration camps where they were experimented on or mined by governments for intelligence. In fact, it made it safer for the Skins when everyone thought all Martians still looked like the first-arrival Martians.

Sitting at his desk, Doctor Were contemplated the sea beyond the cypress hedge. He wished he could go out there and submerge himself for several hours in salt water, his natural habitat. But there was work to do.

He looked at the framed photograph beside his computer: Dafune Kawabata had been gone for 12 years and he still missed her. His ardour for her had puzzled even his most open-minded and perverse Martian colleagues. Some had warned against forming any kind of alliance with humans, in case it weakened his commitment to the cause. Others feared worse: a psychological aberration. After a while Doctor Were had stopped talking about his lover to them, hoping they'd forget she existed.

'Dando looks more and more like you every day,' he said to her image.

He smiled at the impassive Japanese face, recalling their years together. Dafune had been adventurous, with a wicked sense of humour, willing to take enormous risks for the thrill of it, being pushed to the edge for the sake of feeling alive. She had taken up with him, knowing full well he was a Martian. She'd thoroughly enjoyed the use to which he put his cranial tentacles on various parts of her anatomy; it gave the term 'giving head' entirely new meaning.

Over time, she clung to him ever more desperately and he had been attached to her after a fashion, their lovemaking becoming riskier and more frenzied when Dafune realised she could not conceive with him. Martians, he explained to her early in their association, were asexual and could not reproduce in the conventional human sense. Resembling hydras, a type of invertebrate related to jellyfish, Martians reproduced by developing genetically identical polyps that protrude from the parent to eventually break from the parent body to form a new organism.

'You can be a mummy and a daddy,' Dafune teased one day. 'Me, I'm just a vessel for pleasure. I can take anything you dish out.'

In the end, that had proven to be a highly erroneous supposition.

'Don't worry,' he said to Dafune's photo now, 'I will keep this family intact.'

He gave a small reflexive bow of the head, the way Dafune had in life. Idly, he pointed the remote control at the large flat-screen television. The 24-hour local news station splashed across the display.

Twenty-five Martians had been rounded up in Victoria's Western District the previous day and taken to Griffith Island, off the coast of Port Fairy. The miserable creatures' telltale forms – large bulbous eyes, triangular beaklike mouth and four sweeping antennae on each head – ensured they had no hope of hiding. Gone was their menace. They were shrunken, pitiable figures, confused, huddled together and afraid on the exposed windy island.

On the mainland, across the narrow channel from the island, a female reporter shoved a large microphone into a familiar face.

'What do you think about what's happening here today?' she asked.

'I say kill 'em all!' Spit flecked the man's lips.

Doctor Were turned off the volume. He'd treated the man for the flu only recently. To hear such abominable words being spoken about his fellow creatures, even if they were drones, knowing there was no hope for them, made his gut churn. Yet there was nothing he could do to help them, even if he wanted to. He didn't dare. He had to think of Dando. The boy's survival was his first and only priority.

The reporter's face filled the screen, mouth moving silently as she turned expectant eyes to the skies. A Royal Australian Air Force jet soared high above. Two incendiary bombs dropped in quick succession and plummeted to earth. In seconds Griffith Island with its captive Martian population was engulfed by furious rushing flame, setting alight the pathetic creatures amid a tumult of scuttling forms and swaying antennae. People cheered and clapped from the safety of the mainland.

Doctor Were turned away, switching the television off. Sickened, he reflected once again on the viciousness of human beings. They were far more hostile than anyone on Mars had dared think. Perhaps that was why they'd underestimated their quarry.

Nor had there been until recently any doubt he was doing the right thing in eradicating them from the face of the planet. Seeing Martians burn made him almost glad that for the last five years, each time there was need for him to medicate a human, he fed them a cocktail of chemicals that would in the long-term cause horrific genetic mutations, undermining their immune system and leaving them open to predatory bacteria. The other Skins did the same thing in other countries.

More than anything, though, the doctor was appalled by how

quickly human betrayed human, willing to work with Martians against their own kind so long as they profited financially. Especially politicians, priests and bankers.

No Martian would stoop that low.

Let them all die, he thought. Even so, a small part of his mind was not so sure anymore. After having lived in a human skin and loved a human woman, he saw things with slightly different eyes.

He turned to the computer, accessed the deep web, and opened a private messaging system. He sent out a coded question to the Skins: *Are you having problems with the skin?*

Almost immediately, two messages arrived. One from China. The other from Hungary. Both answered *No*. Over the next half hour 252 messages filtered through. All in the negative.

It looked like he was the only one.

When messages stopped, he did what he always did when he needed to think without thinking, and clicked on an audiovisual file. Doctor Were leaned back in his chair to watch the images for the millionth time.

Dando stood on the topmost floor of the lighthouse, in the cramped space beside the giant lens, and gazed through the filthy glass at the ocean. It was twilight. Mellow light fell on the heave and boil of waves all the way to the bending horizon.

'The South Pole is somewhere out there,' said the voice in his head. 'Melting away, filling up the oceans and causing sea levels to rise.'

Dando had been speaking to the voice for the last 15 minutes, but he had not revealed the real reason he had summoned her.

'It's ironic,' he said aloud. 'Martians came to Earth to escape a dying planet only to find Earth is dying too.'

The voice was silent for a while. Then it said, 'That's good, isn't it?'

Dando walked around the dusty lens. 'It is,' he said. 'Father says that on Mars the entire population lives in a series of large, interconnected underground seas. Most are now dry. What humans don't realise is that Earth, almost entirely covered by water, suits the original Invaders. They are largely aquatic.'

'And you,' the voice crowed, 'you are the pioneering invertebrate that will crawl out of the waves to begin the next stage of evolution.'

Dando didn't know about ushering in an evolution. All he knew was that he had to survive. No matter what. His father had drilled that into him from the moment he was born.

'That's not why you called me today, is it?' the voice said.

'No.'

'Tell me.'

'It's about Dad.'

'Ah, yes…'

'He thinks I'm the answer to Martian survival on Earth.'

'Aren't you?'

'He's always conducting experiments with my blood, saying it will benefit the Skins.'

'I see.'

'I don't want to be his guinea pig anymore.'

'Why not?'

Dando hesitated before speaking, but when he did speak all the anger and resentment spilled out of him in a gush.

'I don't care about the Martians. I'm me. I'm different from them. They have nothing to do with me. I've never met one. Just Dad. I'm different from humans, too, and I want Dad to let me leave here and live my own life.'

He looked longingly over the treetops, inland at the world spread before him in all its unexplored splendour.

'You are a pioneering invertebrate,' the voice repeated. 'And you will bring the next stage of evolution.'

'I don't want to hurt Dad.'

'You must do what you must do.'

'You can say that?'

'It's been a long time since I was human, Dando.'

Dando drew himself up. 'I'm not Martian. Nor fully human. I'm something new. And I will have life.'

'What are you going to do?'

'Leave. Even if…'

'Even if what?'

Dando had been walking around the lantern room as they spoke, taking in the view and admiring the fiery sunset. Facing due north, he stopped and focussed on something in the distance. Car headlights moved on the road that cut across the promontory, through low coastal vegetation, to the lighthouse.

'What do you see?' the voice asked, as if it peered shortsightedly over his shoulder.

'A car.'

It was still many kilometres away; wouldn't reach them for another 10 or 15 minutes.

'You better tell your father.'

Dando gazed down on the roof of the cottage directly beneath. Then he fully undressed, slid open the glass door and stepped out on the narrow gallery at the top of the lighthouse.

'Hold on,' he said to the voice, the soft summer breeze blowing his hair across his face.

'Please be careful,' the voice cried. 'Oh, I'll never get used to this.'

The transformation was instant. Dando shrugged forward his shoulders and his arms and legs turned into long, slender, pincer-like appendages with sharp segmented pale green claws at the end. Four more limbs of a similar nature sprouted out the side of his torso so he could stick to the masonry like a centipede and crawl face down along the tower.

Dafune Kawabata's face filled the computer screen. Naked, she lay on a white pillow, her usually neat black hair in disarray and her dark eyes staring at the camera with a lust and intensity that lit up her face. Still staring at the camera, she put a thumb in her mouth and sucked on it with a combination of innocence and adult knowing. She smiled. Then she grinned, threw open her arms and beckoned. The camera jiggled before settling on a stable surface to the left of the rumpled bed.

An octopus-like creature slightly bigger than Dafune appeared at her feet. Using four thick tentacles, it dragged the distended cranium with the pulsating lips and bulbous eyes the length of the woman's parted legs. When it reached Dafune's knees, it raised its head, looked at her, and then began to tickle the woman's vulva with an extended tentacle. Dafune arched her back and let out a small mewling sound. After teasing her like this for a while, it plunged two tentacles into the woman's nearest orifices. Dafune threw back her head, clamped both hands on the cranium and pressed it further into herself as the remaining two tentacles attached themselves to her nipples. The woman closed her eyes, cried out in a combination of pain and ecstasy, and thrust her pelvis rhythmically up to the creature, grinding her hips and encouraging it to push further with the two limbs that disappeared almost entirely in her anus and vagina.

Dafune's cries reached new heights, filling the study as Doctor Were sat mesmerised by the images. The large desk faced the room's sole window so that he sat with his back to the study door, staring fixedly at himself in his natural form, doing his utmost to satisfy Dafune's demands. She liked to talk during the act, coaching him in the arts of pleasuring a woman. He of course received no physical satisfaction from it; only the enjoyment of her pleasure, and he had found that he enjoyed taking orders from her.

His eyes moved from the computer screen to Dafune's framed picture beside it and back again. Here was the only human he had cared for, still and silent as the grave in one image and very much alive in the other.

He had watched the video many times over the years; it no longer exerted erotic power over him. Nevertheless, he watched because he wanted to see the end. The tragic results of their violent love making and their combined carelessness.

It was difficult to distinguish human from Martian now, so entangled had the two become as the creature that called itself Doctor John Were swarmed over his human consort, the woman's arms and legs wrapped tightly around him as he drove and plunged the tentacles into the gaps that allowed access to her in-most parts. After a while, it was impossible to know if Dafune cried with pain or delectation.

Finally, she did cry out, a long drawn out howl followed by a deep, contented moan that seemed to go on forever. Her pelvis thrust up to meet his urgent ramming, and then it happened.

He saw it on the screen in the sudden arch of her spine, the way she froze in the middle of her convulsions. His own Martian form halted, as if the unexpected had occurred, and then Dafune said, 'Don't stop.'

'Something's happened,' he said, pulling out the tentacles from her breaches.

The tentacle in her anus came out intact. The one in her vagina had sheared off at half point, the wound already closed. Dafune laughed at the expression on his Martian face.

'I can feel it inside me,' she said. 'It's wriggling, going in deeper.' She threw back her head and laughed again.

'We have to take it out.' The urgency in his voice froze her laughter.

'What is it?'

On screen, Doctor Were's human covering closed over the Martian body in seconds, sheathing the translucent gelatinous body with pink skin. A naked man sat on the bed between Dafune's legs.

'We have to take it out immediately,' he repeated. 'It can't remain inside you. There's a polyp on it.'

Several minutes later Doctor Were admitted defeat. His arm was inside her almost to the elbow and he still could not find the sheared-off tentacle. By this stage, Dafune had realised she was in trouble. She leaned against the bedstead with her knees drawn up and legs wide apart to allow access, or perhaps to push the appendage out with her own muscular contractions, her face drawn in a grimace as her lover prodded inside her with a human hand. It looked as if she was in considerable pain.

They looked at each other and he said, 'We have to operate.'

'It's too late for that, my love.'

Twelve years later, Doctor Were leaned back in his desk chair and watched helplessly. Dafune's face stretched in a rictus grin of pain. Her lips pulled back, baring white even teeth. Sweat broke on her forehead. From a sitting position, she slid on her backside along the soaked mattress and gripped her abdomen. A long groan escaped as her stomach ballooned, the skin pulled tight as a drum on her belly. She bent her knees as if she were about to give birth.

Doctor Were watched the terrible image on the screen. 'It's happening,' he whispered.

'It's happening,' said his naked counterpart in the video.

'What's happening?' Dafune screamed, her eyes swivelling in her head.

The doctor gripped her right hand. 'The polyp. It's taken hold in your womb and it's growing into a life form.'

'I'm giving birth?'

'If only…'

Dafune caved in on herself. It was as if she were made of plastic and a sadist had unplugged the nozzle to let out the air. Her face tightened, showing in sharp relief the skull beneath. The hazel eyes almost popped out of her head as the cheeks drew in and hollowed, the lips pulled back in a hideous grimace. The same happened to the chest and abdomen. Everything fell inward, pushing out the ribcage so that each rib stood out and could be counted beneath the pallid strip of skin that remained. Her breasts were reduced to brown nipples stretched tight across the top part of her body. Yet the stomach remained large and swollen, an unmoving monolith, healthily pink, blue veins showing through the skin, as it fed off the shrunken body, pulling the organs into a central vortex.

In the end, Dafune was a large belly with a withered head, arms and legs poking out the sides. A grotesque caricature of womanhood. She looked at the doctor, managed to whisper 'John' before everything was pulled into the mountainous abdomen.

It was only when Dafune disappeared entirely, leaving behind a round flesh ball on the bed, that the flushed belly deflated. As it shrank, it took the form of a tiny human being, no bigger than a man's forearm, writhing beneath the skin folds, its extremities in jerky movement.

When it was over, a baby boy with glossy black hair lay on the crumpled bed sheets. It opened large green eyes, took its first look at its father, and let out a bellicose cry.

The doctor was glued to the computer screen. He pressed pause so that baby Dando's image froze on the monitor. Even at that age it was unmistakably Dafune's face.

He heard a muffled gasp from behind. And that's when he saw.

Dando stood behind him by the study door, reflected on the computer screen over his own motionless image as a newborn. The doctor's eyes shot across to Dafune's photo, as if seeking reassurance or support, and again he beheld his son superimposed over Dafune's likeness.

Like mother, like son, he thought, swivelling in his office chair to face the music.

'I killed my mother,' Dando said in a subdued voice.

'How long have you been there?' the doctor asked, folding his hands in his lap.

'Long enough.'

Doctor Were nodded and waited for Dando to make the first move.

'I killed my mother,' Dando repeated. He was naked. Feet bare. Hands splayed. The pincers retracted.

'Not exactly.'

'She died giving birth to me. That's pretty exact.'

'That's what you infer from what you saw,' the doctor said calmly. 'It's not what happened. Dando, get dressed and let me explain.'

Dando shook his head, remaining where he was.

'I assure you,' his father said, 'you did not kill Dafune.'

'Then what happened?'

'The polyp absorbed her as it took form inside her to shape you.'

'That's why I look like her,' Dando said.

Doctor Were nodded. 'And why you naturally have the likeness of a human being. Not to mention DNA with much promise.'

'I'm my own mother?'

'You're more me. The polyp inside Dafune carried my DNA. You have Dafune's form, but you are a genetic replica of me. If you hadn't absorbed her, you would look like me.'

'The Martian you or the human you?' Dando asked, though the answer was obvious.

'Martian, of course.'

Dando suppressed an inward shudder and mumbled, 'I hear her.'

The doctor leaned forward. 'What did you say?'

'She speaks to me. A voice in my head.' Dando tapped his forehead.

'How long?'

'Always.'

'How do you know it's Dafune?'

'She said.'

Doctor Were couldn't believe his ears. 'You should have told me.'

'She said not to.'

'Why?'

Doctor Were wanted to stand, go to the boy – to Dafune – but his legs were too weak. They would not carry him. Besides, he trembled inside, knowing she was near. Could he control himself if he came too close to Dando? It was hard enough as it was. The doctor remained seated, one human leg crossed over the other, maintaining a semblance of self-mastery when all the while he shivered and stared at the boy who stood, still as a statue, by the door.

Dando moved his head and his depthless eyes caught the fading light coming through the window behind his father. 'She said it's our secret. It would hurt you to know.'

Overcoming his weakness, Doctor Were stood and took a step towards his son. Behind him came the soft ping of more messages arriving. He ignored them.

He felt his resolve weaken. The constant deception, the hiding and the need to survive, the covert war he waged on his patients…And now, Dafune being here all along, without his knowledge. With never a word to him.

No sooner did that last thought pass through his mind than the concentration required to maintain his appearance fell away entirely. No longer was he a man walking towards his son, but a monster with hungry eyes, a bloated cranium, and tentacles writhing like Medusa's hair.

Movement outside the window behind his father caught Dando's attention and he recalled the reason he had come down – to warn him about the approaching car. But now, seeing who was casting the shadow on the glass, he decided on a new course of action.

Dando's eyes widened with alarm. He cowered back, reached out a hand and cried, 'No, don't. Get back.'

There was a shattering sound. The window behind the doctor exploded, sending shards flying in the room. Two bullets slammed through the back of Doctor Were's head and came out the front through his eyes. Another bullet neatly sliced a tentacle before he collapsed face first on the floor, twitching in his death throes and spraying Dando with red.

The boy screamed and fell against the wall as another bullet lodged in the plaster beside him. Sobbing, naked but for the covering of his father's blood, he crawled behind the study door and crouched in a corner, hands over his head.

That's where Constable Phillip Badcock, a tall ginger-bearded man in his mid-30s, found him. Ann Robinson, his partner, brought up the rear.

They had seen the monster advancing on the naked boy, and taken the only course of action that seemed right.

'Well,' Constable Robinson said. 'Looks like Helene Loos was right. He was a Martian and it looks like he's kidnapped the kid. He was probably going to experiment on him.'

She cradled Dando in her arms, regardless of the gore on his body. 'There, there,' she said. 'You're safe. We're here. Don't worry.'

Across the room, Constable Badcock replaced the gun in his holster and prodded the dead Martian with a boot.

'Another one down,' he said, his voice flat as he looked at the boy in Constable Robinson's arms. 'Is he okay?'

'I think so,' Constable Robinson said. 'I don't think it's his blood. Is that right, love? It's not your blood, is it? Are you injured?'

Dando curled into her, making himself small and vulnerable. He shook his head wordlessly. He didn't trust himself to speak. Sacrificing his father was a deliberate choice, but that didn't make it easier.

'We got here on time,' Constable Robinson said, rising and pulling the boy with her. 'I think he's all right.'

Constable Badcock approached with a blanket from the couch. He draped it over Dando and said, 'What's your name?'

'Play dumb,' the voice in Dando's head advised. 'Or they will kill you.'

Dando cast his eyes to the floor and tried not to look at his father's corpse, the demolished head.

'I don't know,' he said to the police officer. 'I woke up here.' He looked around the room as if he'd not seen it before. 'Where am I?'

'Where do you live?'

Dando shook his head. 'I can't remember. Please, I'm scared.'

He stared at the police officer, face smeared with congealed blood, and tried to create the impression of a normal boy waking up in hell, frightened and bewildered after an ordeal, with the creature of his nightmares dead at his feet. Yet a wild, jubilant joy rushed through his system.

I will soon be free, he thought. I will be out of this house. Free.

'Let's get him out of here,' Constable Robinson said to her partner; she glanced meaningfully at the dead monstrosity. 'Better to ask questions back at the station.'

'Good idea.' Constable Badcock paused at the study door and shook his head. 'Blow me down,' he added. 'If you told me yesterday Doctor Were was a Martian, I wouldn't have believed you. I mean the man's delivered more than half the babies in town and cared for more sick than you've made arrests. Goes to show, doesn't it, you just never know where the buggers are hiding?'

'The quicker we exterminate them, the better.'

Constable Robinson took Dando to the police car and waited for Constable Badcock to secure the crime scene. Dando sat beside her, wrapped in a blanket that carried his father's scent, the sense of betrayal washing over him like a tide that threatened to sweep him away. He knew he would never see the house again. It was rigged so that it would self-combust 15 minutes after Doctor John Were's death, incinerating the body and eradicating his life's work. The pain washed over Dando. He turned around and sat facing forward. He only wanted to get away from there, to see what lay beyond the spit of land that had been his prison for 12 long years.

'I killed my father.'

At first he wasn't sure if he had spoken the words aloud or if he just thought them.

He knew which it was when the voice in his head spoke, and the cops remained silent.

'You didn't kill him,' his mother stated plainly. 'He lives on in you. As do I. Now we are a family, sharing one body.'

Dando wasn't sure how he felt about that. But he had to live with it for the time being. He also understood that he had to disappear.

Get away from Port Fairy, go to the next town, and then the next. Lay low. Integrate himself into the general populace, find a girl, have a baby, propagate. He'd have to go to the city eventually. Melbourne or Sydney. Not even other Martians could know he existed, until he was ready to reveal himself. First he would work from the inside to pave the way for a new way of being on Earth.

'My son, the Trojan horse,' the voice crowed.

Dando liked the idea of being a Trojan horse among humans better than the notion of one body housing a family of three. He smiled. 'I'm a Trojan,' he said.

'Pardon, love?' Constable Robinson said.

Dando looked out the window. 'Nothing,' he said. 'I just said, I'm chosen.'

'You are. You were chosen by God to survive your ordeal,' she said. 'Promise me you're going to grow up and have a good, happy life with lots of children.'

'I'm going to grow up and have lots of children,' Dando repeated, grinning.

'Good boy.'

Nothing Missed

Angela Meyer

After her father died in the war, her mother's hair grew grey and out. Her mother sits at the kitchen table on her laptop, searching and connecting, her hair reaching out like static, the room becoming dark.

They still live in a version of lockdown, with Sam only supposed to go from the front door to the bus, from the bus across the rubble into school, and then back home. There had been dancing on the street at the defeat, but after that the suburb had returned to a respectful grieving silence. There had, after all, been so much loss. The sight from the bus of their neighbour, Patel, watering the garden, for example, only reminds Sam of the fact her father will never do that again. Every act of living is a contrast to what does not exist anymore.

But one day Sam's teacher, Mrs Laman, is teaching the class about the properties of water, air, light, and Sam remembers the outdoors, and she walks out the gate at lunchtime and down to her old favourite place by the creek. She used to go here just for the sound of the water, knowing it was a bit strange, but having a desire for it. She would mute her device, back then, so she could concentrate properly on the rushing, soothing water. But they'd all gotten used to living without devices, in the hiding, so this was no longer a concern. Her mother is the only one she knows who has reattached. All day in that kitchen, on the laptop. Even Mrs Laman still uses the books the government delivered during the war.

She sits and listens to the rushing soothing, closing her eyes, leaves crackling beneath her palms. She opens her eyes, watching the water make white forks around sharp rocks, and the dark blue meandering. She takes off her school shoes so she might feel the cool trickle through her toes. At the water's edge she looks along the shaft of water right and left, the trees bending in above.

The soldier, hat in hand on the doorstep, told her that when her father fell he landed softly in water. He told her this detail, but for some reason did not tell her mother.

Looking to the left at the water's edge she sees a slimy lump in the grey colour of her nightmares. It's the particular grey-shade of the dead, she sees, and surely it is just a rock anyway. The military scanned and swept for bodies weeks ago. She edges gently towards it, as her heart rate increases. It cannot be. It is. Indeed, it is one of them. Well, it is the back of a head, that she can see, with the neck shredded by some instrument cruder than a laser. How could it have been missed? And then she remembers her mother talking about it, in that flat voice she now uses, about how they scan for the hearts to find the bodies. That it is the shape of the alien heart and how different it is from a human's that can identify them. Their other organs are too similar in shape and placement to our own.

She stares at the back of it for a long time before walking around to the front, anticipating that its eyes could be open. But they are not. The large grey lids are closed over, the mouth pressed shut. She knows it could be her imagining but she does feel a presence, some beckoning from the pursed mouth. A shiver goes through her body, and she walks back to her shoes, and then back out through the trees and towards the school, wondering who she should report this to.

She hesitates at Mrs Laman's desk on the way out of the afternoon English class, but Mrs Laman sighs in a way that indicates exhaustion, and Sam does not want to burden her. She can tell her tomorrow.

Jess and Lea are walking slowly in front of her, thin arms linked tenderly, and Sam slows so she does not have to overtake them. Lea has a new hand-poked tattoo on her forearm, her mother's name in cursive: *Angelica.* Sam had been staring at it in class. She wonders if it still hurts, if it stings lightly with each brush of Jess's hand. Her own arm tingles at the thought.

Her mother is at the kitchen table, thinner, her hair crackling out from her shoulders on either side. Sam puts two slices of bread in the toaster, then adds jam. Her mother does not take butter. It reminds her of alien blood.

Her mother's hand reaches for the toast, and she takes a bite, without looking up. Sam feels her own muscles relax a little. Her mother chews for an age. Then she looks up, startled to see her daughter there.

'What if we missed something?'

It was the same thing her mother asked yesterday.

'What if there is a message we have missed?'

Sam does not know what to say to the pained face of her mother. 'Mum...will you finish your toast?'

'A message from God...the higher intelligence. It was meant to come from technological self-awareness, but could we have missed a sign? I can barely connect the way I could before. I had taken God into my body. In my eyes and ears. And now there is just this.' She points to the laptop.

Sam knows she means her device is no longer connected; her body is no longer aided by technology. And their religion contains the idea that God is in the way the technology empowers and connects them; that they, collectively, become God: Theosis.

'How can this be? We followed all the signs, we followed His path.'

'I don't know, Mum.'

Her mother's face begins to distort, not to sadness, but rage. 'How can this be? What sign have we missed?'

Sam gets up from the table and walks out of the kitchen. She has no answer for her mother. And it is painful, not to share the same questions, in this aftermath.

At some point in the night, lying under her thin blanket, Sam hears the kitchen chair scrape back and her mother's footsteps pad to her bedroom. Only then can Sam fall asleep. She wakes sharply again at first light, at the heat, and throws off her blanket. She thinks about sharp needles piercing her skin and ink mixing with blood and that calms her, so she can close her eyes again for a while.

The alien. She will check it is still there before she tells anybody. How awful it would be to drag someone there for no reason. How humiliating. Both she and her mother will be dragged off on the next sweep-through, taken to a dirty hospital with no privacy. Privacy and quiet are elements of the hiding, and aftermath, she has embraced. They give her room for the thoughts, the figuring out and the grief. Her mother fills the quiet with message boards, the obsessive revisiting of the idea of the failed singularity.

What have we missed?

Sam wishes she could help her.

At lunchtime she sneaks down to the river, and it is still there, still grey and round, not diminished. They must decay more slowly than us, she thinks. And then has a terrible flash vision of her father's body bloated with water. She could beat the head to a pulp. She could slice it into pieces. She could yell at it until spittle rains on its flat, dead eyelids. But it is all over and done, and it has already suffered. Its race has suffered. They were defeated. Wiped out. We won.

And she touches her hand to the bulbous head, curious about the feel of the skin.

When her hand connects, her palm and fingertips – each point of connection – tingle. She pulls her hand back. This is a dead thing; that should not happen. It is probably just her body's fearful response, she tells herself. She moves from a crouch to sit beside it. She touches an elbow to the head. The same: tingling, and pleasant, like sunlight on eyelids. She thinks about the poked tattoo, arms brushing arms, and she places a palm flat on the head and this time closes her eyes and lets the tingling spread up her forearm, bicep, shoulders, across her chest and back, and as it comes into her neck and then her head, she exhales, deeply. Because there is nothingness. There is space and blankness and calm. Her mouth goes slack; she lies down on the warm grass and dirt, keeping her hand all the while on the head. Nothing good or bad. Just nothing.

THE MILITARY WOULD KNOW, she thinks, later, distracted, in class. They would have all the other heads in a laboratory. Or maybe it is the skin itself – the whole body. And is it when they live, or only when they are dead? Is it to help with the grieving? Do they touch one another's dead bodies after they have expired in order to not feel anything bad, to feel nothing and be able to move on? An evolved grief-mechanism? From having travelled to many planets and having lost so many lives?

She has to get onto her mother's laptop. Surely there are leaks in the message boards, first-hand accounts under code names. Or maybe no one would risk it.

And so, when she reports it, does she tell her teacher what she knows? Or would that put them both at risk? And her mother, too.

She needs help. She needs an opinion, a friend. Lea used to pass her notes but then latched on to Jess. Sam aches to look at them, holding hands under the desk. She craves instantly to go back to the alien head and wipe out the feeling. But maybe this could reconnect them. Lea's tattoo, she knows, is over her scars – self-inflicted. It was something they'd noticed in each other. It was something that had kept them from making other friends. Sam doesn't know why Jess got past this, has become so special to Lea. Perhaps her effect is like the harming, or like the alien head – instilling calm blankness.

Sam notices her fists are curled, and she stretches out the fingers. Mrs Laman is teaching them about photons – particles of light – a subject Sam was interested in last week. But now, her mind is looping: the head, the aliens, the nothingness. What her father had to feel. The loop was dangerous. The loop was her mother. *We must have missed something. How could He let this happen? Where are my eyes, my ears?*

THAT NIGHT SAM WAITS for the chair to scrape back. And waits, and waits. Her mother's thoughts static out through the house, all night. And so she cannot access the laptop.

She comes into the kitchen at first light, puts bread in the toaster. When she turns around her mother is looking at her.

'There's something different about you.' Her face is cruel, accusatory.

'Mum?' Internally, she is folding. She doesn't want to be the saner one, the adult. She wants her mum to rise, to lead her to the bedroom and tuck her in and tell her everything will change, and get better.

'You are different. You have been touched.'

She stares at her mother, wondering how she is picking up on her energy, the fact she is hiding something.

'I think you should get some sleep, Mum.'

'I can't sleep without him.'

She doesn't know if her mother means her father, or God: the parts that enhanced her and made her one with Him. Her mother feels halved, Sam knows. Sam does not feel halved. She feels instead that grief has expanded her insides, unbearably. That she is carrying water and images and noise. She would happily never reconnect, except that she itches to get to the laptop to know more about the alien's effect, the numbing.

When she gets to school there is an army jeep in the carpark. A man and a woman in neat uniforms, jumping down from the front seats. She keeps her head down.

Halfway through the first class they enter. Mrs Laman nods, must have been briefed. The woman steps forward of the man; they are both smiling, seemingly to put the students at ease. Sam tries her best to look relaxed.

'Good morning,' the woman says, looking around at the faces of the students. 'We're just passing through the area, talking to people. We want to make sure you are aware that you should report anything, anything at all, out of the ordinary, to this number.'

The man writes on the whiteboard.

Lea raises her hand. 'Is there something we should be worried about?'

Sam notices she is sitting alone today.

The woman smiles patiently. Sam keeps her eyes on the woman's face but can tell that behind her, the man is scanning faces, looking for someone who may be hiding something.

'Absolutely not,' she says. 'In this time after victory, we're just interested in getting everything back to normal.' She glances at the books on Mrs Laman's desk. 'Of course, we're working with the government on reinstating the full capacity network as quickly as possible.' Some of the students whooped. 'So if you see us around, or flying over, we're just locating the biggest damage points and working as fast as we can to fix them.'

Sam nods, keeps her face clear and bright.

At lunch time, the jeep drives away from the school, towards the centre of town. This could be Sam's only chance. She leaves her books on her desk, goes down to the spot and sits by the head. She opens her backpack. She lifts the head, heavy as her own, the brain the exact same size, and pushes it in. Nothing oozes; there is no stench. Just the tingling up her arms, but she has moved quickly enough to avoid the nothingness. Though she wants it, now, to take away the worry. She presses her hand into her bag and lets the alien head empty her thoughts. Blank. Blanched. Gone.

After a while, distantly, she hears the bell. She zips up her backpack and runs, with difficulty, back to class. She will have to sit there all afternoon with the head in her backpack, because if she leaves just after the army visit, she may look suspicious. The forest is behind the library so everyone will assume she has been in the library, which is plausible. The library is another place she goes, to sit alone.

She keeps her head down all afternoon, heart thumping. She carries the books she needs for that night's homework out of the classroom.

She is rushing, she hasn't looked, and of course she has run right into Lea, going back in for something. The bag tumbles and Lea goes straight for it, apologising. *No.*

'Jesus Christ, what do you have in here?' Lea asks, holding it by one strap.

'Just books,' Sam says with a wavery voice, snatching back the bag.

'Mmokay,' Lea says. She doesn't move out of the way. 'Doing okay?' Her eyes are pale blue, like the white-water in the creek.

'Yeah, yeah, not too bad.' She tries not to be out of breath. 'Um, you?'

'Yeah I'm fine,' she says. 'Except Jess is…not well.'

'I'm sorry to hear.'

'Yeah,' she steps to the side. 'Well, see ya mate.'

'See you.' Sam walks off as casually as possible. Doesn't look back. Knows Lea is watching her.

She wondered: could she have left it there? Would everything have been okay? But her prints. DNA. Evidence of her. They would have found it. No doubt. They would need to quarantine her, or put her away so she didn't speak. But still, she could have risked it. This was worse. But she has an idea.

Her mother is at the table, sun coming through grey threads of her hair like silken spiderweb. She looks up as soon as Sam enters, this time. Her face is the face of pain – gaunt and sharp, so pale it is almost blue. Sam sits her backpack on the table.

'Mum.'

'Yes?'

'I know what we missed.'

'You do?'

'But you can't tell anyone in your forums. This is between us and God.'

'Between us and God.' She nods. She glances agitatedly at her laptop, but then slowly presses it closed. 'What is it?'

'You have to close your eyes.'

Her mother frowns. Then nods. 'Okay.'

Sam brings another dining chair around next to her mother, gets her bag and sits it on the chair.

'Will it hurt?' her mother asks. Sam experiences a spasm of frustration at her mother's child-like voice.

'No, Mum. Close your eyes.'

Her mother does so. Sam unzips the bag, just enough so a hand can enter. She guides her mother's hand to the opening.

'It will tingle, but don't pull away.'

She presses her mother's hand against the grey inside. Her mother gasps. Sam watches her face, and she knows the moment when the nothingness sweeps her. Her mother un-lines; her pink tongue falls to the bottom of her palate.

'Oh,' she says.

Sam pulls her hand away. Her mother opens her eyes, looks at Sam with wonder.

'What is it? How did you…?'

How could she tell her it was the same thing that killed her father, that killed so many people?

'Mum,' she swallows. 'In the teachings our connection with God, our becoming, is exponential, slow. But what if it was meant to be sudden? Through…'

She wanted to say: through an encounter. What if it was intended as an encounter, not an invasion? Of course, that is what had been argued by many commentators, at the start. And then the violence was all there was.

'Through touch, through a combining?'

Her mother nods, slowly, considering. She looks with wonder down at the backpack, now closed. Then she looks around at the room.

'It has gotten very dusty in here. And dark. I should open a window.' She stands and pulls a hair tie from her robe pocket and wraps her hair back into a ponytail, and then walks into the kitchen and parts the curtains above the sink.

She turns around and smiles at Sam.

'I think God has rebooted me.'

She should bury it. Deep, somewhere. Her mother seems to have just trusted in her daughter, in a mysterious power, in it being an act of God. Or maybe deep down she knows, but doesn't want to. Sam already feels lighter, having her mother back. She shouldn't hold on to the head anymore. She shouldn't use it, like the harming, like a drug. A deep, deep burial. Maybe they won't find it for years. Maybe the dirt will cover the DNA. But it now feels hard to let it go.

She looks at Lea, hunched over at her desk. Jess is still not back. From the whispers she has heard, Jess may never be back. She took too many pills and is in a coma. Sam wonders why Lea is even at school. Perhaps it is preferable than thinking all day. Perhaps her father is forcing her.

At the end of the day, she asks Lea if she would like to come over, distract herself for a bit.

Lea sighs, like she doesn't have a choice. 'I guess.'

They get on the bus together. Sam doesn't press her to talk. She sits still, but calm, taking on her waves of pain. Lea's thin wrists are bruised. Sam wants to hold them gently. She won't. Lea doesn't feel that way about her anymore.

It is quiet in the house, but that is not unusual. It is, at least, cleaner and brighter.

'Mum?' she calls. Nothing. Perhaps she has ventured out, the way she did yesterday, finally going out in the world, for light and air and exercise.

And so when they walk into her bedroom she does not expect the sight. Her mother, lying on the floor, a knife in one hand, but her eyes closed and her other hand on the alien head, fully exposed, found. The clothes it was wrapped in under the bed, strewn around. Sam makes a quick calculation – she must have found it, been terrified and angry, got the knife, then realised that was what she had touched.

Lea is right behind her. She screams.

Sam's mother's eyes jolt open and she lets go of the head and leaps to her feet with the knife.

Lea turns to run.

'Lea, wait! It's...not real. I can explain!'

She chases Lea and her mother is coming in behind her.

'Mum, let go of the knife!'

'She will ruin the plan,' her mother says.

Sam stops chasing Lea and grabs her mother's wrist with full force. Her mother is still weak. She drops the knife.

Lea is out the front door and running down the street.

Sam does not know what to do. She has ruined everything.

'Mum, listen to me. You never touched it. Okay?'

'But I...'

Sam runs back to her room, bundles the head into her backpack, and then goes back out the front door. She runs after Lea, the heavy pack bouncing.

'Lea! Please stop for one second. Please. It wasn't real. My mum hasn't been the same since the war.'

Lea slows. Looks at Sam incredulously.

'Please, just stop for a second. I'm sorry you had to see that weirdness.'

Lea stops, puts her hands on her hips. 'What the fuck? Seriously.'

'It's a punishment ritual. She blames herself.'

Lea pants, shakes her head. 'It's too weird. I can't deal with this today.'

'I know, I'm sorry. You have enough on your mind. That's why I was inviting you over, to try and distract you, watch a movie or something.' Sam gets closer. Shifts her backpack on one arm. She could try. It was something she could just try.

She simultaneously slips one hand in her backpack and reaches for Lea's hand with the other.

'I'm sorry things have been hard for you.' She tries to lock her eyes on Lea's – gentle, reassuring. The sweeping tingling is taking her body, she tries not to gape, to retain the eye contact, to retain the touch. 'It's going to be okay.' Her jaw drops just as Lea looks down at their hands, puzzling.

'I feel all tingly,' she says. And then, 'Oh.'

They go down together, onto Patel's lawn. Onto nothing. Into nothing. Momentary and eternal nothingness. Empty. Together.

'Are you girls okay?' Patel's voice, cutting through. They pull apart. Sam's hand comes out of the bag. She closes her mouth, clears her throat.

'Fine, sorry…' she manages, sitting up. 'Just enjoying this weather.'

'O…kay,' he says. Walks back up his driveway.

Lea sits up, looks around. 'I feel like everything is new,' she says. 'I have to get home to Dad.'

Sam hopes it has been enough.

She watches Lea walk away, slowly. Lea turns. 'See you tomorrow.'

'See you mate,' Sam says.

It is getting dark, but the helicopters have stopped for the day, and she has been paying attention to the sweeps. They have already done here, the school, the creek, three times, coming in from three different angles. The sweeps were moving west.

She will wash it, and then she will bury it. And hope that's enough.

She puts on the gloves she bought and she holds the head under in the deeper part of the creek, where she can perch on a large dry rock. Get all this natural water, silt, gunk, whatever, all over it. Mask the fingerprints, the sweat.

Then she carries it, dark enough now, un-bagged (seems right) to beneath a tree near her secret entrance to the little creek clearing. And she digs with her small trowel, and it takes a while, but she makes a deep hole. She places the head in gently, to the bottom. And then covers it over. She bags the gloves, and then she walks back to where her mother is waiting in the car.

When Jess is back at school, sometimes Sam sees Lea walking with her, arm in arm, towards the library, and she sees her looking around, and then they go around the side and to the back. And she doesn't want to be rude, but she sometimes follows after a while and just takes a peek at them, sitting on a blanket under that tree, holding hands with their eyes closed.

Cat and Mouse

Bill Congreve

IT HAPPENED AGAIN. THIS TIME A DEAD RABBIT, A HOLE IN ITS GUTS THE size of a pickaxe, a thin slime around the hole that stank of dead seaweed and red dust.

Another mark had appeared overnight on the sandstone wall on the far side of the carpark: IIIII IIIII IIIII II

Seventeen days I've been in here. It was counting. It wants me to get desperate and run outside.

I'd heard once there were so many bones in a rabbit that you should bone it before cooking.

Cooking. Why was the gas still working? Why was there gas at all in a building this old? The water was also okay, but cold only. No electricity.

I cut the stinking slime out of the guts of the rabbit, then broiled it long and slow. Nothing to cook it with but salt and pepper, but I kept the high, shallow window open even in the cold of the evening and made sure the smell wafted out to the thing outside.

It was a carnivore. Let it suffer.

21 JANUARY

> Damned Diary, heh, nothing else to do, might as well write it down. Either that or read, and there's only one book in the

place. Found it on the shelf in the toilet. Somebody's idea of a sense of humour.

How do you make sure your employees don't spend all day sitting on the loo when they should be watching data scrolling by on a computer screen? Give them nothing to read but a turgid Russian sermon about life in gulag.

One Day in the Life of Ivan Denisovich was the title.

Company sponsored literature – let the workers realise how good they actually had it.

Thank heavens it was short. Siberia? At least it isn't cold here, wherever here is.

Eighteen days now. I only realised what the cricket score meant after I noticed that the bottom row kept changing, day after day. It was the only change I could see outside, except for where it parked the car. The 18 marks for my incarceration made the last of about 30 rows of cricket scores etched into the sandstone. The shortest only four days long, the longest about six months.

After the first week, I was hoping the book was longer, not because it suddenly became escapist power fantasy, but because it was alone. There it sat on a pine-wood shelf, a single novel, not even 200 pages long, its only companions a catalogue for Federation-look raw pine furniture and a fresh roll of toilet paper.

As for the shelf, that was a different story: made in a home workshop, rough joints, sanded, routed edges, over-engineered to buggery, no staining, oil or paint, yet still rustic and beautiful in a way, strong enough to climb on if I wanted to, yet all it needed to hold was a thin paperback, a catalogue and a roll of toilet paper.

A labour of love for somebody who didn't quite know what they were doing; for somebody who loved the kind of kitsch furniture illustrated in the catalogue. I could imagine Ivan Denisovich building it in a gulag workshop if the Russians had ever allowed their political prisoners that freedom.

I had another look outside this morning, just before it threw another rabbit in. Got to the end of the corridor that's the only entrance to this place. As usual during the day, the rusty iron-barred gate stood open. I looked outside.

No car.

Just for a moment I thought I was home free.

I got ready to run, planned my route: 20 metres of cracking bitumen overgrown with weeds, hurdle the copper log fence, and then take the first real cover – a huge, old chestnut with branches drooping close to the ground.

The number of times I've looked out at that tree the last two and a half weeks, and the chain link fence and mountain bushland on the far side of it. The tree wasn't protection, not against the thing, but at least I would be out of sight under those branches.

It was beautiful, 20 metres tall, dense foliage, dried male catkins dropping to the ground, nuts starting to swell inside the needle-sharp spikes of their seed pods.

If I'm still here in autumn the leaves will turn orange and fall, and the ground will be covered in drying brown seedpods ripped apart and thrown down by the white cockatoos searching for nuts.

God forbid I'll be here in autumn.

I got a little closer to the door, saw a faint edge of deep bruising red out of the corner of my eye, in the far corner of the carpark, and the faintest twitch of movement in front of the door, in the shadow of the building.

The car *was* here.

The shadow swum into focus.

It was on the roof.

I dived back, felt the scrabble of a metal claw against the sole of one foot, the rattle of its metal tentacle against the sandstone blocks of the corridor, scratching dust and pebble-sized rocks from the stone, heard the gasbag-like wheeze of its frustration, and then the clanking thud of its mass against the rusting metal door frame.

Missed me, again.

Stupid, stupid! The door was open. Of course it was here!

I turned my back on it, bent over, dropped my pants, and farted.

It bounced in one leap to a nearby gum tree and swung a tentacle. The trunk shattered. It pointed another tentacle at the stump, holding a metal box with a small dish antenna. The trunk burst into flame.

It turned towards me, pointing a tentacle at the doorway, waving, all the colours of the rainbow rippling over its surface.

'Ula ula ula,' I heard.

23 January

Damned Diary, let's call it what it is: a Martian, just like the stuffed and tanned corpses in the museums, but it is too big to get inside.

You might wonder when all this started. A job interview at a tiny employment agency, in a single office down a side alley on the eastern side of Katoomba Street.

I walked down the alley. Nobody home. A sign on the door said to come inside, take a seat, and wait.

It was a cold, misty day with the temperature in the mid-teens, the kind of day the Blue Mountains could throw at you even in the height of summer: cold, dank, murky, the air filled with a drifting mist that was more cloud than rain, but wet enough to saturate you and cold enough to give you hypothermia.

In the carpark outside the office was a deep, blood-red, 1970 Ford Falcon, immaculately kept, shining almost translucent through the misty grey. One of the most classic of Australian-built classic cars, this was the two-door sports model, the Futura Club coupe. I found it impossible not to walk over and take a closer look.

The driver's seat had been taken out, replaced by a padded board the height of the rear seat bench, making a long, L-shaped platform big enough for a bear to lie on. In the passenger seat sat an almost perfect store mannequin, power-dressed in a black business suit with the skirt cut high on the thighs, thick lush blonde hair, bare feet, sunglasses – drop-dead gorgeous, but oh so plastic.

It was with some regret that I turned back to the office. I went inside, had a drink from the refrigerated jug of water and glasses that had been left out on a tray, and sat in a surprisingly comfortable but obviously homemade Federation pine couch. That was the last thing I remember before waking up in this place.

God knows what the children think. Their mother would know better. She'd think: here we go again. But this time, she was wrong.

Did the Martian drug me or did I fall asleep? Doesn't matter. It had me.

Today was breakthrough day.

There are dozens of places like this in the mountains, old government buildings locked away down dirt roads behind rusting gates, not appearing on any maps. Who knew what they were? Some dated from the Second World War, the older ones dated from late in the 19th century when the railway first penetrated to the upper mountains, just before the Martians arrived.

This was one of the older buildings and had walls of sandstone block half a metre thick. There was one big room, a combination kitchen, sitting room and bedroom, with a haphazard arrangement of furniture, all of it handmade, bulky, over-engineered pine that didn't quite fit its surroundings. Some of it made for children, some of it made for a person half a metre taller than me. One chair at the kitchen table – if I sat in it my feet swung in the air, and I'm 190 cm tall.

The kitchen included a sink, a gas stove, and a small cupboard obviously intended to be a pantry. In the cupboard was salt, pepper, a jar of 1950s Nescafe instant coffee, bicarb of soda, several unidentifiable pieces of metal, a solid old metal cheese grater, a thin notebook, some gumtree bark, and a cake of soap.

I was using the notebook and pencil for my diary.

For cutlery I had a knife, a fork, and a spoon, all plastic.

All the windows were high up on the walls, too short to climb through, and barred from the outside. There was barely enough light inside to read. There was a fireplace, stocked with well-seasoned hardwood, but no kindling.

The toilet was a separate cubicle, no door. There was no shower or bath.

The corridor from outside ended in the middle of the large room. It was a strange arrangement, but there were marks on the floor and ceiling where walls had been removed. In one wall there were two locked steel doors. A musty smell came from behind one of them.

In all, it was a prison designed by a clever mind that didn't quite understand the way things worked on this planet. Everything had been thought out, but nothing gelled.

I had discovered that a splinter of the seasoned hardwood in the fireplace was enough to scrape at the failing mortar holding the sandstone blocks together, and between the two locked doors was the end of a sandstone block wall. Every second block at the end of the wall would be a half block, but which ones?

It took me five days to realise what it meant and start scraping, but over the last 16 days I'd had plenty of time to make progress. Just to be sure, I worked on four lines of mortar at once.

Damned diary, 25th January

> Yesterday was the day. Now I can plan.
>
> The first sandstone block was the hardest. The first block shifted slightly, but not enough to provide real encouragement. I moved to the third block down of the set I had been working on. Solid as rock. Heh, heh. So I went back to the first and used a lump of hardwood as a hammer, bashing gently from one side and then the other. It took an hour to reach the point where I could get my fingers under it, pull from side to side and gently lever it out.
>
> I reached through the gap and found the lock. No deadbolts here. I turned the latch on the first door. The room was large, almost the size of the main room I had been living in, but it was empty except for a rusty old bin of coal sitting abandoned in one corner. I've been thinking about that coal all afternoon.
>
> The second room was much smaller, the size of a large walk-in wardrobe. Shelving lined the walls. On the shelves were skeletons.

That took some getting used to. I slammed the door, went to the toilet and vomited.

For some time I just sat there, breathing heavily, head in my hands. Now that I know what the thing has done, the lines of cricket scores on the wall terrify me.

After that I picked up the old paperback. I wonder how many sets of hands have held it; how many people, now dead, had sat where I was sitting, reading about Ivan Denisovich, not realising they were waiting to die.

I read for a moment: Ivan queueing for gruel that was half sawdust, laying mortar that froze before it set, cleaning the guardhouse while ill. But Ivan also had the occasional win and made friends. Horror in a gulag, but with a slice of humanity and a portion of hope. None of that here.

What did you do, Ivan? What was your crime so that Stalin locked you away in that place?

I heard the car drive up, ran to the end of the corridor and looked out through the bars like a prisoner.

The bruising red of the driver's side door opened. The thing climbed out. It was a protracted process for the Martian, and looked so awkward as to be painful.

It was shaped like a giant oval of metal, but it had to hold itself on one side to make it through the door. One tentacle clasped the door frame above, another clasped a handle bolted into the A-frame near the dash. The other three tentacles – it had five in all, just like the Martian robots Wells mentioned in his history – supported its weight.

It was covered in metal, top to bottom, to the metal claws on the tips of its tentacles. A wide translucent area shimmered in an eye-catching way on one side. I suspected it might be some kind of one-way glass. It moved like a spider with five legs: a disturbing alien motion both ungainly yet co-ordinated and surprisingly fast. A Martian in an exoskeleton.

It reached back into the car and dragged out a grey-haired old man.

The man slowly climbed to his feet.

I called out, 'Run!' and rattled the bars. He turned to look at me. His right foot stepped out.

The seamless surface of the Martian's armour opened and a new tentacle emerged. This one was grey, wet-looking, and very organic. The Martian wrapped it around the man's neck. A fresh protuberance slithered out of the tentacle and pushed down the man's throat. Other protuberances pushed into the side of his neck.

The man sank to his knees and fell sideways to the ground, his grey hair lying on the bitumen.

The grey tentacle pulsed. The old man seemed to shrink against the ground.

After a horrible minute the grey tentacle withdrew, and all the colours of the rainbow shimmered over the thing's surface in what I suspected was pleasure or laughter.

It picked the old man up effortlessly in one tentacle and carried the body to the door.

'I'm not going to eat him!' I shouted.

'Ula, ula, ula.'

26th January

Damned diary, the old man is still alive. Don't know how. He's got no blood left, and the holes in his neck ooze without clotting.

I've given him some water, made a thin gruel from the latest piece of carrion, this time a possum, and gave him that. The poor bugger can't even speak.

How had the Martian survived? It had made a life for itself in the back-blocks of the Blue Mountains, preying on humanity. It was obviously behind some of the stranger legends and missing person stories of the area. It ate well.

It kept itself amused building bad furniture. It was a classic car buff (that Falcon was beautiful). It kept itself hidden. It used a modicum of camouflage, the car, the store mannequin, and that was just strange enough to blend with some of the more esoteric samples of humanity who lived here. It stayed in touch with its inner self by playing tantalising games involving glimpses of freedom followed by swift, fatal retribution.

Inner self? I sound like a new age therapist.

Damned Diary, I've gotta go. Got work to do.

A piece of coal. A 1940s vintage cheese grater. They don't make them like that anymore, but thank God they once did.

Half an hour later I had a small pile of coal dust, less than half a teaspoon, on the kitchen table in front of me. I turned on the gas, lit a splinter of wood, put it in the sink. Then I ducked below the level of the sink and threw half my little supply of coal dust over the edge.

Nothing.

The splinter had gone out.

The second time I made a small fire in the sink before throwing in the rest of the dust.

It wasn't an explosion so much as a loud whooshing like a recording of a car backfire played at one tenth speed. The flame reached the ceiling. The fire in the sink was blown out, the twigs scattered.

That was all the experimenting I could afford. If I did that twice, the Martian would be onto me before I was ready for it.

28th January

Damned Diary, the old man died last night.

I rearranged the bones on one shelf in the storeroom so that there was room, and carried him in.

I didn't even know his name. I mumbled something about not dying alone, and being laid to rest with friends. I can't remember the words. I closed the door on him, reached up through where the sandstone block had been, and threw the lock. At least he wasn't alone.

Then I went to the toilet, sat on the seat and read Ivan Denisovich cover to cover. There is hope and dignity in the book. Ivan Denisovich is not a violent man. Neither am I. But I need to be.

> I was wrong before. Of course it can get inside if it turns sideways and sidles through the door. And once through the corridor there's no part of this place it can't access.

The corridor is the place for the ambush. That's the only place where an explosion might be confined, and where the Martian would be limited in its movements.

Line the ceiling of the corridor with little woollen sacks of coal dust, I'd need a couple of kilos at least, and something, even a piece of string, to open them so the dust would pour out into the air.

I'd need a way of lighting it at that moment, while the dust was in suspension in the air. And a way of not blowing myself up as well. The Martian's homemade kitchen table would help there, and the sandstone blocks of the corridor itself. I'll wet the old woollen blanket from the bed, use the mattress as well, anything to hide behind and under.

It's really starting to smell in here.

Gotta grind more coal dust. The cheese grater is done for, but I'm having luck grinding lumps of coal against the metal hinges of the door to the storeroom. I wonder if I'll ever get the ground-in black dust out of my hands.

30th January

> Damned Diary, I think that's the date. The cricket score of date marks on the wall outside is up to 27. I've lost count myself, been too busy.
>
> Getting hungry now. It *does* expect me to eat the old man.
>
> It being able to get inside answers a number of questions: the bones in the storeroom, the furniture, how I got in here in the first place…
>
> So why doesn't it? We were playing cat and mouse.
>
> I thought of the rows of cricket scores, the bones in the storeroom, my kids. This stops here. Maybe for me, so be it. But hopefully for the Martian too.
>
> Goodnight diary.

I don't know if I'll see Tom and Melissa again. Maybe they'll see their Dad on the TV news and wonder just what the story was about. Six and eight they are, too young to know much about it, old enough to sense the dread driving the narrative. I'd missed four weekends with them so far. Hopefully they will see something, and forgive me.

Will they realise that a menace humanity thought had been dealt with a hundred years earlier was slowly re-emerging? Perhaps humanity would be strong enough this time, and not have to rely on the Earth itself to be its saviour.

I had kilos of coal dust now. Some of it ground down as fine as talcum powder.

Would it work? What was the explosive limit?

Would a gust of wind just blow it all away?

Questions, no answers.

The bruising red of the 1970 Falcon sat in the carpark. I could drive it if I had the keys. Where would a Martian keep car keys? In its pockets?

I had to laugh.

I started tearing up one end of the old blanket.

Dear Diary

Last entry.

I read Ivan Denisovich for the last time. This time I paid a little more attention. Ivan's crime was that he got caught by the Nazis during the war. His own people thought he had been brainwashed and turned into a spy, because that was what *they* did to others.

Ivan Denisovich, prisoner of war, twice over.

I was a prisoner as well, and this was a war. I understood that clearly now, but unlike Ivan I have choices.

Yesterday I pulled the wooden shelf out of the bathroom. That took some doing. I set it on fire with the gas stove, carried it down the corridor and threw it into the car park. Maybe burning its playthings in front of it will make it mad.

It sat at the end of the corridor for half an hour, staring in at me. I sat inside in the over-sized kitchen chair, swinging my legs, staring back out at it.

Real man stuff. Real mature. The kids' mother would have laughed her head off.

Thank heavens it didn't come in, I wasn't ready for it.

The hunger is starting to bite now, and I'm feeling weak.

I've got no choice, I must make something happen while I still can. Not long now.

Goodbye diary.

Beautiful morning, crisp and clear. Perfect day for a perfect, shiny little war.

The ceiling of the sandstone corridor was lined with half a dozen small woollen sacks of coal dust, about 100 grams in each. There were more sacks, torn from the old blanket, high up along each wall.

How much was too much? I'd seen photos of impressive coal dust explosions, but I had no idea how much coal was involved. The bags were joined by threads of wool. Pull the wool, the bags would tip and release their dust into the air the length of the corridor.

Would it come inside for me?

I'll keep throwing burning bits of broken furniture out the door until it *does* come in.

Then I'll throw a sack of coal dust up in the air. Hold the woollen thread, jerk back as the sack reaches the end of the thread. Strike a match. Throw the match around the corner. Dive for the floor.

All while I'm wrapped in half a wet blanket, hiding under a mattress, under a table.

Heh.

Do it all again if I had time.

If I was really, really, lucky, the first one might go off.

I carried a few broken pieces of furniture down the corridor and went back for a burning brand.

The pine caught easily. The corridor slowly filled with smoke.

After a couple of minutes, I grabbed the burning leg of one of its precious chairs from the fire and swung it out into the carpark.

'Ula!' Loud and close, it dropped off the roof in front of the door and stared in at me.

That was quick. I ran back inside, scrabbling, thumping noises filling the corridor behind me.

A sandstone block in the wall next to the storeroom exploded. The heat ray.

I reached for the first bag of dust, and realised. The Martian was inside. There was a fire in the corridor. Bags of coal dust lined the ceiling.

'Sucker!' I shouted, pulled the woollen thread, and dived towards…

Earth engineering versus Martian engineering. Whose machine would reign supreme?

It had left the keys in the ignition, but it took me 10 minutes to crawl that far. The skin was burned off my right arm, the flesh blackened and weeping. Whenever I moved, I gave a little scream of pain.

My back felt worse. And already my arse was sticking to the Falcon's seat. No eyebrows or eyelashes. The hair on the front and the right side of my scalp singed back in little curling fragments that shattered and fell into my eyes. I don't know how I'll ever get out of this car.

The Martian stared back at me across the carpark from where it sat in the rubble. Its tentacles stirred. One was broken off halfway along its length, another had been blown off entirely. The remaining three lifted it a metre or so above the cracked bitumen – a caricature of the Martian war machine in the museum. The heat ray was gone. One eye was out. The other glared at me, shining grey. The carapace of its exoskeleton was dented and torn, a slow curl of green steam dissipating in the atmosphere.

Would the Earth kill it after it had survived all this time?

Could I just drive away?

No.

It began moving towards me, a broken tripod gait on its remaining three legs, coming faster now. Let Isaac Newton decide who wins. I revved the engine, dropped the clutch and the classic Falcon surged ahead.

The mannequin's hair streamed back in the wind.

Even Less Than Zero

Jenny Valentish

THE WAITING ROOM IS PAINTED MUTED PINK. I GUESS IT'S TO COMPLEMENT, yet not upstage, the flesh in the catalogues, scattered around the frosted-glass coffee tables. Doctor Alpert, the man with the scalpel, is on the TV screen opposite me. He's wearing freshly starched scrubs and talking animatedly about being the best version of yourself.

The woman beneath the TV screen is with what looks to be her boyfriend, judging by the 20-year age gap. If there's a girl in this industry who doesn't have daddy issues, I'm yet to meet her. The girl is so slight that her collar bones gather deeply at her sternum, but you could fit the width of your forearm between her solid breasts. Unbidden, I'm hit by an image of her on set, hemmed in by man-flanks. There's a POV camera in her face and liquid pooling in those hollows.

She meets my eyes IRL and I hastily look down. The catalogue in my lap is open to the mouths. More than just filler, I'm looking for an entire re-sculpting. In fact, I think I might recognise the lips I have in mind. They look to me like Saskia French, though it's difficult to say.

My phone vibrates loudly in my purse and I look around guiltily before pulling it out. *Don't forget, bitch x* the message says. I'd told Sonya I'd give her the painkillers from my surgery. They're useless to me. *Yeah bitch x* I type back.

I hope Doctor Alpert is legit. Frank, my agent, sends all his talent here. But then, botched isn't necessarily bad for his business.

'Kali?' the chick on reception calls. The guy next to me has been flicking through a catalogue too, looking at pecs and breathing heavily. Now he turns his head and looks me up and down. I feel myself shrinking away. Mine is not a conventional beauty, but I thought by now we'd embraced the idea that there is more than one way to be beautiful. Not least since the Australasia Treaty.

I rise with dignity and head into the consulting room.

'Kali?' Doctor Alpert says, rising to his feet and holding out a hand. On his large mahogany desk there's a paperweight with what looks to be labia suspended in it. 'Great to meet you, Kali. So, what's the story? Got a new contract?'

'Oh, kinda,' I say. 'You know. There are offers on the table, but–'

He nods once, losing interest.

As he cranes forward I can feel a trail of saliva wending its way out of what will soon be my mouth. I wipe it away delicately and giggle.

'You know,' I say, gesturing at from whence it came. 'It's too 'V'. I'd like it to be more round.'

He holds up a mirror to my face and runs a finger around my central aperture. I try not to meet my eyes.

'Uh, huh,' he says, leaning in so close that I can smell the onion salad he had for lunch. And behind that, something darker.

As soon as my new mouth heals I'm back on the circuit. The first shoot is one of those casting couch interviews that turns into sex with the director, as a precursor for more sex with the director and possibly his buddy whose name you won't catch. I had told Frank I was done with this amateur shit. I can hardly pretend I'm the new kid on the block when I've been working for two years.

My expectations dip even lower when I walk onto the set and it's done up like something out of a *Last Samurai* flick. There are traditional Japanese screens blocking off the rest of the studio and a kimono hanging artfully from – for god's sake – a coathanger. The only thing missing is a sword.

Look, I get it. Tentacle erotica has been a perve thing in Japan since the early 1800s, so of course it was the first genre they thought to revisit when casting my type. I've generally moved beyond the niche fetish stuff, though, so it's disappointing that we're taking a step backwards here.

As directed by the receptionist, I take a seat on the sofa. After a while, a man I recognise to be Colin Smasher walks in.

'Oh hey,' he says. And then, lower, to the clipboard holder in his wake: '*Get it a glass of water, will you?*'

'I go by *they*,' I say.

They exchange looks.

'Okay, sweetie. We do this your way,' he says. And then: 'Are we rolling?'

We are.

'What do you do with yourself, Kali, when you're not milking multiple cocks?'

'I'm in my freshman year, taking Gender, Sexuality and Diversity Studies,' I smile demurely. This is not true, but I've heard that the producers of Headfuck particularly like working with feminists. For the record, I'm actually a Theatre Studies graduate.

'You are, huh?' he says, like it's the sexiest thing ever. We talk a little about what I love doing most. Predictably, he quickly brings it on to blood regurgitation.

Frank says that 'Kali' is quickly becoming an industry verb for platelet play. It's gained me a certain notoriety (Heather and Saffron were already doing it, though not with humans), but it hasn't translated to the dollars that people probably imagine. And, contrary to popular belief, I didn't get where I am because of my specialist skills. I've always prided myself on being on time, professional and pleasant to work with.

'I bet you'd like to 'gurge on this, wouldn't you baby?' he's saying, having unzipped his pants. I murmur my assent. 'Yeah, you like that, huh?' He makes an animal noise and starts rubbing my lower aperture, way too hard to be pleasurable. I make the corresponding noise.

Being third-generation Martian-Australian, I didn't grow up using literal lingo like 'apertures', but I guess I've come to revert – in irony, or maybe in defensiveness – to the clinical language used by my elders when I was just a polyp. My grandparent (you'd call them a nonna) would describe this very scene as: *The homo sapien male docks the corpus of his external intromittent organ into the female's frontal aperture and moves it in a back-and-forth motion at approximately 58bpm.*

I like to recall that sort of neutrality when I'm being treated clinically myself. Increasingly, hearing my nonna's voice in my head brings me some strange comfort.

Don't trust the flesh puppets, my nonna would urge of humans, out of earshot of the others.

A buff naked guy walks in, carrying a samurai sword. As predicted.

'Oh yeah,' I say. But I pull my tentacles in tight.

Afterwards, Sonya meets me outside and hands me a green juice.

'Hi, ho,' she says, as ever.

'Can we just walk for a bit?' I say. My new lips are killing me, particularly after that scene, and I'm in a bit of a funk.

Sonya is, too. As we take a slow stroll down the main drag, which is a conveyor belt of Subways and Taco Bells, she complains about her movies always getting the stepmom hashtag on www.xxxhub.com, despite her only being 23, or thereabouts.

'I get that too,' I tell her, but she's still talking.

'I feel like this whole incest thing has to move on,' she says. 'I mean, Mario's actually my age, right? It's an insult.'

I sigh inwardly at this human privilege. I'll tell you what's an insult. XXXHub refuses to even feature any of my films in its first hundred results. They reserve that for all the vanilla human double-penetration stuff, whitewashing my kind out of the picture. That's despite the fact that 'polyp prolapse' and 'brutal blood games' are among the website's top searches. No, but you won't read that in the stats they make available to the media.

The production companies are scarcely better. Like last week, I turned up to a shoot by a reputable – in inverted commas – production company. They'd built an Australian-themed set as imagined by Los Angeleans: *Mad Max* meets *Crocodile Dundee*. There was a backdrop of twisted tripods painted onto a desert scene, and vines hanging from the lighting rig.

Lani de Rio came on dressed like Bindi Irwin. She looked at me and kind of shuddered, then forced a pinchy little smile. 'This khaki will totally wash out my skin tone,' she confided, like that was the problem. But what's more awkward is that I happened to know from Frank that she'd complained about doing a crossover scene with me. When actually, I'm more at risk of bacterial infection than she is.

The director explained to us there would be a voiceover; something about bringing the public an eyewitness account about the invaders having escaped from the colony. Then he handed Lani a dog leash, and suddenly her uniform was looking more Guantanamo than Australia Zoo.

It was the last straw when Paul McCock walked in. He was wearing a gas mask for some reason. It felt personal. 'Now *that's* a knife,' he said, coming towards me and brandishing a fixed blade.

In our last green-juice-and-stroll session, Sonya had commiserated with me over this.

'Girls like Lani complain that it's Martians driving down their value, when in fact they're just unreliable bitches,' she said. 'They know you have to work 10 times as hard as they do.'

Now she's rummaging in her handbag for her cigarettes, pushing past the tube of arnica I can see bobbing at the top. Sonya's always bruised all over. She puts her battered little hardbody through all kinds of tests in the worst kinds of movies, but it's in the name of personal best, not pornography. At school she was an athlete and she still prides herself on her endurance. She could out-tough any man I've met. She's what my nonna would have called *tenderised.*

I worry about her. I don't like her boyfriend. I haven't liked any of her boyfriends, but this one I've heard referring to my type as *flubbers*, and he puts her down in public, too.

Sonya shows me some dresses on her phone that she's planning to wear on the red carpet at the Adult Industry Awards at the end of the month. I tell her I like the Herve Leger bandage dress best. I don't know what I'm going to wear yet. I can't muster up any enthusiasm for our industry's night of nights this year.

Sonya says she'll catch me later and heads off to her kickboxing class. That girl. Always collecting bruises.

Frank meets me backstage at the adult entertainment expo as arranged. He's wired as usual, and holding up a T-shirt with me as Cthulhu, the Lovecraft creature. So insulting, like we all look the same.

'What the fuck?' I say, but I've got no fight in me today. I'm totally sleep deprived after last night's shoot slogged on into the morning. I follow him out into the conference hall, which is packed with porn fanboys. The smell is of synthetic lube and unwashed gym towels.

There's a girl onstage gyrating to P!nk. She has stripper-tattoos from her jawline right down to her toes; she must have stopped counting them years ago. Sonya is always hassling me to get a tattoo. I've told her, they don't look so good on my skin. It just looks like I've started to spoil.

The girl's song ends and she stalks off, replaced by a Martian with gold bands on their tentacles. They're dancing to Killing Joke's *Love Like Blood*, and when they shimmy around I realise I recognise them. They did a Reddit 'Ask Me Anything' session a few months back, and I liked what they had to say about going down the feature-dancing route as a side hustle to making movies. They explained you had to cut out the middle-man and line only your own pockets. When your kind has been consistently typecast and misrepresented over the decades, that kind of empowerment can't be understated.

Are you really happy? I ask them silently. They keep dancing, but one eye slides towards me. *Happiness is futile,* they reply. *Ask yourself what really matters.*

A new smell permeates my senses. The smell is, overpoweringly, of meat. Then a flash goes off in my eyes and breaks the spell. I recoil irritably from a fan's camera-phone. I hate the up-tentacle angle.

'There she is,' I hear.

I vaguely recognise Madeline Gambutto, the ex-actress and advocate for Women Against Adult Industry Exploitation, powering towards me. She's got a younger woman bobbing by her elbow who she's probably mentoring for an immodest fee.

'I wonder if you got my email via your agent?' she's saying to me.

'Probably not, I'd imagine, given your appearance in *Martians are Assholes*. Did he book that?'

'I guess,' I say.

'I had the misfortune of seeing it. Those scenes are tantamount to abuse,' she says, her eyes going all intense. She's still very busty beneath her suit, a surgical double G. But my nonna would have described her as *gristle femella.*

Madeline catches herself and adopts a cordial tone. 'We're looking for a diverse range of ambassadors for WAAIE. We think you could be just the sort of representative the cause needs.'

'I'm not an adult,' I say, tartly. Strictly speaking I have to reach 53 Earth years before reaching sexual maturity.

Her eyes harden. But you know what? I'm done with being saved. If it's not women telling you you're being exploited, it's women telling you that your type can't co-opt the word "cunt". This one talks about "empowerment", but neither she nor her hanger-on look like me.

'Look, I'm just trying to survive,' I say flatly.

'What about the survival of your culture?' she fires back.

'I've got to sign,' I say, and walk off to my table.

There's quite a queue already, thank god. Back when I was a newbie I only got a few curious stragglers and diehard fetishists. First up is a plump little fangirl with purple hair and 60s glasses. She's wearing my T-shirt from the last expo. The authorised T-shirt.

'You were great in *Back to the Deep* she says, thrusting out an eight by 10 for me to sign. It's me in a lagoon made out of rolls of blue cellophane, which was also great for catching spills. 'Is Ariane Faithful as nice in real life? What's your favourite flavour of Milo?'

I can tell the questions are going to come thick and fast. 'You're cute,' I smile, stretching my new mouth. 'Thank you so much for coming.'

She hands me a packet of crocodile jerky as a parting gift. The gnarly meat rouses something in me, but not too much.

Not enough.

What really matters is vengeance and blood, suggests not-Nonna, and the room starts to swim.

I cling to the table for support.

Next up is a regular I've seen perspiring in queues across the western seaboard. Josh. Fucking Josh.

'I saw you in *Martians are Assholes*,' he says, wiping a palm on his jeans. 'I just want to say they shouldn't treat you like that.'

'Oh, those guys,' I say.

'My heart bleeds for you,' he says urgently.

But I've had that sort of stuff bred out of me.

'I'm clean and willing to do blood play,' he blurts out desperately.

'Try craigslist,' I say, smiling sympathetically. 'It was so nice meeting you again, Josh.'

I'm in the limo with Sonya, on the way to our night of nights. As Downtown Los Angeles skims past our tinted windows, I can smell layer upon layer of Sonya. A tang of musk beneath the Dove deodorant. The smell of her scalp at her hairline. And she's about to get her period.

She's wearing the Herve Leger bandage dress. I've got a Gerber knife in my Kate Spade handbag.

Sonya offers me the rolled-up note to be polite and I shake my head. I have a weird reaction to cocaine. Last time, I started hallucinating that my tentacles were withering in front of my eyes. I look at the vein in Sonya's neck as she leans forward to the tray on her knees and sniffs hard so that the stubby line of white powder disappears up one nostril. She tosses her head back, looks at me and laughs.

I wonder what Sonya would look like with a V for a mouth.

Section 3: The Future

Riding the Snails

Jason Fischer

YARNI FIRST SAW THE SNAILS THROUGH THE AIR-SLATS ON THE SIDE OF the transport. Coughing and eyes watering from the dust, she could make out the immense bulk of the creatures on the horizon, each a looming shadow that blocked out the dawn sun.

Inside the transport it was pure misery. The men and women were packed in on hard bench seats, and they cried out as the vehicle crashed over the last of the alkali flats. Then they eased into the sea-legs swaying of a trip into the desert proper.

Some slept. Others were criminals like her. They did not.

Then the transport slammed to an abrupt stop, and both the sleeping and the fretting were dashed around, many of them bruised and even bloody. Then someone threw the doors open and there was shouting.

'Out. Emerge. Assemble!'

This was Earth Creole, the only acceptable language, a pidgin of dead languages including Chinese, English and Spanish. Certain words had been removed from the lexicon, such as *rebellion*, *revolution*, and *justice*. To help the invaders understand it, every word was peppered with the hissing and booming inflections the invaders favoured, or as much as the human throat could handle.

The people screaming into the transport were wearing the chicken-scratch glyph of the Authority on their breasts. When people were too slow to emerge, the Authority goons laid about with bright silver whips, the tips cracking out with unerring accuracy. Yarni caught a whip across the cheek, and it was pain honed to perfection, her nerves amplifying the slightest brush into a deep wound that wasn't real.

She screamed like the others, and pushed over strangers just to get out onto the desert sands. No friends here, no dignity, just pain and panic.

Yarni blinked against the searing sunrise, and for one moment she saw the rest of the transport, dozens of carriages linked into a road-train, packed with workers for the mines, with farmhands, service staff, mechanics and sex workers.

Then there were the saddest carriages, sealed tightly and marked with that final glyph. The one that translated into *Cattle*.

At the very front of the road-train was a teeming horde of beasts, somewhere between lizards and oxen. At some unseen signal they surged against their harnesses, all tails and skittering feet and sand. In moments the train was swallowed by the dunes and gone.

'Be still! Submit!'

Yarni stood in a line with the other new arrivals, suffering through the measurement of her retinae, the jab of rude needles. A wind kicked up, and she could hear the faint hiss of the loose sand blowing across the red dunes.

'Go! Walk that way!'

The whips cracked, and Yarni did walk that way, and the red sand slowly gave way to the grey, and then they slid and slipped across the mats of lichen, past the patrolling Invaders watching from their war tripods, into a project built on the grandest scale.

By the time Yarni and the others arrived into the camp, the snails had fully retreated into their shells, hiding from the heat of the day. Their shells curled in the same old Fibonacci spiral of their tinier Earth cousins, but there the resemblance ended. The full-grown snails were over 50 metres from toe to crown, and Yarni felt a thrill of vertigo as she looked to the very top of the nearest shell, to the ramshackle structures and rope-ladders fixed into the uncaring beasts.

The top of each snail seemed to hold a village in the sky, and the people tending to the machines and cranes were tiny dots, lice crawling on the backs of these terrifying creatures. While the snail was asleep they worked at a quick speed, winching up supplies and tying everything down. Others were descending with the tents and gear for the camp – snail crews slumbered through the day when the snails did.

A series of valves ran along the outer rim of the shell, and these opened suddenly, venting a dark liquid out onto the sands below. Some of the ground workers danced away from the splashing muck and cursed upwards. They received nothing but mocking jeers from their friends in the sky.

Other people were abseiling down ropes, polishing parts of the shell as they went. Some worked with etching tools, scratching an intricate mural into the shell. Each snail told a different story, and they appeared to be Martian morality tales.

She'd seen these in the cities and the work camps, had learnt the hard way that these were the only approved art-form. The story always went as follows: the evils of the old world, humans at war, killing their planet and their own kind, and then finally their benefactors arriving from another world, freeing them from ignorance and gifting them with enlightenment.

This was more of the same beautiful propaganda, curling around the spiral. Some of the workers clambered across the outer shell, elaborating old carvings on the parts of the shell that had grown, while others worked closer to the centre curl, scratching new scenes into the fresh keratin.

Mars and her glory, retold on the flanks of giants.

Their ships, falling from the heavens. Their tripod war-machines, destroying the earth's defences, razing the cities, subjugating the primitive human race. Then the gifting of technology, the ending of hunger and all want.

The masses, knelt in supplication. The leaders of humanity, hands clutching tentacles, heads bowed in surrender. A great celebration, Earthfolk and Martians celebrating an awesome union.

She stared at the mural, hands clenched into fists, consumed with hatred until she missed an instruction. A silver whip fell across her back, sending her to her knees with a gasp.

'Go there! Work now!' an Authority woman yelled. Yarni ran where she pointed, fearing another lashing. She ran and ran, until she stood in the shadow of the colossal snail, and she did not know where to go.

The workers were raising their day-tents in the shade of the giant, and in minutes a meticulous grid of canvas appeared, without so much as a peg out of place. Yarni hovered around the work, but she could not match the rhythm of the snail crew. Each peg or rope she touched was immediately pulled loose and fixed by those around her.

A hand on the shoulder, and she flinched. An Authority man, but this one was relaxed, his whip still on his belt.

'You go up,' he said, pointing to the top of the snail. 'The boss said.'

Lips suddenly dry, she nodded. If Yarni could not do the work, the only option for her was the next Cattle car, and that was the end of her.

She climbed into one of the last hoists still running, trying not to look down. Half a dozen workers passed her on the way down, and they watched her silently. Was it pity or contempt that she saw in their eyes?

She felt insignificant against the whorls of the shell, and this close the enormous carvings made little sense: scratched out nightmare figures beyond all sense of proportion. Then the hoist shuddered and came to a stop, locking in place to a small type of dock.

Yarni spun with the vertigo of it all. She saw all of the snails, dozens of behemoths asleep, and a city of tents across the plain. The dull green squares of the lichen mats, fighting the red of the desert sands. Surrounding the camp were perhaps a dozen of the Martian's tripod war machines, making a lazy circuit of this grand project.

Trembling and clutching at the safety rail, Yarni walked onto the top of the shell. This snail sported a small village upon its back, with work huts and algae looms, as well as numerous machines and vats that fed into the innards of the snail itself.

Whoever had bred this snail back on Mars had sculpted the shell with pockets and folds across the top, ersatz caves to store supplies, a small temple to the Martian ancestor-gods, and finally a large hollow, the only dwelling on the colossal creature. Yarni walked towards this, head low, heart hammering.

She stood on the threshold of the cave for a long moment, and then a voice synthesiser screeched out, making her jump.

'Enter. Enter now!'

The dawn was approaching at a side-angle, leaving the interior of the cave in a deep gloom. Yarni stepped inside, and the bands of the shell beneath her lit up with each footstep, leaving a luminescent print that glowed for a long moment.

The cave was decorated in the austere Martian fashion, but fashioned for a human servant. A bed, a table and chair, and a hygiene cocoon in the corner. The walls were daubed with a grand Martian mural, etched out on the red planet hundreds of years ago. A story of their old civil war, of heroics and villainy that made little sense in the mandated retelling.

The cave's owner had carved a new addition into the wall above the bed. Three glyphs in the conqueror's language. The Three-Fold Law was all the justice that a human needed to know:

One Government

One Language

One Law

She heard a rustle from the far end of the cave, and an algae lamp fizzed into life, bathing the complex in a green glow. A figure came towards her, lamp raised, and Yarni took to her knee, head bowed.

'Enough of that,' the synthesiser crackled. Yarni looked up to see a man supported by a clattering spider-frame, his muscles wasted away from lack of use. He had the gills implanted already. His face was pale behind a fishbowl glass helmet. A network of clear tubes were inserted into the hollows between his ribs, pumping a pale blue goop into his innards.

What once was a human was now an Aspirant. When this favoured soul finished his process, there would be little left to show what he'd once been.

'You were Authority?'

'Once,' Yarni admitted. 'Hall of Linguistics.'

'Impressive. Why have you fallen?'

'I broke a culture law.'

'No small thing,' the Aspirant warbled through his synthesiser. 'How so?'

'Illegal poetry reading,' Yarni said. 'Blake and Dickenson in English.'

He reached out a frail hand, and a mechanical claw shot forward, tapping on the wall glyph. *One Language.*

'Foolish to worship a dead culture. Our masters have superior narratives. Was it worth it?'

Her heart said yes, but she shook her head for no.

'I saw you on the consignment. Criminal. I have claimed you for this snail. Her name is Derghymmid, a grand old girl. I am her Captain, Suharto.'

He gestured her towards the table, where a meal had been set out for her. Suharto was already beyond such mundane requirements, but Yarni fell onto the plate, shovelling down plankton paste and rice cakes into her two-days-empty stomach. Fresh water, and she drank down so much that her stomach started to hurt.

'Obey, and you will find kindness. Perhaps a return to the Authority, if you please us.'

Yarni could not believe her ears. She pushed aside her empty plate and looked up at her benefactor, sought out his eyes that no longer blinked in the depths of his casing.

'Come. Now, time to prove your worth.'

She followed the Aspirant across his home, her two footsteps out of rhythm with the tappity-tap-tap of the spider frame. She drew up short, skin crawling, frozen in place with fear.

Rising from a low pallet was a horror, an invader, one of the masters. A bulbous head supported by a bed of tentacles, all wrapped in a flexible suit of clear casing like the Aspirant wore. Pipes and liquids and respirators, keeping the Martian alive in a world that was deadly to its whole awful race. It peered at Yarni with eyes of pure night, inspecting her for a dreadful moment.

She had seen a few of the Martians in the city, in parades or when they addressed her department, but never so close. She'd never known a world without the masters, but no familiarity could outweigh their sheer alien-ness, and her own human urge to either crush this thing or flee from it.

'This is my friend, Quophanis,' Suharto said. 'A high official. Quophanis has caught the black spots.'

She could see the marks on the Martian's tentacles, and big clusters of them around its forehead. The infection meant a slow death, and had doomed several waves of the initial invaders.

'They cannot suicide,' Suharto said. 'It is taboo. I cannot kill my friend, though it suffers. The Authority would thank me for my kindness, but by custom I could no longer be Aspirant.'

He waved at his pipes, his mechanical aids, everything that would one day make him a floating brain with tentacles. Reaching into a storage cube, Suharto fetched out an object, placing it in Yarni's hands.

A gun, heavy and cold.

'They will end me,' she protested. 'I will be Cattle.'

'Contradiction. If you perform this mercy, you will be restored to the Authority. You may have your own snail.'

She held the gun, considered the sick alien before her, and then she immediately placed the gun on the floor, abasing herself.

'Forgive me for holding a weapon in your presence, Master,' she said to the Martian. 'Violence upon a Master is wrong, no matter the intent.'

'THAT IS CORRECT,' the Martian boomed out through its own synthesiser. It rose up upon all its tentacles, and was no longer faking an illness. It skittered towards her, the black spots fading back into its skin. It raised other patterns across its face and limbs, its subcutaneous ink sacs rising up to form new glyphs. The same three signs marked across the cities and townships, the Three-Fold Law.

'THIS ONE MAY EARN PENANCE,' the Martian said, scooping up the abandoned weapon. It handed it back to Suharto, who placed it reverently back into the storage cube.

'A relic, from the old days of violence and resistance,' Suharto said. 'It no longer works, save to test those who we fear are troubled.'

'Those who fail?'

'They become Cattle, on the spot.'

Yarni looked at the sharp beak of the Martian, the sinuous twist of its tentacles, and she shook openly with fear. The Martian chittered in delight.

They started her out on the vats, stirring up muck from dusk until dawn. It was exhausting work, and she felt the nerve-whips more than once when she was too slow to drain nutrients down into the snail, or when her algae slurry refused to take. They had a chemist on the snail, an obnoxious little Authority woman named Gee-Gee, and she screeched into ears, slapped faces, and pulled out hair by the fistful.

It was all Yarni could do not to push Gee-Gee into an emptying vat, sending her down into the guts of mighty Derghymmid. But day after day, she took the beatings and the abuse, and learnt the art of crafting slurry, the delicate balance between product and waste.

'You go to the looms now,' Gee-Gee told Yarni one day. 'Fail, and you will stir my vats until you take the jump.'

Gee-Gee indicated the open space beyond Derghymmid's shell, the faint curve that was a dizzying height from the ground. Yarni never went close to the edge, and clutched the ropes white-knuckled whenever she caught the hoist.

It wasn't even a week until she saw the first jumper, another criminal from her transport. The man was white-eyed, twitching from a thousand whip-strokes. They'd starved him for his work errors, and the man barely slept through the day for worry of what dusk might bring.

Bent over the algae looms, Yarni felt the elbow of her knowing neighbour, a weaver who pointed out the moment when the man dropped his stirring ladle into the vat, took his first step, a free and casual walk that turned into two, three steps, and then he was running, fighting off the cracking silver whips that licked into him as he ran through the laughing Authority goons.

No-one stopped the man as he simply launched himself from the top of the snail's shell at a flat-out sprint. Yarni saw his arms pin-wheel for that split second, and then he was gone.

The weaver held up one finger, then a second, then a third, and then she clapped her hands together, face lighting up in a grin. Yarni learnt that this was a great sport to veterans of the snail. They kept a book on the new arrivals, gambling food and drugs on who would next jump.

'I had a bet on you,' another weaver said to Yarni.

'I am not sorry,' Yarni said.

'Keep your bet going,' the first weaver said. 'She might still jump.'

Yarni learnt to weave the algae lattice, and her fingers proved nimble, even when soaked and raw by night's end. The weaver who'd mocked her gave her to the lichen crew, and she spent many hours teasing up the little buds and fronds through the substrate, squirting on the nutrients to speed up growth.

'Fruticose. Foliose. Crustose. Squamulose. Leprose,' she whispered to herself as she wove together that sodden mass. There were other words to describe the components of lichen, approved words, but they never sat right on her tongue, felt sharp and Martian as she hacked them out. Below her, the snail powered through the night, churning up the desert, and hers was the company of the stars and of her long-dead Latin.

Yarni never exactly loved the snailing life, but she worked hard and kept out of trouble, and this saw her shared out across the bulk of Derghymmid, given jobs with the hoist crews, grilling up algae cakes with the cooks, and scrubbing the muck from the snail's valves, even while others carefully scratched away at the enormous mosaic, etching out Martians in a weird flat Egyptian style, all profiles and gesturing tentacles.

That work she was not invited to do.

She spent weeks working with the lattice planters, hanging from hooks dug into Derghymmid's tail, rolling out the fresh lichen into the churned up desert sand, setting it out in the slime and the discarded casings from the snail's passage.

In a year or two they would pass back this way, the snail devouring a lichen forest now grown three feet in height. With every crossing of the great desert, these enormous ploughshares were slowly turning it into a land fertile for Martian crops.

'Fifty years? A hundred? We'll be long dead,' one of the planters scoffed when she asked how long the project would take. The finality of his words sank in.

She was going to live her entire life and die on the back of a snail.

From the ground she admired the growing artwork on Derghymmid's shell. The artists spent a few hours of the off-shift marking out new figures to carve, while others worked on filling in detail.

The scale was immense, like the Nazca carvings. Martians and their war-machines, and the beginnings of script detailing a story, with the approved markings for dialogue and context. What humans featured in the story so far were as a subclass, enemies, comedy relief. As always, the Martians were the heroes. From what she knew of their narratives, the two main characters were Tollyp and Daeserat, infamous warrior friends from the Martian civil war, who set out on a quest to destroy a great enemy.

When the artists finally gave up on their work and rappelled down to the camp, Yarni tried to strike up a conversation, to ask about their great work. The artists shared a knowing look and walked past her, not even saying a word.

Yarni increased her efforts, hoping to win favour and freedom from her servitude. Suharto had established a type of midshipman caste in his crew, the Learners, and the clattering old Aspirant invited her into this august circle, an exhausted brood that laboured by night and studied half the day.

Soon Yarni was reading books by daylight while her lucky tent-mates snored away. Even with years of experience she still fought to follow the Martian script, which never quite married up with Earth Creole. It was an ambiguous language, weighted towards the needs of the invaders, and no-one was ever truly fluent in it. It was the most binding of all the Martian's chains, the one they'd wrapped around the human tongue.

Yarni remembered her time in the Exile's University. A dissatisfied Authority from her Department had brought her into that hidden world, where each book was worth more than a life; where conjugations and clauses were taught in a terrified whisper.

She'd gobbled up every forbidden word. English, Latin,

Indonesian, Japanese, it was all delicious. Over time, the University relaxed. They got stupid.

She still remembered the night of the last poetry reading, and perhaps she always would. She remembered resting her head upon a lover's shoulder, as her friends smiled and took it in turns to read from Blake's *Songs of Innocence and Experience.* Then that awful moment of discovery, when the doors flew open, and everything was screaming and silver whips and a trial that lasted perhaps 30 seconds in all.

Now, she read a book about the damn snail, and memorised every painful word.

She was reading about how to tweak the acid levels in snail mucous when she heard the clatter of the spider-frame, and no less than Suharto whipped open the flaps of the tent, waking Yarni's sleeping tent-mates.

'On your feet,' he barked. 'Attend me.'

Emerging into the bright desert sun, Yarni saw Derghymmid's entire crew assembled, kept well clear of the comforting shadow of the snail. Beyond that, the entire crew of young gastropod Coshitellak, and even those who rode on the brood-mares Urchooquash and Jahbulax. All of these workers were arranged in a grid, kept in place with the licking of silver whips as they fussed and grizzled.

Then, a commotion. A handful of workers were frog-marched forward by the Authority and cast down to the red sand, then a dozen hulking brutes in Authority riot-gear fell upon them, hammering the terrified group with fists, boots, and the dance of endless whips.

Someone gave a warbling blat on a claxon, and the goons instantly stopped the beating, standing around the bloody scene with straight spines and calm faces.

Quophanis strode through the crews, spider-legs scrabbling through the sand as he stood over the beaten workers. 'DESERTION!' he addressed all of the crews in creole, his synthesiser set to maximum volume.

'THIS HOIST CREW OF COSHITELLAK WISHED TO LEAVE,' Quophanis said, gesturing with a tentacle towards the flat horizon. 'PLANS WERE MADE.'

The Martian hovered over the broken escapees, passing its tentacles across their faces, tasting delicately of their spilled blood. It drew back with a delighted sigh.

'A LOYAL WORKER ALERTED US TO THIS CRIME,' Quophanis said. 'TIME NOW FOR OUR JUDGEMENT.'

The Martian raised the condemned to their feet, hoisting them up with tentacles and mechanical arms, and gently placed them in a neat row, as if arranging toys or dolls.

'OUR JUDGEMENT. YOU MAY LEAVE.'

It gestured to the horizon, emphasised this again when the condemned paused. Unable to believe their luck, they trotted away, churning up plumes of red sand with each footstep. One man was so badly beaten that he could not stand up unaided, and two of his fellows helped to carry him, struggling to escape this bizarre Martian who freed his slaves.

Yarni could not believe what she was seeing, but all around her the slaves watched this judgement stoically. There was no outcry over this strange clemency. Nothing but the whisk of the red sand, the slow shifting creak of the sleeping snails, and silence from every mouth.

For many minutes, the condemned continued their escape into the depths of the desert, with no supplies. Certain death, but a free death. Perhaps they would turn cannibal on the weaker ones, and one or two of the escapees would make it out of the desert and back into kinder lands.

A tapping on her shoulder, and Yarni saw the extended claw of Suharto's spider-frame. He pushed through his workers, settling down next to her.

'Mark this lesson well, my poet,' he said.

She was confused, and nearly said as much, when an entire sand dune seemed to stand up, shaking off sheets of red sand. It was a Martian war-machine, tripod legs flexing and lifting it clear from its hiding place.

Another, and another, and then the three war-machines took off after the escapees, honking and chittering with excitement. The people ran, darting in all directions, abandoning their wounded friend, while the war-machines danced around them, nipping at their feet with heat-rays, teasing the humans for many long minutes.

At a signal from Quophanis, the toying stopped. One war-machine sent heat-rays into the group, burning humans into ash. The second one tore its prey apart with its great metal claws. The third machine dumped black smoke onto those who remained, who huddled together and wailed as death fell around them.

Yarni excelled at her studies, and soon she was allowed onto Derghymmid's head, guiding the great snail on his path. Slight pressure on this eye-stalk would send him left by five degrees. A hook driven into this pressure point would speed up the snail. One driven into the space precisely between its eyestalks would bring the beast to a complete stop.

'When I am completed, I will visit the breeding caves on Mars,' Suharto confided in her. 'A whole brace of snails, bringing life back to the blasted places. You, continue to please me, and I shall give you your own snail. You may be the first to till the Fanshpaddoy into a green place.'

The Simpson Desert, she wanted to say, but it was an old name, and not a fight worth having with an Aspirant. She'd shared a crumbling Atlas with a friend who died in the raid, and felt the magic of gazing upon a long dead world. This was Mosskari now, but once people had called this land Australia. The snails were criss-crossing the Yugripaddoy and turning it into farmland, but once this red wasteland had been known as the Strzelecki Desert.

At the 3am meal, Yarni sat with the other Learners in Suharto's cave. Some of her fellow students were hooked up to surgical tubing, siphoning off their blood and feeding a red dribble into the bulbous head of Quophanis. The Martian was ecstatic, flush with a red glow, and in gratitude it displayed many symbols on its subcutaneous ink-sacs, mostly Martian philosophy and advanced snail techniques. The Learned madly took notes.

Suharto was probably a few years from needing blood transfusions to sustain himself, but he watched the proceedings with a keen, almost lustful eye.

'You do not donate, Yarni the poet?' he said.

'We have the Cattle for that.'

'If all gave the gift, then no need for Cattle.'

Over time, the edge of Yarni's fear had subsided around the Martian. She was cautious now, and kept her distance.

'Why does Master Quophanis travel with the snails?' she asked. 'The others stay on Mars. Or in the cities.'

'He is an observer.'

'A master wants to watch us plough a desert?'

'Oh no,' Suharto chuckled wetly, the sound disturbing through his synthesiser. 'He is interested in the shell etchings.'

'Does he wish to see his propaganda done correctly?' Yarni said, a note of bitterness falling from her mouth.

Sudharto scowled behind his clear casing. 'Watch your tone. And no, Mars did not command the etchings.'

'They – the artists – *want* to do that?'

'Yes. It puzzles the masters on Mars. So they have sent Quophanis to investigate. Now, you have your answer.'

She became obsessed with the volunteer artists. Most of the workers snatched at every hour of sleep, yet these folks laboured into noon most days, working feverishly to complete the mural. Sometimes Yarni noticed Quophanis leaning over the deck railings above, monitoring the work, making recordings of the art with the Martian instruments that were half alive.

Now that she was Learned, the rank-and-file workers did not trust her, and her questions were rebuffed, so when she saw a large group leaving the tents before dusk, she did not ask questions, simply pulled on a sand-cloak to follow them.

The group was heading towards Coshitellak, the handsome young snail with a jade-green shell. His etchings had recently been completed, black shapes against the green, and the group arranged themselves at a distance, seating themselves on the sunlit side of the giant.

'Attend!' one of the workers cried out, a man with wild eyes and a matted black beard. He had a repaired synthesiser, which crackled and spat as he addressed the crowd.

'The tragedy of noble Wrokalorn! Hero of the Martian Civil War! Wrokalorn seeks vengeance upon the Gnasher of Barsoom, the beast of 10,000 teeth. See how our hero defies the ancestor-gods, and gathers a force to hunt down the Gnasher. Wrokalorn does not turn from the hunt, and shows scorn for logic and planning. All of Wrokalorn's comrades are doomed. Wrokalorn and the Gnasher slay each other. Revenge is folly!'

Now that they had delivered a story synopsis in the Martian style, the bearded man was joined by several actors from the crowd, who played out the roles of Wrokalorn and its companions, and even the Gnasher.

From her Authority days, Yarni had seen many Martian narratives, but this was something entirely new. A story featuring Martian protagonists, told in the Martian style, but the story itself was a human invention.

She looked closely at the figures, read over their dialogue and context tags. The story was incredibly complex, even when married to the plodding and unsubtle Martian style.

Quophanis and Suharto were in attendance, as were the masters of five other snails, but they made no move to stop the performance. Save for the folly of Wrokalorn, a historical figure who fell into disgrace, it praised the Martian characters, and exemplified their morals.

When the others left for their work shifts, she sat still for a long time, pondering the story on Coshitellak's shell. The man with the tangled beard sat next to her in the sand.

'So, the Learned one comes to learn,' the man finally said. 'We work to honour the morality of our masters.'

'You're such a liar,' Yarni scoffed.

'How so?' the man said, watching her carefully.

'That's *Moby Dick*.'

Suharto and Quophanis told her such soothing lies, but Yarni knew she was going to spend her life as a snailer. Many hard years awaited her, carving up wastelands and bringing them to life, one shuddering mile at a time. But now, she climbed down in a harness each dawn, scratching into Derghymmid's shell with hammer and chisel. She filled in the outlines of the carved Martians with solid infill, sending slivers of golden snail shell tumbling to the sands below.

When finished, this snail was going to tell the epic of Gilgamesh, hidden underneath the Martian trappings. Another crew was working on Jahbulax, rewriting the book of Genesis, a very tricky secret to hide. Those on Urchooquash had just finished their great work, the tale of the Monkey King.

Quophanis had left with great pomp last month, and the Martian heaped praise upon the volunteer artists, who glorified their captors in this pleasing manner. The Martian took the bearded man with him, and promised to allow him to spread the art form further, into the cities and even to Mars itself.

The snails were expected to live for many years before the toxic Earth environment killed them, and even then a snail's shell was considered sacred by the Martians, to be cleaned and stored in great open graveyards.

In her later years, Yarni became a high priestess of the Earthling's Martian cult, and was permitted to visit the snail cemeteries with those of her order. Her favourite graveyard was the site in the centre of Yugripaddoy, the Strzelecki Desert now blooming with crops and life. She took thousands of children through the holy site, and made them visit each snail's shell.

'Look beyond the Martians,' she whispered in a child's ear. 'It all makes sense when you imagine they are gone.'

She taught the children about Chaucer, the Bronte sisters, Don Quixote and Sun Tzu; and Stephen King, Spider-Man, the Simpsons – every story that ever mattered to a keen-eared listener, every character that ever thrilled a heart.

The Martians had burnt down all the libraries, only to assemble every written work on a medium that would outlast the Pyramids. These secret libraries were all over the world now, even back on the invaders' home planet. The Martians were revering the sum total of human culture in their holy places, and to Yarni that was the only victory that could ever matter.

The Sixth Falling-Star

Kaaron Warren

JENA KNEW BEFORE SHE ENTERED THE HOUSE SHE SHOULDN'T TAKE THE body; it was just a question of how she'd tell the family. That particular smell of decay was the indicator; her first mate said: 'No fucking way,' holding his nose and gagging as if they didn't smell this smell half of their days.

'You stay here then,' she said.

The old man opened the massive oak door eventually. Damp rose a metre from the ground in the dark concrete of the house and she wondered how much longer he'd be able to stay here. It would be hard for him to get away; the place was full of people who relied on him. They shook hands.

'Ah, our intrepid barge captain,' he said. 'Our pirate, our wild woman, our wonderful mistress of the dead.' He bowed, and Jena laughed. How he maintained his sense of humour she didn't know, but she hoped she too could avoid jadedness at that age. 'Will you come in, you and your crew? We have a plethora of plums, a very good season, so there's plum wine if you like it.' He winked at her because he knew she liked wine and he had seen her dance for a room full of people under the influence.

She wrinkled her nose. 'I'm not sure my crew would like that. In and out, that's the way with them. You're looking well,' she said, although he looked awful.

'Better than my friend over here.' He gestured towards the body, having the grace to duck his head, hunch his shoulders. They both knew he hadn't done the job, made sure this person had taken the dosages needed before he died. She relented, nevertheless.

'Go on, give us a look,' she said.

The body had a blue tinge, not a red one, and she could smell the decay powerfully here. She felt a small satisfaction in knowing her job as well as she did, but her annoyance in him was increased. She'd taken dozens of bodies from him over the years; he knew perfectly well she'd dump this one.

'He was greatly loved,' the old man said. He winked at her again. 'And yet what does it matter, once the soul is departed? What does it matter what happens to these mortal remains?'

He wanted her to take the body anyway. If he paid well enough perhaps she would. She appreciated that he didn't try to blackmail her into it, to use past actions against her. Instead, he filled a box with jars of plum wine, and handed her a bag of the current currency.

Jena waited for the rest of the story. They always liked to tell a story, give some background, make her care. The old man just nodded though, and she wondered why. They were paid to take bodies; who's to say what they did with them? So long as they dumped it before too long, they'd barely be affected. Sure, it'd take up space needed for more viable bodies, but at the moment they were far from capacity. Who would be hurt by this one extra, which they'd dump as soon as they reached the deep part of the canal?

'Next time just do the right thing,' Jena said, trying to be stern. But the jar of plum wine she'd already swallowed had gone straight to her head.

'We will,' he said.

She should have asked him why they hadn't done it. She should have examined the body there and then, and asked more questions.

Never mind. All that on the next journey.

She and the old man wrapped the body in a red sheet and Jena called for the second mate to help her carry it out. They were less squeamish than her first mate, who had lived a very sheltered life. In all honesty he brought very little to their crew and she would consider ways to leave him behind.

Jena called up to the Cloud, 'One body, blue-tinged.'

'Ugh,' the second mate said, dropping her end of the body. 'The head's all soft. Feels like a pillow.'

Jena turned the body over roughly and saw that the back of the skull was caved in. She shook her head. 'They've killed him. Someone's killed him.' She called up to the cloud. 'One body, skull caved in.' That way it was recorded and wouldn't come back on them.

They laid the body down in the hold.

'Come on,' the first mate said. 'I'm feeling frisky.'

That night he seemed colder than usual. His fingers were always cold, something she liked about him, but now his whole body seemed chilled to the bone. 'Are you sick or something?' she said.

He shook his head quickly; no one liked to be sick. He bent forward and kissed her gently on the lips, and he stroked her with his long cold fingers, inside and out, until she felt as if her bones melted. The soft feel of his stomach made her think of the dead man's head, though, and she curled over into herself, focussing on the longsong to take her mind off it. The sound of a rat chewing in the corner, probably a crust it had stolen from the deck, got on her nerves and she threw a shoe at it.

'Settle down,' the first mate said, and she decided then and there she needed a new lover. The sheets were damper than usual; she'd been lazy in hanging them out. Still, exhausted, she slept.

They sailed along for the next half day, the barge rocking softly along the canal. The red-misted sky darkened mid-afternoon and Jena told the driver to pull into the next sheltered corner he saw. There was a storm on the way and they didn't want to be in the open water when that struck.

The first mate was agitated, too full of energy to stay aboard, so he ran ahead, back and forth. He pointed out interesting things he found. A bricked over burial mound ('There's 290 of them in there,' he said. 'Not named. Do not enter, it says.') and the ground around it darkened, muddy, poisoned from the chemical war 300 years earlier.

It was sites like this one that made Jena feel invincible, as if her family had survived something remarkable. They'd lived through the first five Martian landings, and this war; perhaps they could survive anything.

A bike rider, passing them at speed along the bike track, called out, 'You'll find a good spot up ahead. Village of Barndioota.'

The first mate ran ahead, calling out, 'Don't worry, I'll sort it,' as if it needed sorting by him.

They pulled into an inlet, where three locals waited to help them tie up and disembark. Usually these people were not particularly friendly but today they were lively and bright, waving bottles of dark liquid, calling out, 'Join us! Join us!'

'This looks alright,' the second mate said, and she jumped on shore, her hand already out for a bottle.

They spent three hours ashore in the pub while the storm rolled over outside. In the end it wasn't as bad as expected, although the lightning filled the room with brightness every few minutes and the clash of thunder shook the glasses that weren't being held. As evening fell, Jena began to gather her people. The longsong played as they ate and drank. The villagers, most of whom had never been more than 100km from home, wanted to hear stories of distant places, of travel, of other people.

They didn't ask about what lay at journey's end.

The first mate was drunk in the corner, curled up in a ball, covered in sawdust. Jena decided she'd leave him there. She spoke in an aside to the second mate, 'Pack his things. We're leaving him ashore,' and the girl gave her a look, excited and pleased all in one. The first mate was popular with no one.

'Many thanks for your hospitality,' she told the townspeople as they departed. 'We'll owe you, if ever you need something taken away. No charge.' She'd taken only one body from them, a long while hence, and even then they said it wasn't one of theirs.

'I did have a favour to ask,' one of the men said. He showed her a young girl of about 25, squatting in the dirt. Jena hadn't noticed her before. She swayed forward and back, toe to heel, heel to toe. 'Margrit's not happy on solid ground. Do you have room in the crew for one more?'

'Does she have any skills?'

'She's got a green thumb. Can grow herbs no matter what the soil or how much sun. She's pleasant enough when she's happy. She's happy when she's playing music.'

'She just wants to be on the water,' a woman said.

'Why has no one else taken her?'

'We've not asked anyone 'til now. Your crew always seems to be the friendliest, the steadiest. We've been waiting for you.'

'I'll do you a swap,' Jena said, pointing at the first mate. 'I'm not going to lie to you; Jason's not much of a catch. But he'll be happier onshore and he can cook. He has a strong back. He'll be able to help out in one way or another.'

They shook hands, sealing the deal, and Jena led Margrit out. 'Does she have any things?' Jena asked, and the man handed her a hessian bag, cram packed and heavy.

Jena called up to the Cloud, 'On board, Margrit. On shore, Jason.'

They set off. A dozen or more stops and they would be there. Six more sun rises, Jena thought. On the barges they ignored Longplayer Time because it would give them mornings that were nights, nights that were mornings.

Once it stopped, perhaps, the time zones would be reconsidered.

Despite herself, she missed the first mate's running commentary of what he found on the side of the road. She thought how angry he'd be to be left behind and kept looking back to see if he was chasing after. They'd try to avoid stopping there on the way back and hope that he'd moved on the next time they did have to stop. She chewed on red ferns, feeling the pleasant numbness wash over her, letting the sound of the water, the sway of the overhanging trees, the hum of the longsong lull her into rest.

They pulled into a small offshoot road and sent the barge into sleep mode once Jena felt they were secure. They were supposed to meet a client here but weren't sure they'd show up; they had the kind of skittish voice she expected from young kids being forced to do chores. They pushed through long red tendrils, thicker here than back up the canal, using long sticks.

'Just use your hands,' Jena called out, but the crew ignored her.

Their fears were possibly well founded but the extra time they took to do anything was infuriating.

Margrit played a tune using her mouth and a spoon, which should have been awful but was actually entertaining. For all her irritating ways (circling the barge whenever she could, humming, making these tunes in all circumstances) she did bring a sense of calm to the crew, and her knowledge of the longsong was unmatched. She talked a lot about the world ending when the longsong did, at the end of the millennium by usual counting.

The longsong slowed, playing over the loudspeakers a long drawn out note that sounded like a mournful cry. Jena swore the song was much slower than it was when she was a child, but they say that is an illusion; one many experience, for sure. As time speeds up the music slows.

A young man, not more than 30, came out with a naked body, covered in red threads. Many of them looked like this but she was particularly lovely. He wept as the crew took the body from him. Most people had learned to accept death, not to grieve. Impossible, others said. By the nature of love and friendship, of community, we miss people when they are no longer around.

'She was an artist,' the young man said.

One thing Jena learned early on is that everyone loved to tell their story. They may not know they want to, but work hard enough and out that story comes.

And while they're talking their mind is in the way back, not in the right now, and she could take whatever she wanted.

Mostly she didn't want anything except their name on her list of the dead to be. But some of them had stuff they didn't need, and the barge could do very well with. While the young man wept and talked of lost talent, Jena sent the second mate into his small house to see if there was anything worthwhile. The second mate came out nodding, with some fresh fruit. The bereaved wouldn't notice; why let it go to rot?

The young man paid the fee. Jena always haggled over the price, maintaining the illusion that her family weren't wealthy. They spent it if they travelled far from home where no one knew them. The bereaved man went for a walk while they transferred the body. She was lighter than Jena thought she'd be, with her skin still soft. Her blood still being remembered.

Over the loudspeaker a voice repeated more of what Margrit had said, about the end of the longsong heralding the end of the world.

A contingent from the next town walked out to meet them, travelling along the canal path.

'Ahoy!' one of them called. 'Are you stopping by us?'

'Do you need me to stop by you?' Jena asked.

At that, they were silent.

'Is everything alright? Is the person prepared?'

'It was sudden. We had no time.'

'What sort of death?'

'A drowning. We found him face down in the canal.'

'Did you get him into salt?'

The spokesperson shook his head.

'Run ahead and tell them do it now. Do you have plenty of salt?'

He shook his head again.

'Here,' she said, reaching over to give them a large cloth sack. The salt stocks would never be depleted, it was assumed, with so much of it revealed when the water pulled back. Thank goodness the people back then had the foresight to collect and store it. Everything was underwater now, only these villages they stopped at, nestled on what once were hills, had dry homes now.

They reached the village a few hours later.

'He drowned, you say?'

'He did. He didn't want the same death as the rest of us, we think.'

'He did it on purpose?'

'We think. There is no bruising, and he was holding onto a rope anchored to the canal's floor.'

Suicide was almost unheard of, so much so that Jena found this hard to believe.

'You're supposed to all take the treatment. You need to do it as a matter of habit. The chemical is healthy. No side effects. You should all start doing it. We can't take him. We can't dispose of an unprepared body.'

'He is in salt, though.'

She inspected the body and could see that the boy had swallowed a lot of canal water before dying. His skin was pinkish, his tongue swollen, red-veined.

'We'll take him.'

The man fell to his knees and wrapped his arms around her legs. 'Thank you, thank you.' He was strong; she could feel his arm muscles. And his hair was thick and dark red. She ran her fingers through it.

The longsong chimed and rang and he lifted his head. 'You smell good,' he said. 'Salty and sweet all in one.'

They chewed red ferns and Jena told her crew to take some time, which they happily did, and she and this man spent a good hour together.

The next pick up was an old man who had been dying on the last three or four trips. He'd been given his treatment. He was pissed off, angry, couldn't fuck anymore. You don't get to that age hating fucking, do you? Everybody knew the treatment could cause impotence and lack of motivation. That was a good thing at times.

The last time through, his urine was red. When urine was red and the skin veined, you are ready. Red tears. You know it is working then. He cried as they left last time. Gave them gifts, begged them to take him.

'Next time,' Jena had said, and here they were. He was perfectly prepared and they laid him down with the other bodies.

At the next stop, a dozen or more adults were crying and the mother, a girl of 14 or so, was bundled up like a baby as if they could coddle the grief out of her. The baby body was covered with red fibres that appeared to grow out of its skin.

Jena took a thick blanket and directed the people to wrap the baby. She wasn't going to touch it. There was blood pooled on the ground and she could see crystals in it. She wasn't sure how that would affect things, so called up: 'One infant. Crystals in blood.'

Their last stop was heralded for a week away. They called this stretch the doldrums, because it was long, slow, uneventful.

Jena sat on the step, looking down at those she'd collected so far. observing them, ensuring they were all well covered. Their ghosts wouldn't come to her until the last stretch; it was always the way. She never told the others what she heard; none of them believed in anything beyond this long life.

There were 15 in the hold. She'd periodically come back and check them: some of the crew wanted to have sex with any that were good looking and still warm. She didn't abide by that, not for the memory of their charges, nor for the health of the crew members.

In deeper water, they dumped the murdered body. Such a thing would have them turned away, for sure. The eels would get to work and the skeleton would sink to the canal bed to rest with all the other bones.

They travelled on towards end point. This last stretch was the longest. They passed fields of old 'cars', left rusting for hundreds of years. They made good storage units for non-perishable goods that could deal with weather. Sometimes they came across one in the water and those would have to be avoided. Usually it was gone by the next trip.

Everywhere was lush, overgrown, jungle-like in parts. Red weed grew everywhere. Cactus-like branches. Carmine fringe.

Ghosts clamoured to take the seat beside her. She had no control over them. The artist woman's ghost said, 'Beech trees are burning.' It was nothing but a memory.

'Is that it, now? We're full?' Margrit said. As she neared Jena, the ghosts disappeared one by one. They vanished if anyone came near. Only Jena could see them. She did wonder if they were real but they were far too interesting to be her imagination.

She and Margrit stood together, the longsong playing gently, the world passing by. Old barges bumped along the side of the canal, covered with red weeds and ferns. Constant lapping of the water. Uneven edges to the canal and trees and bushes and grass over the edge. Bikes rode past, much faster. It wasn't a quick journey but there aren't any real roads, no way for road transport to get through. The reflection on the water; sky, clouds, trees. The water red tinged as the sky was. Other barges passed slowly. A wave as they went by. Each of them had their own business, their own thing to do, their own destination.

'So much water,' Margrit said.

'You've seen water,' Jena said.

'It's different to see it like this. It's so empty, isn't it? You could imagine we were the only ones left alive.'

They stood in silence, the slap of the water, the calls of the birds the only sounds. 'So empty,' the girl said.

'This bit is,' Jena said.

The second mate joined them. Margrit played him a tune, a beautiful thing. Jena wondered if she was trying to seduce him; it would probably work. She looked at him with a different eye and decided he could be the new first mate.

'Oh, that's so sad. So sad.'

'It signifies the end of the longsong. It's the voices of all those who are close by, who circle and circle and circle and will be bereft when the music ends.'

'I knew a guy who went there and came back. He walked with a limp forever after. He helped to power it. He says it is amazing.' She bent and turned up the radio, tuned in as always to the song.

'If he has heard the longsong up close, I hope you said goodbye to him. When it stops, all those who have heard it for real will choose to die. We'll have a warning in this way. We don't want to see the world collapse.'

Jena agreed that many felt a deep sense of loss and anxiety but she thought it was because of this nonsense, spouted by many. Not because a song that had been playing for a thousand years was about to stop.

They stopped to refuel at the lichen point, handing over too much money to have the people fill the tank. It was a long, awful job and she would always pay someone else to do it. Jena had her second mate supervise. He turned red and said, 'I'm flattered. I'll do a good job. You won't be sorry,' and set to.

He did do good job, but did it in a too-loud voice that made her wince. She was mildly deaf but some sounds were piercing.

Rats offloaded at this point as they often did; the smell of food here was strong. They liked the lichen and liked that it was all gathered in one place.

Fully fuelled, they set off on the last leg.

They ate dinner, rice and onions. Jena cursed whoever made it (probably Anto, laziest of all men) because there were tiny stones in it and one lodged between two back teeth. She couldn't move it with her tongue so looked around for a suitable stick, and this is how they found her, her mouth wide open and the stick shoved in there.

'Digging for gold?' Anto said. 'You should stop. You're making me feel ill.'

She spat on the ground, a small red globule.

'Revolting,' he said. She found him revolting, too.

'This is the worst meal I've ever eaten, and I've eaten rotten rats stewed in foetid water,' she said.

'Yeah, well,' Anto said. His only comeback was to jump off the barge, carrying his small bag of professional equipment. He'd jump on the next barge, if he felt like it. Canal crews were decided at random, day by day. Jena called it 52 pick-up, because it was like a pack of cards thrown in the air and then placed into piles. There's your crew. Always changing.

She usually picked one person per crew to have sex with. The crew changed periodically; the only steady thing was Jena, whose hand had been on the tiller of this boat for 20 years. She swapped her lover whenever one disembarked. Might be one month, might be a year, but always one at a time. She'd seen what happened otherwise. They'd packed crew members down in the hold with the other bodies – that was otherwise. She'd had her eye on the cook at one stage, except his lack of skill annoyed her, so good riddance.

In the meantime the second mate would do.

The first mate called out. They'd seen a mountain of plastics. This seemed unlikely; such a thing hadn't been seen in decades. 'I'm sure of it this time!' She was always on the lookout for something to get rich on.

Jena left the lot of them there to trek over plains of red dirt to the plastic. She'd collect them on the way back. It was a kindness none of them understood. It was almost all red dirt, now they lived in the centre of Australia. Water had drowned the rest.

In the utterly beautiful silence (apart from the longsong but that she barely noticed) she ate a meal in solitude. Red weeds had been brewing for hours, since early morning, and were sweet now and tender.

The ghosts stayed with her, though. Not all of them had told their story. The story was always different to the one she heard on collection. Sometimes in big ways, sometimes in small. They never showed themselves, it was just the voices, and she knew perfectly well there was every chance it was her own inner voice, telling herself stories, distracting her. But just in case, she listened. She owed them that much.

'Tell me your true stories,' she said.

The further she travelled alone, the redder the plants, the clearer the water. The longsong faded as she travelled and another sort of music took over; the hum and beat of the Martians. Turn by turn she drew closer to the Red Fog that was Port Stephens.

On the shore, figures waited. On the hill behind them, three or four long cylinders stretched to the sky, shiny, reflecting the red around them, red ash falling from the distant lip.

The music rose as she approached. She called up to the Cloud, 'Fifteen. Bringing fifteen. One possibly unclean,' because she wasn't sure about the suicidal boy. She should have dumped him furlongs up the canal, away from sight, but they wouldn't mind. As long as she didn't try to trick them.

She manoeuvred the barge into a well-maintained docking area. It, too, was covered in red weed and she was glad she didn't have to walk on it. They would do it all, once she brought the bodies to the deck.

Four of them waited. Big, grey rounded bulk, the size of fat horses, they glistened like wet stones. Two dark, large eyes, monstrously vital and inhuman, set deep in a rounded head, above lipless mouths that drooled and quivered. They had no chins; instead the flesh seemed to merge into the thick, ridged skin below. They heaved and pulsated. It had taken her many years to understand this was not a form of agitation but their standard way of being. Some had two long tentacle arms, others had four. She thought they lost them fairly easily but had not yet figured out if they grew them back or not.

Machines in the background made a musical clanking, which pushed her to work more quickly. This was why she came; for the metals they produced, seemingly out of nothing. Metals that afforded the family great wealth. She shared some with the crew, to keep them quiet, but only just enough.

There were others, lolling in the reddish water, only their eyes emerging, watching her as she moved one body after another within reach.

She heard from the Cloud, 'Which one unclean?'

'I'll leave it on the boat,' she called out.

The rhythm of their voices was comforting. 'Ulla, Ulla,' which sounded to her like a mournful call for help but she thought it was the opposite. They kept time using the beat of the longsong, *Ulla la Ulla la la la Ulla la*

They chewed through red ferns and, knowing how it made a human body feel, Jena assumed they felt a similar way. Dulled but less angry.

Rusty pumps caked with a thick red solid mass, see-through, almost like Amber.

She felt the rats around her ankles, smelt them, their old wood stink. They had the sense to stay onboard here.

She pulled her barge up to shore. The young ones waited for her, leaping about as best they could. They looked so lumbering, slow compared to humans who were limber and lithe.

'Hello!' she called out. She saw on approach that one of them was adapted. She spoke to that one, a prejudice deep-seated that time and time again has proven worthwhile. Those who've had some appendages removed looked more human and had more human responses. They knew some of the language.

She dragged the bodies out, laid them close to the edge.

She'd seen it before, a kind of frenzy if there is too much of a thing. Really there would be unlimited bodies if everyone would agree to it, but most, even after all these long years (over a thousand) of living with the Martians, people still found them abhorrent.

As usual they swarmed towards her as she approached. She liked watching them move; they seemed to flow like lava, red-hot, liquid.

They lifted the bodies off the deck and carried them away, suckering sneaky slurps of blood. They fell upon her cargo, long teeth out ready to feed, but a great 'Ulla' made them drop to the ground. Her ears rang with it but her mild deafness protected her from a painful response.

'Ulla', quieter now.

Again she blessed her deafness so she couldn't hear them feeding. If she turned her back she could imagine it wasn't happening.

'The water is so pure now. We can taste it in the blood,' one said to the Cloud.

There were stories about how awful the water once was. How people poured waste into it, rubbish and filth and the toilets flushed straight into the water. This before the drawback and then the rains, when the Martians appeared from the base of the sea where they'd slept for hundreds of years. All the creatures of the sea would thank them, if they could.

One by one, the bodies were lifted and drained. She watched as the young woman was dragged across the sand, and the baby, and the old man.

A long straw like protuberance emerged from the back of the Martian's throat. There were gargling noises. Then the long, slow draining of the blood, leaving a husk, like a discarded onion skin. Brown and brittle.

On previous deliveries she tried to tell them the stories of the bodies she gave them, but they blinked at her with their massive eyes, waved their arms around across their sharp mouths as if to say, *be quiet.*

She filled the barge's compartments with body-preservation chemicals and many precious things like aluminium. As she worked, she talked with the Martian she called Will. They'd said their name, once they understood what she meant, but Jena knew that was an invention, something they made up because they thought they should. They were always more talkative after a big meal.

'Tell me about the waters,' Will said. They liked to hear how well they'd done, how clean the world was. The Martians liked the humans to be healthy and clean, to have clean blood.

'It's so clean, you can see the canal floor all the way along. And the lakes are so pure they are like crystal. Clean water keeps us all healthy,' she said.

Jena sweated, and bent over to splash water over her face. She didn't like the water here; too many had bled into it. But she was so hot.

'Will it be cooler soon?' Will asked. They had learned that humans liked to talk about the weather. They had learned a lot in the centuries since they were revealed in the drawback. They had adapted their food habits, and they had spread their plants everywhere, cleansing the water wherever they went.

They had rusted the metals, destroyed the plastics. They didn't talk anymore about 'the others', those Martians who were not on Earth, but Jena knew that it was a future possibility. Some believed the longsong was a signal; when it stopped, other Martians would arrive.

'What do you think of that?' she asked. 'About new ones arriving here?'

Will didn't answer.

'Are you happy about it?'

'We don't know what happy is. We are hungry and not hungry, tired and not tired.'

'And yet you work harder than most humans.'

'We want Earth clean for when the others get back. The longsong is a comfort. You have seen it playing.'

She had been to the longsong herself, a form of pilgrimage. She had met a lover there, more than one, and to be honest had been distracted in that way. She had circled, as others did, but she did not leave changed as most did.

The sound of Martians talking or calling was similar.

'We are hungry,' Will said. 'Bring more next time.'

Jena steered back to collect her crew.

They had found a small amount of plastic, they said, but it was so old and decayed it crumbled to red dust in their fingers. The creeping red destroyed all plastics no matter how vital.

The hold was full of stuff the Martians gave her. Various metals and materials they made. This they would sell along the way.

'You've done well.'

It was her old lover, Jason. He'd caught up with them. 'Did you miss me?' he said, and she had, really. His replacement was dull and sweaty.

'He left,' the first mate said. 'Went for a swim and never came back. I guess he liked the feel of the eels on his skin.' He wriggled, mimicking an eel, and she laughed.

'I have another for the eels,' she said.

'That boy? Should we do something about it? Find out how he died?'

They looked at each other. 'Not our business,' she said. 'Nothing we can do about it. I fed to the eels already, anyway. This one is a suicide.'

'We'll skip them next time, then. We don't need the fuss.'

'No, we bloody won't. We need the income,' she said. They tipped the body over the side and watched the eels flurry around it. It reminded her of the Martians feeding and she looked away, ill to her stomach. Her clothing chafed at her and she wished she could be dry, just for a little while.

There were new babies along the canal. It felt as if more than ever, but perhaps something had triggered in her. Red-veined babies, squalling and vomiting, laughing. She saw the looks they gave their parents and wondered; *Should I? Could I?*

The Martian numbers hadn't grown much since The Long War. From time to time small ones appeared; no one knew how. No one had managed to study them because it was impossible to keep them in captivity. Locked up, they shut down, dried up like an octopus out of water.

The longsong played, slower, slower, slower. Margrit tapped her on the shoulder. 'Are you all right? You seem sad.'

Jena was always this way after seeing the Martians. 'Tell me about the longsong,' she said.

'People circle it, around and around, wearing a deep groove in the ground. That's someone's whole job, filling in that groove! What a job! I can hear it ringing in my ears. Not sure if the song is real any more or if the memory is so strong in my head that I will hear the notes long after the song has stopped.'

Margrit was only with them to earn enough to go back to the longsong. Many cared for the long player. It doesn't need much upkeep. And perhaps is of no importance to humans. One or the other. Vital or forgotten.

'It's slower, isn't it? Tell me I'm not imagining it,' Jena said.

Margrit said, 'It hasn't changed in a thousand years. Perhaps you are tired, feeling slow. Perhaps you are sluggish.'

'Or perhaps the pedallers are slowing down,' Jena said, offended. She had seen them herself; people on bikes, pedalling to keep the song going.

Jason interrupted them. He was excited, jumping on his toes.

'I've been walking ahead and you won't believe it. You will not! They are roasting a pig ahead. It's been on the spit for a day. They've invited us.'

They swapped some of the Martian's materials for food and ate until they couldn't move. There was laughter and joy. The spit fire was burnt to coals but nearby a bonfire warmed them, leading them into a deep sense of satisfaction.

'The long player will stop in a couple of days.' Jena said it casually but everyone knew to the minute how much longer.

This journey they took the old man who made plum wine. He was a good man and had been well-prepared. She stayed with his people for a day, because it was the closest she had to a family. She didn't tell them she knew what they'd done; the old man had marks around his neck, finger impressions. Someone had killed him. She thought *on the way back we need to do something. We can't let this slide.*

When she caught up with the barge it was loaded to the roof; there had been an accident in Quorn, the collapse of a roof, and dozens killed. One was a young man who must have died not long before they collected him. His blood was still shiny on his skin.

Jason said, 'Let me come with you this time.'

Margrit, too. 'The longsong will end and none of us should be alone. We are a crew.'

Everybody agreed. They would be together.

They were close to the Martian jetty when the music stopped.

Jena's ears rang in the silence and absence, because in that moment she couldn't hear the song.

Then, 'Ulla,' they heard, 'Ulla,' but this seemed different to her, with an edge of fear, as if they were saying, 'leave us alone, leave us.'

On the boat, a similar cry went up, because the sky glowed with lights, hundreds of them, growing larger and brighter as they neared the planet.

Jena thought, *so the longsong was like a timer, set to alert them when the earth is clean again.*

She thought of all the islands, all the places where barges delivered food to the Martians. It was a good relationship, developed over hundreds of years. They could see the Martians on the shore, now, and although emotion was impossible to read, Jena thought they looked fearful.

If they fear their own kind, she thought, *what does that mean for us?*

Blood pulsing, they watched as the new machines landed. And as the hatches slowly opened and the new Martians emerged, Jena knew it no longer mattered who murdered the old man, or who loved who, or anything at all.

The Second Coming of the Martians

Sean Williams

> This is already the vastest war in history. It is war not of nations, but of mankind. It is a war to exorcise a world-madness and end an age.
>
> – H. G. Wells, *The War That Will End War*

THE STORM HAD A RAGE DISORDER UNLIKE ANYTHING IN JOEL'S experience, and he'd recently interviewed a man convicted of bludgeoning nine people to death. One moment the screaming wind retreated to the point where he could stand, if leaning at a heavy list; the next he was battered flat, clinging to ice for dear life.

Pressing on seemed increasingly pointless. He couldn't see anything, and his compass was useless so close to the South Pole. Every metre he wrested from the elements might be leading him in completely the wrong direction. He could keep moving for warmth, but the wind snatched that away from him through tiny chinks in his thermal armour. Better, he told himself, to dig in and wait for the blizzard to pass. Which it had to eventually, surely.

Dropping to all fours, he slid his heavy pack with its grisly burden off his shoulders and un-stowed a collapsible shovel.

The ice beneath him, however, had been scoured free of loose snow and what remained was as hard as rock. He needed to find the lee of something and burrow into its 'blizz tail', as the expeditioners in Mawson station called the snow dunes that remained when the fury of the storm had passed.

Crawling, skidding occasionally, barely able to see even his fingertips, he blundered in a blind zig-zag in search of shelter.

For the first time, he felt fear.

Everyone had warned him that Antarctica was a fool's errand, and a dangerous one at that, but he had refused to listen. Nature didn't kill investigative reporters: war zones or ex-spouses did. Now, as his limbs grew heavy under him and treacherous sleep beckoned, he wondered if he should have paid more heed. Death was a high price for chasing a phantom that might not even exist.

'Fuck you,' he shouted into the storm. 'I didn't come all this way for nothing!'

An answer was the last thing he expected, and indeed he received none.

Only later, in the grey nimbus between life and death, when all strength had fled and his breath froze into a hard crust on his lips, did a dark figure step out of the storm with a ponderous tread and scoop him up in chill limbs that curved unnaturally around him.

Joel stirred, moaning weakly. Through ice-dusted eyelashes he glimpsed the distinctive shape of his rescuer, and came immediately to full consciousness. The fire of discovery – of being proven *right* – banished all thought of dying.

'You!'

Sleep, whispered an alien voice in his mind. *Forget.*

'Wait…I have…to ask…' He shook his head, fighting incipient torpor with all his will.

No. The answer was as firm as the footfalls beneath him.

'One question!' Wriggling in the embrace of the tentacles that held him tight, he reached for his pack. 'I bring…payment!'

You have nothing I desire.

'That's not true. Blood…*human* blood…You've never tasted it. I know, because of the stories they tell about you. The ghost of the ice. Rescuing the lost and injured and bringing them back to the station. Never seen. Never...*feeding*. Haven't you ever wondered what you missed out on?'

For a long moment, all Joel could hear was the wailing of the wind and the walking machine's steady, three-beat plod. Did the latter falter, just for a moment?

'You must be draining seals and fish,' he pressed on. 'Maybe the odd bird. Sterilising the plasma somehow. By boiling it? That can't be satisfying. What I have is clean. Pure.'

Yours?

The question shocked him, unexpectedly. He was tempted to lie, in case such an intimacy would tip the scales in his favour. Who knew what this strange, lonely being at the end of the world might crave most?

Truth, however, was ever the best mask for deceit.

'Three volunteers from the station,' he said. 'I paid them well.'

The walking machine let out a hiss and came to a swaying halt. The wind squalled around them like a ferment of banshees.

What is your question?

Joel swallowed, his throat suddenly thick. If his suspicions proved correct, the reply he received would cast the previous century in an entirely new light – and make him a celebrity into the bargain.

'Who are the real Martians?'

I do not understand.

'I think you do, but I'll clarify so there's no ambiguity between us. The architects of the Great War...the ones who sent the cylinders to Earth in 1894...sowing the Red Weed and killing millions...Who were they? I know it wasn't you lot, so spare me that fable, please. You were shock troops, not tacticians; the bullet in the gun and someone else pulled the trigger. I want to know who that was, and you are going to tell me. You, the last, the sole, perhaps...survivor of the original invasion. Who heard the original orders. You alone will remember who gave them.'

How do you know I will tell you?

'Because you're hiding out here, helping the ones you once wanted to kill. Out of guilt, right? So consider this an unburdening. A shriving. An expiation. I'll throw that in for free, along with the blood.' Joel suppressed a rising tide of triumph: he wasn't there yet. 'Do we have a deal?'

The creature considered for a minute that felt like an eternity, warring, no doubt, between habitual secrecy and the need to let go of the past. In Joel's experience, need trumped habit every time. He risked everything on the assumption that this held true for every species.

Very well. I will answer your question.

Breath whooshed out of his lungs. 'Thank you.'

The blood first.

'Of course. It's in my pack. Put me down and I'll get it for you.'

Not here.

The massive walking machine lurched into life, turning about and heading back the way they had come, presumably away from Mawson research station and the warmth of human safety.

Joel felt his heart pounding in his throat. Adrenalin made him feel unnaturally alert. At last, he would discover the truth that no one else in a century had even suspected.

He, and he alone, would know the true face of humanity's enemy!

The alien walked for half an hour to a patch of wind-ravaged ice that seemed to Joel's eyes little different to any other they had crossed. Parallel ripples of sastrugi stretched to the edge of visibility, casting feathered lines of snow from their summits. The storm had eased from full-throated rage to mild fury: it no longer hurt Joel's eyes to open them to their fullest extent. He could clearly make out the domed summit of the walking machine above him, rocking with every swing of its three, many-jointed legs.

There was a faint hitch in its gait, the cause of which became immediately apparent when they arrived and the machine crouched, relaxed its tentacles, and allowed Joel to tumble free.

Joel tested his extremities for frostbite or other injuries, observing as he did so that the walking machine had also endured much hardship in its sojourn in Antarctica. There was evidence of repair in every strut and joint. Materials from another machine had been employed to replace that which had been damaged beyond repair, creating a patchwork effect all down one side. The hood where the pilot sat opened with a drawn-out groan that spoke of poorly-lubricated bearings.

Lithe feeding tubes – *they* worked just fine – snaked from beneath the hood.

Joel kept a close eye on them as he opened his pack and produced the first of three carefully labelled blood bags, each containing about a litre of precious fluid.

He hefted the bag in one hand, proffered it. 'Female, Eurasian, 43. A meteorologist with a very pleasing singing voice.'

The thin tubes lifted the bag out of his hands and, with a sucking noise, drained the liquid contents. Crimson threads snaked up to where the alien sat at the controls of the machine, a metre above him. Beneath a broad, leathery-brown scalp, two immense eyes regarded him impassively as the creature drank.

Joel had met so-called Martians before, and marvelled at the frond around their mouths that operated as hands and the giant ear on their backs, but none was like this one, this relic of a war older than his great-grandparents. He felt an atavistic thrill that wasn't anticipation or dread or fear, but contained a little of each. Was this what the first proto-human to subdue a sabretooth tiger had felt? Facing down the monster, finally!

'How does it taste?'

Sweet.

'I'll give you the next in a moment. You have to give me something in return, first.'

The cylinder…landed off-course, it told him. *Our intention was not to attack this continent, for it was uninhabited at the time. I, the only survivor, tried to contact the masters and my fellows here on Earth, but no one was listening for me here, at first. My call went unnoticed, and then…my fellows fell silent.*

'The masters…' Joel said, unable to keep a certain smugness from his tone. 'Is that what you called them? They didn't anticipate the bacteria that wiped you out, poor fools – like you wiped out the feedstock you brought with you. We found the drained bodies of your passengers in the cylinders after you were defeated. You ate them just like you ate us, and then the bacteria ate you.'

Yes. Here, I was safe from the pathogens, provided I was careful.

'Home sweet home,' he said, with a shiver. Antarctica, the coldest and driest place on Earth, where it never rained, was often described as the most like Mars in nature. 'Where is your species originally from?'

We evolved in the oceans of Mars, then migrated below the surface when our water retreated.

'So you *are* Martians after all! I thought you might be slaves from another planet.'

There is a hierarchy of species on my home world.

'Yes, I see,' Joel said. 'It might have been the same here, once, before we wiped out the Neanderthals and the hobbits. That was my clue, you know. You were selfish enough to prey on an intelligent race, and yet you threw yourself carelessly into battle. Who does this? Someone taking orders, that's who, from someone else – the masters – to whom you were as disposable as your feedstock.'

This is true. You reason well.

'Tell me more about them.'

Where my species harvest blood, they harvest thought. Except... "thought" is not entirely correct. Your mind lacks the concept. Perhaps this analogy will make it clear. Blood contains nutrients necessary for the survival of the body; those nutrients can be stolen by predators, if they evolve a means of removing the blood from the body. Imagine if you can that your mind is sustained by your thoughts in a fashion similar to body and blood. One creates the other, but without the other, the one could not exist.

'I think I get it. The masters are psychic vampires.'

I do not mean thoughts such as the means by which I communicate with you: your lips and ears contain blood, but the spoken word travels through quite a different medium. Perhaps "cognition" is a better word...or "consciousness".

'So they eat your thoughts or whatever you call them and you eat the blood of the feedstock. What do *they* eat, or does the hierarchy, the food chain, stop there?'

They prey upon another specialised species. Mars is an ancient world that changes slowly, unlike yours. Equilibrium, once established, is embraced and only reluctantly abandoned.

'Hence the Great Invasion, I suppose. There are lots of theories about what led you – sorry, the masters – to invade, but they've all felt incomplete to me, because they don't explain the enormous *need* behind this vast effort to conquer another world. You don't do that on a whim. You do it because you have to.'

All equilibria fail, in time.

'But that's no reason to just lie down and die, no. Things went wrong with the hierarchy on Mars, so the masters sought to build a new one on Earth. They sent you and the feedstock to soften us up. They obviously planned to follow, but then the bacteria got the better of you. You fell foul of our own food chain.'

Yes.

'And then…nothing. No second invasion. Why not? That's always been the flaw in my reasoning, or so people have been eager to point out. Was it a revolution? Did your kind turn on the masters for sending you to your deaths? Are you now top of the food chain? Or was there someone above *them*, who shut their efforts down?'

Neither.

'So why *did* a super-species of Martian with the technological ability and will to invade Earth give up at the first hurdle?'

Perhaps they did not.

'Bullshit. I'm sure we would have noticed a second attack.'

Perhaps you were looking in the wrong place.

Joel had slumped into a relatively sheltered nook and wrapped his arms around his knees, forming the closest thing to a sphere the human body was able to achieve. Now, he sat upright and studied the Martian closely. It was still in the hood of the walking machine, still inscrutable, but he sensed something new in its mental tone.

'What are you trying to tell me?' he asked. 'That there *was* a second attack, and it happened here, far from civilisation? In Antarctica?'

He looked around, struck by the thought that *this* nook might be the hollow under a fighting-machine's knee-joint, or that *that* sastrugi might be the side of a cylinder.

Nothing so…prosaic, the Martian told him.

Joel returned his attention to the enormous eyes, watching him closely. Did he see amusement in their alien depths?

Or hunger?

He fished in his pack for the second bag.

'Perhaps this will help you find the concepts you need to explain.'

While the creature drank of a male Islander electrician, the youngest of the three who had agreed to donate their blood, Joel took a moment to assemble what he had learned so far.

Mars had once possessed a highly stratified and threatened ecosystem. Seeking to avoid the consequences of environmental collapse, the apex predators of that ecosystem cast their eyes towards Earth, where a veritable bounty of "thought", "cognition" or "consciousness" awaited. Not to mention blood for their shock troops. It was a perfect plan, with just one, tiny, unforeseen flaw: the bacteria, the pathogens.

This picture felt more authentic to him than many of the alternatives. It was clearly, however, not yet complete.

'I refuse to believe that the others like you who live here now are some kind of fifth column,' he said when the lines of blood snaking up the feeding tubes ceased. 'If bacterial species were on the retreat, I would wonder, but they're getting stronger, more virulent if anything…'

Indeed. The ecosystem of Earth is one of constant internecine conflict. To survive here, Martians must assimilate, becoming no longer entirely Martian. Such was far from the masters' desire after their defeat in the Great Invasion.

'Go on.'

Consider this war of worlds, the striving for dominance, less between two populations than between two entire philosophies of life. For Martians to win Earth, the entire natural order must be overturned. Humans have made their own attempt at doing that by subduing the very same pathogens that mercilessly attacked us: however, as you observe, the pathogens merely and mindlessly evolved new means of assault. The masters, therefore, accepted the impossibility of owning Earth, and chose instead to harvest its bounty from afar. Consider: the sustenance they craved was not material, and their ability to connect with us, their shock troops, was not affected by distance–

'My god!' Joel exclaimed. 'They attacked us telepathically?'

In a manner of speaking. Once the masters understood the futility of subjugating humanity using their instruments, they embarked on a plan to subdue your ranks using your own. Hierarchy is not unknown here, after all. The masters exercised their superior minds in order to create puppets who altered your development, thereby creating a new herd species for the masters' sole benefit.

'Speak sense, will you? They did no such thing.'

They very nearly succeeded.

'What are you talking about? There's no evidence of any such attack, no proof–'

The proof is littered all through the middle of your 20th Century. Mass education, migrations, baby booms – mechanisms intended to increase the fecundity of Earth's thought. Communism, Fascism, Capitalism – the means to facilitate its harvest. There is no part of your recent history that was not influenced by the masters of Mars.

'Impossible!'

Even as he protested, however, Joel felt his certainty undermined. He had come looking for answers, and he had found nothing to offend his reason until now. What had this forlorn creature to gain by lying to him? Unless it was itself mistaken…

But was it? The picture it painted, of human puppet-tyrants and the bloated masses under their control, had no obvious flaws, except that it had previously been invisible to him. The masters must have acted swiftly and in secret while humanity yet lacked the means of reaching Mars. They must, indeed, have put this new plan into effect soon after the Great Invasion itself, the very time all the social upheavals listed began in earnest. The story had a plausible edge to it, however much he wanted to deny its veracity.

'How can you know this? You've been tucked down here all this time, alone…No, I understand! The masters could still talk to you, once they heard your calls. I expect you knew everything they were doing.'

Yes.

'So what went wrong this time? How did we win a war we didn't even know we were fighting?'

You did not win. Do not imagine that the human puppets turned on their new masters. If we could not, they could not.

'But–'

No, the war was won for you, as it was the first time. Just as we foot soldiers of the first invasion were attacked by pathogens hidden in humanity's veins, pathogens that reproduce within and feed off their unwitting hosts, so too were the masters attacked by fragments of thought that live in your minds; tiny, conceptual viruses too small to see from afar that infect all your kind. It was these allies, deadly to the purely rational, that defeated the masters.

Joel was frowning, picturing at first creatures like demons from ancient myth, hebephrenic possessors of the vulnerable…perhaps influenced by this prolix confrontation with a creature from beyond his everyday world.

Then, however, as the 21st century's more modern perspective on the mind re-asserted itself, he began to understand.

'Memes,' he said. 'You're talking about memes! Ideas that spread from mind to mind like diseases. Adversative and…what's the word? Proselytic!'

There is a better noun. Its ancient root, in one of your dead languages, is "to bind".

'…Religion?'

Yes.

Joel gaped more in shock than disbelief. 'The masters caught God…'

They caught irrationality, tribalism, sacrifice, and genocide – concepts against which they had no defences. The result was carnage. Within two of your generations, the masters were decimated, and have trembled on the brink of extinction ever since.

'Hence, we missed them while exploring Mars. This is incredible! I don't know what part of this story is the most appalling: that it happened to us, or that we had no idea what happened to them.'

It was unavoidable.

'If they had reached out in peace, or at least for help–'

Interspecies collaboration is something neither of our species has learned. Survival is predicated on adversarial behaviours that require one or the other to dominate.

'That makes us out to be the villains of the piece, but we did nothing deliberately to harm the masters.'

Would you not have, if you had the means?

'I…can't say. We were never given the chance to prove ourselves!'

You have, many times. As you yourself observed, there were once many hominid species on this world. How long did it take yours to wipe out the Neanderthals and the others?

Joel felt small pains prickle across his cheeks, as blood rushed into his chilled skin.

'That was then,' he said. 'This is now.'

So it is. Tell me, what you will do with the knowledge I have given you? Will you take it back to your people in order to prove your theory dominant? Will they use this knowledge to reveal my kind to be a lesser species than the one you now consider your true enemy? Will this reduced status allow you to discriminate with greater impunity against those of us seeking peaceful asylum on Earth? Will that spell the end of all attempts at assimilation between my people and yours?

'I don't know.'

I do. The only alternative to the dominance of one species over another is for both to change. That process must be allowed to continue. I cannot let you interrupt it.

Instantly alarmed, Joel leaped to his feet. 'We had a deal!'

You have not completed your side of the bargain.

'Here, then!' He tossed the third bag, the one containing the sedative powerful enough to knock out a legion of Martians, so it landed at the walking machine's feet. 'Take it. It's yours.'

I have had my fill.

'Drink it. You've earned it. Then–'

What? Let you go? Without knowing in which direction the base lies, you cannot survive.

'I'll take my chances!'

His legs were stiff from crouching on the ice, and he went from standing to running in a series of wild jerks. The wind snatched him up and bundled him along, whipping the walking machine from his sight, and hopefully he from its.

The alien's implied threat was undoubtable: Joel knew too much to be allowed to live, so his only hope, however slight, was first to get away from it, and then to worry about how to reach the base.

The walking machine boomed heavily behind him. He scrambled up the side of a sastrugi and flung himself over the top. Slipping without control down the other side, he realised that in his haste to escape he had left his pack behind.

Damned fool! Perhaps he could lead the Martian away, then double back to collect it. Without it, he had no chance.

He hit the bottom of the slope and braced himself to stand.

Then came the piercing crack and the thin ice bridge giving way beneath him. With a weightless cry, he fell.

The crevasse wasn't as deep as some, but it was deep enough. Joel regained consciousness with one arm twisted painfully beneath him. Unable to feel anything at all below his waist, he could only grunt uselessly in pain and despair when he tried to move. All around him was blueish ice and fallen snow. Far above, dimly visible in the Antarctic light, grey clouds scudded rapidly across the jagged hole he had left in the ice. Blearily, he supposed that they would be the last thing he'd ever see.

A rounded silhouette blocked the view, and he groaned.

'What, have you come to gloat?'

Be still.

With great care, using legs and tentacles equally, the walking machine positioned itself across the crevasse and began to descend. Cold flakes of ice dusted Joel's face, and once a fist-sized lump thudded against his one uninjured limb. In mere moments, it seemed, he was eye to eye with the Martian once more, the two of them cramped together in the tight confines of his tomb.

This region is densely mazed with such cracks as these, the alien told him. *They form a natural barrier to discovery.*

'And to escape, I suppose,' he said. The bitter words made him cough, which caused him to show more pain than he cared to. 'Ah, god. Soon there'll be one more skeleton for your collection.'

I have no desire for you to die.

'No? Changed your mind, have you?'

That was never my resolve. I stated that I could not let you be an interruption, not that I would kill you. Judge me by your preconceptions rather than my actions, if you will. The blame for this outcome is not mine.

A distant prospect of salvation occurred to him. 'Right, you don't kill people. You save people. What kind of atonement would it be if you let me die?'

I cannot save you now, the alien said with heavy finality. *You are too badly injured. All I can offer is the entire truth, for you do not yet know all.*

'Forget our deal,' he spat in wretched disappointment. 'I was going to betray you anyway. The last blood bag was poisoned.'

I know.

'Read my mind, I suppose.'

I did not. Hidden I might be, here, but I was the masters' conduit for their second assault on Earth. I know more about your kind than I once cared to.

'Conduit…? Oh, I see. The psychic vampires needed a beachhead when the rest of you died. That was you, the last survivor. You were still useful to them.'

Yes. Until I was set free by the poison in your minds.

'So, if not atonement, then what? Gratitude?'

I explained it to you earlier: the only alternative to the dominance of one species over another–

'Is that both must change. And the masters have changed…lost their power, their place in the hierarchy. But how–'

A series of wracking coughs took Joel's voice from him for more than a minute. When regained, it was almost too weak to be heard.

'A new meme. The ghost of the ice…obviously a Martian. Makes you look good, not the enemy, even to the most close-minded…I did think so…Easily fooled, at least…Turns out I was…'

There is no deception. I have no need to lie.

'No. I'll be dead soon enough.' He suppressed a sudden urge to weep. Antarctica had been the end of him, after all, but for a moment he had held the truth in his hands, he alone out of every human on Earth. Hadn't he?

'There's something…you haven't told me.'

The identity of the masters.

'Yes.' He said no more, accepting the Martian's ability to understand him without words.

You already know them. You have seen their face…in the face of Mars itself.

Joel winced, feeling his body's last efforts shivering down into the numbness of his lower limbs. *The face of Mars?* That meant nothing to him. Why did the creature have to be elliptical now, when the remainder of his life could be measured in mere breaths? Better if the Martian came out and just said what it meant, rather than confuse him with the suggestion that some mystery lay hidden behind the perfectly obvious. What everyone knew about Mars was the way it shone in the sky, a symbol of war, and strife…and blood.

Joel might have laughed, then, had he the breath, for understanding came to him in a flash of delicious irony. The heights of the Martian hierarchy? The creatures that had twice assaulted Earth from the depths of space, and might have won had not fortune ruled against them?

The face of Mars was red.

The red of *weed.*

The last true Martian on Earth saw him smile as he died, clutching his good hand close to his chest, as if to take the knowledge with him, where it could do no harm.

Contributors

Carmel Bird was born in Tasmania, lives in Castlemaine and in 2016 was awarded the Patrick White Literary Award. Her first collection of short stories appeared in 1976. Since then she has published novels, essays, anthologies, children's books and manuals on how to write.

Her novels include: *Cherry Ripe, Unholy Writ, Open for Inspection, Cape Grimm, Child of the Twilight and Family Skeleton; The Bluebird Café, The White Garden, and Red Shoes were each shortlisted for the Miles Franklin Award; and The White Garden was also shortlisted for the* NSW Premier's Award, and the Aurealis and Ned Kelly awards.

Lindy Cameron is author of the Kit O'Malley PI trilogy *Blood Guilt, Bleeding Hearts* and *Thicker Than Water*; the archaeological history-mystery *Golden Relic*; the sf-crime novella *Feedback;* and the action thriller, *Redback*. She is the co-author, with Kerry Greenwood, of two short stories: 'A Wild Colonial' for *Sherlock Holmes: The Australian Casebook*; and 'The Saltwater Battle' for *War of the Worlds: Battleground Australia*. She is also co-author of the True Crime collections *Killer in the Family* & *Murder in the Family* (with her sister Fin J Ross).

She is currently working on a series of novellas featuring time-travelling archaeologists, and the great-great granddaughter of Alexander the Great and the Amazon Queen, Thalestris.

Lindy is a founding member and current President of Sisters in Crime Australia, the Publisher of Clan Destine Press.

Bill Congreve is an award-winning writer, editor, critic and independent publisher (MirrorDanse Books). His work has appeared in a number of countries in publications as diverse as *Faerie Reel, Tenebres, Event Horizon, Terror Australis, Aurealis, Borderlands, Bloodsongs, Crosstown Traffic, Monstres!, The Year's Best Australian Fantasy & Horror, Cthulhu: Deep Down Under* and *The Best of the Scream Factory*. His collection of vampire stories is *Epiphanies of Blood*. His most recent collection is *Souls Along the Meridian* (2010). He won the Peter

McNamara Achievement Award in 2012 and has acted as judge for the Aurealis Awards on nine occasions. He works as a policy and procedure writer in the emergency services sector.

Jack Dann has written or edited over 75 books, including the international bestseller *The Memory Cathedral*, *The Rebel*, *The Silent*, and *The Man Who Melted*. He is a recipient of the Nebula Award, the World Fantasy Award (twice), the Australian Aurealis Award (three times), the Chronos Award, the Darrell Award for Best Mid-South Novel, the Ditmar Award (five times), the Peter McNamara Achievement Award and also the Peter McNamara Convenors' Award for Excellence, the Shirley Jackson Award, and the Premios Gilgames de Narrativa Fantastica award. He has also been honoured by the Mark Twain Society (Esteemed Knight).

Library Journal has called him "...a true poet who can create pictures with a few perfect words" and *The Washington Post* Book World compared his novel *The Man Who Melted* with Ingmar Bergman's film *The Seventh Seal*.

Dr. Dann is an Adjunct Senior Research Fellow in the School of Communication and Arts at the University of Queensland. Forthcoming is the Renaissance fantasy novel *Shadows in the Stone*, which Kim Stanley Robinson has called 'such a complete world that Italian history no longer seems comprehensible without [Dann's] cosmic battle of spititual entities behind and within every historical actor and event'.

Jason Fischer is a writer who lives near Adelaide, South Australia. He has won the Colin Thiele Literature Scholarship, an Aurealis Award and the Writers of the Future Contest. In Jason's jack-of-all-trades writing career he has worked on comics, computer games, television, short stories, novellas and novels. He also has a passion for godawful puns, and is known to sing karaoke until the small hours.

Jason Franks is an author and graphic novelist based in Melbourne. He is the writer of the novels *Bloody Waters* and *Faerie Apocalypse*, the *Sixsmiths* graphic novels, and the short story collection *Ungenred*. He has been short-listed for Aurealis, Ledger and Ditmar awards.

Kerry Greenwood is the author of 60 novels and five non-fiction books. Born in Footscray, she has worked as a folk-singer, a translator, a costume-maker, and editor. Kerry has a degree in English and Law from Melbourne University and was admitted to the legal profession on the 1st of April 1982, a day which she finds both soothing and significant.

Kerry is the beloved creator of the 20-book Phryne Fisher mystery series, the Corinna Chapman mysteries (Allen & Unwin); the Delphic Women trilogy – *Medea, Cassandra and Electra*, *Out of the Black Land* and *Herotica* (Clan Destine Press). She holds both the Ned Kelly and Davitt Lifetime Achievement Awards for her crime fiction, and wants another lifetime.

For recent short story anthologies, Kerry co-wrote (with David Greagg) 'Cruel Sister' for *And Then… The Great Big Book of Awesome Adventure Tales* (CDP 2018); and (with Lindy Cameron) 'A Wild Colonial' for *Sherlock Holmes: The Australian Casebook* (Echo 2018); and 'The Saltwater Battle' for *War of the Worlds: Battleground Australia.*

Narrelle M. Harris writes crime, horror, fantasy and romance. Her 30+ works have been published in Australia, the US and the UK. Award nominations include *Fly By Night* (Ned Kelly Awards), *Witch Honour* and *Witch Faith* (George Turner Prize short-listings), and *Walking Shadows* (Chronos Awards). Her story 'Jane' won the Body in the Library Prize at the 2017 Scarlet Stiletto Awards run annually by Sisters in Crime Australia.

Narrelle's work includes vampire novels, erotic spy adventures, het and queer romance, traditional Holmesian mysteries, and Holmes/Watson romances *The Adventure of the Colonial Boy* (2016) and *A Dream to Build a Kiss On* (Improbable Press 2018).

She also writes novellas in her Duo Ex Machina queer crime/romance series on Patreon. Her spec-fic het romance, *Grounded*, was released in March 2019 by Escape Publishing. Other 2019 releases include her short story collection, *Scar Tissue and Other Stories* and urban musical fantasy *Kitty and Cadaver* (CDP).

Dmetri Kakmi is a writer and editor. His memoir *Mother Land* was shortlisted for the New South Wales Premier's Literary Awards; and is published in England and Turkey. He edited the acclaimed children's anthology *When We Were Young.*

Dmetri's ghost story 'The Boy by the Gate' was published in *The New Gothic*, and reprinted in *The Year's Best Australian Fantasy and Horror* 2013. 'Haunting Matilda' was shortlisted in the Aurealis Awards Best Fantasy Novella category in 2015. His essays and short stories appear in anthologies. He lives in Melbourne.

Rick Kennett is a life-long resident of Melbourne, Australia, where he works in the transport industry and has an interest in cemeteries, ghosts and all things spooky. He is the author of the novels *The Devil and the Deep Blue Sea* and *Presumed Dead*, plus the collections *The Dark and What It Said* and *Thirty Minutes for New Hell.*

Rick's stories have appeared in *Aurealis*, *Andromeda Spaceways*, *Weird Tales*, in many anthologies and on several podcasts including Cast of Wonders and Pseudopod. 'The Enemy of the Enemy' is based on a single and often overlooked reference in *The War of the Worlds.*

Angela Meyer's debut novel *A Superior Spectre* (Ventura, Australia/ Sarabrand UK) has been shortlisted for the MUD Literary Prize, an Australian Book Industry Award, and the Aurealis Award for Best Science Fiction novel. Angela's writing has been widely published, including in *Best Australian Stories*, *Island*, *The Big Issue*, *The Australian*, *The Lifted Brow* and *Killings*. She previously published a book of flash fiction, *Captives* (Inkerman & Blunt).

Angela has worked in bookstores, as a book reviewer, in a whisky bar, and for the past few years has published a host of Australian authors for Echo Publishing, including award-winners and an international number one bestseller. She grew up in Northern NSW and lives in Melbourne.

Steve Proposch, Christopher Sequeira & Bryce Stevens are editors and writers who specialise in mystery and speculative fiction under the collective moniker Horror Australis. Together they have edited and written for award-winning anthologies *Cthulhu Deep Down*

Under (Volumes 1-3), and *Cthulhu Land of the Long White Cloud,* and have more future classics in the works.

Sequeira is also the editor of the anthology *Sherlock Holmes: the Australian Casebook* (Echo Publishing) which features some of the same writers as *War of the Worlds: Battleground Australia.*

Alex Proyas is an Egyptian-born, Australian film director/writer/producer, who grew up in inner-city Sydney with a passion for film from an early age. His early shorts were acclaimed, including numerous outstanding short film awards and nominations at London, Melbourne, Cannes et al international film festivals.

Alex made his first feature, *Spirits of the Air; Gremlins of the Clouds* in 1989 and in 1994 he completed *The Crow*, starring Brandon Lee, which went on to major critical and commercial success and bona fide cult status. His 1998 film *Dark City*, starring Rufus Sewell, Keifer Sutherland, Richard O'Brien, Jennifer Connelly and William Hurt, also earned its place as a cult classic.

In 2002 Proyas made *Garage Days* (2002) starring Kick Gurry, Pia Miranda and Maya Stange which was followed by *I, Robot* (2004) starring Will Smith, Proyas' greatest commercial success to date. In 2008 he completed *Knowing* starring Nicolas Cage and Rose Byrne which became another major world-wide success, and most recently *Gods of Egypt* (2016) starring Gerard Butler, Geoffrey Rush and Nikolaj Coster-Waldau. Proyas lives in Sydney with his wife and daughter and is currently planning his next feature, *The New Country.*

J. Scherpenhuizen's comics, illustrations and prose fiction have appeared in a wide range of publications in Australia and the United States, from publishers ranging from small press to giants like Marvel Comics. Jan has acted as both writer and illustrator on a number of projects, ranging from the cute picture-book series *The Wild and Crazy Dinosaurs* to the gritty horror graphic novel *The Time of The Wolves.*

With writer Christopher Sequeira he has developed and created numerous properties including for comics *Mr Blood* and *The Catamorph.* His illustration work includes a number of illustrations in the recent *Sherlock Holmes: The Australian Casebook* to which he also contributed a short story. Currently he is completing a Doctor of Arts at Sydney University which comprises a graphic novel and literary novel interwoven with a thesis.

Lucy Sussex is a New Zealand-born writer living in Australia. Her award-winning work covers many genres, from true crime writing to horror. Her bibliography includes the novel *The Scarlet Rider* (1996, St Martins; reissued Ticonderoga 2015). She has published five short story collections, and also edited anthologies, including the World Fantasy award shortlisted *She's Fantastical.* She has worked at Deakin, Melbourne and La Trobe Universities, while being a researcher, editor and review columnist.

Lucy's literary archaeology (unearthing forgotten writers) work includes *Women Writers and Detectives in C19th Crime Fiction: The Mothers of the Mystery Genre* (Palgrave). She has also edited pioneer crime writers Mary Fortune, and Ellen Davitt; and an anthology of Victorian travel writing, *Saltwater in the Ink* (ASP). Her study of Fergus Hume and his 1886 *The Mystery of a Hansom Cab*, the biggest selling detective novel of the 1800s, was published by Text in 2015, and won the Victorian Community History award.

Sholto Turner is an artist, sculptor and designer. Based in Castlemaine, central Victoria, he originally studied Graphic Design and has spent the last 20 or so years working with various mediums of sculpture (bronze, timber, steel, stone) and drawing. For the last 10 years he has specialised in mould-making, and concrete casting. His illustration for *Battleground Australia* appears on p17.

Jenny Valentish is a journalist, author of the novel *Cherry Bomb* and the non-fiction book *Woman of Substances: A Journey into Addiction and Treatment*, and has contributed to many fiction anthologies. She drew on her stint working at adult magazines – which included ghostwriting the column of Jenna Jameson and visiting porn sets – to write 'Even Less Than Zero'.

Kaaron Warren is a Shirley Jackson Award winner and World Fantasy Award nominee, and has lived in Melbourne, Sydney, Canberra and Fiji. She's sold many short stories, seven short story collections, and five novels – the multi-award-winning *Slights*, *Walking the Tree*, *Mistification*, *The Grief Hole* and *Tide of Stone*. *The Grief Hole* won a Canberra Critic's Circle Award for Fiction, a Ditmar Award, the Australian Shadows Award and the Aurealis Award.

Kaaron's stories have appeared in Australia, the US, the UK and elsewhere in Europe, and have been selected for both Ellen Datlow's and Paula Guran's Year's Best Anthologies. She was a Guest of Honour at World Fantasy Convention in 2018 and Geysercon, NZ, 2019.

Janeen Webb is a multi-award winning writer, editor and critic who has written or edited 10 books and over 100 stories and essays. She is a recipient of the World Fantasy Award, the Peter MacNamara SF Achievement Award, and the Aurealis and Ditmar Awards. Most recently, her short story 'A Pearl Beyond Price' won the 2018 Ditmar Award. Currently, her novella 'The Dragon's Child' is on the Locus Recommended Reading List and is short-listed for both the Aurealis and the Ditmar Awards.

Janeen holds a PhD in Literature from the University of Newcastle, and divides her time between Melbourne and a small farm overlooking the sea near Wilson's Promontory, Australia.

Sean Williams is an award-winning author of over 40 novels and 120 short stories for adults, young adults and children. As well as his genre-confounding original fiction, he has contributed to shared universes such as *Star Wars* and *Doctor Who*, and collaborated with other authors such as Garth Nix (their latest book is *Let Sleeping Dragons Lie*).

In 2017, he was the Australian Antarctic Arts Fellow and spent time on Casey Station, researching this and other stories. His latest novel, *Impossible Music*, is his first to be set entirely in the real world.